It was long after midnight. I opened my eyes to pale light beyond the windows and lay very still. Someone was in the room. A shadowy figure loomed against the light from the picture window —a figure that moved toward my bed. As silently as possible I rolled to the far side and clung to the edge, stiff and waiting. Hands crept toward me across the pillow, shadowy arms extended in my direction, searching, searching. Quite suddenly a voice whispered through the room, *"Listen . . ."* and once more, *"Listen . . ."*

FAWCETT CREST BOOKS:
By Phyllis A. Whitney

BLACK AMBER

BLUE FIRE

COLUMBELLA

DOMINO

EVER AFTER

THE GLASS FLAME

THE GOLDEN UNICORN

HUNTER'S GREEN

LISTEN FOR THE WHISPERER

LOST ISLAND

THE MOONFLOWER

POINCIANA

THE QUICKSILVER POOL

SEA JADE

SEVEN TEARS FOR APOLLO

SILVERHILL

SKYE CAMERON

SNOWFIRE

SPINDRIFT

THE STONE BULL

THUNDER HEIGHTS

THE TREMBLING HILLS

THE TURQUOISE MASK

LISTEN FOR THE WHISPERER

Phyllis A. Whitney

FAWCETT CREST • NEW YORK

A Fawcett Crest Book
Published by Ballantine Books

ISBN 0-449-20419-7

This edition published by arrangement with Doubleday and
Company, Inc.

Selection of the Doubleday Book Club, March 1972

Manufactured in the United States of America

First Fawcett Crest Edition: January 1973
First Ballantine Books Edition: December 1983

In appreciation and admiration for Gunvor V. Blomqvist, who has translated so many of my books with understanding of the mood they are intended to convey.

Chapter 1

I sat in the darkened theater with my hands clasped tensely in my lap and my eyes fixed unblinkingly upon the screen. The man beside me touched my arm and I pulled away from him, not wanting anything to break the spell of the scene that was moving inexorably to its climax.

"Let up, Leigh," Dick whispered. "This is pure corn, even if Laura Worth did win an Oscar nomination for it years ago."

Twenty years ago. *I* knew. But I would not listen to him. I shut him out and watched the screen. I knew the scene by heart, but the impact was always the same. My ambivalence was always the same. I was fascinated by every move the woman on the screen made, yet at the same time I detested her utterly. No one had a better right to detest her.

In the role of Helen Bradley in the movie adaptation of my father's novel, *The Whisperer*, Laura Worth was coming down that famous Victorian staircase that had been almost a character in the book. Not only I, but the entire audience sensed her fear. Terror seemed to emanate from her as she descended the stairs, one hand clinging to the banister, the other held to her throat in dread. She was a woman going to meet death—and knowing it. The audience knew it too. Sure of the outcome, sure she would finally escape, they still felt the fright she meant to convey. Even Dick was silent, watching as she reached the foot of the stairs.

The black and white screen managed to reproduce the eeriness of gaslight; even the furnishings seemed to suggest the gray flicker that was the very color of terror. Helen Bradley knew that she lived in this house with a husband who intended to kill her. She knew that no one would believe her accusation if she made it, and that there was no escape from what was going to happen—very soon. Yet she must go down those stairs, cross the hall, and enter the parlor where he waited for her. The background music was hushed, suitably tense and anticipatory. You forgot this was Laura Worth, the actress. You became Helen Bradley.

Her walk across that dim hallway toward the parlor, her pause before the door was memorable. Surely no one had ever managed so short a walk more graphically. I even knew the exact shade of the dress she wore. Although the screen was black and white, the true color was a rich Venetian red, as it had been in my father's book. Helen's hand was on the china doorknob and the audience held its breath. Some of us who had seen the picture before knew what was coming. As the woman steeled herself to open the door, the chilling voice from nowhere came whispering out of the air.

"*Listen . . .*" And then ominously closer. "*Listen . . .*"

Helen Bradley tore open the door and rushed into the parlor. Anything was better than to stand in the dim hallway and hear that evil whispering.

She rushed into the room, the camera following. For a moment there was only her intense fear—and silence. Even the music held its breath. The camera panned about the room, touching the mantel with its ornate clock, moving toward the dining room door. My hackles rose as they always did at this point—because of what was not there. In an earlier scene an iron doorstop in the shape of a cat had propped open that door. Now the doorstop was gone—and, dreadfully, I knew why. The reason had nothing to do with make-believe and a movie screen.

Then the camera turned upon Helen's face, and you saw the widening of her eyes in new terror. The view flashed to the body of the man who lay upon a rug before the narrow Victorian fireplace—then back to Helen's face. You saw the growing of this new, more dreadful terror as she realized that her husband was not murderer, but victim, that he lay dead across the room. You could see the realization drawn in Helen's eyes that the murderer was unidentified and still about —he was not, after all, the known quantity of the man she had married. Now she was alone in this house with the Whisperer. That was when she screamed, and the sound was one that went echoing down the nerves of every listener for hours afterwards.

I stumbled to my feet and pulled Dick with me. "Let's get out. I don't want to see the rest."

He rose, startled, and followed me from the theater. We stood blinking on the lighted street and for a moment I clung to his arm, shivering, though the spring night was gentle. Be-

hind us theater placards spread Laura Worth's unforgettable
face across the foyer. Above, the lights of the marquee announced the Worth Festival now running.

Dick patted my hand. "I don't blame you," he said. "I take
it all back about corn. She made that scream sound as real as
any scream could be. I've got prickles down my spine."

"It was real," I said. "She knew what she was screaming
about. Walk me back to the house, Dick. I want to go home."

He looked at me curiously as we walked toward Fifty-ninth.
"You've got an obsession about her, haven't you? You really
are a little nutty when it comes to Laura Worth. Is it true that
she was your mother?"

"Not was—is." I could hear the chill in my own voice. I
would not let Dick know all that I was feeling. "She's still
alive, you know. She was fifty-eight a month ago."

"No, I didn't know. She disappeared after *The Whisperer*,
didn't she? Wasn't there a scandal that hurt the picture? So
that she lost out on the Oscar and never played another role?"

He was still curious, but idly so. He didn't really care. And
I cared so deeply that it tore me apart.

We had reached the brownstone town house that had belonged to my father, Victor Hollins, and we paused beside
iron-railed steps.

"Thanks for taking me, Dick," I said. "I'm sorry I got
upset."

He waved a careless hand. "It was worth seeing. Someday
you'll have to tell me the end. I'm sorry if I've asked you too
many questions."

I didn't invite him in, and he did not expect it. We were
friends. He had told me once that at twenty-three it was time
for me to wake up and fall in love. Not necessarily with him.
He had only a small inkling as to how I felt about love. I never
paraded what they might call my aberrations to the men I
knew. Eventually they discovered that I couldn't be reached,
and they either kept me as a friend, or drifted away. No one
got hurt, and that was the way I wanted it.

I ran up the steps and let myself into the house. A lamp
burned in the lower hall, and there were lights on upstairs.
Ruth called to me over the stair rail.

"You're home early, dear. Did you see a good picture?"

I hesitated, not wanting to wound her. She was my step-
mother and very dear to me. But this time hurt would be
necessary if I was to follow my father's wishes. He had died
just a month ago, and he had left a letter for me that was ex-

plicit in its instructions. Ruth knew nothing of the letter. I had locked it away in a drawer until I could decide what I must do. Tonight I had gone deliberately to see *The Whisperer,* and watching Laura Worth on the screen had brought me at last to resolution.

I answered in as gentle a tone as I could. "Dick took me to see a Laura Worth movie."

The faint catching of her breath was audible, but she turned from the rail without answering. I heard her pad back to her room in her fluffy mules. I had never known anyone more gentle and kind and loving—yet somehow it had always made a difference to me that she was not my mother. And even when I was small I had sensed that the love my father gave her was not the same sort of love he had cherished for Laura Worth. This knowledge had been given its final confirmation when my father was dying. He had held Ruth's hand, but he had seen another woman's face, and a strange, touching joy had dawned in his eyes. "Laura," he had murmured. "My darling Laura." And he was gone, leaving me to try to comfort Ruth, with a dark, bitter hatred draining me.

Now I considered running upstairs to put my arms about Ruth's small person, and to tell her why I had gone to see that particular picture at this time. But I must be more certain of myself first.

I went down the hall to my father's study and turned on the lamp that lighted the desk. My desk now. My study. He had taken pride in my writing, though it was so different from his own. He had been even more delighted than I when a newspaper had published my first little "personality" piece. He had always said that this room was to be mine when he was gone—but I had not expected that day to come for a long time. His loss was all about me. It must always wound those who are left when a man's possessions outlive him.

I had kept the room as it had always been, except for adding a few things of my own. His library still packed the shelves. There was a long shelf next to the fireplace that held his books—all the novels he had written. Novels that had made him famous and had once earned him a good living. He had not been clever at saving money, and his books were not as popular as they'd once been, so there was very little left. Ruth would have barely enough to live on—and I wanted nothing. I could earn my own living, and I would help her if it became necessary. But here were the books which had made his reputation, with *Maggie Thornton* first in the row, and all its hardcover and paperback editions lined alongside it. The book had been translated into thirty-two languages, and as a little girl I could remember coming into this room to count the editions as the number increased.

Maggie Thornton was the first book of his made into a screen play for Laura Worth, and he had gone out to Hollywood to write the film script for her. The combination had been so successful that she had won her first nomination for an Academy Award, and that time the Oscar had been hers. It was during the making of the picture that they had fallen in love. Victor Hollins had wanted to marry her, but she had refused. Her work was everything. She meant to have love affairs, but never to be tied down. Victor would not stay in Hollywood and dance attendance to her ego. He had his pride and his own satisfying work, and he had returned home to marry a girl who had been in love with him for a long time.

When I was old enough, he had told me all these things. He had told me how, when he knew that Laura was going to bear his child, he had asked Ruth to take the baby. She had never hesitated, and she had loved me as her own—and I had loved her. At least I had been secure in having my own father.

Nothing in his telling had ever been meant to make me hate Laura. He did not hate her himself, and he felt that there should be room in every human heart for many loves of many kinds, and much forgiveness. Something went wrong with his intent. I saw only the pain in his eyes when he spoke of Laura. I saw only the hurt to Ruth, the injury to me because I'd had a mother who did not want me.

So I grew up with that disturbing ambivalence. I was greedy to learn all I could about Laura Worth. I found old movie magazines which contained pieces about her that were often unflattering and gossip-filled. I could see very clearly that she was a person I would not want to know—yet I went on gathering my secret fund of probably faulty knowledge. Once in school I bragged openly that she was my mother, shocking my teacher and puzzling my schoolmates, only to deny the whole thing the next day. Even in play with my dolls, I was haunted by the specter of a mother who had never wanted to see me. I would tell my doll children that I was their mother, but I was very busy and I could not keep them. Then I would burst into tears because I could not bear to give them up. Afterwards I would try to make it up to them with the kind of love Ruth gave me. But that was never satisfactory because I knew they would never forget the cruel words I had spoken, and they could never love me back.

Laura had been thirty-four when I was born. Four years later she had made *The Whisperer,* though this time my father had not written the script. Laura's career was over before the end of the picture—though she could not have known it then. Often as I grew up I relished the fact. I hoped she had not given up her work willingly. I hoped that she had suffered when it was taken from her. For try as I would, I could not see that she deserved any sympathy or kindness.

I sat at the huge desk where Victor Hollins had written his novels so painstakingly in longhand. My portable typewriter was dwarfed by its mahogany expanse. I pushed the typewriter away, pushed away the unfinished piece I was writing for a magazine, and reached for the framed photograph beyond it. Across the lower right-hand corner a strong feminine hand had written: "For my darling Victor, with all my love—Laura."

I had found the photograph in a locked drawer in my father's desk, and I had set it out deliberately where it would taunt me, goad me, anger me into deciding. Ruth had not understood, and I could not tell her how I felt. She had been able to pity Laura as the years went by—where there was no pity in me.

Now I studied Laura Worth's face. She had been stunningly beautiful, but never with a conventional beauty. Pretty she was not. Her father had been an American who married a fair-haired Norwegian girl, and Laura had taken after him with dark hair and eyes. In the portrait her hair was brushed into the fluffy bob of the early thirties, her chin tilted to show the long beautiful line of her throat. Above those wide cheekbones her great dark eyes wore their naturally thick lashes, and her brows had been darkly penciled. Her strong nose with sensitively flared nostrils and her wide, generous mouth all added to a face that could belong only to Laura Worth. It was a face that would be recognized anywhere, even though it had not been seen on the screen in a new film for all those years since 1950.

I turned the portrait so that it caught the light and the glass became a mirror, with my own face superimposed upon hers. I looked like neither Laura Worth nor Victor Hollins. My chin was not softly rounded like Laura's. It was a chin as strong and stubborn as Laura Worth's nose. My eyes were a hazy blue, my hair a darkish blond that I wore straight in a

cut that fell just below my jawline. I looked nothing at all
like the picture, yet I felt the unwanted resemblance inside
me. I knew I had something of her stormy, indomitable nature. I wanted to be gentle like Ruth. I did not want to feel
so deeply and be so torn by my emotions. This was one reason
why I was wary of love. Love between a man and a woman
was dangerous, hurtful—I wanted none of it.

Once when I was ten my father took me to a movie matinee.
The picture we went to see was *Maggie Thornton.* "I want
you to know what your mother was like," he had told me.

The dynamic woman on the screen fascinated me. Beside
her I felt like a zero. How could any daughter grow up to
equal such a mother? Was that what my father wanted, I
wondered—for me to be like her?

On the way home we were silent, both of us haunted by
what we had seen. When we reached the house Father took
me into his study and perched me on his desk. I did not want
to hear what he might say.

"I don't want to grow up to be like her!" I cried. "She didn't
want me, and I don't want her. I only want you and Ruth. I
hate her—I hate her!"

He held me very close and let me cry out a storm against
his shoulder. I think my wild emotions alarmed and distressed
him. This was not what he had intended.

When I'd spent myself he kissed me gently. "You must
never do that again," he said. "This is the way Laura used to
be. It is necessary for you to forgive her, but not to be like
her."

I never forgave her, and I was terribly afraid that I was like
her.

Two days before his death, my father took me into his study
again.

"I want you to have something," he said.

He opened a locked drawer in the desk and took out an
object I had never seen before. It was a beautiful French paperweight—"millefiori," it was called, he said. Under the glass
were a multitude of tiny glass flowers in red and blue and
green and yellow. I held it reverently in my hands while he
told me about it.

"Laura Worth gave it to me to celebrate the completion of
Maggie Thornton. It is very old and very valuable. I want you
to have it. Keep it to remember us both."

Two days later he was gone. I did not need the paperweight
to remember him by. Now I had his letter, written in the

knowledge that his heart was faulty. In it he told me that he had always wanted me to know my mother, and for her to know me. Now that I was grown it might be possible for me to bridge the gap that she, apparently, had never even tried to bridge. As I knew, she lived in Bergen, Norway, and he wanted me to go to her, make her acquaintance.

"I know you're gathering pieces for a book about great women movie stars of the past," he wrote. "No such book can be complete if it leaves out Laura Worth. She hasn't granted an interview in twenty years, but if you take her the millefiori paperweight, I think she'll see you."

I could understand very well how his letter attempted to trap me. I took pride in the fairness and objectivity with which I wrote the pieces that were beginning to win me a name. If I interviewed Laura Worth, I must look at her without stormy subjective emotions. That was what he intended.

"If you have any difficulty in reaching her," the letter went on, "you are to go to my good friend Gunnar Thoresen. The accompanying letter is for him."

I knew who Gunnar was. He would be about thirty-eight now, but years ago when he was in college he had written my father an unusually perceptive letter about one of his novels, and they had begun their long correspondence. Gunnar's father, now dead, had owned a line of merchant ships that sailed from Bergen, and he had a partnership in the company and worked for it himself. On occasions when Gunnar had been sent to New York, my father and he had met, and had become close friends, in spite of the difference in their ages. Gunnar knew Laura Worth, and I had realized that he sometimes brought my father word of her. I had seen him once or twice when I was younger, but I did not remember him. My father usually met him away from the house, perhaps where no constraint would be set upon their conversation.

"Your own heritage on your mother's side lies in Norway," my father's letter continued, "and it's time you learned what that heritage is. I believe your mother lives in your grandmother's house, and even though the old people are gone, the house, the town, the country, will tell you more about yourself than you're now able to know. It's time for you to forgive and understand your mother. Ruth won't keep you from going. She'll understand."

He closed with loving wishes for my happiness, my future, that brought tears to my eyes. He had worried about me for a long while. This was his way of trying to mend something in me that had been damaged beyond repair long ago. The attached letter to Gunnar Thoresen was sealed, and I did not wonder then what was in it.

Laura Worth and I could never be friends. I might be able to write a piece about her as an actress, but I could never forgive her as a human being. As far as our being mother and daughter, I had a grim need in me to confront her with that. Perhaps to cause her pain, if that was possible.

Watching her tonight in *The Whisperer* had stiffened my resolve. I was going to Bergen. I was going to use all my ingenuity to get to see her. Whatever walls she had built around herself, I would break through. Presented with me in the flesh, she would have to give me something more than the stony silence I had had over the years. Whether she granted me an interview or not, she would have to claim me as being of her own blood. It was time for her to confront what she had done in the past, and to understand that actions have consequences. It did not occur to me that there was a certain arrogance in my attitude that might have been worthy of Laura Worth herself. I only knew that I meant to bring her far more than a millefiori paperweight.

From the picture on the desk her young face looked back at me with that faint mockery she often revealed in her more pungent characterizations. What would she be like at fifty-eight? I had talked to other aging movie stars. I knew how tenderly they preserved their beauty, and I admired them for the life and drive that still kept them active, busy, glamorous figures. But Laura had fled from the very life she had so loved, as she had fled from my father and me.

I knew few details of what had happened after she left Hollywood. She had traveled in Europe for a while. She had married an Englishman who held a position in Oslo at a diplomatic level. They'd lived in Norway for a time, but the marriage had not worked out. There had been a divorce. For a few years all that Laura Worth did was newsworthy. But after the divorce she had moved to her mother's old home in Bergen, and had disappeared entirely from the public eye.

Why had she run away from everything? Why had she *really* run away? Oh, I knew about the scandal that had erupted in Hollywood before the filming of *The Whisperer* was finished. But other actresses had surmounted gossip just as vicious and had continued with their careers. What if the director, Cass Alroy, had been found dead—murdered—on the set of *The Whisperer* that I had seen on the screen tonight?

True, there had been suspicion of Laura Worth in the beginning. There had been a time when it was thought that she might even be brought to trial for his murder. Everyone knew that Cass and Laura had quarreled all the way through this first picture they had made together. It was rumored that they had been lovers—but then, that sort of rumor haunted every star constantly. The gossip columnists waited avidly to pick up the slightest acquaintance and blow it out of all proportion. At least she had been completely exonerated during the inquest, and if rumors continued, they were the sort of thing a woman like Laura Worth would surely have had the strength to live down. So what had caused her crack-up?

The murder case was never solved. It still stood open on the books. But after Laura Worth was freed of all suspicion she had a complete nervous breakdown. Friends spirited her out of sight, took care of her, kept the reporters away. *The Whisperer*—which she had managed to finish—did not gross as much as expected, and someone else won the Oscar. After her recovery she had found that her option was not being picked up by Premier Pictures where she worked, and no one else wanted her services at that moment.

I knew from talking to other stars that a waning popularity could happen suddenly like that. But usually such actresses kept their hand in. Especially if they had the followers, the adulation that Laura Worth commanded. They did stints on the stage when they could, appeared on television, worked abroad. Sooner or later the right vehicle might come along and their stardom prove undimmed. Bette Davis, Joan Crawford, Lillian Gish, Gloria Swanson, were all busy, active women. But Laura Worth had fled.

There were too many questions. I pushed the picture aside and got up from the desk. At one end of the bookshelves Father had kept his scrapbooks and I went to look over the years marked on the matching cover of each. Ruth had kept these books faithfully for him, since he was not one to save every review, every clipping and published picture, or account of talks he had given across the country. But Ruth had treasured them all, and I had her to thank for a complete record of Victor Hollins's professional life. There was just one scrapbook into which he himself had pasted certain items—in this case items that did not concern him personally. I had discovered this book long ago, and I sought it now, carrying it to the desk.

It fell open easily at the place I wanted because I had pored over the story so many times. Pictures of an older, even more beautiful Laura Worth looked up at me from the page. These were no posed pictures, but candid shots caught by news photographers of a woman in tragic trouble. Her eyes were stark, the famous hollows in her cheeks emphasized. Those wide cheekbones gave her face strength and character, the girlish softness of an earlier day was gone. Here was a woman who had suffered deeply—the same woman who had played Helen Bradley so brilliantly in *The Whisperer.*

Lower down the page was a picture of Cass Alroy, with an account of his gifts and accomplishments as a director. I had never liked his face. It was thin, rather ascetic, and somehow the mouth looked cruel to me. He was said to have driven almost despotically the actors with whom he worked. He held them to what he desired at all costs, even resorting to trickery to call forth emotion when he wanted it for the sake of a scene in a picture.

But it was not the news pictures which interested me most at the moment. It was the story of what had happened that night at the studio when Cass Alroy was found murdered, and which my father had clipped so carefully and pasted in this scrapbook. I knew the account by heart, but I read it again.

Sometimes when Laura Worth was working on a picture she would stay in the studio, living in her dressing room, even sleeping there overnight. She had found that she could sustain the mood of a given role and story far better if she did not allow the outside world to intrude. She would study the script, learn her lines for the next day's shooting, sometimes walk about the darkened sound stage, rehearsing scenes for the following day.

On this particular night she had gone to the empty set of stairway, hall, and parlor for *The Whisperer,* and had acted out a scene that was to be shot the next day. Afterwards, she had returned to her dressing room and prepared for bed. Everything had seemed to rustle and creak around the great sound stage, and though she had never been uneasy before when she had stayed in her dressing room, that night she kept listening nervously. When the crash came from the direction of the set, she had flung on a dressing gown and rushed out.

A light was left burning all night, so that the set was partially illumined, as it had been when she had rehearsed earlier. She rushed into the parlor set and almost stumbled over Cass Alroy's body. Terrified, she had run to the door of the stage and screamed for help. One of the studio police had

come in from outside. It was found that Cass had been felled
by a heavy iron doorstop that was one of the props on the
set, his skull crushed by a blow that must have caused immediate death.

Further clippings developed the story. Laura Worth was
being questioned by the police. Laura's quarrels with Cass
Alroy, her reputed affair with him, her resentment of his direction, all were brought out in unpleasant detail. But there
were three circumstances which could not be shaken or
denied, and which eventually won her a waiving of all
suspicion.

First of all, someone else was on the set that night—a
young girl who was a Laura Worth fan had managed to hide
herself in the studio at closing time in the hope of seeing
Laura, and had stayed in the sound stage through the night.

Fans were an integral part of every movie star's life. Any
popular star might have a fan club with membership spread
across the country. Fans were a breed apart and the stars loved
and feared them. They could storm a theater during a personal
appearance and rip the clothes from their idol's back. Or they
could run errands, and answer phones, write letters, do endless small chores, if they were permitted to indulge their wor-
shipful eagerness to serve. Some of them would go to extremes
to be near the star they adored. Most were young and impulsive and emotional.

Laura had such fans all over the country. She had one in
particular in Los Angeles. This girl's name was Rita Bond,
and she was an impulsive eighteen-year-old who had decided
that the best way to be near Laura, perhaps to have a chance
to see her, speak to her, was to hire herself out as an extra
for one of Laura's pictures. Her plan worked better than she
expected and she was given the bit part of a maid in *The
Whisperer*. A face was wanted—a young face, roundly plump,
that could look frightened in the proper scene. Rita must have
looked perpetually timid and frightened, judging from the
news accounts.

This girl discovered that Laura sometimes stayed overnight
in her dressing room near the set, and on this occasion Laura
had announced when the day's filming was over that this was
her plan. Not only Rita, but everyone on the set had known
her intention. Rita had seized an opportunity and hidden herself away among the cranes and vast camera and sound equipment—all the usual clutter that surrounded a set where they
were shooting. She managed to remain in the sound stage

unnoticed when the studio closed. She borrowed a cushion or two from *The Whisperer* set, and made herself a sort of bed near Laura's dressing room. Exactly how she was to approach her idol, she later admitted, she did not know. Being much too excited and thrilled to sleep, she lay awake on her improvised bed.

She heard Laura speaking her lines aloud. She crept after her when she went to the set and walked about rehearsing the next day's scenes. In no way did she intrude upon her. It was enough for her giddy little soul to be permitted to watch such glorious rites. When Laura returned to her dressing room, Rita followed unseen. She lay down again, and again she did not sleep. When the crash came from the set and Laura rushed out of her dressing room, Rita rushed after her, right on her heels. She waited in helpless horror when Laura went to the door and screamed for help. She was there when the police came. And she was there through the weeks of testimony that followed. Fortunately, she had been on guard over Laura all that night, and she had seen every move the actress had made outside her dressing room. She had vouched for the facts of what had happened.

A second circumstance provided even stronger evidence so that Laura could not be seriously suspected, in spite of the rumors that flew around. It was found that the cat-shaped iron doorstop which had killed Cass Alroy was too heavy to have been used as a weapon by either Laura or Rita. Neither could lift it easily, let alone have used it to strike a blow. A big man might have wielded it, but not a woman of Laura's or Rita's build.

There would have been a complete impasse if the third circumstance had not come to light. The police discovered that the fire door at the back of the stage had been opened that night. A day or so before, someone had dumped a pile of fresh earth intended for use in a plant border, in front of the seldom used door. In this earth were the prints of a man's 10½ size shoes made clearly when he had come out the door. There were no entry prints, so he must have gone in by the main door. Fragments of earth trailed for a little way on the asphalt alley, and then disappeared, undoubtedly jarred from his shoes by the act of running away.

Cass had gained more than one enemy over the years—so there were plenty of possibilities. Investigation brought one of these in particular into the picture as a likely suspect. Dr. Miles Fletcher was Laura Worth's personal physician—a man a few years older than she, and rumored to be in love with her. She had been seen about town in his company a number of times recently. He was a tall, well-built, muscular man, and his shoe size matched that of the prints found in the dirt pile. What was more, he had been in the studio that afternoon to attend Miss Worth, when she had been thoroughly upset by an altercation with Cass Alroy. Everyone on the set had heard him exchange heated words with Cass that afternoon. This, however, was all that the police were able to establish. Dr. Fletcher had an ironclad alibi.

He had checked out of the studio gate after he had attended Miss Worth. The discovery of the murder had taken place about eleven o'clock at night. At which time Miles Fletcher had been in the company of his sister, Mrs. Donia Jaffe, watching a play in a downtown theater. There were others present at the theater who attested to seeing him there in Donia's company. Nothing could be done to connect Dr. Fletcher with the murder. Nevertheless, those footprints remained and there was no gainsaying them. The inquest verdict was murder at the hands of a person, or persons unknown. The immediate flap was over.

Laura was free to have her breakdown, and Rita Bond was free to go wherever all ex-adoring teenage fans may go.

The clippings I followed had nearly finished with the story. There was just one more. Dr. Miles Fletcher had attended Laura constantly through her days of uncertainty and trouble. She turned to him as she turned to no one else, and when she finally collapsed it was he who helped to spirit her away to a place where he and his sister nursed her back to health. How she rewarded this devotion was never known. Or at least not made clear in anything I had read about the affair. He too seemed to vanish from the public eye when Laura herself vanished.

That was the strangest thing of all for me to realize—that so many years had passed. The scandal died at last and there was a huge revival of interest in Worth pictures. If she had been willing, contracts would have been offered. Once more in old pictures she flashed across movie and television screens in the full beauty of her youth and young womanhood. For the world she would never age, though in reality she was now nearing sixty. The clippings, a little yellowed in the book before me, had the same sense of current immediacy. They recounted events that had—in the minds of the writers—only just happened. Coming to them after the picture I had viewed tonight, it seemed as though the tragedy must have taken place yesterday. If I turned on the radio, a news broadcast would surely send Laura's name echoing through the air to startle listeners.

Yet, in truth, all those who were young and beautiful were old by this time. Those who were still alive would wear wrinkles and gray hair and sagging flesh. Not one of them would resemble these news pictures from another day.

I carried the scrapbook to the bookcase and put it away with a strange heavyheartedness. There was no sadness for me in knowing that Laura Worth was no longer young. I could not help hoping that she missed her youth and lost beauty. Whatever pain she suffered was merited. She could never make real payment for the harm she had done to others who were good and deserving. Victor, my father, and Ruth, his wife. Not me. I was neither good nor deserving as they were. Nevertheless, having read through the clippings again, the sense of tragedy lay heavy upon my spirit.

When I had turned off the lamp on the desk, I stood for a moment in the darkened hush of my father's study. From outside closed windows came the subdued roar of New York. Pale moonlight fell through panes of glass, touching the carpet, an armchair, the desk. I did not see them. A voice was whispering through my mind. *"Listen . . ."* it said. *"Listen . . ."* In my father's book a dumbwaiter had been used to achieve the illusion of a whispering that came out of the void. I needed no such device. The voice itself seemed to sound through my very pulses, and I was remembering again the scene in *The Whisperer* when Helen Bradley came upon her husband's body— that dreadful moment when she screamed.

Yes, Laura Worth had known how to scream.

Another director had been hired to finish the picture. And Laura, being an actress, had postponed her moment of collapse and played her role through to the end. I wondered how those in the studio—cameramen, propmen, script girl, technicians—all the crew and assistants to director and star, had felt when she screamed. It must have been a moment of horror for them all. Perhaps Cass Alroy's blood had stained the very carpet where actors stood speaking lines that now had a dreadful meaning. They must have all been aware of that door to the dining room where an iron doorstop had stood. It was gone in the final scenes of the picture. No one had made an effort to replace it.

Abruptly I wrenched myself from these imaginings, turned

the lamp on, and looked again into the eyes of the portrait. There was no horror there—that was yet to come. Only that faint trace of mockery, that hint of growing self-assurance, that suggestion of ruthlessness, perhaps, in the wide young mouth that was not altogether soft. But I did not want to search her young face any longer, and I laid the portrait face down on the desk. Then I opened a lower drawer and took out the millefiori paperweight. As my father wished, I would take with me this gift of Laura's to Victor—his gift to me. I hoped her eyes would reveal something of old pain when I gave it to her.

I went upstairs to tell Ruth that I was going to Norway.

Chapter 2

I stood at the window of my comfortable room at the Norge Hotel and looked out at what I could see of Bergen. This part of the city occupied a peninsula that thrust into the waters of the town fjord and held much of the business district. Coming in from the airport I had been oppressively aware of sheer crags of rock overlooked by crouching black mountains, some of them with snow ridging their peaks.

Often there would be a house perched on what looked like an inaccessible crag, its cheerful yellow paint defying the brown and black landscape. A forbidding landscape conquered by a hardy people. I had no sense of belonging here.

From the hotel window I could look down into the busy square where the statue of a violinist stood fiddling. He too stood upon craggy rock. The weather was brisk and chill, for all that it was sunny, and the people on the streets were dressed for winter. I had left forsythia blooming in New York, but here there was snow on the mountains and one's breath rose mistily on the air. Gulls swooped past at window level, and I could hear their raucous screaming.

Over the roofs of opposite buildings the mountain, Flöyen, rose steeply to its rock-faced summit, with rows of red-roofed houses climbing nearly to those heights where dark fir trees took over and marched to the top. To the right, clustering thickly on lower slopes, were more houses, set helter-skelter, as though their streets ran crookedly. Over there was the district of Kalfaret—the district where my Norwegian grandmother had once lived.

I had asked the porter at the desk downstairs if he knew the house of the former American movie star, Laura Worth. He had nodded at her name. Yes, indeed he knew.

"She lives in Kalfaret—the old patrician part of the city. If you walk toward the park you can see the houses. Perhaps you can see them from your room upstairs."

I asked him to give me her address and telephone number, and he looked them up for me, wrote them on a pad.

"You must remember that Miss Worth is half Norwegian," he said, smiling as he pushed the paper toward me across the desk. "She belongs to Bergen now."

I thanked him without comment and returned to the self-service lift with the door that did not open automatically. When I reached my room, I went at once to the phone. Direct action was what I wanted. I had taken time for lunch since I'd come in from the airport, and that had been slow, using up more than an hour. Now I wanted to set the wheels in motion, start what I had come here for.

A woman's voice with an American accent answered my ring. My heart began to thud as I would not have expected it to. When I asked for Miss Worth, my business was promptly demanded. I said I was Leigh Hollins, from New York, and that I wanted to see Laura Worth. She would know who I was.

The woman repeated my name, and I sensed shock in her tone. Miss Worth could not talk to anyone just now, the voice explained. Would I be at my hotel for the next hour? If so, I would be called back.

I had to be satisfied with that. More than an hour had passed and I was growing restless. It began to seem that Laura Worth might not be willing to see me, that my direct approach was too sudden to bring me anything but refusal. No matter. There was still Gunnar Thoresen to fall back upon. My father had been sure that he would help me.

The shrilling of the phone sent me rushing toward it, and once more my heart began to beat in that thick, heavy way. Would her voice sound the same as I remembered it from all those films? I would recognize those smoky tones anywhere, I was sure. But it was a man who answered my "Hello"—only the desk clerk from downstairs.

"Dr. Fletcher is here to see you, Miss Hollins," he said.

Dr. Fletcher? That was a name out of the past. Could he mean that the same Dr. Fletcher who had rescued Laura Worth after the tragedy was here in Bergen?

"He asks if he may come up to see you," the clerk went on. "It concerns Miss Worth, and is very important."

"Yes—yes, of course," I managed. "Ask him to come straight up."

I hung up the phone, adjusting myself to this new turn of events as I moved about the room, whisking a few things out of sight, straightening the chairs and coffee table in the sitting room section.

The knock on my door sounded in less than five minutes and I went to open it. I was prepared for a large man from the newspaper accounts I had read, and the picture I'd seen. He had been forty then, now he was sixty—and perhaps even larger than he had been because he seemed to have filled out considerably. His black hair was untouched by gray, but he combed it from the side across the top of his head to conceal the balding, and he wore a full black mustache that hid his mouth. In the picture I remembered, he had been clean-shaven, and his mouth had looked fairly grim. Perhaps with good cause at that time. There seemed a certain wariness now in his gray eyes, but no lack of self-confidence. This was a man who knew what he wanted, was sure of what he meant to do, but who was, nevertheless, not altogether sure of me.

"Please come in," I said and gestured toward the small sofa.

He crossed the room and stood for a moment beside the window. "You've quite a view of the mountain here, in spite of those buildings. Bergen is a beautiful town. And I see you can watch Ole Bull at his fiddling."

I knew he referred to the statue of the well-known musician and composer below my window. I noticed that he gave the name the Norwegian pronunciation. Just as Gunnar was pronounced "Goonar," the composer was "O-le Bool."

But I did not feel like indulging in chitchat.

"Do you know who I am?" I asked directly.

He turned from the window as I sat down in a chair opposite the sofa. "Yes, of course. You are Victor Hollins's daughter."

"And Laura Worth's," I added.

He lowered his large frame carefully onto the sofa springs. "I've always wondered if that story was really true."

"Of course it's true," I said.

His shrug was questioning, and now he examined me even more closely. I felt the chill of imminent dismissal behind his look, and suspected that if Dr. Fletcher had anything to say about it, I would not see Laura Worth.

"Why have you come here?" he asked, as flatly direct as I had been.

"My father died a month ago, and I found he had left me a letter. He wanted me to meet my mother, but there was another reason besides for my coming here. I've done some writing, though of course I could never follow in his steps. I've had some things published and now I'm doing a book of interviews with famous women stars who were in motion pictures in the thirties and forties. I'd like to do a sketch of Laura Worth to make the book complete."

"Miss Worth never gives interviews. She hasn't done so for twenty years. You must know that."

His eyes troubled me. They were a pale gray which seemed to hold light in them in some strange, brilliant way. They were eyes that missed nothing. They noted my navy blue knit, the dark blond hair that swept my cheeks, they studied my face and obviously found it young and not very interesting. They probed for my motives. They made me defensive. Dr. Fletcher was even more sure of himself now, and confident of holding the winning cards in whatever game he played. I did not like him at all, and I didn't even know the game.

"Perhaps she will want to see me," I said. "I've brought her something from my father. In a sense, I'm a message to her from him."

"It's a bit late in the day for such a message," Dr. Fletcher told me, smiling thinly. "I'm sorry that you've come a long way for nothing. Miss Worth isn't well and such a meeting would be needlessly upsetting for her. I can't permit it."

"As her doctor?"

The smile took on a slight edge of triumph. "As her husband, Miss Hollins."

I gaped at him, far from poised and sure of myself. "I—I didn't know she was married."

"The fact hasn't been widely broadcast," he said. "Miss Worth did me the honor to become my wife two months ago. Fortunately, it was my sister who answered the phone when you called, and of course she recognized your name and came to me at once. We haven't troubled Mrs. Fletcher with the news that you are here. Nor shall we. I must make it very clear, Miss Hollins. Our door will be closed to you. And my wife never answers the telephone herself. I have her health and well-being very much at heart, and I don't intend her to be disturbed by specters out of the past. She has suffered enough."

So now I was a specter out of the past. I studied him helplessly for a moment, and he shrugged again under the force of my stare and rose to his feet.

"I hope we understand each other, Miss Hollins. I thought it best to make this clear to you in person. Mrs. Fletcher, I might say, is well protected from all outside intrusions that she might find wearing and disturbing. It will be useless for you to stay in Bergen. Even if I were sure that you are her daughter, I know that she rejected motherhood long ago. She would not care to see you."

He went past me to the door, and I followed him automatically, unable to think of anything to say. When he had gone, his footsteps fading quickly on the soft hall carpet, I flung myself upon the bed and stared angrily at the ceiling.

There was one way in which I resembled my mother all too well. My father had told me so ruefully more than once. The word "no" was something we could never accept. Even when I was small I had been a difficult child to forbid. Ruth had learned early that I could be persuaded, but I couldn't be negatively commanded.

Laura Worth had once been like that. She was apparently so no longer. She had grown old and ill, and she had finally married Miles Fletcher whom she would not marry in those long-ago days in Hollywood. A husband! This I had not expected to cope with. And especially not with this man who had figured rather unpleasantly in those newspaper clippings I had read so many times. He had been in love with Laura and he had exchanged angry words with Cass Alroy at the studio the afternoon of the murder. But in spite of that matching footprint size in the dirt outside the fire door through which the murderer must have escaped, he'd had a safe alibi. All these things I remembered.

There was no use in thinking about all that, however, or permitting myself to be defeated by this setback. Possibly even Gunnar Thoresen could not help me now, but I must try him as the next step. If he failed me, there would be some other way.

I found the name of his company in the phone book and put the call through. After a small delay, he came on the wire, and I liked his manner of speaking. His voice had a deep timbre, a resonance that was pleasing. His accent was English, rather than American, his speech slightly formal.

"I am Leigh Hollins," I began, "and I've come to Bergen—" but he broke in at once.

"Leigh Hollins! You are Victor's daughter? I am very sad to hear of your father's death."

"I've brought you a letter from him," I said.

"I will be grateful for that. May I take you to dinner tonight? We will have much to talk about."

"Thank you. But first—I'm here for another reason as well.

My father wanted me to see Laura Worth. Perhaps he has told you that I'm writing too. Now I want to do an interview with her for a book I'm planning about women movie stars of her day. But seeing her appears hard to arrange. Apparently I'm not to be allowed to meet her."

He seemed to consider my words, and I wondered if he knew of the relationship between me and Laura.

"Perhaps my father told you?" I added. "She is my mother."

"I know this," he said gently. "And of course you must see her, regardless of Dr. Fletcher."

I liked his quiet confidence, and the fact that he knew at once where my source of trouble lay.

"I will think of something," he said, and I found that I believed him implicitly.

I told him of Miles Fletcher's visit to the hotel and just what he had said.

The deep, quiet voice at the other end of the line pondered aloud. "I have a friend in Laura's household—Irene Varos. I think she will help us."

"Who is Irene Varos?"

"It is difficult to give her a label. She is a Yugoslavian woman whom Laura found years ago when she was traveling in Europe. She engaged her as part secretary, part house-keeper, part personal friend and assistant. Irene does not like Dr. Fletcher. I will prevail upon her. You will see."

"You're saving my life," I told him.

He laughed briefly, and was grave again at once. "You have come at the right time. Laura needs you. You should be very good for her. You may be able to help her."

His words dismayed me. I didn't want to give him a false impression to start off with. "I'm afraid—" I began, but he broke in before I could continue.

"I'm sorry, but there is a long-distance call for me on another wire. I will have to go. If six-thirty is convenient, I shall pick you up at your hotel—the Norge, is it?—and then we may talk. Do not worry. I will make arrangements. Good-bye now, Leigh Hollins."

I could do no more than thank him and agree. For a moment or two after I'd hung up, I sat staring at the phone. Gunnar Thoreson might very well provide the solution to my problem. He had sounded assured, and determined to see that I met Laura. But he was also harboring a mother-daughter illusion about us that had nothing to do with the facts. Perhaps it was just as well that he'd mistaken my motives. If he knew how I really felt about Laura Worth, he might not be so willing to help me. Nevertheless, I felt a little guilty about deceiving him. He was being kind and helpful, and he was my father's friend. I had no wish to make him believe what, unfortunately, could not be true. Yet at the same time, I needed all the help I could get if I was to confront Laura Worth with my double purpose.

Now I had the afternoon on my hands, and I didn't mean to spend it sitting in a hotel room. Bergen was outside, waiting for me, and I might as well start getting acquainted. So far, I had felt no stirring of recognition, no feeling that through my mother I had come from this place. The crowding circle of black mountains—the Seven Mountains that hemmed Bergen in—had only depressed me. But there was something active I could do.

Downstairs I found no cabs at the hotel door, but the doorman told me there was a taxi stand a half block away on Torgalmenning, the main business street of the town. I crossed through traffic and hailed a cab. The driver studied the slip of paper I held out to him and nodded as I settled back in the seat. I was on my way to the area in which Laura Worth lived.

We drove past the expanse of open park with its lake, its central fountain, bandstand, and great museums, and moved along a hillside busy with traffic. There were few stop lights, yet the traffic was not unduly wild at the cross streets. Each driver seemed to bluff gently to see who got across first. The roads were narrow, not built for motor travel, but most of the cars were moderate in size. We passed the old tollgate that had once marked the edge of town and the driver identified it for me. We drove among the lime trees of Kalfaret.

The hillside houses were mostly square and white, though some were brightly colored. They were two-storied, with steeply peaked tile roofs rising to a ridge at the top and well adorned with chimneys. The cab took a side street up the hill and now there was scarcely room for passing, but few cars. The driver slowed and motioned toward a house ahead.

A tall sustaining wall bordered the street, with the house he indicated high above. I could not see it well from the cab window and I asked him to go past. When we were a little distance away around a curve, I told him to stop and wait for me. Then I got out and walked back.

The house was white and set against a hillside which still wore the dead browns of winter. I could glimpse the steeply

slanted blue tiles of the roof rising high above me, with only
the upper dormer windows visible, looking down upon me
blankly, curtained and secluded. There was a garage set into
an indentation near the steps up the hill, and a small car stood
outside its door. Steep steps running parallel with the street
climbed toward the house.

I walked past on the far side and then turned to look back.
Nearby bushes around the opposite house offered a shield and
I stood still for a few moments studying the area. Crooked
streets ran this way and that, and the houses were so built that
each in turn looked upon the chimneys of neighbors lower
down the steep hillside.

My grandmother had once lived in this house. Now Laura
Worth lived here. I said the words to myself, but nothing
happened inside me. They were empty of meaning, of emotion.
No sudden feeling of kinship engulfed me. I did not belong
to Norway.

Sounds from above caught my ear, and I saw that four
people were coming along the side of the house, down a walk
that slanted toward the steep flight of steps. Instinctively I
stepped farther behind the scraggly brown bushes that shielded
me from view.

The man was Dr. Fletcher. A woman leaned upon his arm.
She was enveloped in a coat made from some hazy autumn
color of fur, with the pale, soft collar pulled high about her
face. On the other side she was guarded by a younger woman
who was quite thin, and slightly taller. A second woman came
skipping along energetically behind this entourage—a small
brown, wizened little person in a colorful Norwegian sweater
and green slacks. I made identifications to myself as well as I
could. The woman in fur was of course Laura Worth. I could
not see her face, but she walked like an invalid, as if she were
much older than I knew her to be. The second woman would
be the housekeeper-secretary Gunnar had mentioned—Irene
Varos. The lively, wizened little person must be the doctor's
sister.

Painfully, the woman in fur descended the steps, leaning
upon her supporters. When she reached the street level, she
raised her head for the first time. For the first time I saw her
face and held my breath. It was a white, thin face, devoid of
makeup, its good bone structure visible beneath skin that had
long since lost the bloom of youth. But it was a face I would
have known anywhere. The dark eyes looked sunken, but the
shape and tilt of them was there. And age could never change

the structuring of those facial bones, or destroy the memory of beauty that lay beneath that translucent skin.

The two who helped her led her toward the car, assisted her into it. Then Irene Varos got in beside her, and Dr. Fletcher took the driver's seat. The little woman stood on the steps, watching her brother as he backed the car out and drove away down the street. Then she ran back up the steps and disappeared above me around the side of the house. Just as the car turned away, Laura glanced out the window on her side. She seemed to look directly at me, and for an instant our eyes met, though I doubt that she was aware of me standing there. Then the car was gone down the hill, and I was left staring at a house empty of her presence.

Only then did I discover that I was shaking. In the cool air there was perspiration on my face, and when I opened my handbag to take out a handkerchief, my fingers trembled so that I nearly dropped the bag. My reaction dismayed me. Laura Worth was my adversary. At least that was what I had hoped for. Now I was less sure. Not less sure of my antagonism toward her, but not sure that there was anything there worthy of my steel. The woman in furs had been a wraith, a ghost out of the past. She seemed hardly able to walk by herself, let alone stand up to a daughter she had injured.

But that was not why I was trembling. This was a reaction I did not understand. I blotted my forehead with my handkerchief and stood there for a few moments longer until the shaking subsided. Then I returned to my waiting taxi. It was around the curve, and the driver had seen nothing. I got in and told him to take me about Bergen—anywhere. He could show me the city.

It was a bright, beautiful city made up of both old buildings with steeply peaked gray slate roofs and tall chimneys, and blocks of modern buildings as well. It reached around the waters of the fjord on two sides, with that crowded peninsula thrusting out between, into the center of the harbor. Beyond lay more water and hilly islands, some of them the rocky North Sea skerries I had seen when we were coming in on the plane. It was a city which had been planned by geographic necessity, forced into its pattern by the mountains and water that circled it.

For Norway, May was a month of festivals and holidays, and we passed young people's groups marching in the streets, drilling in uniform with their bands. Some of the boys carried crossbows that were apparently symbolic of the past. There seemed to be Norwegian flags everywhere, flying their red ground with the blue and white cross.

All of it flowed over and around me. I was still haunted by a white, beautiful face framed by fur and turned toward me unseeingly. This was not the way I wanted her to be. I wanted to see her strong and assured, filled with confidence. Only then could I bring her down with a satisfying crash. This pale, faltering woman was not the Laura Worth I had come to see. Perhaps her own life had caught up with her, and there was no need for me to bring her down. But I would not accept that. I had carried a painful and bitter resentment for too long to let it go easily.

I told my driver to take me back to the hotel, where I paid him and went upstairs to my room. I had a feeling of being suspended and not entirely of the world I was in. Certainly I must carry through my plan to meet Laura face to face. But for the moment I could only wait.

Late in the afternoon I dressed carefully for my meeting with Gunnar Thoresen. I wore brown wool, with a white cowl collar and dipping white cuffs. An antique gold pin and earrings were my only jewelry, and I brushed my hair to a darkly blond sheen. I wanted my father's friend to like me and help me, and in a sense my careful grooming would hide my ungroomed feelings toward Laura Worth.

Promptly on time the call came to my room that he waited for me in the lobby. I put on my beige coat, caught up gloves and pocketbook and went downstairs. He was waiting near the lift. We seemed to know each other at once and he met me with an outstretched hand. I liked the look of him—tall, well built, but slender and narrow of face, somewhat ruggedly handsome, with the brown hair and eyes that were more typical of this West Land of Norway. He was friendly, courteous —I was accepted as my father's daughter—yet there was a certain reserve about him that contrasted with the more easy camaraderie of the American. I liked that reserve. I did not want too much friendliness between us. Enough to aid me, but no more.

"I have found a place for my car," he told me. "Parking is something of a problem. It is only a short distance to the restaurant, so if you do not mind walking—"

"I like to walk," I said.

The evening was chill, but clear, and the sky had not darkened at all. The daylight would last in May, I realized.

"This is what we call festival weather," Gunnar said. "In

Bergen it rains a great deal. All through the winter it is likely to rain. We do not have the heavy snows of the rest of Norway. But in May the weather clears and is usually good for our annual festival season."

I knew about Bergen's famous *Festspillene*, the great festival of music, drama, and folklore, held every year in spring, with renowned musicians coming from all over the world to the place which had given birth to Edvard Grieg and Ole Bull.

We walked together up the street from the square as it climbed toward the huge gray stone building of the National Theater looming above. Gunnar chatted pleasantly as we walked, and neither of us mentioned Laura. All in good time, his manner seemed to say.

The restaurant was across from the theater and we went up a tiny circular stairway to reach the second floor. There we had a table set in an alcove beside a casement window that overlooked the theater garden. Light beige cloths and electric blue napkins graced the tables, and there were green plants hanging in pots from the ceiling. Only one other couple was dining across the small room.

"This is not our usual dining hour in Bergen," Gunnar said. "We go early to business and leave our offices early. A man expects to be home by four-thirty or five, to begin what we call our second day—the time we spend at home with our families. Then we have our main meal at that time, with perhaps a snack around nine in the evening. At this present hour we go to restaurants only to talk and drink beer. This is a university town, and you will find students filling many restaurants now."

I let him order for me and he chose the salmon, which he said I would like. When the waitress had gone, I faced him purposefully, feeling that I'd waited long enough.

"I saw Laura Worth this afternoon," I told him.

He showed no surprise, but was silent while I explained. I had not been able to wait, I said. I'd been eager to look at my grandmother's house.

"I got there just in time to see Laura come down those steep steps with Dr. Fletcher and a woman I suppose was Miss Varos. They helped her into a car and drove away. A small woman—Dr. Fletcher's sister?—stayed behind."

"Of course," he said. "They were running from you. You must have startled Dr. Fletcher for some reason. I wonder why."

"Then—then I won't be able to see her?"

"Perhaps you will." He gave me his slow, rather beautiful smile. He was a grave man, and I had not seen him smile before. "I was able to reach Irene on the telephone after I talked to you. She was not able to speak freely from the house, but she went outside to call me back. She said that Dr. Fletcher had seemed disturbed when he returned from his trip downtown, and he had persuaded Laura that it would be pleasant to visit the cottage she owns on a small lake near Fantoft. Mrs. Jaffe, the doctor's sister, is staying in the Kalfaret house here in Bergen, but Irene was to go with Laura and look after her. We think it is all a plan to keep Laura from meeting you, should you become persistent. But like me, Irene thinks it may be good for her to meet you."

"She looked quite ill," I said.

Gunnar nodded soberly. "This illness has come on her only lately."

Since her marriage? I wondered.

"It appears to be an illness of apathy," Gunnar went on. "I have seen her a few times, and it is as though she had suddenly given up all desire to live."

This time I wondered aloud. "It's strange that she should make such a late marriage. Now that she no longer has her beauty, her youth—"

He contradicted me a little sternly, and I sensed that while there might be gentleness and kindness in this man, there was also a firm layer of bedrock.

"You do not know her, Leigh Hollins. I may call you Leigh? She can be a fascinating woman. There is more to beauty than a surface veneer, though perhaps someone as young as yourself has not yet discovered this."

I bristled inwardly at his words. He was not all that old himself, and I did not like being put down.

"She's also a very wealthy woman," I said with some asperity. "Dr. Fletcher might not overlook that."

"There is that possibility, of course. Though perhaps you are leaping to a conclusion."

"It could be that she's finally reaping everything she's built for herself in the past," I said, piqued enough to forget for the moment that I must be on guard with Gunnar Thoresen.

His dark eyes regarded me thoughtfully, and with the same disapproval I had already glimpsed in them.

"We all build for ourselves what we eventually reap. Is not that the cliché? I have known Laura Worth for many years,

Leigh. Our families have, as you may know, been close. My father was devoted to her during his life, and so is my mother. She is a brave woman, a sad woman, who until now has not been broken by the years."

I was grateful for the waitress's interruption as she set soup plates before us and dry bread to break into the soup. Avoiding Gunnar's eyes, I gave my attention to the delicious mushroom soup that was made with plentiful fresh mushrooms. I knew even more about Laura Worth and the past than he did. But for the moment I must keep what I knew and felt to myself.

"Irene and I had a discussion on the telephone," Gunnar went on when the waitress had gone. His slightly formal manner of speech had a pleasant sound in contrast to the more slurred speech of Americans. I was beginning to tune into it. "We have decided that it is wiser if we do not immediately tell Laura that you are her daughter. In her present weak state, the thought of meeting the daughter she has not seen since the child was newborn may be too much for her. If she meets you first as a journalist, she may rouse herself to make a good appearance. She is quite capable of doing so. Then the next step of letting her know your identity will be easier. Perhaps you can use another name temporarily and merely identify yourself as a writer who is eager to interview her. I have suggested Mary Thomas as a possible name, since we had to settle on one. If you have no objection."

I sensed a certain male assurance in these arrangements, but I had no objection. They might even suit my own purpose better.

"Then I'm to meet her after all?"

"We have planned something—if you do not mind." At least he seemed to recognize a certain high-handedness in these arrangements. "At Fantoft, where she has gone, there is a place in which she often likes to walk. Our famous *stavkirke* is there—one of Norway's few remaining stave churches. It is in a small pleasant park of walks and rocky hills. Irene will take Laura there at ten o'clock tomorrow morning, after Dr. Fletcher has driven back to town. If these plans suit you, I will drive you to Fantoft and Irene will bring Laura there. An extra car is kept at the cottage, which she may use. Then you can speak with each other alone."

"She'll have been told about me ahead of time?"

"Yes. That is, she will be told that you are a young writer

from America who wishes to interview her for a book you are working on."

"But if she has refused interviews for so long?"

"I believe Irene will persuade her. During the last few years she has begun to believe she is forgotten in America. It is even possible that she will welcome an interest great enough to bring you here."

"I see. Then I'm to interview here there, if she will allow it? Is that all?"

"You Americans have a phrase," Gunnar said. "To play something by ear—is it not? You must see how she responds. Nothing can be forced, but perhaps you will ask for another meeting."

"What if Dr. Fletcher finds out and says no?"

"Laura will have been warned that he has already said no. It is a word she did not care for in the past. Possibly she will not accept it now. Possibly she is like yourself in this?"

I smiled at him, agreeing. He was perceptive, this lean Norwegian with the handsome, narrow face. Perhaps there was a certain obstinacy in him as well. I suspected that he did not like Miles Fletcher.

"Does Laura know about my father's death?" I asked.

"Yes. It was in the papers here. Though I do not know how it affected her. Since her marriage, I do not see her often, and she has said nothing."

"What has her life been like since she's lived in Bergen?"

"Rather quiet. When she came here she seemed a woman badly hurt. She had made a foolish marriage which had not gone well and there had just been a divorce. She had been injured only a few years before by what had happened in Hollywood, and by the suspicions the public held against her in America, in spite of her exoneration by the law from any guilt. Where in the past she had lived in the public eye, she now hid from its gaze. In Bergen we do not trouble her. We tend to mind our own business and to leave alone anyone who wishes to be left alone. There has been a certain pride in the fact that this famous woman was born in Bergen. I believe her mother insisted upon returning to her own home for the birth of her child—even though she quickly took the baby back to her American husband. It is not overlooked that Laura Worth lives in our midst now. But we do not disturb her."

"What did she do with herself during all those years?"

"She accepted certain friendships. My father and mother,

and then myself were among them. She became interested in our winter sports, our summer hiking. She reads a great deal."

"But all that is merely marking time," I said. "It's hard to picture someone who lived as Laura Worth did going into retreat, giving up a great career so completely."

The waitress took our plates away, brought boiled salmon with small white potatoes and a side sauce of sour cream. When we had been served, Gunnar returned to my last question.

"She has not been altogether unhappy, I think. Perhaps not entirely happy, either. Who is? But that is enough talk about Laura Worth. I would like to know about you. This writing—it interests you greatly?"

His own interest seemed sincere and warm, and in spite of the flashes when he regarded me like an autocratic uncle, I was drawn to him increasingly. I still had not disillusioned him of his notion that I was a proper daughter seeking her mother. Yet while I didn't deliberately deceive him, I held back from a truth which might make him refuse to help me. Now I attempted to tell him a little about myself.

"My father always encouraged me to write," I said, and tried to describe the sort of things I'd had published. I wanted him to know that I was working hard toward success in my field.

"You paint an unusual picture," he said when I paused. "You have great ambition, but what of the rest of your life? Do you make room for play, for enjoyment?"

"The most interesting sort of play is satisfying work." Since I didn't want to be lectured about a balanced life, I asked a question of my own. "Do you have a family, Gunnar?"

"Only my mother, who lives with me. My wife, Astrid, died several years ago. We had no children. She was always rather frail."

"I'm sorry," I said. I had to ask the next question. "You were happy together?"

"Very happy." His tone told me how much he had missed her.

We ate in silence for a little while, and I found the salmon as good as he had promised. There was no strain in our quiet. We had both lost those we loved and there was kinship in that.

When it was time for dessert he insisted that I must try the cloudberries—those delicious yellow berries that grow in the mountains of Norway. Not until we were having coffee did he return to the subject of Laura Worth. What I had said earlier must have stayed with him, troubling his thoughts.

"You will be gentle with her?" he asked me.

"I'm not sure that I'm a gentle person," I said. "I'm likely to be direct."

"An admirable trait. The Bergenser is direct also. But this is a vulnerable woman. You can wound her easily because you are her daughter. When she learns this, she will remember everything you have said to her."

He was overlooking my own vulnerability. Laura Worth had wounded my father cruelly and turned away from me. I too carried wounds—for both my father and myself. I answered him carefully.

"I shouldn't think she would care about my being her daughter. She made her own choice long ago. She decided against my father, and against me. So why should my existence trouble her now?"

"There is such a thing as the blood tie, is there not? Perhaps it is a thing more of the heart than of the mind. Did you perhaps feel it when you saw her today?"

He had put his perceptive finger upon something I didn't want to admit to myself, let alone to him. I didn't want to remember that fit of trembling that had possessed me so unexpectedly, so unreasonably. Had that been it—the blood tie that flowed through my pulses and responded to Laura Worth against my conscious will?

"She's a stranger to me!" I said a little too hotly. "I haven't any feeling that she's my mother. She interests me as an actress—an artist in her work. I can become excited about her career. I can—" I broke off, knowing that I protested too much.

I must be more careful with this man. He could probe too deeply. And if he knew how I truly felt about Laura Worth, I suspected that he would stop our meeting without the slightest qualm. He was her friend, not mine. He was my father's friend and Laura's, and there was in him a rough granite that would bruise anyone who flung herself heedlessly against it. My earlier feeling that I didn't want to deceive him about Laura was fading. He would be a difficult man to fool and my one objective now was to go through with this planned meeting. What happened afterward would have to be met in its own due time.

"I suppose, more than anything else, I admire the fact that

she's been so single-minded about her career," I went on. "I want to be like that myself. But of course I know there's a price that must be paid in time and energy and concentration. Nothing outside must interfere, even though it might seem attractive at the moment." I didn't add that I meant to be even more single-minded than Laura had been. I would not be so foolish as to fall into emotional traps that would hurt others, as she had done.

"I wonder what such ambition is like?" he mused. "This is something I have not felt. I am fond of the sea and ships. I am fond of painting, at which I dabble a little. I enjoy the mountains in the winter, and the lakes and fjords in summer. I like to live my day fully, with work and pleasure mixed. We Norwegians sometimes wonder if Americans do not miss the best part of living because of this very rush and hurry and determination to—what is it you say?—to get somewhere?"

"When I'm working, I'm happy. I'm satisfied."

Again he gave me his grave, rather winning smile, and now I saw that his brown eyes could twinkle a little.

"Perhaps you are only happy because you have not taken time to taste the other things. Perhaps while you are here you will let me introduce you to some of what we enjoy."

"Thank you," I said, and knew I sounded unenthusiastic. Gunnar Thoresen was not part of my purposeful concentration. It was Laura upon whom I must focus, and I had no time for distractions. It didn't really matter whether he liked me, or I liked him, providing he helped me. I assured myself of that quite firmly, resisting any appeal he might have for me. I had no time for anything but Laura.

We walked back to the hotel through an evening that was just beginning to grow a little dark, and we parted in the lobby with the word that Gunnar would call for me at nine-thirty the next morning.

I went upstairs to my room feeling unduly weary, and knew that the change of time, the little sleeping I had done on the plane, all were beginning to catch up with me. Plus a depression that I didn't altogether understand. A depression that seemed to grow from the effort it took to be my individual self, purposefully and unwaveringly. Gunnar, if he knew my intentions, would try to sway me from them—or simply stop me entirely. It was difficult to be constantly on guard, as I must be.

After a steaming hot bath, I went gratefully to bed, discovering for the first time the luxury of a Norwegian eider-down which tucked me in like a sleeping bag and lulled me quickly to oblivion.

Chapter 3

Apparently the university students roaming the streets stayed up a good deal later than the rest of Bergen. Until early in the morning there were outbursts of laughter, shouting, snatches of song. But I heard them dimly through my dreams and came wide awake only once during the night. Then I thought it was morning because of daylight that flooded through my window. My watch told me it was three-thirty, and I got up and closed the draperies, went back to my eiderdown.

By seven-thirty I was refreshed and ready for the day. I found there was a certain brisk lift to my steps as I moved about the room, dressing. My depression was gone and I was ready for the meeting with Laura Worth. Today I would make sure that I saw her only as an actress, and I would lull her into accepting me as a writer. That must be the relationship between us at first. There would be no more shivering and trembling at the sight of her. No more "blood line" betrayal. No weakening of my original purpose.

I dressed in a plaid skirt and woolly white sweater, and slipped my feet into sturdy brown walking shoes. I was hungry by the time I went downstairs to breakfast.

The breakfast room was on the second floor, and already there were English and American hotel guests lining up to serve themselves from the *koldtbord*. I found I could have all I cared to eat of an assortment of cereals, breads, meat, herring, cheeses, and a choice of fruit juice, and coffee and tea.

I filled my plate and found a table near a window, where I could watch my fellows as they moved about the room. Early May was still well ahead of the real tourist influx, but there were already a number of visitors in Bergen, aside from businessmen who were here from Oslo or other parts of Scandinavia. Bergen was a busy commercial city, with shipping and fishing its main industries.

Breakfast, including the goat cheese, which I liked, girded

41

me further for the day, and when Gunnar called me from the lobby I went downstairs cheerfully to greet him.

I knew at once that he had read my father's letter, and that whatever it contained had set him on guard against me. In a way, I was sorry for this. I had liked Gunnar Thoresen, but I could not afford to let the wary change in him defeat me. Undoubtedly my father had written something about my attitude toward Laura, and Gunnar was ready to ally himself against me at my first betraying word. But I knew how to meet the danger. I set myself to being wholly a writer this morning, my senses alert to everything around me, my notebook ready to take down impressions. I used it once or twice on the drive to Fantoft in Gunnar's Mercedes, and it seemed to allay his suspicions of me to some extent. I was not wholly fooling him. I *was* a writer.

The drive proved to be a pleasant one. The road ran around the base of Ulriken, the great hulk of black mountain next to Flöyen. That was where the cable cars went up, Gunnar told me. They were still skiing on Ulriken, and he had a hut up there that had belonged to his father.

"It is not permitted for private persons to build up there any more," he told me. "But I am able to keep my father's hut. We will go up there before you leave Bergen. Perhaps we will even take Laura with us."

So at least he was not going to back away if I tried to form a continuing relationship with her. Now and then as we drove, I glanced at his rugged profile, and saw in him more than ever the strong crags of rock that were Norway. I must move carefully now, very carefully.

The countryside was still brown and sere, but little lakes shone blue under the morning sky, and small houses graced the islands that floated in them. When we reached Fantoft, Gunnar drove at once to the *stavkirke* and parked his car in a clearing. We got out and he stood beside me in the strong sunlight that fell between leafless branches, looking even more lean and tall than I'd remembered him from yesterday.

"We are early," he said. "I wanted to show you the church first. It is something you will see nowhere else in the world. I believe a copy has been built in your Middle West, but this is one of the ancient buildings."

I was keyed for my private war, not for sightseeing, but I had no choice. The church was hidden from us over the brow of a hill, and together we climbed among pines and gray beeches, with the earth still brown from winter on either side of the steeply winding path. Except for a single outdoor work-man, there was no one about. These were not sightseeing hours, and the church would not be open until afternoon, Gunnar told me.

The place had a somber mood of its own, wild and lonely and set apart, with all the tawny, bleak color of a time when snows are gone, and the earth has not yet quickened to green life. Only the pines gave an accent of green, and they were dark and austere.

As we neared the top of the hill, the church came into view. It was set in an enclosed rectangle, with a mound of rock frowning upon it from one side, and the hilly ground slipping away unevenly on the other three. I stopped to stare in aston-ishment at a past that had only just supplanted the pagan in Norway. The building was a tall, narrow structure made en-tirely of wood, and painted dead black. It rose thinly toward the sky, with its steep, shingled roofs overlapping one another like layers of armor, from the pointed rod at the top of the tower to sturdy supporting pillars which rose from the ground —the staves which gave these churches their common name.

It was all that lightless black which disturbed me most—so unexpected in a church. Everywhere there was hand carving. Every shingle had been lovingly carved to channel the rain, and from high ridges carved ornamentation thrust the heads of dragons and serpents into the air. Outside the walled enclosure beeches raised bony branches, as if in mimicry of dragon and serpent. I was stopped by some feeling that oppressed me, held me disquieted. There was a sense throughout this place of evil warring with good. That, of course, was why the building had been raised—to combat the thronging evils of a pagan world.

"Tell me about it." I spoke softly, not wanting to disturb the hush.

Gunnar answered as quietly. "The building was moved here —I believe in 1884, when it was about to be torn down in another place. But much of it probably dates from the twelfth century. Norwegians have always loved wood, loved to work with it, and carve it, and their skills were very great, even in those times. When there is a gale, the building moves with the wind like a good ship, but no wind have ever damaged it."

"Why is it black?"

"That's only the tar with which it has been coated to pre-serve the wood. Otherwise it would disintegrate."

"And the serpent heads? The dragons?"

"You'll find the same motifs on the prows of Viking ships.

They signified the evil spirits which might try to enter, but are caused to flee instead. The inner holiness triumphs, you see."

We went up the path and around to the shingled entrance gate of the enclosure. Inside, at the left of the gate, was a brown mound of earth with a huge black stone cross surmounting it.

"That cross belongs to a time when Christianity was fighting paganism in Norway," Gunnar said. "There were no churches in the year 1000. People used to gather to worship in the open about such crosses long before churches were built. At one time there were many of these *stavkirkes,* but now there are only about twenty-eight left. We preserve them lovingly."

A narrow, arched walk had been built around the outside, close to the walls, and protected by the lower roofs. The front door was closed against us and we moved out into the chill, sunny morning to sit on a low stone wall that surrounded the enclosure.

I looked doubtfully down upon the path we had just climbed. "If Laura is ill, how will she ever get up here?"

"If necessary I will help Irene bring her up. But I suspect she will rouse herself to make the effort. Perhaps her apathy and weakness are an armor she wears. She may be curious about you. Remember that you are Mary Thomas."

I was content with the masquerade. It might be better for my purpose if Laura had no warning about my identity ahead of time.

We waited in silence in this silent place, and I raised my face to the warming touch of the sun, as though it might heal me of disquiet. I felt no peace in this quiet haven. It was as if the evil dragons and serpents found their counterparts warring inside me, and would not let me be.

In a few moments we heard the sound of voices on the path below, and I felt the quickened thumping of my heart. But today I was prepared. I would not be shaken. I steeled myself against any betrayal of the blood.

She came ahead of Irene up the path and she leaned on no one's arm. She wore brown slacks and a gaily figured Norwegian sweater that set off her still remarkable figure. Her dark head was bare and no fur collar shielded her face from view. She wore her hair waved slightly back from a central part and wound into a Grecian coil on the back of her head. No traces of gray had been permitted to show in the dark brown strands. Above the rolled neck of the sweater her head rose proudly, the chin lifted, delicate, slightly flared nostrils breathing the clear, piny air, luminous eyes raised to search the enclosure above her. Today she wore lipstick and there was a faint blush of rouge on the wide cheekbones, brightening her deep-set eyes. She saw us and waved, then came on more briskly. Irene, who was far younger, followed her, puffing.

"She's marvelous," Gunnar said softly. "I have never seen her fail to rise to a challenge. As I thought, you will be good for her. Let her know your admiration quickly. Give her a fresh audience." There was a certain command in his tone. He didn't mean to let me get out of hand.

I too marveled that the weak, helpless woman I had seen yesterday, a woman barely able to descend a flight of steps and get into a car, should turn into this radiant person who climbed the hill toward us. I realized what she was doing. She was making an entrance, putting on a performance for my benefit, and it was doing her a great deal of good. In spite of myself, I was forced to admire the effort.

She reached the summit and came through the gate as though she wanted to escape the worried pursuit of Irene Varos, who hurried after her looking thoroughly distressed. I had time for only a glance at this companion and saw the thin, quiet woman in a brown coat, with a brown beret pulled over black hair that was drawn into a smooth bun at the back of her neck. She was probably less than forty, yet for the moment Laura Worth, by her manner of moving, seemed the younger of the two.

"My dear Gunnar!" Laura said, as she came toward him with both hands held out. I knew her voice at once.

He took her hands in his and bent to kiss her cheek. "You are looking splendid, Laura. I have brought someone to meet you. This is Miss Thomas from New York."

She turned to me, graciously charming and welcoming, yet not overdoing the welcome. I was the suppliant, not she.

Her hand felt cold in my warm hand from which I'd quickly stripped the glove. Her thin face wore the ravages that I had glimpsed yesterday, but rouge and lipstick and delicately applied eye shadow gave a surface illusion of youth that her manner supported. Laura Worth, I sensed, could, if she chose, fool the beholder into thinking he saw what was no longer there. I felt no pity in clasping her hand, no shock of dismay. This was Laura Worth the actress who greeted me, and I was glad that it should be that way.

"Miss Thomas—how very kind that you wanted to meet me. That you believe I am remembered."

I was on safe enough ground now. "But of course you're remembered. There's a Worth Festival of your pictures running in New York now. I saw *The Whisperer* again only a few days ago. I've always thought you were magnificent in it."

"Thank you. As you might guess, it is not my favorite picture. Its associations are too painful. Have you seen any of my others?"

"As many as possible," I told her. "There have been several revivals. I think I was ten years old when I went to see my first picture of yours. My father took me. He was a great Laura Worth admirer."

Gunnar coughed gently and I glanced at him and went on. "Of course you've been popular on television too, so you're remembered even outside of New York where there are no Worth revivals."

"You're very kind. We must talk a bit. I want to know about this book which Gunnar tells me you are writing. Come and sit here beside me." She patted the stone wall as she seated herself upon it. Then she waved a gently imperious hand of dismissal at Irene and Gunnar. "You don't mind leaving us alone for a little? I want to talk to this charming young woman from New York."

I caught Gunnar's warning glance as I sat on the wall beside her. I was quite content to have her think me "charming." Content to have her trusting and unsuspicious.

"Now then," she said, "tell me what it is you want of me. You know it has been my rule for many years never to be interviewed."

"Perhaps it's time for that silence to be broken," I said. "Among young people at home there's a growing Laura Worth cult. And of course you're remembered by the older generations. Perhaps this is the time to let the world meet you again."

"Through you?" She smiled at me, but she was not quite so trusting as I had thought. I must remember that this was a sophisticated, knowledgeable woman. There was a slight skepticism in her eyes, and I bristled.

"I've had a number of pieces published in papers and magazines," I said. "Even though I'm young, I'm not a beginner. Several famous women stars who know my work have agreed to let me interview them."

"I see. Mary Thomas? I don't believe I've read any of your

writing. But then, I don't read many American papers or magazines any more."

"My book wouldn't be complete without you."

There must have been a ring of sincerity in my voice, for she reached out and touched my arm in the sort of endearing gesture I had seen her make on the screen so many times. My flesh seemed to burn at her touch and I had to make an effort not to draw away.

"You must remember that I've sometimes been badly treated in print," she said. "That's one reason I've made the rule of no interviews. That and the fact that I was bothered so much for a while that reporters became a great nuisance for me. I'm not altogether sure I should break my own rule now. Gunnar has been persuasive. That's why I've agreed to see you. He persuaded Irene, who talked to me. He's a good friend, and if he thinks this is wise—then perhaps—"

"You will do it, won't you?" I said.

Her warm smile lightened the lines of her face and made it momentarily young. "Then begin," she said. "We'll try this out. What is it you want to ask me?"

"Not here." I shook my head. "I'll need more time. I'll need the opportunity to sit down quietly with you where we can talk and I can make notes. Can that be arranged?"

Her smile trembled into uncertainty and the lines deepened once more. "I'm not sure that would be possible."

"Why not?" I asked bluntly.

She looked away from me, looked at the black, peaked church rising above us, her eyes moving to the nearest dragon's head. Then she shivered and gestured toward Irene.

"May I have my jacket, please? It seems a little cold. I'm sorry, Miss Thomas, but I haven't been well, and I'm afraid what you ask is impossible."

Gunnar heard her and came forward as Irene put the jacket around Laura's shoulders.

"Nonsense! Whatever it is you are being asked to do, I am sure you can manage it. Miss Thomas will be good for you. In this little while she has made you seem like the Laura I remember. Give her what she wishes. Share yourself with the world. You are part of a time that must not be lost."

Her thick lashes fluttered briefly and she flung him a sidelong, upward glance that was age-old in its charming coquetry.

"I suppose I have lived long enough to be historic. But do you really think I'm that old?"

"I think you are eternally young." He was not mocking her,

or teasing. His eyes were warm with admiration and affection. "Nevertheless, you have grown a great deal as a woman since the time when you were a star. You have more to give in an interview then you had then. You have the judgment with which to look back. I have no knowledge as to whether Miss Thomas can do you justice. I, too, have not read her writing. But you must let her try."

Irene Varos had been standing by silently, her dark eyes concerned, as though she too weighed and judged me. I sensed a certain guardianship, a single-minded protection toward Laura which had grown out of long years of companionship and trust between them. If Irene opposed me, I might be in for trouble.

"Will you help me?" I said, turning to her directly. It was as if I willed her to remember the secret of my identity that had not yet been spoken. I wanted to remind Irene that I was Laura Worth's daughter. I wanted her to think that because I was her daughter, I might bring her something of comfort and rejuvenation which nothing else could supply. It would be the natural thing for her to expect.

"It may be difficult to bring Miss Worth out every day," Irene said doubtfully. Her words carried only a trace of accent in the intonation. Apparently her long association with Laura, her years away from her own country had given her a comfortable mastery of English.

Laura looked at her directly. "I wasn't planning to leave the house every day in order to have meetings with Miss Thomas. I would prefer to return to my house in town, and have her visit me there."

"Dr. Fletcher—" Irene began hesitantly, but Laura suddenly clapped her hands with an air of youthful decision.

"No—better still!—Miss Thomas shall come to stay at the house! I've not had a house guest for a long while. We can work more sensibly there. Miss Thomas, I have a room filled with memorabilia. At the house I can show you everything. I can tell you stories that you could never hear anywhere else. I can even show you my beginnings, since I was born in that house."

"Bravo!" Gunnar cried. "It is a perfect solution."

Irene remained doubtful, not entirely convinced. "We have no guest room," she reminded Laura. "Mrs. Jaffe is staying in the room we used for guests."

Laura's great dark eyes were alive with purpose and amusement. "There's a possible solution. It can be arranged. We'll talk about it later. Will you come, Miss Thomas?"

"Of course," I said promptly. I could scarcely have asked for anything better.

Irene gave in. "If this is what you wish. But Dr. Fletcher has told us that he is against publicity of any sort, and he will not permit this. He will be angry as it is, when he learns about today's meeting."

Laura stood away from the wall, drawing herself up so that she seemed taller than she was.

"You mustn't worry about Miles, Irene. If I say that Miss Thomas is to visit me, then I'm sure he will indulge me. After all, it's my well-being that concerns him."

"Yesterday—" Irene began doubtfully.

"Yesterday I didn't care. Yesterday I'd given up. But thanks to my good friend here"—she smiled at Gunnar, and her beautiful ravaged face seemed almost gay—"and thanks to this young lady, I am alive again."

She turned to me swiftly so that her back was toward the others and she faced me alone. The look of gaiety was instantly gone. Her eyes seemed to flash a message of entreaty that took me by surprise.

"You *will* come?" she said. "Please come, even if there are difficulties. I'll arrange everything. I can do it if you are there. I can find the strength."

It was as if she begged me for something, signaled some special need to me. She wanted me in that house. She wanted me for reasons she might not have confided to Gunnar and Irene. I sensed the urgency in her, and something strangely close to fear.

"I've said I'll come," I told her. "I'm not afraid of difficulties, so long as you want me there and will give me what I ask for."

With a quick gesture she put her hands on my shoulders and kissed me lightly on the cheek. I stepped back as sharply as though she had slapped me, but fortunately she did not notice. She had already whirled to face the other two.

"We must go home at once," she said to Irene. "We must make the house ready for a guest. Tomorrow Miss Thomas will come. No—let her come this afternoon. There must be no delay!"

Delay would defeat her, I thought. She was carrying this off on a wave of nervous energy. By nighttime she might collapse. I suspected that Irene Varos thought that too, and that part of her reluctance to carry out this plan grew from the knowledge that Laura's strength was ephemeral at best.

"I'm sure Gunnar will bring me at whatever hour you wish," I agreed, and turned to him questioningly.

"Of course," he said. "I am at your service, Laura. I am delighted that you will make this effort. You are already looking better than you have in months."

She was obviously pleased by his words, and he was the next to be swiftly kissed on the cheek. He held her affectionately for a moment, and then she turned back to me.

"It's settled, then. I shall look forward to our visits. And I must know more about you. This isn't to be altogether one-sided."

I smiled and took her hand, thanking her. In the end it would not be one-sided. There were surprises that I had in store for her, and now that I was to be allowed past her guardians, I would be able to deliver them. Though first I would be the writer. The rest could come later.

By the time she and Irene started down the path together, her energy had begun to flag a little. The other woman took her arm as they descended the path, though Laura still kept her head high, the gallant lift of her chin that I had seen so many times on the screen still evident.

We watched them go without speaking. When I finally looked at Gunnar I found his eyes upon me.

"You carried it off very well," he said. "You kept a rein on your own emotions."

I had, indeed, but in spite of my father's letter, I did not think he fully guessed what those emotions were.

"If you can stay a little," he went on, "there is something I would like to show you here."

He was still looking at me with that studying gaze which probed and went deeper than I wanted it to. For my eventual purpose, it might be better if I saw as little as possible of Gunnar Thoresen.

"I've nothing to do," I said. "But what about you? Haven't I already cut badly into your working day? Perhaps you shouldn't call for me this afternoon. I can manage easily by taxi."

He started toward the gate to the enclosure and I went with him. "There is nothing pressing at the office that needs my attention at the moment. The letter from your father has made you my responsibility. It is possible I will take a few days off while you are here."

He sounded as though it was a responsibility he didn't altogether welcome, but would carry out because it was his duty. I wondered again about that letter, and exactly what Victor Hollins might have told him about me.

"I don't want to be anyone's responsibility," I assured him.

His smile was as grave as ever. "Perhaps you have no choice in the matter. Perhaps this is something between Victor Hollins and me."

We crossed the path by which we had climbed to the plateau of the church, and I went with him. His words disturbed me, but I had no quick answer for him as we started up the small hill that rose opposite the enclosure. A well-trodden trail wound upward, leading away from the rocky face to which moss gave a touch of green.

"I want to show you one of my favorite spots," he said.

The path mounted in hairpin turns and finally wound behind the hill to mount it from the rear. At the top was a bare brown clearing, circled by trees. We could look down between straight gray trunks toward the church. It seemed to me like a tall-masted ship—a black pirate ship sailing against a blue sky. Inside there would be sanctity, and I had a feeling that the evils of the world had come up against that grim outer armor, never to penetrate, to be defeated against those black shingles. Yet it seemed that the building was somehow a focal point of attraction. Was that because good must always attract evil?

"From the other side you can see a bit of Bergen and the mountains that guard it to the south," Gunnar said. "A splendid view."

I turned obediently to admire the scene. Nearer at hand there was a lake, a few houses, and farther away those ubiquitous arms of the sea that thrust into the coast in fjords everywhere. The immediate quiet was so intense that distant voices reached us, and a dog rustling through underbrush far down the hill made an explosive sound in dead leaves. I could see his master lying upon an outcropping of rock, stripped to the waist to soak in the warming rays of the sun.

Gunnar smiled. "We have a mystique about health and sun and the outdoors, you know. Whenever the sun is bright you will find Norwegians drinking it in. We build our houses to receive it. Perhaps that is our natural reaction to long dark winters."

I looked again at the church, imagining how it would stand dreary in black winter rain, with the sky dark overhead. On such a day it would need to be bright and holy within. I shivered, as Laura had done, and clasped my arms about me. I don't know whether I believe in premonition or not. Perhaps one can always color any happening in the light of after knowledge. But it seemed to me that this place promised me something from the first that was dark and ominous and threatening.

Gunnar drew me back to the present. "What do you think of Laura Worth? You guarded yourself well, but I wondered what you were feeling."

"I had no feeling that I was her daughter, if that's what you mean," I said. "I had no sense of inner recognition." That had come yesterday, but I would not tell him so. "I wasn't acting any part. I was being what I am—a writer with a chance to do a rare interview that I must give everything to."

"It is a good thing that you are going to the house this afternoon. Now you will have the chance to tell her the truth. That you are Victor's daughter—and hers. You will have won her confidence a little first, and that will be in your favor."

"Tell her? At once?" I knew I sounded alarmed. "But if she knows, she's likely to be angry and turn me away."

"You cannot be sure of that. There are several reasons why you must tell her as soon as possible. You cannot in good conscience stay in her house without telling her the truth. Otherwise, I too shall feel that I am misleading my old friend. You cannot expect Irene, who is also her friend, to keep the truth from her indefinitely. And there is, of course, the matter of Dr. Fletcher, who knows who you are."

I had already been worrying about Miles Fletcher and his visit to the hotel yesterday. If he got to her first and heard about this plan to have me stay in the house, if he told her of my identity before I could—everything might collapse.

"Yes, I must tell her," I agreed. "I'd thought I might get my interview first. It's likely that she would talk more frankly to a stranger than to her own daughter."

"Not necessarily. It may mean a great deal more to her if the admiration you feel for her work comes also from someone who is of her own blood. Possibly you will find that you can give her more than mere admiration."

I turned from his searching look, lest I let him see too much. I could not change my own inner feelings. They rose from too fundamental a cause.

"One thing you have already brought her that she has not had for many years," he said gently. "You have given her appreciation for her work, Leigh, and word that she is not forgotten. This may prove the breath of life to her. Once she lived on the world's adulation, as a woman like Laura must. She has starved for a very long time."

"Then why did she give it all up? Why did she run away?"

"As I understand it, there was no place for her. Her studio was afraid of the scandal. No one would touch her then. But times have changed, you know."

"She could have fought that," I said. "Others have. The stage wouldn't have barred her. Or she could have gone abroad and acted. She never tried. She ran away. Why?"

Gunnar shook his head gravely. "I have no idea. She never talks about what happened. I believe she has talked to some extent to Irene, who will never betray her confidence. But she will not discuss these things with anyone else."

"And now she's married this man who belongs to that time," I said. "This seems a strange thing to do."

"She is a complex person. It is not a simple thing to understand what motivates her."

If I got my interview, I might probe a little, I thought. There were questions I would ask her. Whether she would answer or not was another matter.

"I will take you back to the hotel now," Gunnar said. "Suppose I call for you this afternoon around two o'clock?"

"And if Dr. Fletcher gets home before that?"

"Irene believes he will be out all afternoon. And he thinks Laura is at the cottage. Of course there is the sister. She is an odd person. There is no telling what she may do, or how much she knows about you. We'll have to take that chance. If you find that Laura has been told the truth before your arrival, then—" He shrugged helplessly.

"Then—I will play it by ear," I said, quoting him.

He did not smile. "Yes. I should think you are rather good at that."

We started down the hill together, and I pondered his meaning. Was there an intended sting? I found I did not want Gunnar Thoresen to think ill of me—as he was likely to do before this affair of Laura Worth was over. But there was nothing I could do about that, one way or another, and I said no more on the way to the car.

He was silent as well on our return drive to Bergen. Now and then he would point out some interesting sight. And I managed to ask him about Kalfaret, the district in which Laura's house was situated.

"The word means Calvary," he said. "In the early 1900's a number of well-to-do Bergen families settled there, building the sturdy, rather attractive houses you see there today. This was the fine residential section of the city, near enough to downtown to be convenient, but far enough up the hill to have marvelous views."

"I wish I could find myself here," I said. "Nothing in Norway speaks to me. It's all interesting, but strange. I keep feeling there should be something more."

He glanced sideways at me, then quickly ahead at the road. "Perhaps you have spent too much time stifling your own feelings. Perhaps you have done a dangerous thing in refusing to feel—except in one direction."

"What do you mean—in one direction?" I asked uneasily.

"It is possible to give oneself as much to hating as to loving. Is that not so?"

I could feel the flush mounting into my face. I was suddenly angry with him. And with myself and my father and Laura. And I was hurt as well. It was not my fault that I felt as I did. The damage had been done *to* me, after all. I was not to blame.

"What did my father say in his letter to you?" I asked coolly.

His own voice had an equal coolness when he answered. "I do not think I will tell you. At any rate, not just now."

Tears burned my eyes. I might have known that my father would betray me. Undoubtedly for my own good—as he would have thought. But I felt miserably betrayed, nevertheless. Betrayed and hurt and wounded. It wasn't true that I couldn't feel. I was lacerated by pain, and the man beside me knew it.

Unexpectedly, he reached over with one hand and covered my own where it lay in my lap. He squeezed my hand briefly and let it go. I did not want it to be so, but his touch was comforting. He needed to speak no words. His touch told me that he did not condemn me for whatever I was feeling, and he would let me be and let me get over it. Nevertheless, I knew that he had silently set himself in opposition to the emotions which drove me, and I dared not accept him fully as a friend.

Neither of us spoke until we were back in Ole Bull's Plass before the hotel, and by that time I had myself more firmly in hand. I thanked him and told him I would be ready at two o'clock. As I turned away, his eyes were grave.

"You are very young, Leigh," he said. "This, inevitably, will be cured,"—thus dealing me the final wound.

I fled from him through the revolving doors into the lobby. The lift was unbearably slow in getting me upstairs, but at least I had the car to myself. I unlocked my door with a hand that shook, and bolted into the room, closing it behind me, turning the lock. In a moment I had tossed my coat and hand-bag into a chair and cast myself full length upon the bed, to burst into stormy tears.

Young! I had never been young as other girls were young. You matured very fast when you knew you had a mother who didn't want you—who only wanted to be famous and rich and successful. It was not youth I suffered from—but a too early maturing. I'd had to face my life as it was, as it must be, long ago. How little Gunnar Thoresen knew about me. As little as Victor Hollins had known. Whatever my father had written in his letter to Gunnar, it had not given him the truth. It had been a betrayal of me and all that I felt most deeply.

Once my father had told me that love was the most important thing in the world. I knew about love. I had loved him dearly, and I loved Ruth. But he had meant the love between a man and a woman—the damaging sort of love that brought happiness to no one. I had never yet slept with a man, but I was quite sure that I would make that choice if it appealed to me, before I would fall in love. I had only to look at how Victor had suffered. And Ruth too. To say nothing of myself —all because my father had fallen foolishly in love with a woman like Laura Worth. She in turn had apparently had many loves—and had not been happy for it.

My weeping quieted as I clarified my own resolve, my own feelings. What could Gunnar Thoresen know out of that cold Norwegian reserve of his? How had he dared tell me that I might have stifled my own ability to feel?—and how wrong he had been! I was feeling now, stormily, painfully, in a way he was probably not capable of.

After a while my thoughts stopped churning. I must bathe my face and go downstairs and get something to eat. I needed to be strong for the ordeal ahead of me. It was not an ordeal I altogether dreaded. The storm that had wracked me had in a sense prepared me for battle. I was glad that I could feel nothing toward Laura Worth when it came to her being my mother. I wanted to keep my anger pure and clear so that it could burn free when I needed it.

There was one thing that still troubled me. Why was Gunnar Thoresen willing to let me get anywhere near Laura Worth if my father had told him how I felt about her? Why was he willing to take this risk, since it was undoubtedly in my power to wound and hurt Laura as he must not want to see her wounded or hurt?

For this I had no answer.

Chapter 4

The white house, with its four-sided, steeply slanting roof of
blue tiles, rose high above us as we climbed the narrow flight
of steps from the road. At the top we followed a paved walk
toward the entrance at the side rear. Many of these houses,
Gunnar said, had entrances toward the back like this. It was
a plan that freed the front of the house for windows and
garden doors, all of which let in the light.

While I stood looking about, he climbed the few steps and
rang the doorbell. A garden apparently surrounded the house,
restrained by a white picket fence on two sides, with the tall
supporting wall that rose from the street running across the
front. The rear yard ran straight up the hill at a steep angle
to end at a neighbor's wire fence above. All about Laura's
house other houses were set at odd angles to suit the curving
of the hillside and the roads that sectioned it into various
levels.

Laura herself came promptly to the door at his ring, and
opened it in welcome. She wore a flowing, floor-length gown
of Burgundy velvet that was too wide in the shoulders and
belonged to another day, yet was ageless in its ability to en-
hance and flatter. I wondered if it was a Paquin or a Chanel.
There were gold beads at her throat, and gold earrings dripping from her earlobes. Her makeup had been tenderly cared
for, and her darkened lashes were her own, and as long as I
remembered them from her portrait. I suspected that she had
dressed for me, and she looked thoroughly the movie star.

For Gunnar she had an affectionate embrace—as though
she had not seen him for a long while, and to me she gave her
hand in gracious welcome. I knew at once that Miles Fletcher
had not returned, and that no one had told her anything about
me.

On the screen she had never been nervously animated, but
always vitally alive, and this was the manner she wore now as
she drew us into the dim anteroom that was the inner hall of

57

the house. It was a small square room, with doors opening on
all sides, and narrow turning stairs running upward at my
right. The walls were of natural wood that added to the
gloom, for all that a lamp burned on a table near the foot of
the stairs. Somehow I felt a secretiveness about the house,
contributed to by shadowy doorways and dark stairs.

A sound on the stairway caught my ear and I looked up to
see Donia Jaffe, Miles's sister, again wearing the green slacks
and bright sweater I'd seen her in yesterday. She was small,
with eyes that were too big for the delicate oval of her face.
She wore her hair in a boyish cut that left its streaks of grey
plainly showing in the brown. When she saw me looking up at
her, she ran quickly down the remaining steps and pushed past
Irene Varos, who hovered in the background.

Laura saw her and introduced me as Miss Thomas, with an
apparent reluctance to draw the little woman into the scene.

Donia Jaffe held out her hand and murmured, "Miss
Thomas," politely, but her huge dark eyes told me slyly that
she knew better, though for the moment she would hold her
peace.

"Irene, will you take care of Miss Thomas's bag?" Laura
said over her shoulder, and Miss Varos came forward to take
the bag from Gunnar's hand. She disappeared with it into a
room at the rear, while Laura led me through double doors
to a long room that ran across the front of the house.

This was a spacious living room, with doors opening into
the garden at the front, and many windows to entice the light.
The walls had been painted an off-white, but the gloomy
woodwork remained, and overhead the ceiling was timbered
with dark wood. Much of the furniture was massive and dark
and deeply carved. There was a use of brown leather and brass
nails that reminded one of Spain, though I learned this was
native Norwegian work.

At one end of the room was a section set slightly apart in a
sort of alcove. Gunnar, noting the direction of my gaze, explained that these houses always had a "gentlemen's room,"
where the master used to retire to smoke and talk with his
friends.

At this end of the room, above a brown-upholstered sofa,
the wall was hung with oil paintings, frame touching frame,
most of them old. The backgrounds were predominantly
gloomy—dark forests and bristling black mountains, stark
winter scenes, storms at sea, animals at bay.

Laura waved a hand at the paintings. "There you have the

somber Norwegian character—hardy in dealing with the elements, and with a tendency toward melancholy. I'm thankful this was tempered in me by my American father with his English descent."

"That gloomy picture Miss Worth has painted isn't the whole Norwegian, by any means," Gunnar put in. "You'll find we have a lighter side as well."

Laura smiled at him fondly, and went on with her tour of the room. "I have left everything as it was except for a few possessions of my own. My mother's family built this house. It's not terribly old, but it belongs to a special time, and I treasure it."

Donia Jaffe stood back while Laura conducted me about, as if she preferred to watch rather than to join in. Irene had disposed of my bag and stood in the doorway, her eyes not upon Laura, but following Donia's movements with no liking in them. She scarcely troubled to hide her distrust of Miles's sister.

Laura seemed oblivious to the tension of others, though it was quickly clear that this was not a contented household. With her Burgundy velvet flowing in lines of grace, she went past the grand piano on which delicate French porcelains had been set, and called me to admire the corner fireplace that was typically Norwegian. Its porcelain front had been rounded in form to fill the corner, and at the back of the hearth was a cast-iron shell with a bas-relief scene of three goats and a troll. When flames were leaping, I could imagine that these figures from an old folktale would come to life.

"I must show you everything," Laura said. "All of this is a part of what made me—a part of Laura Worth." She seemed to fill the room with a glowing vitality that denied the pale apathy I had seen yesterday.

"But you didn't grow up here," I said. "So how can you feel that this is part of you?" I might have added that I did not feel it was any part of me.

She turned to face me, her eyes warm with happy memory. "My mother sometimes brought me home to visit when I was a child. It was always a delight to come to Norway—Bergen —this house. And of course she returned to it herself to live here later. Look—I must show you something else."

As she swept past Gunnar, the full skirt of her gown brushing him, he reached out to catch her gently by the arm. "Quietly, Laura—quietly! Irene is already frowning at me for causing all this. You must not burn yourself out in a blaze of energy. Miss Thomas will be here for as long as you wish."

But she would be not be stilled. The very lines of her face had lifted and the pleased excitement of a child looked out of her eyes. I watched her uneasily and knew it was wise of Gunnar to try to quiet her. Irene, as he said, looked as though she too wanted to interfere.

From the piano Laura took a framed picture and held it out to me. "It is of Norway's King Haakon—you must look at it!"

The king was in full uniform—a fine and dignified figure. He had signed his name across one corner of the photograph. There was another name above it—Laura's family name on her mother's side. My grandmother's name—Thrane.

"This was signed for my uncle, Einar Thrane," Laura said. "When the Germans invaded Norway, my uncle helped to hide the king in the forests near what was then our country home. He helped to save him, and the king never forgot."

She set the picture proudly back upon the piano and turned to Gunnar. "You were a child during the war but you must remember something of that time in Norway. Your father was involved, wasn't he?"

"I was eleven when the war ended," Gunnar said. "I remember a great deal. Yes, my father worked with the underground. My greatest regret at the time was that I could not be of adult use."

"Norway was a brave, small country," said Laura warmly. "I love all the stories of her courage."

She moved on, her Burgundy satin slippers stepping lightly across the rug that was clearly Norwegian craftwork—a rust design on beige, with a wide, rust-colored border.

"Enough of the room—you must admire my view!" she cried.

I had been stealing glimpses of the view as I followed her lead, and now I went to stand beside her at the wide window. We were, I discovered, of nearly the same height. She wore a fragrance that spoke of Paris, and it seemed to drift from her softly waved brown hair, from her gown as she moved, from her hands as she gestured toward the window. I did not any longer question her fascination or her charm. But I was not the right person to respond as she wished.

We could look out over the town of Bergen, with its lakes and indentations of deep bays, its buildings and bridges and mountains. The great long mountain on the far side of town wore snow well down from the peak and below it red-roofed buildings clustered. Laura turned from me to draw Gunnar to her other side, and he came readily as she slipped her arm through his.

"Our city is beautiful, isn't it, Gunnar? One of the most beautiful in Europe." She glanced up with a flicker of dark lashes, and he returned her look with an affection laced by a trace of tolerant amusement. She loved to coquette with him, and he responded gravely, playing his role well.

She doesn't know she's old, I thought, faintly contemptuous. *And he doesn't seem to know it either.*

Then I was aware that his look had shifted to me, and I knew his meaning. It was as if he had said, "You cannot go on fooling her. You will have to tell her soon." He had less tolerance for me than for Laura.

I stepped back from the view. "All of this is lovely and interesting, but it's Laura Worth I've come to see. When may we begin to talk?"

She came with me away from the window.

"You're afraid I'll change my mind, aren't you? But I shan't. I haven't talked to anyone for years about those days in California, and I'm eager to begin. You will have to listen to me for a long while, once I start."

Her glance moved past me toward the two women who lingered near the door, and I sensed a certain defiance in her words, as if she expected some attempt to stop her. Neither woman spoke, and Laura put her hand on my arm.

"First, I must show you the room where you are to stay while you visit me. Gunnar, have you guessed where I will put her?"

There was no halting this woman on her course. She was like a ship of her own Vikings. She swept past the two women who watched her from the doorway—Irene gloomy with foreboding, but alert, ready to reach Laura's side at the slightest sign of faltering; Donia, her eyes bright with something like malice, as if she awaited with interest an inevitable collapse.

Gunnar came with me in Laura's wake. "Be gentle with her." He spoke softly, but almost severely. "She needs you more than she knows."

I said nothing. I would not meet his eyes, and I could sense his doubt and mistrust of me.

Laura crossed the inner hallway and stepped to a door at the rear. As I followed her, I had a glimpse on my right of a long, elegant dining room, with glass doors beyond that gave upon a terrace. Then Laura had flung open a door upon a room that stood momentarily in deep gloom. As she flicked a switch an overhead lamp with a Tiffany shade came on, and the room flashed to subdued life. She stepped to its center, her arms outstretched as if she engulfed the very walls, and drew to her with pride and love all that the room contained.

I stood riveted in the doorway and looked about me with a sense of growing fascination and not a little alarm. Alarm because everything here spoke to me emotionally. The room was furnished, in the sense that it possessed a sofa, a low coffee table, and a chair or two, but these things floated upon a sea of what, by this time, were probably museum items. There were dress forms on which gowns from Laura's past successes were lovingly fitted. There were props that I remembered—a vase that had been featured in one of her pictures, an Empress Eugénie hat tossed upon the sofa. Piled on a long table were scrapbooks, and on the walls were hung endless photographs. There were still scenes from various movies, and picture after picture of Laura Worth as this character or that. Gunnar stood beside me, his fingers pressing my arm in warning, though he said nothing.

Laura dropped her arms to her sides and turned to face me, and I saw tears glistening in her eyes.

"I haven't entered this room for a long time," she told me. "I couldn't bear to look at any of these things. I've considered having them all packed up and taken away—burned, destroyed, anything! Anything so that I would never have to see them again and remember the past. Miles thinks this is what I must do. He feels that it's morbid to cling to all this, when I've turned my back on that world so long ago."

"My brother is right," Donia Jaffe said, and there was a slight edge to her voice that grated like metal.

"Perhaps"—Gunnar spoke softly—"there may be a healthy medium between a total ignoring of a part of one's life, a pretense that it has never been, and an angry preoccupation with it because it exists too sharply in memory. There is—acceptance."

Laura seemed to droop a little under his eyes. The exultation that had filled her faded, but she made an effort and walked to a dressing table that stood against one wall. She did not answer Gunnar as her fingers moved to the makeup mirror with its circle of tinted bulbs.

"This was the very makeup table I used in my dressing

room on the lot," she said. "Imagine what this glass has reflected! I don't want to look into it any more."

"If you looked into it," Gunnar said, "—that is, if you looked into it honestly, you would see a lady of great beauty and courage who has long ago outgrown the pretty girl who once used it."

Tears swam in her eyes and her lips quivered, but she did not bend to look into the mirror.

I did not want to watch her, and I let my fascination with the room win over my alarm as I moved about.

"If you intend to let me stay here while I visit you, nothing could be more wonderful," I said. "There's so much here that I can write about. So much of Laura Worth!"

In her volatile way, Laura brightened and blinked the tears away, but she had tired visibly.

"You can look at all this later," she said. "Come upstairs with me now. I'll take you to my room where we can be alone. Gunnar, thank you for bringing this child to me. I'll say good-bye now. But I hope to see you again soon."

He took her hand and bowed over it gravely, formally. "I hope you will not be sorry because I have brought her here." His eyes sought mine for a moment and there was a clear, stern demand in them.

I met it smiling. "I have a great deal to discuss with Miss Worth."

He gave me a slight nod of the head. "This will be your opportunity. If you need me again, you have only to call."

I knew what he meant. When I had told Laura Worth what I had to tell her, I might not be staying in this house after all. And that would be too bad, I thought, with another quick glance around the room before I followed Laura back to the hall. The writer in me was eager to absorb all I could.

Donia seemed to fade out of sight as Laura saw Gunnar to the door, but Irene Varos stood at the foot of the stairs, waiting, as though she did not mean to leave Laura alone with me, if she could help it. Laura settled the matter.

"Please see that no one disturbs us, Irene. Miss Thomas and I must begin." She held out her hand to me. "Come—we'll go up to my room where we can be alone. Have you your notebook, or whatever you need?"

"I have what I need," I said, and followed her up the narrow, turning stairway.

The bare wooden staircase had been built against one wall, so that it took up as little space as possible. Its curving, wedged steps and turning rail were polished and decorative, but Norwegian stairs were apparently not meant to deal grandly with space. The steps opened at the top upon an inner hall, like the one below, with doors on all sides. A hanging light fixture illumined the space, and there were Norwegian rugs on the floor, and woven hangings on the walls.

Laura led the way to the open door of a large front room that ran part way across the front of the house. Here the old-fashioned divided windows had been replaced with a modern picture window that framed the tremendous view. Glass doors opened upon a balcony where one could sit in the sun. The sloping ceiling slanted down on one side to a dormer, and in the alcove formed by the slope of the roof Laura's double bed had been set. Here all dark woodwork had been banished and the room was done in soft cream and beiges, with bold accents of wine color. The furniture was modern and probably Swedish, light wood, upholstered in a design of beige and green and wine. Laura's Burgundy gown gave the room heart and focus, and one knew she had planned it that way.

However, there was nothing in this room to remind one of Laura Worth, the actress. This setting had been planned for a beautiful woman, with no thought of the past. On a table stood a photograph of Dr. Miles Fletcher in a silver frame. There were no other photos in the room, but over the chaise longue hung a painting of a ship in distress on a stormy sea. Above its masts the sky was aboil with storm clouds, and dark waves edged with spume leaped against its fragile sides. Dimly seen in the background was a black and rocky coastline. Yet this painting had the touch of more modern execution than those I had seen downstairs.

"More of Norway?" I said. "It's a stunning picture, but how can you live with it?"

"Live with terror, do you mean? Ah, but this *is* Norway. The ship will win. I like the picture because it speaks of unquenchable courage. You know, the rest of Scandinavia regards the Norwegians as country cousins, but we are the adventurous ones, the bold ones. The Swedes are too proper, and the Danes too commercial. Not that the Bergensere haven't done well on the score of commerce." Where, a few moments ago, she had mentioned her English heritage, now she was identifying with the Norwegians.

But—unquenchable courage? I found it strange that she admired such a trait, when she herself had long ago run away.

"Of course, one reason I treasure the picture," she went on, "is because Gunnar Thoresen painted it."

I stepped closer to study the scene more carefully. "It's very good. I should think he could be a fine painter if he does work like this."

"Gunnar paints for his own amusement," she told me. "He lacks the drive and ambition to make a real artist. That's what comes of being well adjusted. I'm thankful I never was."

I caught her up quickly. "Tell me about that. This is what I want to know. What made you the way you were?"

She closed the door to the hall, then went to the chaise longue and lay back in it, waving me to a comfortable chair opposite.

"Were! Ah—that's the operative word, isn't it? I *was*, but I no longer *am*."

"That depends on what you want to attach to those words," I said. "You must have accepted the fact that you were no longer an actress when you chose to give up that life."

She closed her eyes for a moment, shutting out the sight of me. "You are going to ask me painful questions. Irene said you would. She said you'd distress and wound me—but perhaps that will be good for me. At least you're here, and that's what matters."

She opened her eyes and stared at me across the room. In the full light from the windows I saw that her dark eyes were more sunken beneath the bone structure than they had once been, and it seemed to me that there was a strange shading in them of something uneasy. But what could there be in Laura Worth's life now which would make her afraid and uneasy?

"Is it important to you that I've come here to open up the past?" I asked.

"It's important that someone has come. Someone who cares about what I used to be. Someone who may be able to help me. Though perhaps that's foolish. Perhaps there's no help for me any longer." She flung out her hands in a gesture of defeat, and let them drop.

She was dramatizing, I thought, playing a role for me, and I began to feel impatient. I still had to do Gunnar's bidding—and I meant to. First, however, I hoped to get something more for the piece I might write, even if she could not bear the sight of me once I'd told her the truth of my identity. But so far she had answered no questions, she had drifted around them in some sort of emotional mist through which I could not find my way. My feeling persisted that she seemed almost fright-

ened at times. Yesterday when I'd first seen her she had been
a woman who had obviously despaired of living. But what
there was for her to fear, I didn't know—and it did not seem
likely that she would tell me.

Perhaps it would help a little if I went about this like a
proper interview, instead of merely trying to draw her out. I
opened my handbag and reached into it for my notebook and
pencil. My fingers touched the tissue-wrapped millefiori paperweight and closed about it. Should I dispense with the mockery of an interview and do at once what I had come to do?
No—I pulled out the notebook and flipped it open. I would
get something out of this meeting first. I would use her as a
reporter before I confronted her as a daughter.

She was watching me. Her eyes noted the open pages, the
poised pencil, and they were not without suspicion. "I have
been treated very badly by the press. Why should I trust you?"

"You're quite right," I agreed. "Never trust a reporter.
You've just told me you're glad that I'm here, but if you won't
talk to me, I might as well go away. Perhaps I'll write a story
about a lady imprisoned in a house built upon the black rock
of a Norwegian mountainside."

"Imprisoned!" she echoed and there was a sudden dark note
in her voice that made my flesh creep. I had to remind myself
that she was an actress.

"Imprisoned with memories she fears and resents?" I suggested. "With a room full of things she probably keeps locked
from sight most of the time because there is an old Pandora's
box she fears to open?"

"You look so young," she said. "Young and eager and
harmless. But there is a bite in you. I like that. I think you'd
be afraid of very little. As I was not afraid when I was your
age. The younger are foolishly brave. What questions do you
want to ask me? Though we'll not begin with Pandora's box,
if you please."

"I'll repeat the question I asked before. What gave you the
drive to become an actress—a great actress? Can you find the
answer in your past?"

She shrugged and began to recite clipped phrases. "My
father died when I was in my teens. My mother and I had no
money. We were living in the Middle West—Minneapolis. I'd
always had a flair for performing. I'd taken dancing lessons
and often had the lead in school plays because I was pretty.
My mother dreamed of the movies, while I thought I would
like the stage. We went to Hollywood. She worked in a de-

partment store and enrolled me in an actors' school. My father used to say, 'Whatever you are doing, Laura, be the best.' Not, 'do it well,' but 'be the best.' I'd loved him very much and I was still trying to please him . . . but Miss Thomas, you're not writing."

My pencil had not moved because the thought had come to me that these were my grandparents she was talking about. That I was here now because they had lived—these people I had never heard about before.

"I don't need to write all the time. These are things I'll remember," I assured her.

"The rest is not spectacular. My mother fought for opportunities for me. She denied herself constantly. I wish I could have loved her the way I loved my father. He had been everything to me, but I could never feel close to my mother."

I bit at the eraser on the end of the pencil. Had life come full circle for her? Now that she had a daughter, who in turn had loved her father . . .

She regarded me questioningly. "You look strange. Am I shocking you so soon? I must tell you the truth, you know. That's all that matters now, though it was something I used to hide in the old days because I was ashamed not to love my mother."

"The truth is what I want," I said.

"Good. As I say, the beginning was not spectacular. I was noticed. I was given a screen test. It was not very good, but apparently I had something which came across in front of a camera. When you have it you can be above average—if you work. Providing, of course, that you want to enough. By that time I wanted to enormously. I was still trying to show my father that I could be at the top of whatever ladder I tried to climb. The small parts came. I was not bad. They were watching me. My option was picked up and I was given a contract with what looked to Mother and me like a princely salary."

She paused, shaking her head in dissatisfaction.

"I'm giving you nothing. I'm giving you a summary of facts. Facts you probably know. But I can't talk about that time with any great enthusiasm. Mostly it was drudgery. I had no dates. I went to no parties. There was only time for work. I knew only the people in the studio with me. And my teachers. I was studying voice. Talking pictures had come in and I had to learn to speak properly. My voice was naturally good."

Yes—her voice was naturally good. I listened to the timbre

she had not lost. It was a voice which could play the whole scale, yet its natural tones were faintly smoky.

"*Distant Thunder* was your first starring vehicle, wasn't it?" I prompted.

She brightened a little. "Yes. That was the start, really. The critics were very kind. I received a raise and the chance for better roles. But of course I had no opportunity to choose my pictures then, and after that many of them were mediocre. Yet I was gaining a name, a certain popularity. My pictures were good box office. I was being turned into a star. The public, it seemed, liked mediocrity."

"Until you met Victor Hollins?" I said.

She went on as though I had not spoken. "My leading men were the best of that day. Some of them became stars in their own right. Some of them I was in love with. That happened quite often, you know. Actors sometimes begin to believe they are the characters portrayed, and they fall in love with each other's roles. There's usually a rude awakening when the traits they admire evaporate."

"But you never married at that time? You always stepped aside?" I was drawing close now—close to the quick.

She was silent for a moment. Her eyes were closed again and thick, dark lashes lay upon her cheeks. For some reason, with her eyes closed, she seemed younger, more vulnerable. Perhaps because hers were eyes filled with memory and knowledge.

"You've chosen a good phrase," she said. "Yes—I always stepped aside in time. I was married to my work. It was all I really wanted, and it wouldn't have been fair to a husband to present him with a wife like that."

So she had excused herself, I thought. Made herself believe that she did any man who loved her a favor by not marrying him. Perhaps that had been true. I made the motion of writing something on my empty pages. She would have to return to the name she had circled away from if I gave her time. I would wait.

"Maggie Thornton was the best role I ever played!" She opened her eyes and there was pain in them, as well as knowledge. No wonder she seemed younger when she shut that look away. "I deserved my Oscar. The role deserved it, and I deserved to win because of what I brought to the role. Victor Hollins was a fine writer. The best. We worked together superbly. He wrote the script for me. He strengthened the role for me. The picture was better than the book. Have you read Victor Hollins?"

"I've read everything he ever wrote," I said quietly. "I do not think the picture was better than the book."

"You've read him? That's strange, considering that he's no longer popular with the present generation. I understand that he has been forgotten in America."

"That isn't entirely true. *Maggie Thornton* is still recommended reading in colleges. And *The Whisperer* has become something of a classic in its genre."

"Because of the picture," Laura said. "That was a case where the picture made the book."

This time I agreed. "Because of your playing of the role of Helen Bradley. You should have had the Oscar that year as well. Why didn't you get it?"

"You know so much, Miss Thomas—I think you know the answer to that as well."

"The scandal injured you?" My words were blunt and I watched for her reaction.

Dark lashes lowered again, so that I could not read what lay behind them.

"Of course that would have been temporary," I went on. "You could have returned if you had waited a while longer. Your public loved you enough. Why did you run away?"

"No!" The word came explosively. She repeated it. "No! I've told you I won't open Pandora's box!" She flung herself up from the chaise longue and strode to the balcony door, moving like a queen—in command like a queen.

She frightened me a little. I wanted more from her. I wanted to probe as deeply as I dared—and not only because of what I meant to write. For the first time I was beginning to feel a kinship—though not of love. There was no affection for her in what I felt, but there was a certain grudging admiration. And the feeling that I had sprung from this woman's bone and blood and sinew—that there was more of her in me than I'd ever wanted to acknowledge. Now I wanted, not to acknowledge, but to know. To know all I could learn about Laura Worth. Yet I had pressed very nearly as far as I could go—without going that last step farther.

When she held her head like that, with the chin bravely tilted, she could look far taller than she was. Critics had spoken of her "authority." I could see what they meant. Even in a room, playing to an audience of one—a resentful and critical one—she had authority. She stepped onto the balcony, standing with her back to me, her hands resting on the wooden rail, looking out upon the city, and she commanded my attention. It was a moment of drama, and I think she relished it. Perhaps she had not played Laura Worth, the actress, for a very long time.

I applauded softly, rather maliciously.

The sound shocked her, swung her around, and she came back into the room. I supposed one had to walk like that as an actress—with all that grace and assurance. She came straight to my chair and stood before me.

"You've done your homework well. You've read Victor Hollins's books. You've seen my pictures. Do you give as much research as this to every actress you interview?"

I smiled at her. "No, I don't. Only to you." The moment had come. I could carry this on no longer. I reached into the handbag I had dropped beside my chair and brought out the tissue-wrapped paperweight. "I have something for you," I said, and stood up to hand it to her.

She raised her hand, not turning it palm up at once, and I noted the speckling of brown on the back, the raised veins. Age could be denied and disguised in almost every way except in the hands. Laura Worth's hands seemed older than her fifty-eight years. Then she took the small package from me.

The tissue came away readily and she held the glass weight up to the light. Tiny, bright flowers glowed in slanting sunlight from the balcony doors and her look was caught by them, transfixed.

"Where did you get this?" she asked. The authority was gone from her voice. It was thin and wavering.

"Victor Hollins sent it to you. When he died he left a letter asking me to bring it to you. He was my father. My name isn't Mary Thomas. It's Leigh Hollins."

I thought for a moment that she was going to faint. Her pallor was alarming. But when I would have reached out to support her, she moved past me to the chaise longue and sat down. This time she did not lie back and close her eyes. She stared at me with an unwavering gaze and moved the paperweight hypnotically from one hand to the other, back and forth, over and over again.

"You look nothing like me," she said at last. "Nor do you look like Victor." She spoke quietly, without emotion. The moment of weakness was gone, and color had returned to her cheeks.

Whatever I had expected from her, it was not this—that we should discuss my appearance.

"I look like myself," I said. "For which I'm thankful."

Her gaze swept me up and down and I felt suddenly awkward standing before her, being measured—and apparently found wanting.

"Why didn't you tell me at once?" she asked.

"I told Dr. Fletcher who I was when I saw him yesterday," I said. "He wouldn't let me see you. He wouldn't have you disturbed by my sudden appearance. So I had to find some other way of meeting you. My father left me a letter for Gunnar Thoresen, and I went to him. He talked to Miss Varos, and our meeting yesterday was arranged. They thought it best not to tell you my identity at once. Gunnar felt it would be good for you to meet someone who was interested in your film career. If you knew who I was, you might refuse to see me."

"He's taken a good deal upon himself—that young man! I'll have to talk to him."

"He knows my interest in writing this piece is genuine," I said. "He warned me that I'd have to tell you the truth as soon as possible. But I haven't played entirely fair."

"How old are you?"

I blinked in surprise. "Twenty-three."

She pouted her lips in a slight grimace. "Your birthday is not a date I've wanted to remember. You make me feel very old."

I could feel myself stiffening with old hurt and anger. No, she wouldn't have remembered my birthday. Strange that I should know hers so well.

"Of course I won't stay," I assured her stiffly. "You can forget me as soon as I've gone. There's no need for you to do anything about me now. Everything you've done was done in the past. It doesn't matter any more."

Angry as I was, I was not saying the things I had come to say. Disappointingly, I knew there would be no use in saying them. Any accusations or reproaches would be shed without pain by the woman before me. She might remember Victor with feeling. Her pallor on seeing the paperweight had told me that. But I meant no more to her as his daughter—and hers—than I ever had.

"If you're my daughter, you're not a coward," she said.

Again I was surprised. What she meant I didn't know, but I answered indignantly.

"I don't see that it has anything to do with you—but I don't think I'm a coward. You're the one who has run away. You've run away at least three times that I know of. When you wouldn't marry my father. When you let me go. And when you gave up your career."

For a moment or two she looked at me almost sleepily. It was a look I had seen on the screen, and it was a warning. The smoky voice was almost a caress, though her words mocked me.

"What a foolish young thing you are! As it happens, in all three cases I took the action which most called for courage. But that's no business of yours. So you think you're not a coward?"

"I don't believe I am." I knew I sounded grim.

"Then why are you talking about not staying here? You came for an interview, didn't you? Why not see it through? Are you afraid of me, now that I know who you are?"

I gaped at her. "You mean—that you'll still talk to me?"

"Why ever not? To be interviewed by my own daughter—it sounds like a scene from one of Victor's books! Except that there was sentiment in Victor—and there is none in me. When I'm playing a role I can feel passionately, but in real life I've long ago lost any talent for emotion. So if you expect a sentimental reunion, I will disappoint you."

"I'm not sentimental either," I told her, and heard the quiver in my voice. She was getting past my guard and angering me far more than I was getting past hers. "If you'll let me stay and interview you, then that's what I'll do," I said flatly.

She reached out and set the paperweight carefully on a coffee table. Then she held out her hand to me, still mocking. "It's settled, then. A bargain. Nothing is changed. I'm still Laura Worth, and you are a young woman who wants to write about me. Anything else can be forgotten."

As I took her hand reluctantly, I remembered the words Gunnar Thoresen had spoken to me. "Be gentle with her," he'd said. As if she needed gentleness! With her cool, firm clasp of my hand, I was committed to staying in spite of the anger that flared up in me. Now I had to be an actress too. More than ever I owed her a debt that I wanted to pay—a debt of resentment and hurt for old wrongs, for callousness and cruelty. For indifference. I wanted to hurt her as she had hurt others.

"Now then," she said, "—I can't go on calling you Miss

Thomas, or Miss Hollins. Your father named you Leigh, after
an aunt, I believe. So I'll call you that."

I matched her tone as well as I could. "And I can't go on
calling you Miss Worth, or Mrs. Fletcher. So I'll call you
Laura." There was another name I could have used—a sentimental term we both rejected.

The hint of a smile touched her wide, beautiful mouth.
"You may call me Laura, of course. You needn't be defiant
about it. That tilt of your chin when you look like that—you
must have caught it from watching my pictures."

I lowered the betraying tilt. The last thing I wanted was to
resemble her in any way. She laughed softly.

There was a tap on the dor and Laura called, "Come in."

Irene Varos came into the room, looking quickly from
Laura to me and back again.

"I've been told the truth," Laura said dryly. "Leigh is to remain with us for a time. I understand that you and Mr.
Thoresen have been conniving."

Irene paid no attention to this accusation. "Now you will
have to talk with Dr. Fletcher. He has returned home, and in
a few moments he will come upstairs. Mrs. Jaffe is telling him
about Miss Hollins's arrival."

"I'll talk to him," Laura said. "Miss Hollins and I will wait
for him here."

"Perhaps you'd rather—" I began, but she waved a hand at
me.

"Stay with me. We'll talk to him together. Irene, will you
tell Dr. Fletcher I would like to see him, please?"

Irene hesitated at the door, as though she was undecided
about something. Then she went out.

When she had gone, the woman in Burgundy velvet drew
a deep, slow breath, as though she prepared herself for a
coming engagement of forces.

Outside on the stairs I heard footsteps. I swallowed hard,
waiting. Nothing had gone as I had expected, or as I'd wanted
it to. I didn't know what was coming next.

Chapter 5

What came next startled me. Laura lay back against the chaise longue, with the lovely lines of her gown flowing about her. She let one arm droop limply toward the floor. The planes of her face seemed to loosen and change as apathy took over. She was once more a woman who cared about nothing. I dropped into a nearby chair, watching her suspiciously. What game was she playing now?

Dr. Fletcher came into the room with a firm, decisive step. He flicked me a look of recognition and dismissal. Plainly he wanted none of me. He went directly to where Laura lay and bent to kiss her cheek.

"Hello, darling. How are you feeling?"

"I'm all right." The words came faintly. "You've met Leigh Hollins, I understand? My daughter."

He had to acknowledge me and we exchanged stiff greetings. Then he picked up Laura's hand by the wrist and felt for her pulse.

"Too fast," he said. "This meeting has excited you. And now you're worn out."

I could imagine that Laura was damning her giveaway pulse. She opened her eyes and smiled at her husband weakly. "It has been tiring. But this is something I must do. Gunnar is right. This is something I owe to the world."

"Just what do you owe the world?" Dr. Fletcher pulled a chair close to his wife and sat down. At this moment, with sunlight falling upon him, he seemed younger than she, although he was older. His dark hair and mustache did not age him.

Laura answered gently, and there was a note of pleading in her voice. "You've forgotten that I used to be Laura Worth. Leigh tells me that I'm still remembered in the States. And Gunnar thinks I should grant this interview. There are people who want to know what has become of me, where I am, how I live."

"What people will want to know," Miles said evenly, "is about Cass Alroy's death. Your so-called public will be avid for scandal, as always." He flung me a quick look. "Isn't that true, Miss Hollins?"

"I suppose people are always titillated by scandal," I said, "but there are many who are interested in her art. Laura can talk to me about whatever she chooses."

He shook his head at me. "It won't work out that way. This is something I can't permit. As I told you at the hotel yesterday, you will only upset and disturb my wife. Obviously, you've already done that."

"I've invited Leigh to stay for a few days." Laura's voice was faint, weary. "Please, let's not have any fuss about it. It's much easier to go along with what she asks than to quarrel over it."

"There will be no quarrel," Miles said. "I must simply forbid her staying here."

He had turned toward me, and I saw the dark flash in Laura's eyes that he missed. "You forbid her to stay in my house? When she is my daughter?"

He turned back to her at once, studying her thoughtfully as he realized that her apathy was not as complete as it appeared. For a moment he seemed to conduct an inward debate, as if he might be considering whether or not to face her down. Then he acquiesced gracefully.

"I'm sorry, love. You know I'm thinking of your health, your strength."

"I'm feeling better since I've talked to Leigh," she said. "Perhaps it will be good for me to remember who I am."

"We'll see," he told her. "If you stay, Miss Hollins, can I count on you to disturb my wife as little as possible?"

That was not entirely what I planned, but I nodded meekly enough, and he rose and went to the door. "I'll leave you for now. I hope we can make you comfortable, Miss Hollins. The house, as you may realize, is somewhat crowded at the moment."

"She's going to stay in my downstairs room," Laura said. "She can interview the room, as well as me."

For some reason this seemed to startle him, and he looked less pleased than ever. "As Laura knows, I've wished she would get rid of all those things. She belongs to another life now, and such memories can only be painful."

"Why?" I asked directly. "I should think there would be an enormous satisfaction in looking back at a success like Laura

Worth's. There must be so many gratifying details to remember."

"All ending in disaster," Miles said. "It's better put away—forgotten."

"You were there at the time, weren't you?" My question was calculated. There was no reason why I should pull my punches with this man. I had Laura on my side now, and I knew she meant to keep me in the house. So I might as well challenge him with some of the questions I wanted to ask. "I believe you were in the studio that very afternoon—if I remember the newspaper reports correctly."

But it was Laura who stopped me. "That door will stay closed, or I won't talk to you at all."

Miles leaned toward her. "You're trembling, darling." He seemed to be watching her closely, probing for something. "None of these things can touch you now. It's all finished by twenty years."

She clung to his hand and looked up at him with her eyes brimming, while he patted and soothed her. It was a very touching scene, I thought, believing none of it.

"I still feel this isn't good for you," Miles said. "The shock of seeing your daughter—"

"The mother-daughter aspect needn't worry you," I interrupted. "There's more to being a mother, or a daughter, than the mere matter of blood. The ingredients have been left out of both of us. Laura and I are agreed on that. So you needn't worry about the shock to either of us."

He looked at me curiously with those gray eyes that seemed to catch the light, weighing me in some sense, perhaps not knowing exactly how to take me, but definitely not liking me.

"Leigh is quite right," Laura agreed. "She's neither asking nor being given any family privileges."

"You're cool about it, both of you. I must say that's reassuring, in a way."

"Reassuring because of Victor?" Again I was challenging. "Because of the legend concerning my father, so that you'd prefer no sentiment there?"

His face changed from its wary, watchful quality to something oddly sad, and I was suddenly uncomfortable. I saw myself with abrupt clarity as someone who plunged into deep waters I knew nothing about. Legend also had it that Miles Fletcher had loved Laura Worth a long time ago. Loved her enough to bring her back to life from her illness after the tragedy, and to receive nothing tangible for his efforts. Until now, perhaps. Could he really have remained in love with her for all this time? And if she had never been in love with him, why had she married him after all these years? What hold might each have over the other?

He did not answer me, but his manner had a certain dignity that set me in my place. With a brief nod to Laura, he went out of the room.

She did not stir from her chair. She looked bone tired, and all her strength and animation had seeped away. Her very voice was weary as she spoke to me.

"Perhaps you'd better understand to start with that Miles and I have a very real affection for each other. Love changes with the years. We bring each other something different now than we may have expected years ago, but it's nevertheless real. I won't have you baiting or challenging him. If that needs doing, I'll do it. Do you understand?"

I returned her look angrily, discounting her words. I didn't believe that Miles Fletcher had married Laura for love at this late date, or that she could return his affection.

When she saw I didn't mean to answer, she sighed wearily. "You're too much like me, Leigh. You've a sharp tongue that you don't curb. It was unnecessary to hurt him with Victor's name. It can't be a happy thing for him to have you here."

Her words shamed me, and my anger died. "I know that," I said contritely. "I wished at once that I hadn't spoken. He made me furious and I wanted to strike at him."

"We're all vulnerable. You, too—perhaps more than you think. And especially me. I've not made the best of lives for myself. A sacrificed career. A marriage that didn't work out. Lost love. A child I never acknowledged. I wonder that you want to write about me."

"I don't want to write about any of those things. I want to write about Laura Worth the actress."

"Someone who existed only in the parts she played? Someone who was nothing otherwise?"

"That's self-pity," I said.

Her laughter startled me. "The quick tongue again. But you're right, of course. I can feel sorry for myself at times. That's why I'm glad you've come."

"Because I can help you to regain your pride in what you've been?"

She swung herself up from the chaise longue. "No, my earnest young interviewer. Because you are one more person in this house. And I want it as full as possible. I want no more empty corners where shadows can lurk. Nowhere a whisperer can hide."

I felt a chill along my spine. I had been right earlier when I'd thought that at times she looked haunted by fear. There were traces of it in her dark eyes now.

"A *whisperer*?" I repeated softly.

For a long moment she stared at me as though she challenged me to deny her words. "You—with the sharp tongue! What will you say if I tell you that I've heard him more than once lately? The whisperer!"

"Perhaps you're hearing with your memory, because you've grown tired and discouraged. People do, you know—hear voices when they're exhausted. Have you told your husband?"

"And be put on some drug to cure my hallucinations? No. I've told no one but you. I can tell you because you are safely my enemy."

Her words startled me and I made some involuntary sound of denial, even though they were true. But she rushed on.

"Oh, yes—I recognized it at once. An actress is watchful, you know. We're forever on the lookout for the ways in which those around us betray themselves. So that we can imitate. It's a habit that never dies. But I prefer you that way. You can be objective. The others are too close to me. They would fuss and carry on and pretend. But you—will listen. That's why I want you here. Because you are a listening ear."

Again, I believed none of this. "If there's a voice, what does it say?"

"What does it always say?"

I remembered my father's book and the secret play.

"Do you mean the word *listen*?"

She raised her shoulders in a faint shudder. "Of course. But now *you* will become the listener. That's what I ask of you. In repayment I'll give you the material for your chapter—up to a certain point. You must accept the taboo. I won't ever talk about Cass Alroy's death."

I nodded, but I gave her no verbal promise. There were questions I must eventually ask. In the meantime, I would do as she wished and give her my listening presence. If she really suffered from hallucinations, then perhaps I could help her to recognize and banish them. And she would reward me by answering my questions. In the end she would have to answer because I would find the means of pressing her.

She broke in on my thoughts. "Whatever you are plotting, you're unlikely to succeed. You have an open young face that gives you away. A pretty face. Or it could be. Not beautiful, but acceptable. . . . But now—it's only an hour or two till dinnertime, and I want to rest. Dinner is at seven. We don't follow the Norwegian customs here."

I moved self-consciously toward the door, my emotions in a state of confusion that would take some sorting out. In the course of these last hours I had been ashamed, angered, humiliated, rejected, complimented, and appealed to. Now I was being dismissed.

"I'll see you later," I told her stiffly and went out of the room.

In the dim upper hall where there was only one small window next to the stairs, I stood quietly for a moment, trying to get a grip on my own indignation, and at the same time orient myself to the house.

The closed door at the front next to Laura's would be Miles Fletcher's room, undoubtedly. The two doors at the side were the other bedrooms—Irene's and Donia's. The good-sized modern bathroom and various closets were at the rear. As I looked about, one of the side doors opened and Irene Varos came toward me earnestly.

"You're good for her, after all," she told me in her slightly accented voice.

"I'm not sure she's good for me," I countered.

She paid no attention, but looked quickly around, as though she did not want to be heard. "I wasn't sure about you at first, Miss Hollins. Mr. Thoresen urged me to accept you, and I trust his judgment. But still—it seemed a risk. Miss Worth's *daughter* . . ."

I wondered how well Miles accepted Irene's habit of calling his wife "Miss Worth."

"It's only Laura Worth's career I'm interested in," I assured her, "and I think perhaps she enjoys someone new. She looks better than she did yesterday."

"Yes?" The faintest smile touched the woman's straight mouth. "Of course with Miss Worth it's not always possible to be sure."

"I've already discovered that. She must bewilder any doctor."

There was a certain pride with which she answered. "She makes them think what she pleases."

"I've gathered that." I moved toward the stairs and she followed me to the top step.

"We've tried to make you comfortable in the downstairs

room, Miss Hollins. The sofa is a daybed—a good one. And
there's a downstairs bath you can have for yourself. I hope
the—atmosphere of the room won't disturb you."

"Atmosphere?"

"All those faces out of the past. I agree with Dr. Fletcher
that all those things should be disposed of. Given to some
theatrical museum in America, perhaps."

I started down the stairs and she came after me.

"Did you know Laura Worth when she was an actress?" I
asked over my shoulder.

"No. I've never been to Hollywood. We met in Dubrovnik,
in my country, after she had left the films. Perhaps that's why
the things in that room disturb me. They belong to a time I
don't understand."

We had reached the closed door of the lower room, and I
put my hand on the knob. "I'm going to rest for a while before dinner. I'm still trying to catch up from my trip."

"Yes—yes, of course. It takes a few days to adjust." But
she looked faintly disappointed, as though she would have
liked to come into the room with me and further discuss her
distaste for memorabilia.

"Don't worry about me," I said. "I'm fascinated by anything that has to do with Laura Worth as an actress. I'll feel
at home in this room. I'd like to write a very good piece about
her."

"She has talked to me a little—about that time," Irene said.
"If I can be of any help—"

I looked at her in surprise, wondering what she might offer
me that Laura could not, wondering at what she was hinting.

"Thank you," I said, and opened the door of the room.

All the blinds were closed, but the overhead light with the
Tiffany shade was burning, so that the center of the room
glowed yellow, while the outskirts were shadowy. The odor of
dust and camphor was stifling. No one had thought to air it
for me. Or was it that they preferred me to be uncomfortable?
And so not stay too long.

On the far side there was unexpected movement and I
paused in the doorway, with Irene looking over my shoulder.

"I've been waiting for you," said a light voice from the
shadows across the room.

I could see her now. Donia Jaffe sat perched upon a trunk,
her short legs crossed, not touching the floor. She had changed
from sweater and slacks to a bright green and purple print
that sent a jungle design sprawling over her small person. If

Miles was sixty, she must be about ten years younger—if I remembered the news write-ups correctly.

Behind me Irene made a slight sound of disapproval. At once Donia waved a small, bony hand in her direction.

"It's all right, Miss Varos. I'll take care of Miss Hollins's comfort. You can run along back to Laura."

Without a word Irene went away, but I could sense the offense she took from the stiff manner of her going. I walked into the room and glanced longingly at the sofa. If Donia noted my look, she paid no attention.

"How lovely that they've put you in this room!" she cried. "That makes it stop being out of bounds. Imagine living in a house where there's a Bluebeard's room that's forbidden to everyone!"

I regarded her with a writer's interest, giving up my longing for the sofa. Like an actress, a writer too must be watchful and alert for the signs which depict character and betray inner meaning.

"I shouldn't think Laura Worth's career was very mysterious," I said. "In a sense, all these things belong in the public domain. They've been written about and talked about, photographed and recorded."

"And then closed up in a locked room." Donia hopped down from the trunk and tapped the top of it with her long fingernails. "This trunk, for instance. Why should it be locked since my brother and I have come here? You're a reporter—you should be interested."

"I'm not exactly a reporter," I said. "I don't concentrate on fresh news. I'm interested in personalities."

Oh, I know about you. I used the wrong word. I've read your things. That piece about Barbra Streisand was less than kind. But very well done. You're an excellent writer. Are you going to be as sharp with Laura Worth?"

"I happen to be a buff when it comes to Worth pictures. And I suppose I really prefer to write about that period in Hollywood, when there was still something of the old glamour."

She watched me out of bright, shrewd eyes. "My husband was in film work and we lived in Beverly Hills before we were divorced. Underneath the glamour it was pretty tawdry. I hated it when my brother began to attend Hollywood celebs in his practice. Of course they had money. Some of the time. But Miles became too involved. He'd have done better to leave them alone."

What she meant was that he'd have done better to leave Laura Worth alone. I didn't know how well she had known Laura in the old days, but she certainly had a viewpoint that I should learn more about. And she seemed quite ready to talk. If only the room didn't stifle me with its locked and ancient odors.

"Is it possible to let more light and air into this room?" I asked, and moved to open shuttered doors that gave onto the rear yard. When they'd been spread wide, I found myself looking up the steeply pitched hill to the house and garden above. Fresh, cold air swept in, bringing with it a smell of the sea, laced by a scent of sun-warmed pines. Donia took her cue from me and opened the shutters of two side windows. The room grew brighter and the smell of dust and camphor lessened. I would certainly need to leave everything open tonight.

"About that trunk—" Donia said, and returned to flick the lock with a long fingernail, the jungle vine of her dress seeming to twine about her as she moved, "—you should waste no time getting to your research. Why not open it now?"

"Do you have a key?" I asked. No one had told me not to look at whatever I pleased, and I agreed that no time should be lost.

"It's not up to me to unlock it," said Donia virtuously.

That, I thought, meant that she didn't know where the key was. I smiled at her.

"You're dying of curiosity. Perhaps the key's been left somewhere in the room. Let's explore."

I went to the makeup table that had once served in Laura's dressing room, and poked about on its top. There was a sandalwood box with a carved lid, and I opened it. Inside was a ring of keys. I jingled them in my fingers as I went back to the trunk.

The third key fitted the lock and the hasp lifted. Donia, alive with her odd, young-old avidity, was beside me. A wave of camphor rose with the lid of the trunk and I had to step back, choking.

At once Donia pounced upon the top article in the trunk. It appeared to be a bolt of red cloth, rolled into a bundle. "Let's unpack it all!" she cried.

I took the bundle from her, feeling my first qualm of uncertainty. "Perhaps I'd better ask permission first."

"And if she says you can't go through the trunk?" Donia

demanded. "Then you'll lose your chance. Don't wait—go ahead!"

She was like a child in her eagerness, for all that she wore a wizened monkey face. I felt a revulsion toward her urgency.

"At least I think I should go through it with Laura," I said. "Then she can tell me about these things as we unpack them. It's really no use to do it myself."

I started to replace the rolled bundle of cloth, but Donia stopped me with an outstretched hand.

"There's something in that. You can feel how heavy it is. Unwrap it and see."

I began to unroll the cloth, and as it came free in my hands I recognized what it was, and drew in my breath. I was holding the very costume that Laura Worth had worn as Helen Bradley in *The Whisperer*. The heavy object that had been wrapped in its folds fell to the carpet and I paid no attention as I shook out the creased and wrinkled garment that had once played a role in the picture made from my father's book.

Its color—as it had been in the book—was Venetian red. It was trimmed with gray bands of caracul, and embroidered with black silk on the fitted bodice and skirt. Though the dress had photographed black, I remembered the glint of silk embroidery, the soft look of the fur. The tight bodice had set off Laura's figure beautifully—and she had never looked more entrancingly feminine, more touchingly lost.

My toe struck the object that had dropped from the gown's wrapping and I bent to pick up a tall candlestick. Its brass had long ago tarnished to a dingy green-gold, but once it must have been a handsome article. A Chinese dragon coiled upward around the candlestick's column, lifting its fanged head beneath the candle holder. Polished, the dragon's scales would have gleamed in candlelight.

Donia gave a small, shuddering cry. "That's the candlestick! That's the dragon candlestick!"

I didn't know what she meant, but it was a beautiful thing. I flung Laura's costume across the open trunk and carried the candlestick to the garden doors, so that I could better examine it in the light.

Laura saw me there when she came through the door from the hall. She saw the candlestick in my hands and like Donia she cried out—in a sound of pain and distress. I could only look at her in astonishment as she sped toward me across the room and snatched it from me. Donia retreated to a far corner, where she hovered, watching with malicious zest.

Laura carried the candlestick back to the trunk without a word and dropped it into the top tray. Then she saw the Venetian red gown and caught it up almost in disbelief. The purple-red of her Burgundy velvet and the brownish Venetian red merged into each other, mingling like a flow of blood. She held the costume to her breast, her face growing pale, her eyes sunken and dark.

"I'd forgotten that I'd kept this," she said, and put out a hand to steady herself against the open lide of the trunk.

I spoke softly. "I'd like to see you wear that costume again. You haven't grown heavier. It would still fit you beautifully."

Donia giggled, but it was only a nervous sound. Her face wore a frightened look when I glanced at her.

With an effort, Laura seemed to recover herself. She rolled the dress into a wad and stuffed it down in the trunk. Then she let the lid fall with a slam.

"Where are the keys?" she said.

The ring had dropped to the floor and I picked it up for her. She took the keys from my hand and found the right one. When the trunk was locked she closed her fingers about the ring. For the first time since she had come into the room she looked directly at me.

"I'd forgotten something," she said. "That's why I came downstairs. To tell you that there are certain things in this room which must not be disturbed. This trunk is one of them. Do you understand me, Miss Hollins?"

All her authority, her stage presence were there as she commanded me. The very use of my last name was a reproach, an accusation. She stepped back from the trunk, turned toward the door—and without warning crumpled into a heap on the floor, fainting dead away. I remember hearing the clatter of the keys as they fell from her hand. I remember a sudden scuttling from the corner as Donia snatched at the ring and caught it up. Then I ran to the door and called for help.

Miles hurried downstairs, with Irene following. He knelt beside Laura for a moment, and then lifted her in his arms and carried her to the sofa across the room. Irene went to the dressing table and picked up a bottle from its top. Without a word she handed it to Miles, and I saw the green glass crown stopper of an old-fashioned bottle of smelling salts.

He held the open bottle briefly beneath Laura's nose, and she gasped at the whiff of ammonia and began to breathe heavily. Dark lashes flashed up from her cheeks and she looked dazedly about the room.

"What frightened her?" Miles spoke over his shoulder to Donia and me.

His sister answered quickly. "It was that red dress she wore in one of her pictures. Miss Hollins found it in the trunk over there and Laura seemed terribly upset at the sight of it."

Miles glanced at me with distaste. "Naturally she would be. She must stay out of this room."

Laura put her hand on his arm. "Of course I must not stay out of it, Miles dear. I must come here often to help Leigh with all she needs to learn about me. It was very foolish and weak of me to faint. The dress brought it all back too vividly. The dress and—" she broke off and closed her eyes, breathing rapidly.

"The dress and what?" Miles asked.

She turned her head from side to side, not answering.

"There was a brass candlestick," I said. "She dropped it back in the trunk."

"A candlestick!" There seemed a note of surprise in Miles's voice.

"With a Chinese dragon wound about it," I said.

"Help me to my room, please." Laura sat up, and Irene came to her quickly.

"I'll take her upstairs, Dr. Fletcher. This has happened before. It passes. I think she'll be able to walk now."

Laura suffered Irene to help her from the sofa, then she thrust her hands away and stood alone. "I'm sorry. It's a ridiculous weakness." She turned to me. "If you please—I prefer not to have that trunk opened at all. There's nothing in it for your chapter about me."

Momentarily she seemed a pitiful figure—forcing herself to stand alone and erect, trying vainly to summon that authority she needed more than ever. She could not command me now. And because she was not commanding, I gave in.

"I won't ask you questions about the trunk," I promised her.

She seemed to grow stronger under my eyes and she gave me her quick radiant smile as she moved toward the door. She did not look at Miles again, and she rejected the offer of Irene's supporting arm as she crossed the hall and went up the stairs.

Donia rushed to the doorway and watched her go. Then she turned back to her brother. "It was the candlestick that frightened her. I saw her face when she glimpsed it in Miss Hollins's hands. It was not the dress. I only said that."

Miles went to the trunk and tried to lift the lid. "It's locked," he said.

"I have the keys." Donia was quick.

For a moment he seemed to hesitate. Then he glanced at me and shook his head. "Let it go," he told his sister, and he followed Laura out of the room.

Donia stood looking after him and there was a strangeness in her face. It was as if love mingled with distrust of her brother, and confused her, so that she did not know which took precedence. She gave herself a curious little shake that set the green and purple vine twisting about her slight figure, and went rushing out of the room with the nervous swiftness of movement that seemed to characterize her. In a moment she was back, looking in at me, her eyes bright and baleful.

"That was very clever of you—to promise her no *questions* about the trunk. But of course that will not keep us from going through it some other time, will it?"

I think she saw by my face that she had better not wait for an answer. This time she disappeared for good, and I heard her clattering up the stairs. When I was alone I went to the sofa where Laura had lain, and stretched out upon it full length. I felt utterly weary and totally confused. There were threatening currents abroad in this house, and I was beginning to hope that I could gather the material for my piece quickly and get away. My own ambivalence toward Laura Worth was part of my confusion. It had always been there, but in the past I had accepted the fact that I could admire her as an actress and detest her as a woman.

Now the contradictions were worse than before. When she was arrogant she angered me—and she could humiliate me as well. She made me long for a chance to use whatever weapons I could find against her. Then a moment later she would look frail and weak, and I would be disarmed—even though unwillingly—because I could not fight so fragile a foe. There were even moments when I found myself admiring her as a woman of some courage, only to think her utterly foolish an instant later. How was I to write about a woman like this? And how foolish I had been to promise her no questions about the trunk. With so many contradictions in evidence, I needed a key to the secret of her complex character. That key lay buried in a past she had shared in part with Miles Fletcher, and perhaps even with his sister Donia. As well as with a man who was dead—Cass Alroy. I wondered if there would be a picture of Cass Alroy in that trunk.

Driven by sudden curiosity, I left the sofa and went to Laura's dressing table. I meant only to look in the sandalwood box for the keys, but there was a quilted chair in front of the kidney-shaped table, and I pulled it out and sat down, facing my own dim reflection in the mirror. Behind me bright daylight radiated from garden doors and side windows, leaving my face in shadow. There were bulbs of tinted glass around the mirror, and I found a switch and pressed it.

The light was merciless upon my face. It showed me youth that was somehow marred. Laura had said I had an open young face. But the openness seemed only to betray emotions that were less than attractive. I probably showed anger and resentment quickly. Only when I thought of my father did the look soften a little, while my eyes welled with tears. I had come here because of him, really. But not for any purpose he would have approved. He was too forgiving—Victor Hollins. He had been gentle and loving and kind, and Laura had wounded him cruelly. I must not forget that. I would never forgive it. I must not look at her in her moments of frailty and forget what she had been, what she had done.

With a gesture of rejection for my very self, I touched the switch to turn off the lights around the mirror. The sandalwood box stood near my hand and I flipped up the lid and looked inside. The keys were there. Donia had put them back. I smiled to myself, but I only closed the box with a click. My decision about the trunk would have to come later.

Somewhere in the house a phone sounded. I heard steps upstairs and an answering voice. Then Irene came running down to call me.

"It's for you, Miss Hollins. There's an extension in the downstairs hall."

Gunnar! I thought. It could be no one else, and my spirits lifted as I went to pick up the receiver. After a few hours in this house, he spelled light and clear air and honesty. I forgot his disapproval of me. I had almost forgotten that Norway lay outside these windows and that I need not brood inside forever.

"This is Leigh Hollins," I said, and the sound of my lifting spirits was in my voice.

"So you have told her who you are," he said. "Good. You sound cheerful."

He seemed pleased, and I did not contradict him.

"Yes, I've told her. It makes no difference to her who I am, so long as I can write a story."

He made no comment on that. "I have called to see if you can come to lunch with me tomorrow. It is a holiday and I'll be away from the office."

"I'd love to." I accepted without hesitation. There was much that I wanted to tell him. He might be able to help my confusion of thought, since he knew Laura so much better than I did.

"That is fine," he said. "I suggest that we drive part way up Flöyen and leave the car. Then we can walk the rest of the way to the restaurant at the top. You like to walk, I believe?"

"I love it," I said. I was elated by the prospect of escape, and of being with someone who was not wrapped in the past or driven by old horrors.

"Bring Laura with you, if you can," he said.

My elation evaporated. I said, "Oh?" rather blankly.

"If she isn't able to make the climb, we'll go up in the funicular," he told me. "This isn't an official invitation, you understand. It is up to you to persuade her to come with you."

I could guess what he meant. If he invited her formally, he would have to ask Miles as well, and plainly he did not want that.

"I'll do my best," I said, and in a moment we hung up.

Laura was tired and did not come down to dinner that night, so I had to postpone seeing her. Miles and Donia and I dined in the long, elegant dining room. There was a huge rectangular table with tall-backed leather chairs set around it, and Miles was seated at one end, Laura's empty place at the other. Donia and I faced each other across the table's width. I had changed from my sweater and skirt to a beige knit dress, but she still wore her winding green and purple vine.

Again there was dark woodwork, and many paintings hung around the walls. Exquisite blue and white plates from China had been set on a rack above one door, and there was a wedged cabinet made to fit the corner, with a scene on the front of it done in deep carving—of dogs and men, with a mountain behind. A great tankard sat upon the carved sideboard, with a tollgate scene etched upon its silver.

At dinner that night I learned more about how the household was run. Help was practically nonexistent in Bergen, though Laura had found a cleaning woman to come in twice a week. Irene cooked and served the meals and kept a general eye out for management of the house, for all of which she

was well paid. Often Donia did the dishes. The wealthy home
with many servants was a thing of the past.

Irene had learned something about Norwegian cooking, and
we had a popular dish that night—reindeer roast, served in a
sauce made of sour cream, thickened with a little melted goat
cheese, and garnished with green grapes. Miles pointed out
that the wild game of Norway had no gamy taste because it
was marinated in milk ahead of time to neutralize the flavor.
There were the usual boiled potatoes, and a fresh cucumber
salad.

Donia chattered incessantly while we ate, and sometimes
her talk carried small barbs directed at me, sometimes at
Laura. I sensed that Irene served her reluctantly and would
have been pleased to have her out of the house. Miles roused
himself to make some effort toward conversation, but he was
not a talkative man and there was something brooding about
his presence. I wished him free of that dark mustache, so that
I could see the shape of his mouth and judge his emotions
accordingly.

Our talk dealt with Bergen and Norway, with customs and
living conditions, with the interest in outdoor sports. Donia
was eager to learn to ski. Miles was not, though apparently
Laura still did some skiing when she was able. Unlike the
sport in America, it was mostly cross-country skiing in Norway. Nothing anyone said touched upon the past, or upon
Laura's career. Once or twice when I tried to turn the conversation in a direction that might aid me in my writing, Miles
switched quickly to other matters.

I was glad enough when the meal was over. Without asking
anyone's permission, or lingering long enough to be stopped, I
ran upstairs to Laura's room and tapped on the dark wood
paneling of her door.

Her voice, not altogether recovered in strength, called to me
to come in. Outside, the evening was still bright, but Laura
had lighted a handsome lamp made from a tall blue vase of
Royal Copenhagen china that stood beside her easy chair. Her
Burgundy gown had been replaced by a sand-colored caftan
robe, embroidered in brown and gold. On her feet were
jeweled slippers from India. When I admired the robe, she
said with pleasure that Miles had given it to her.

She had been reading, and the tray Irene had served her sat
upon a nearby table, the food hardly touched.

"I've brought you an invitation from Gunnar Thoresen," I

said. "He'd like to take us both to lunch up on the mountain tomorrow."

For an instant her eyes brightened. Then she shook her head. "Go with him and enjoy yourself. It's a holiday and Miles may have plans. I don't want to spoil them."

Again there was indication of her fondness for Miles, and a more sincere consideration for him than he seemed to show her, for all his apparent watchfulness of her health. I was relieved that she chose not to go, and I didn't urge her.

"We'll be able to talk tomorrow morning before Gunnar comes?" I asked.

"I hope so." She did not sound eager.

"I must try to do what I've come for," I reminded her. "I'd like to write a really good piece about you. But there's so much talking we must do first. Have you the strength for it?"

She roused herself and stared me down. This was a woman who wanted no sympathy, who asked for no quarter. Against my will I had to respect her.

"Of course I have the strength. I don't often have such attacks as I had this afternoon. I was unprepared to see that dress again. For a moment it was too much for me."

"Then it was the gown from *The Whisperer* that upset you? Mrs. Jaffe told your husband that it was the candlestick."

Her pallor seemed more intense, but this time she showed no faintness. "What candlestick?" she asked, and there was that arrogance in her manner which challenged me.

I turned to leave. She was playacting again, and I wanted none of it. I was beginning to see that my difficulty with her was always to be that I would never know what was real, what was a performance. I wondered if she knew herself. Was there a real Laura Fletcher? Or were there only the many masks of the roles she played as Laura Worth? Had she any real inner being?

"I'll say good night," I told her. "I'm looking forward to spending some time with your room downstairs."

If that made her uneasy, she said nothing, and I went out, closing the door behind me. Irene hovered in the hall as if she watched for me, and I tried to reassure her.

"She's very tired," I said. "I won't trouble her any further tonight."

The woman nodded solemn approval and went to Laura's door. I descended the stairs to the empty hall below. A shaft of light fell through the living room door, and I gathered that Donia and Miles were in there, spending a quiet evening. I

distant gaze of hers, that unbearable arrogance—but *I* was real, and she must still deal with me. She could not escape wholly into make-believe.

I moved on about the room, taking my time, relishing each discovery as though I relived the period that had created it, still cradled in that curious ambivalence that had been mine since I was a child. It was possible—almost—to shut out the corroding resentments, the jealousy of what she had been that I was not, the deep, tearing hurt that went back to the first days when I had known about her and begun to understand. I could, instead, glow with the delight of an inveterate movie buff who is given a chance to step into the world of a long-admired idol. It no longer seemed strange to me that these two opposite passions should exist in me at the same time, yet with neither entirely destroying the other. I simply accepted and postponed the time of war between them.

I found a pair of blue shoes Laura had worn in *Sands of Fortune*. They were made with T-straps and Cuban heels, entirely unsuited for walking in the sand. I remembered the scene in which she had kicked them off and stumbled on through the desert in her stocking feet, while the camera panned in to focus on bright blue slippers resting against the tawny sand. In the picture it had been sad to see them there, left abandoned to the desert heat—as the woman in the story must surely be abandoned, if rescue did not come.

Of course it had come. It always came in the movies of that day. Perhaps that was what made them satisfying. It was good to feel that matters would be neatly tied and brought to a happy conclusion—when in real life that was not the way at all. In real life the woman who had worn these shoes sat alone and weak and frightened in a room upstairs.

The train of my thoughts startled me. Alone? weak? frightened? Why did I think of her in that way? She was anything but alone. She quickly summoned arrogance to overcome any physical weakness, and she was the least frightened person I had ever known—most of the time. And yet—somehow—these things had impressed themselves upon me and left me questioning. There *had* been moments when she was afraid.

I picked up one blue shoe and slipped my hand into the toe. Unbelievably, there were grains of sand still clinging to the inner sole. She must never have put them on again. And now they brought a hot western American desert into this Norwegian room. I set the shoe down carefully so as not to jar out the crumbs of sand. They were part of memory.

On I moved about the room. I was nearing the doors to the outside now, and against a shadowy wall where light bypassed it, there hung another picture. This was much larger than any of the others, and as I stepped close to make it out I saw that it hung with its face to the wall. My curiosity demanded at once that I turn it about. The frame was heavy in my hands as I lifted it from its hook and carried it to the bright evening light that fell through the door.

Someone had done an excellent painting of Laura Worth at the peak of her success. It was a three-quarters portrait of her seated figure. She wore a red gown that I thought for a moment was the dress from *The Whisperer*. Then I saw that it was not. Red was always her color, but this style was different, with a V neck that showed the beautiful line of her throat, the familiar tilt of her chin. The artist had caught the luminous look of her dark eyes, and her thick dark hair fell about her face, giving her a gypsy look. Her reddened lips were slightly parted, as though her breath came quickly. Her hands lay open in her lap, palms up, unlike the carefully posed hands of the usual portrait. It was somehow a sultry picture. She looked like a woman awakening and eager for love—eager to give love. She, who had never been able to give it at all!

I carried the portrait back to its place, wondering why it had been turned with its face to the fall. Surely it was a picture Laura Worth would be proud of, would treasure. Had it been she, then, who had turned it from view? Here was a puzzle easily solved. Tomorrow I would ask about it. In the meantime, I would leave that lovely painted face turned toward the room, so that I, at least, could enjoy this younger glimpse of Laura, the actress.

I had, however, lost my interest in exploring the rest of the room. The turned-to-the-wall portrait had left me uneasy. Miles Fletcher had said that all paths of exploration must lead to disaster. Perhaps no one here dared explore the past. There had been a murderer who was never apprehended, and he belonged to a time Laura would not touch or talk about. A time she kept locked in a trunk with that gown she had worn in *The Whisperer*. Was I the one who would explore—the one who might bring about disaster, or free her from some long-ago threat which still haunted her?

I began to busy myself with everyday things because I needed a sense of reality to steady me. Irene had opened the sofa bed and its Norwegian eiderdown awaited me. Quickly I unpacked a few more things and slipped into my terry robe.

Open windows and doors had made the room chill, but I did not want to close them. I would take a hot bath and go to bed, no matter how bright the day light might be. Weariness was once more engulfing me and I did not want to think about Laura Worth or anything to do with the past. Not even my own meager past. Only the thought of meeting my father's friend, Gunnar Thoresen, tomorrow could buoy me up. I would go to sleep quickly and let tomorrow come.

A light burned dimly in the square hall outside my room. A radio was playing and the sound of music came from the living room—a BBC broadcast from London, as I could tell by the announcer's voice.

The small downstairs bathroom opened off an alcove beneath the stairs. As I went toward it I saw that here again were many pictures hung close together. These were all rather small photographs in oval black frames, and they were clearly family pictures. I paused to look at them with interest. If I could identify them, these were undoubtedly my grandmother's family. There were uncles and aunts and great-grandparents. There were children of all ages—perhaps some of them were my cousins. Strangely, I found myself wondering which was the face of my grandmother. I wanted to know what she had looked like. I must ask Laura to tell me. I must not go home without taking some knowledge of my Norwegian ancestors with me.

I went through the bathroom door and closed it behind me. The tub was a lovely old-fashioned one—enormous and deep enough to float in. I turned on the faucets and sprinkled in my favorite bath salts.

When I had luxuriated sufficiently in an aura of rose geranium, and was warmed to my very toes, I returned to my room. Laura's room. I had left the Tiffany lamp burning, but someone had opened the door and frugally turned it off. I turned it on again and saw that the garden doors and the windows had been closed. Already the odors of camphor and dust were creeping back.

I flew across to open each window, and set the doors ajar. I did not think that anything would intrude upon me from outside during the night. This was safe Norway. This was quiet Bergen.

Against the wall near the doors hung Laura's portrait. Someone had already turned it back to face the wall. I let it stay that way. It was less likely to disturb my dreams. All this was Irene's doing, of course. Tomorrow perhaps I would ask her about the picture.

The eiderdown welcomed me. This was no puff of an English comforter. It was slipped into a big cloth cover which was tied with blue ribbons along the side. It was the exact size of the bed and was not intended to be tucked under the mattress, but only under the sleeper. The sides and bottom were folded under on top of the bed, and I learned to slip into this sleeping bag effect carefully and let it enfold me in lovely warmth. I closed my eyes against the light evening, and in spite of everything went soundly to sleep.

When I woke up suddenly the room was dark and my heart was pounding. I didn't know what I had been dreaming, but something had disturbed me. Awake in the dark, I could feel the room pressing in around me. The shadowy figures of the dress forms seemed about to move—invaders of my privacy. The staring eyes of the photographs watched me from the walls, and I was intensely aware of the Venetian red gown hidden from me by the closed lid of the trunk, glowing in its enclosed world of darkness.

The night seemed very still, though there were distant sounds of traffic. No board creaked within the house. The other members of the household were undoubtedly asleep upstairs, and I felt alone on this lower floor, with no one nearby in a strange house.

The whisper came so softly that at first I thought it my own imagining. And then I knew it was real.

"Listen . . ." it said. And while I listened with my entire being, it came again from farther away. "Listen . . ."

The sound was utterly eerie and utterly devastating because my mind, my emotions, were ready for it in this room. I could not tell what direction it had come from. A whisper can seem disembodied, directionless, neither male nor female. When I'd lain very still for another moment or two and the sound had not come again, I got out of bed into the cold air and thrust my feet into slippers. I fumbled for my robe and pulled it on, stood in the center of the room, waiting, listening. I was half afraid that the whisperer stood in the room with me, alert and watching the darkness. If I dared to turn on the light, some dreadful truth might be revealed to me.

I did not dare, and I heard nothing more. There was no one in the room. Had the voice come from my open windows? From the garden doors? I went to the inner door that led to the hall and found it barely ajar, though I had closed it when

I'd gone to bed. When I pulled it open and listened intently to the house it was as still as though it too held its breath. I closed the door again securely and wished I could lock it.

Grazing Laura's trunk with my knee, I crossed the room in the dark and stepped through the open doors to the garden. Overhead the sky was a night sky, but not altogether dark, and the stars were barely visible. How brightly they must gleam in the black sky of winter. Beneath my slippers the dead grass of the lawn was rough and stubbly as I walked around the side of the house and into the wide front garden. There was no one about. No shadowy figure fled my coming.

It must not be very late because many of the lights of Bergen still burned in a carpet of shining jewels at my feet. Around Lille Lungegårdsvann, the little lake in the park, the walks were lighted. Streets made wandering paths of light interlaced with dark, and the waters of the larger lake were a deep blue under the sky, with the bridge a row of jewels from point to point. All around, dark mountains encircled the city in guardian arms, and a light glowed from the communications tower atop Ulriken. The snow peaks lay sleeping, waiting for spring. Out of doors the traffic sounds were louder, but no voice whispered eerily, commanding me to "listen."

Had the sound been part of my dreaming? Was it possible that Laura's imaginings had so haunted my dreams that they seemed momentarily real? I couldn't tell.

Down the hill in Kalfaret a party was going on in a private home, and strains of music reached me. Strange music for Norway, I thought, for this was like the sound of a bagpipe playing as it should be played, in the open—as though the player stood on a balcony. I listened for a little while longer, but it was cold outside and I pulled my terry collar up to my ears and scuffed my way back to my room.

The moment I stepped through the double doors, I sensed the change. I knew someone was there in the room, waiting for me. The door to the hall was open again, and a shaft of light cut through, touching a shadowy figure which stood before Laura's picture. There was something ghostly about the stillness of that figure, about the long white gown which clothed it. The electric switch was far across the room from where I stood, and I waited, frozen, not daring to speak or move, more frightened than I'd ever been in my life. By going outdoors, I had given over the room to this presence.

Then someone came in from the hall, touched the switch near the door, lighting the Tiffany lamp. The sudden illumination blinded me for an instant, and then I saw that it was Laura who stood before her own portrait, dressed in a long white gown with a lacy yoke and ribbons at her throat. The painting had been turned toward her, and she stood facing it. In one hand she held a pair of shears, the pointed blades gleaming in lamp light. For some reason the sight of those shining blades in Laura's hand was so terrifying, that I had scarcely a glance for the man who stood in the doorway. The whispering voice could have been Laura's. She could have come here to frighten me, to do me some harm. If that were true, then surely I must question her very reason. I felt a little sick, as well as fearful.

From the doorway Miles saw me and touched a finger to his lips. Then he came into the room in his foulard dressing gown and pajamas. He went to his wife's side and gently took the scissors from her, laid them on a table.

Laura did not appear to recognize him. Her face was rapt, her eyes staring, and I realized with a further touch of horror that she was asleep. Miles stared past her at the portrait for a moment, then without speaking touched Laura's elbow, guiding her with the lightest pressure, so that she turned to walk docilely across the room to the hall, and went with him up the stairs. I stepped into the hall after them and watched them go up. At the turn of the stairs Miles looked down at me, and there was some sort of dark warning in his face.

I found I was trembling when I went back to my room. This time when I closed the hall door, I set a chair atilt beneath the knob. I lowered each window to an inch or two, and closed the garden doors. Then I went to stand before the portrait, where Laura had stood—and now I saw the dreadful destruction that had been wrought.

Shockingly, marring the painting from frame to frame, ran the deep lines and cross lines of a terrible game. A vandal's hand had scarred the portrait across and across in a game of tic-tac-toe. Naughts and crosses had been cut roughly into nearly every space for the game in progress—a contest that was nearly finished. Two crosses marked the diagonal, with just one more to be put in place for X to win.

Strangely, the vicious, destructive game had been cut into the canvas below Laura's face. No jagged scar marred her beauty. The cuts ran across her breast, her lap, her open, giving hands. I reached for the scissors where Miles had placed them and picked them up in fingers that were shaking. Bits of canvas and pigment clung to the sharp points, giving evidence of the use to which they had been put. When I'd set them aside as if they burned me, I looked again at the portrait.

Whose turn was it now? I wondered in eerie fascination. Would O have a chance to block the winning of the game? Or would X perform the *coup de grâce* at the next turn? And who was O? Who was X?

I wondered if Miles had succeeded in getting Laura upstairs without waking her. When she wakened, would she know what she had done? Perhaps it was better if she didn't learn. Perhaps the oddly warning look Miles had given me meant just that—that I was to say nothing to her of what I had seen. I turned the portrait gingerly about with its face to the wall, as Irene had hung it. I did not like to touch something that had turned evil and threatening almost before my eyes.

My bed was still warm and I crawled gratefully into it and lay there shivering. It was a good thing I was to see Gunnar Thoresen tomorrow. Already he stood for sanity and common sense in my eyes. I would tell him about all that had happened, and he would reassure me. He would give me his quiet, rather beautiful smile—and I would be reassured. As a matter of fact, when the time came, he did none of these things. But it helped me to go to sleep by believing that he would.

When I awakened in the morning, it had been light for a long time. Probably from three o'clock on. But at least I had slept and I woke up rested, and almost convinced that I had never heard that whispering voice in the night. There was still the portrait, however, and the scissors which lay upon a nearby table. I was glad that the picture faced the wall, for I had no desire to look again at that dreadful game of tic-tac-toe.

Breakfast was the breakfast of home. Laura had taught Irene her own American ways. There was bacon and eggs and toast, with delicious hot coffee. Coffee that suited my palate better than the bitter European brand served at the hotel. I ate alone because I had risen late, and I was glad enough to be without company except for Irene Varos.

She said nothing about Laura's walking in her sleep, or about the damage to the portrait, and I wondered if she knew about either. For some reason she seemed pleased with me this morning. She sat at the table across from me for a second cup of coffee and told me that Laura was up and feeling refreshed, that she was eager to talk to me. Which meant that Miles must have said nothing to his wife about what had happened last night. But eventually she would have to know—

unless that picture was kept always with its face to the wall, so that she never looked at it.

Here, at least, was my opportunity to talk to Irene, perhaps to draw her out a little. Carefully I circled away from danger, looking at her for the first time as a woman in her own right, rather than merely as resident dragon. If I knew more about Irene, she might help me to better understand Laura.

Her thin, rather solemn face, beneath straight black brows, was not unattractive. Her dark hair was pulled back too severely. If it had been loosened a litttle it would have framed her face more appealingly. She wasn't a handsome woman, but there was strength and character in her face. For many years she had been close to Laura, and I knew she could tell me things as an observer that Laura herself might be unaware of. Yesterday she had even hinted that she might help me.

"Do you have any family, Miss Varos?" I asked conversationally. My interviewing had begun.

She shook her head. "My parents are dead, and so is my older brother. I had no one when Miss Worth and I met in Yugoslavia, and she asked me to come and work for her. I was assigned to her there for a little while, and we became acquainted."

"Was it difficult for you to leave your country?"

"Miss Worth had friends in high places at that time. It was arranged."

I pressed her a little more boldly because it was necessary to find the tender places. They were what told you most about a man or woman, and Irene Varos was very close to Laura.

"Hasn't working for Laura Worth curtailed your own life?" I asked.

Her smile was stiff, as though she did not use it very often. There was no great amusement in it.

"Mr. Thoresen has warned me that you're here to ask questions and we mustn't mind. Of course everything which surrounds Miss Worth must be of interest and value to you. Therefore, I suppose I am of interest and value."

"I'm glad you understand," I said.

Her face grew solemn again, and a little sad. "There was a man whom I might have married. He—he died. If that had gone differently I might never have left my country."

"I'm sorry," I said.

She raised her coffee cup in thin fingers. "It was long ago. I can't remember his face. It's quite possible that I could have made a different life. But there were circumstances . . . Perhaps Miss Worth has been my work and my child." Again she gave me the stiff little smile. Irene was in her thirties, Laura in her fifties, but I knew what she meant.

"May I ask you other questions? Ones less personal?"

"Of course. I'll try to answer."

"I'm fascinated by Laura Worth's collection of things from her great days in pictures. They all seem to have been arranged lovingly and carefully. When did she have the heart for that? She seems to have put her career out of her life for a good many years."

"It was when we first came to Bergen," Irene said, and her face softened a little, grew younger. "This was the first time she had a place for her collection, and I helped her arrange the room. She still had thoughts of returning to pictures then, and all these things meant a great deal to her. They meant all the more after her marriage and divorce. She wanted them carefully preserved and labeled, so that the room might be a showplace where she could bring her friends. I learned while I assisted her. She told me a great deal about her life in Hollywood when she was making pictures."

"Have you ever seen any of her pictures?"

"Of course. She has copies of several films. When we first came here she would sometimes show them to a few friends."

"Does she have the film of *The Whisperer?*"

"She has it, but this is one she never likes to show. The memories are too painful."

"Did she ever tell you about that time? About the tragedy?"

"Yes—she told me." The words, the tone, were suddenly clipped, and I knew that Irene would not talk to me about the night when Cass Alroy had died. I plunged toward a problem more immediate, hoping to catch her off guard, so that she'd talk to me frankly.

"Did you know that Laura walked in her sleep last night?"

She did not seem particularly startled. "Last night? No, I didn't know. Sometimes she does leave her bed at night. I try to watch and follow her. Last night I'm afraid I slept soundly. What did she do?"

"She came into my room. I'd gone outdoors for a little while to—to see what Bergen looked like at night. When I came back in she was standing before that portrait that you'd turned with its face to the wall. She had a pair of scissors in her hand."

"Scissors?"

"Yes. Dr. Fletcher must have missed her, because he came

down and found her. He took the scissors away from her and
got her back upstairs."

Irene shook her head sorrowfully. "She shouldn't be left
alone at night. There was a time when I found her outside at
two o'clock in the morning. She'd climbed the retaining wall
that rises from the street. If I hadn't rescued her in time she
might have fallen and been seriously injured."

This added to the picture of a neurotic and deeply disturbed woman and I felt a growing sense of uneasiness about
her. But it was what had happened last night that interested
me most.

"Before Dr. Fletcher found her," I went on, "she defaced
her own portrait. With that pair of scissors she held."

Irene stared at me for a moment and then left the table. I
followed her to the room and watched while she took the picture from its peg and turned it face out. The jagged scars of
the game were even more clear by daylight. Irene put out a
hand and traced the lines, touched the X's and O's with the
tip of one finger.

"It's a game," she said wonderingly.

"An unfinished game. What do you think it means?"

"How can it mean anything when it's something she's done
in her sleep?"

"Perhaps that's the very time when the deepest meanings
surface," I said. "And you can see that she didn't scar the
face of the portrait. All the grooves are cut into it below the
face. Isn't there some significance in that?"

Irene gave me a sudden intent look. "When did you see Dr.
Fletcher?"

"When he came into the room from the hall. He must have
missed her and come downstairs a little while after she left her
bed. Has he told her what happened, do you think? Did she
say anything to you this morning?"

"Nothing. Nothing at all."

"Then he can't have told her."

"No—not yet." With a sudden agitated motion Irene
reached toward the picture and turned it once more toward
the wall. "She mustn't come in here and be shocked by this."

"But she'll have to know," I said. "Isn't it better if she's
told before she accidentally discovers it by herself?"

"Perhaps Dr. Fletcher is waiting for an opportune moment." Irene's tone was dry and faintly bitter.

"What do you mean?"

She turned from the picture and went back to the dining

room, with me in her wake. We sat down at the table and she poured me a hot cup of coffee. My questions hung in the air between us.

"Perhaps he would like to do her an injury," she said at last.

"An injury? You mean he might tell her about this in some hurtful way?"

"That wouldn't surprise me," Irene said. "She has an affection for him. He can hurt her when he wants to."

"Then why don't you tell her first?"

"And have Dr. Fletcher send me away from the house for upsetting her? He'd like to do that. He'd like her to be unguarded. Perhaps she even senses this. That's one reason why she wants you here."

"Perhaps I'll tell her myself then."

"In that case, you must do it very gently."

I shook my head, already rejecting the idea. "No—I don't want to tell her at all."

"Yet someone will," Irene said quietly. "But it cannot be me."

I finished my coffee and pushed my chair back from the table. "Is Dr. Fletcher in now? Perhaps I'll talk to him, find out what he plans."

"He has an appointment, and he's gone out. She's alone upstairs, waiting for you."

"What does he do around Bergen that he always seems to have appointments? Especially since today is a holiday. I thought he was retired."

"I believe he's arranging for a new practice. Doctors are always wanted. Miss Worth tells me he's looking for a suitable office. She wants to stay in Bergen, and he doesn't care to be entirely idle. There are those he could see, even on a holiday."

"I'll go to her now," I said. "Thank you for talking to me about these things, Irene. You are very good to Laura."

She smiled for the first time and began to clear away the dishes quietly. I went upstairs to Laura's bedroom. Her call to "Come in," was cheerful and strong. Even in speaking two words, she sounded like the Laura Worth I knew on the screen and I had a momentary sense of unreality as I entered the room. How could I be here, talking to this legend of a woman? And how did everything else I was learning about her fit that legend?

This morning she had forsaken the chaise longue, and was standing at the balcony door. Again she wore one of her fabulous long gowns from another day. This one was of palest aqua chiffon that floated when she moved—all grace and flattery. On another woman, this dressing in styles of the past might have seemed pathetic—but not in Laura Worth. She knew what looked well on her, and she had the confidence to make her own style. As though the world might still follow her. It was hard to reconcile this vital, confident woman with the staring sleepwalker I had seen last night.

She turned with the bright balcony behind her, her face in shadow so that for a moment she gave the illusion of youth.

"Good morning, Leigh Hollins! I've slept well for once. Nothing disturbed me, and I've eaten a huge breakfast."

I wanted to say, "No sleepwalking?" but I held my tongue. Today I was more partisan than I'd been yesterday, and I did not feel like hurting her, no matter what had happened in the night. Today she would be Laura Worth, and I the writer, and our being mother and daughter would not come into it at all. I slammed a door in my mind upon a voice of protest. "Later," I told it, "later."

She floated toward me into the room, gestured me into one chair, and took another. The arrangement was calculated. My chair faced the bright clear light from the picture window and balcony, while her own was in shadow. I did not mind being manipulated. I would get more from her this way. It was the actress I had come to interview.

She gave me no chance to begin, however. "I know what I shall tell you about," she informed me, sitting erect in the brocade chair, with her knees crossed so that aqua chiffon made a lovely line of thigh and leg. I found myself sitting pigeon-toed, with my notebook on my knees and my pencil clutched like a child's above an exercise book. I hadn't felt so self-conscious at other interviews I'd done, but now I was aware of straightening my toes and pulling back my shoulders from their hunching.

Laura did not seem to notice. I don't think she was much aware of me as a person—she was too wrapped in her own performance.

"Will you hand me the paperweight, please," she said, motioning gracefully, not waiting for me to begin my questions, but taking command without a by-your-leave.

The paperweight was not something I wanted to talk about, but I had no choice. I picked up the glass sphere from the low table and carried it to her. She held it up to the light so the tiny glass flowers sparkled with color.

"I want to tell you about the day I gave this to Victor Hollins," she said.

I laid my pencil down across the page that had so little writing on it from yesterday, and braced myself inwardly. Whatever I might write about Laura Worth, it would not be this. I did not even want to hear, and my heart began its deep, rebellious thudding. With only a few words she was destroying my ability to interview.

"We'd just finished making *Maggie Thornton*," she said. "We knew it was good. Victor assured me that I would win an award for my performance, and I told him it was because of his writing. We were terribly in love."

"Please—" I said. I had to stop her. I wanted to listen to none of this.

She did not hear me. She played to me, but she forgot me as anything more than an audience.

"He was marvelously good looking in those days. He reminded me a little of Leslie Howard. He had the same gentleness, the kindness that Leslie used to portray in his roles. But there was a greater virility in Victor and sometimes he forgot to be kind and spoke with the same bite he could use in his writing."

I made some sound of resistance, of protest. I wanted to see Victor only through my own eyes. She went right on.

"When the picture was finished and we were sure there would be no more remakes, he told me we were going away together. I put myself in his hands. I didn't even ask where. And we came to Scandinavia, because he knew my roots were here. In Copenhagen we sat in Tivoli Gardens and watched the world go by. We shopped in Strøget. We climbed the Round Tower, where Catherine the Great once drove her horse-drawn carriage around the wide ramp to the top. We saw Copenhagen from the tower at night, with the bright streets radiating away from us.

"The next day we came to Bergen. I saw it for the first time in my adult years with Victor Hollins. We climbed Ulriken and walked in the snow. We took a boat out to the skerries. We visited the *stavkirke* at Fantoft and Victor fell in love with that place. It appealed to his writer's imagination. He said there was an immense feeling there of good struggling against evil. He said that was what all fiction writing was about—that eternal battle between good and evil. In his books he wanted the good to win. Perhaps that's why they are considered old-fashioned today."

I too had felt that warring of good and evil at Fantoft, and I heard Laura in wonder. More than I knew, I was my father's daughter.

The smoky voice that built pictures in my mind which I didn't want to see fell silent for a little while. Perhaps she was thinking of yesterday at Fantoft, of meeting me there. Was that why she liked to walk in that place—because she had once gone there happily with my father?

"We took the train over the mountains to Oslo." She picked up her story. "We looked from the train windows into the deep fjords and over the valleys. We went from spring to winter, up where the streets of tiny skyline towns ran between high walls of packed snow. It was all beautiful because we were together, sharing it. In Oslo we walked among the Vigeland statues and saw all of life depicted in those enormous works. After Oslo we sailed to Stockholm."

The paperweight lay in her lap and she picked it up, turned it about in her fingers, as if it were a crystal ball in which she saw the past.

"Stockholm was the end of our trip together. The end of our time together. We stayed in one of those grand old nineteenth-century hotels near the place where the waters of Lake Mälaren meet the waters of the Baltic below the bridge. It was late afternoon when we went into Gamla Sta'n, the old town. When it began to rain we didn't care. We walked those narrow cobblestoned streets arm in arm with the old copper towers above us, and I wanted it to be always like that.

"The clock tower looked down at us, and on every side there were tiny shops with their counters cluttered with antique treasure. I pulled Victor into one of them because I wanted to buy him something that would remind him always of that day. The millefiori paperweight was waiting for me. I asked the girl to wrap it for me, while Victor was in another part of the shop. I carried it in my purse as we went back to the rainy streets.

"We found an unexpectedly elegant little restaurant right off the narrow sidewalk, and when the rain came down too hard we ducked into it. I don't remember what we ate that evening, but there were candles on the tables, and because it was early there was no one else there. When the waitress had gone away with our order I gave him the paperweight, and we held hands across the table. When we went home, he said, we would be married. It must always be like this for us. I was the only woman he had ever truly loved. He told me that, and because it was Victor I believed him. Of course I knew it couldn't always be like that, but I smiled at him and said nothing. He told me he could see the candlelight in my eyes.

"It was still drizzling when we walked back to the hotel, but I was very warm and happy inside. We walked across the empty courtyard of the palace, and we crossed the bridge where the black waters were roiling angrily, as if lake and sea could not bear to mingle. When we got back to our high room the evening was gray, but there was a saffron streak in the sky beyond the opera building and a great black storm cloud was cutting into it. The eastern sky was still pale and there was somehow a sense of melancholy, perhaps a too recent memory of winter, even though we'd seen forsythia blooming. I can still remember the sorrowful sound of the gulls. When I hear them in Bergen, I remember. But it was warm in our room. And our love was warm."

I was crying. I hated her for making me cry. Getting my handkerchief from my purse was awkward, but I had to wipe my tears. I could barely see her face in shadow, but there were no tears in her voice—only that husky quality that carried emotion on its tones.

"We had to leave for home the next day." She had stopped turning the paperweight about and held it still in her hands. "I waited until we were back in Hollywood before I told him I couldn't marry him. He was very angry with me, but he knew I meant it. He flew back to New York without even letting me know he was leaving. A month later I suspected that I was going to have a baby. I didn't tell him. Not then. He might have tried to use that as an excuse to force my hand. Of course I didn't expect that he would be so angry with me, or that he would marry Ruth as quickly as he did. Months later, I let him know about the child. What could I do with a baby in Hollywood?"

What indeed! I bent my head over the empty pages of the notebook so that she couldn't see my face and know how torn and shaken I was.

"Victor did the wise thing," she said. "He wanted his daughter. So I let the baby go. It was the only way."

The baby, the child, his daughter—these were the words she used. Never "you" in direct reference to me.

"I thought you might like to know about the paperweight," she said gently.

As though she had given me some priceless gift! It was

likely that I had been conceived that night in Stockholm—yet she talked to me about a paperweight.

I flung the word back at her. "Paperweight! What about my father's love that you threw away? What about me? What about the way I would grow up without a mother?"

She was unruffled, but her role had turned compassionate. "You had a better mother in Ruth than you could ever have had in me. I know that because Victor wrote me about you from time to time—until you were grown up, and then he stopped. He never sent me the pieces you had written, or told me what you were like now. Ruth gave you both the happy, contented lives you deserved, and which I could never have given either of you. Any more than I could give myself a happy, contented life."

"That's the way you excuse yourself, forgive yourself!" I flailed out at her. "That's the way you've been able to stay free and irresponsible."

"You're crying," Laura said in wonderment. "But none of this should matter to you now. You are your own person, just as I am my own person. We have agreed that we owe each other nothing—except as writer and actress. So why should you cry for something I don't cry about?"

"You're monstrous!" I spat the word at her. "I'm crying because my father died only a little while ago, and you've brought it home to me how much you hurt him, and how little you cared."

I could feel hysteria rising in me. Her very look of slightly amused tolerance destroyed me. I lifted my head and stared at her angrily, no longer ashamed of my tear-stained face.

"Now I can understand something!" I cried. "Now I can understand what drove you to go downstairs to that room last night and destroy the portrait of yourself. If you hadn't done it, *I* would like to do it. I can't imagine anything more wonderful than to feel those scissors in my hand as I slashed that painting across and across."

Her eyes were enormous and there was a glassy shine to them. Her pallor had a leaden hue.

"What are you talking about?"

"You might as well know!" I flung at her. "You walked in your sleep last night. Miles found you in my room after you'd mutilated the picture, and took you back upstairs. You can go down and see it for yourself."

She looked quite dreadful and I knew in horror what I had done—how I'd shocked and frightened her. Angry as I was, I hadn't meant to do anything as dreadful as this. But before I could speak to her, or try to soften my words, she jumped to her feet with the paperweight raised in her hand. With a single wild gesture she flung it straight through the picture window. There was an enormous crash of breaking glass, and then a tinkling as small pieces fell from the jagged opening.

"Get out!" she said to me. "Get out of my sight. I never want to see you again."

"Of course," I told her. "I'll pack my bag and leave at once. There's nothing more we can say to each other. Not ever."

I banged the door behind me with some of the fury she had shown, and pitched myself down the stairs with dangerous speed. Fortunately, there was no one around. In Laura's room of pictures and costumes, I closed the door behind me and stood trembling in its center. Across the room the scarred portrait hung with its face to the wall as Irene wanted it to hang.

I was too distraught to pack, to do anything sensible. My stomach was churning with emotion. I had to breathe fresh, cold air. In a moment I was through the doors to the garden and had walked around the house to the front.

Near a flower bed where nothing was yet blooming, Donia Jaffe stood with the paperweight in her hands. She was almost as pale as Laura had been. She held the ball of glass flowers toward me in fingers that were shaking.

"She tried to kill me," she said, and her lively dark eyes sped toward the broken window of the room above. "This paperweight just missed my head."

I took it from her and examined it closely as if its perfection was the most important thing in the world. Miraculously, it had not even been chipped in its flight through glass, and its fall to soft earth had preserved it. I tried to breathe deeply so my voice wouldn't shake.

"She didn't throw it at you," I said. "She was angry with me and she flung it away in a rage."

Donia continued to stare at the window. "She's sick and dangerous. Unbalanced. For twenty years she's brought my brother nothing but grief and suffering. For her, everything that happened that night in Hollywood is still going on. She has never let any of it go. It will be forever on her conscience. She can only end it if she dies. She should be put somewhere so that she can do no more harm."

For some unfathomable reason I turned the dregs of my anger upon Donia in defense of Laura. "If you mean that she's mentally ill—she's not! And she's not dangerous. If she was, she'd have thrown that paperweight at me. I goaded her into what she did. She made me angry, and I goaded her. Actors are highly strung people."

"I knew you'd bring trouble," Donia said. "My brother was against your coming here. She was quiet and we were having no difficulty with her. And then you came to stir her up."

"At least she's alive again," I said. "In the state you call quiet she was half dead."

"Which is the only way she can lay the ghosts that haunt her."

How long we'd have glared at each other, I don't know, but just then Gunnar Thoresen came around the side of the house toward the front garden.

"Good morning," he said cheerfully. "I heard voices, so I came around."

I ran toward him and very nearly flung myself upon him. He looked to me like an old and dear friend upon whom I could count for support and comfort. I remembered in time that he was none of these things, and held out my hand lamely.

"I'm glad to see you," I said, and clung to his hand a moment too long.

"There is something wrong." It was a statement.

"Just about everything!"

"Then you must tell me what you wish me to do, and we will try to make what is wrong better." After a brief nod in Donia's direction, he looked only at me.

Donia sniffed in displeasure and went toward the house. "When my brother comes home, I'll tell him about this. Don't think that I've been fooled by your excusing Laura. I know what she just tried to do."

Gunnar looked after her gravely, his brown, slightly wavy hair shining in the sun. "There *is* trouble. Perhaps you must tell me a little."

He looked wonderful to me with his strong, narrow face and perceptive eyes. I wanted to throw my arms about him and hug him for all that quiet Norwegian strength. Instead, I showed him the paperweight and gestured toward the broken window above. He glanced up at it with understanding, and smiled slightly.

"I should have warned you that Laura has a great temper. She did not have a proper Norwegian upbringing, I am afraid. We are indulgent and loving toward our children, but we also discipline them. In any case, I had a fear that all might not go smoothly at first, so I came early to see if I could be of use."

"She told me to get out. So I'd better go now and pack, and you can take me back to the hotel until I'm able to catch a plane for home."

He shook his head and the twinkle I had seen before was in his eyes. "She will change her mind. You must give her time. She will regret and she will want you here. So it is better if you come with me now, and leave the packing for later."

I had no wish to go flying home. I simply wanted to stay longer in the company of Gunnar Thoresen. I wanted to tell him everything that had happened since I'd last seen him. Whether I stayed in this house or not, I wanted him to know all that had occurred.

"You have been crying?" he said. "Because she threw the paperweight?"

"No—not because of that. Because of what went before."

"Then go and wash your face. And put on your lipstick so that you will feel like a woman. Then fetch your coat and we will go. It is better if I do not enter the house during this crisis. I will wait for you in my car."

I ran to do his bidding. If ever I could fall in love, I thought irrelevantly, it would be with a man like this. And that would not be wise. Not for me.

When my face had been refreshed with cold water and my lipstick brightened, my coat flung about my shoulders, I went into the hall and found Irene Varos standing at the foot of the stairs as though she waited for me.

"She's been throwing things again?"

"Is it a habit, then?"

"Not so much any more," Irene said.

"Have you been up to see her?"

"Not yet. It's better to let her quiet herself first. Then she's less likely to throw something at me."

"I told her about the picture," I said. "I told her that she walked in her sleep last night, and I didn't tell her gently. Perhaps you'd better know as well that Mrs. Jaffe thinks the paperweight Laura threw was aimed at her. Of course it wasn't. It wasn't even aimed at me, though Laura was angry with me. But Mrs. Jaffe is talking about her being sick and dangerous and unbalanced. She said she should be put somewhere so that she couldn't hurt anyone."

A look of intense disliking flashed in Irene's eyes. "Mrs. *Jaffe* ought to be put somewhere herself! But thank you for telling me. Nothing of the sort will be done while we are here to protect her."

"Don't count on any *we*," I said, and let myself out the front door.

It was wonderful to leave the house behind me and drive up the mountain in the Mercedes.

Chapter 7

The winding road snaked back and forth along the hillside, with trim, bright houses arranged in mounting levels. After a turn or two I could look down upon the dark blue tiles of Laura Worth's house. Everywhere the gardens were neat, almost ready to burst into bloom, and often there were plants in the windows. Far below, Bergen reached its peninsula into the waters of the fjord and spread its buildings around on either side. I could see boats at anchor in the larger space of water on the left. On the opposite shore, far to the right, were the wharfs, with steamships alongside, and the peaked roofs of old Bryggen on the street that paralleled Vagen, the inner harbor.

"It's beautiful—your city," I said. "Heavenly."

He nodded, quite complacent. "Yes. It is difficult to understand why anyone would live elsewhere. Though the Oslovian thinks us countrified here in Bergen. Of course he is wrong. We are the gateway to the west. We have nine hundred years behind us, and we are the door that opened to let in the influences of England and the other countries of Europe. How difficult to get over the mountains to Oslo in the old days. Now the trains run through all winter."

He was talking to amuse me, to cheer me, until I was ready to talk to him. I let him go on. I didn't want to begin my story while he was driving on a mountain road. Besides, it was pleasant to lean back in the seat and relax, to watch the vast scene grow beneath us as we climbed, and for a little while to think of nothing.

When the road had wound as high up Flöyen as was possible, Gunnar parked the car near a sign that warned us we could drive no farther. We got out and started up a road that soon began to rise steeply, with the black rock face of the mountain towering high above us. At the very top dark fir trees stood silhouetted against the sky.

We were not alone. The sun had brought people pouring into the open, and a number of them had chosen this holiday to climb the mountain. Children climbed as sturdily as their parents, and we even saw a baby carriage or two being wheeled up the steep road. There was the bright red of sweaters everywhere. Norwegians loved the color red. Yet the little groups did not trouble one another. We traveled in small islands and tended to our own affairs.

When we reached a bench that had been placed at a high lookout point, we climbed up to it and sat where we could see the entire countryside. My eyes followed the road that wound past the neighboring mountain, Ulriken, and ran out toward Fantoft, around little lakes and into the country.

The steady traffic sounds of Bergen were more distant now, but we could hear intermittently what was coming to be familiar—the curious "hee-haw" scream the ambulances made. There was a sound of band music too, from the center of town, for this being a holiday, the marching groups were out, the young people and the parades. From the water far below came the roar of a motorboat, and a plane hummed overhead. Behind us among forest trees birds were singing.

"Last night," I told him, "I'm sure I heard a bagpipe playing. Is that possible in Bergen?"

He smiled. "It is not likely. Undoubtedly what you heard was one of our Hardanger fiddles. Though the bagpipe is a wind instrument, and the fiddle is string, the sounds are similar. I have such a fiddle myself. One time soon I will play it for you. The music is distinctive—it belongs to Norway."

"The party seemed to go on very late," I said idly.

"That is the way with Norwegian parties. Before you leave, we must give one for you. You will never know what being toasted is like until you have been toasted at a Norwegian supper party. We begin very formally with great dignity. We do not loosen up easily. But as the aquavit flows, we become extremely witty and clever. Or so we like to believe. Of course no one drives his car to such parties, since the government does not look kindly upon those who drive after drinking. So we all come in taxis, and in the early morning hours, feeling very gay indeed, we all go home in taxis."

He was speaking lightly, with the unexpected ability of the Norwegian to laugh gently at himself, and his inconsequential talk had the effect upon me that he intended.

I was quiet now. Now I could tell him without tears the story Laura had given me of that time in Stockholm. The time when she and Victor had been in love. He listened intently and did not speak until I was through.

Then he said, "What a fine gift she has made you."

"Gift?" I was startled.

"It is a good thing to know that one has been born of so tender a loving."

Something in me hardened against him. "I don't think Laura Worth knows anything about love. Or about tenderness. She's only played at it, acted it."

"You are here," Gunnar said. "And she even remembers the saffron sky over Stockholm. One does not recall small things unless the moment was important. But now you must tell me the rest. Tell me how the throwing of the paperweight came about."

Calmly he guided me away from arguments or attack. I had to go back to the beginning before he could understand about the broken window. I told him what Laura had said about hearing a whispered voice. I told him about the costume in the trunk, and the dragon candlestick, and how Laura had fainted. I told him about Donia's behavior, and about the voice I had heard in the night. And though I didn't want to—because of the aftermath—I told him about her sleepwalking, about the scarred picture, and of Miles Fletcher coming to take his wife back to bed.

Gunnar minimized nothing I said, but in the end he questioned me. "Do you think she would really do such a thing—deface her portrait, even in her sleep?"

"She had the scissors in her hand. And when I looked at them later, I found bits of canvas and paint stuck to the blades."

He shook his head solemnly and there was a frown between his dark brows. "I do not like this. Did she waken? Does she know what she has done?"

"She didn't know then. Dr. Fletcher apparently got her back upstairs without waking her. And Irene said he'd told her nothing. But she knows now."

"How is that?"

I could not look at him. "I lost my temper this morning when we were talking. I was so angry that I blurted out the whole thing. I told her just what she had done. That was when she threw the paperweight through the window."

Gunnar's long narrow hands rested upon his knees. I saw his fingers curl under and clench upon themselves, and I knew he was angry—with me. All the kindness and tolerance had gone out of him. There was nothing I could do to lessen his indignation over my actions, no extenuation I could offer, but

I found myself bristling against him. He couldn't know what Laura had been like—how cold and removed from me, how indifferent to anything I might be feeling. How she had said that each of us was her own person—and that was the end of it.

When he spoke there was a chill disapproval in his voice that I had not heard to this degree before. His anger took a cold, wounding turn, like the thrust of steel.

"So you have succeeded even better than you expected in your purpose in coming here? I should never have let you see her. I should have torn up your father's letter and sent you home at once."

I swallowed hard against the shock of his words, but I met chill with chill.

"I've wondered why you didn't. Perhaps now you can tell me what the letter said."

"It was a kind letter. Perhaps kinder than you deserved. Your father was concerned with you. He wrote that while you might bring some healing of old wounds to Laura, it was not she who mattered. He said that she had lived her life and made her choices—and if she was hurt now, he did not think it was very important. But you were important to him. He felt that you could not make a life for yourself until you were rid of the angers that consumed you. There was nothing he could do about these, though he had tried. He felt to blame that it had happened this way to you, but he did not himself know the cure. He hoped that this meeting with Laura might accomplish what nothing else could. You mattered to him very much."

Tears burned behind my eyelids, and I blinked furiously to keep them from falling.

"It was foolish of him to believe that," I said.

"Yes, it was foolish. I cannot agree at all with Victor that Laura does not matter. He could write that because it was so long since he had seen her, and he felt you were more important, being young. But I am here. I know and respect her. I have a great affection for Laura Worth. She is not all artifice as you think. There is a woman deep inside who deserves to escape from some prison in which she has enclosed herself. It could have been your opportunity, indeed your privilege to free her. But now you have failed in this."

I wanted to fight him, to fling angry words back at him, but they would not come. I couldn't tell him so, but with part of me I knew how right he was. He would have been quite justified in sending me away, and never permitting me to see Laura. I had begun, all too successfully, the purpose for which I'd come to Bergen, and I could take no satisfaction in my success. I would still finish what I had come to do, but I would not enjoy it as I'd expected to.

I got abruptly to my feet, and he rose with me.

"If there's more mountain to climb, let's climb it," I said.

He answered me as curtly. "There is more."

I went with him down from the rocky place where the bench was set, and as we started up the road a change came over him. He moved a little ahead of me, as if he were alone. He seemed to forget me in the sheer satisfaction of being where he liked best to be—in the outdoors, under a sunny sky, with great trees all around harboring glens cushioned with pine needles, a stream that rushed noisily under a bridge we crossed, and the black rock of the mountain shining above us in the clear air. He seemed to be following the road toward the top as if new life flowed in him again after the long winter. He made me no part of this, yet, strangely, I too seemed to belong—as though I had lived here and knew the endless black days, the rain and snow, the darkness of the water, the storms—and now was released to the warming sun.

We did not talk. I had lost my chance to learn what he thought of the earlier happenings at the house in Kalfaret. We needed our breath for the fast walking. The road turned inward away from the panorama of view, and moved less steeply over the broad top of the mountain. Flöyen had no sharp peak like Ulriken. It simply flattened out into rolling ground. Under the trees were great patches of snow, and sometimes these covered portions of the road, so that we crunched through the melting crust. Around a turn in the path the vista opened before us and I saw the high mountain lake he had brought me to. Its clear, shining surface was a thin coating of ice, with occasional cloud shadows drifting across it. All around, tall fir trees stood like dark guardians, and beyond them rose another mountain peak, its snow fields brilliantly white in the sun. This was Norway as I had imagined it. Now it spoke to me.

"To come this way is the long road around," he said. "But I thought you might wish to see this place."

"Thank you," I said, and perhaps he heard the slight lift in my voice. He glanced at me briefly and then looked away.

"It is not worthy of you to be jealous of her," he told me unexpectedly. "You have no need to resent the fact that you do not resemble her outwardly. As yourself, you are undoubtedly a cause of great envy for her, even pain. You are young and attractive and talented. And you have certain strengths in your character that are equal, perhaps even superior, to hers. Life is very much ahead of you. It cannot be easy for her to discover you, and to make her own comparisons."

He spoke impersonally, from a distance, and I wondered why I had ever thought him perceptive. He could think of Laura Worth, but not of me. What I was, what I might have felt and suffered, and longed for, he did not in the least understand.

"If you think I'm jealous, you know nothing about me," I said, and walked faster than before. He came with me in silence, and I only wished I could be away from him, free of his condemning presence.

We saw hardly anyone now. Most hikers had turned off to take the shorter route to the restaurant that topped the mountain. We met a boy and girl in bright sweaters and slacks, and an elderly gentleman in the knickers that were commonplace walking wear for the older generation. They smiled at us politely in passing.

The road at last wound away from the lake and we had only a short walk before we came out upon a flagstone terrace in front of the low building on top of Flöyen. Here there were small white tables with black chairs set about them, well occupied with people of every age sipping beer and soft drinks. Dogs had arrived up the mountain along with their families —rather well-behaved dogs which did not run about and make a disturbance. The baby carriages had arrived too, though not all had been wheeled up the road. There was the funicular on the far side of the terrace, making its regular trips up and down the heights, servicing the streets along the mountain from several stations. Flags of Norway and other nations rimmed the terrace, blowing in the wind from their high poles. Beyond lay the steep drop of the rocky cliff—with all of Bergen and its waters and far islands spread out below, clear to the North Sea.

"Shall we find a table in the sun?" Gunnar asked.

I nodded, but before we could seat ourselves, a waiter in a white coat came hurrying toward us.

"There is a table inside," he told us. "The lady is waiting for you."

Gunnar and I looked at each other—and knew.

My spirits plummeted. She had come here to accuse me, to reproach me before Gunnar. There would be further dreadful scenes.

"I won't have lunch with her," I told him. "I don't want any more of this. I can take the funicular down. You needn't bother about me."

He took my arm gently, but firmly, brooking no resistance. "I insist. It will be better if you see her now. After what you have done, you owe her that."

I owed her nothing, and I wanted only to cross the terrace to reach the funicular, leaving them to each other. But Gunnar drew me with him in a manner that allowed no opposition, and we followed the waiter into the building.

A long, glassed-in veranda was set above the terrace, with white-clad tables in a long row, where diners could sit sheltered and still look out upon the terrace and the view. The ceiling slanted steeply overhead, and there were skylights and hanging lamps. At a table halfway down Laura Worth sat waiting for us.

She wore a gray wool suit that became her, and a tiny gray hat of uncertain but charming vintage, and she looked beautiful and young and happy. Both hands were held out to Gunnar, who bent to kiss her cheek. Then she greeted me with an outstretched hand and drew me into a red chair beside her.

I sat down stiffly, unable to follow with ease this emotional transformation. Gunnar accepted it more readily than I, though he threw me a watchful glance, sensing my astonishment at this turnabout.

"I knew I could get here ahead of you by the funicular," she told us. "I've been watching for you to appear. Your cheeks are pink, Leigh. Norway is good for you."

Gunnar took the chair opposite us, and the waiter brought menus. I was glad to study mine. I could find no words to speak to her. What had become of her horror and shock over being told that she had done such a dreadful thing to her own portrait? What had become of her anger with me? I simply couldn't change gears like this. She had ordered me from the house. She had been furious enough with me to break a window by flinging the paperweight through it. And now she sat smiling at me as though some of her affection for Gunnar had spilled over to me. Such amiability left me astonished. And helplessly indignant. I had been put through an emotional upheval, I had alienated Gunnar thoroughly—and all, apparently, for nothing.

"Unless you want something heavier for lunch," she said to me, "we must introduce you to our open-faced sandwiches. Will you order for us, Gunnar, please."

The waiter went away, taking the menus with him, and I had nothing to distract my attention. I could only look at Gunnar and Laura as they took frank pleasure in each other's company. He was clearly devoted to her, and despite the difference in their ages, she was still woman enough to provide that fillip of spice in the company of an attractive man.

I watched the terrace for a while, noting the pink legs of little girls, the clear white skin of a blond mother, the beards on the faces of young men. Below the edge of the cliff gulls swooped and soared, enjoying the air drafts formed by the mountain.

I felt thoroughly upset and confused and uncertain. Laura's smile was radiant, her eyes bright, and there was that illusion of youth about her. If I had shocked and injured her in any way, it didn't show, and I felt somehow that it should have. Gunnar need not have worried, but he had, and he had not forgiven me. His formal manner toward me told me that.

"What do you think of all this?" she asked him. "That at this late date I find myself with a daugher. A young girl of twenty-three who is very much like me."

"Like you?" I echoed in exasperation.

She touched my arm lightly with one of her small, caressing gestures. "Of course. Before you stormed out of my room in a temper, I looked at you—and saw myself. We were mirroring each other, the two of us—all those lost tempers and furious reactions. But we're over it all very quickly, aren't we?"

If she could dismiss her own desperate actions so lightly, I could not. I couldn't dismiss either hers or mine. What had happened had been real.

"I can't fly around like that," I said. "I don't forgive so easily."

She paid no attention. Perhaps she took it for granted that she would be forgiven—as she always was. "I saw you in the garden with the paperweight in your hands. I hope it wasn't damaged. I'd like to have it back."

"It's not damaged," I said. I didn't know whether I would give it back or not. It was in my handbag, but I didn't bring it out. "Mrs. Jaffe is convinced that you threw it at her head. She thinks you tried to kill her."

Laura's laughter was as delightful as I remembered it on the screen, and as free of any darkness. "That's wonderful! I didn't know I could frighten the little beast. I'll have to try it again."

Gunnar was watching us both, his manner sober, unamused. "You object to Dr. Fletcher's sister?"

"I detest her!"

"Then must you have her stay in your home?"

"I don't want her there, believe me. Miles is sorry for her. He says she has no place to go, and I can't hurt him by insisting that she leave. Sometimes there is a close tie between brother and sister, and the rest of their family is gone. Perhaps it will only be for a little while. I think he doesn't entirely realize the spite she feels toward me."

Gunnar accepted her explanation. "Tell us now," he said, "—you did not come up here merely to surprise us."

"No, of course not. Miles had no plan for the holiday, after all. So I ran away. I went out and found a taxi to take me to the funicular. I came for myself—for the pleasure of lunching with you both on the mountain."

She was still playing at being young and carefree, but now the edge of the mask had slipped a little, and I was aware of something tense underneath. All this gaiety was covering something up. It was not to be taken entirely at face value as I'd thought.

"Leigh has told me what has been happening," Gunnar said. "It is not going well with you, Laura?"

She had kept her veined, betraying hands under the table, but now she brought them out in a little gesture of pleading.

"Will you intervene with my daughter for me, Gunnar? Please ask her to come back to the house and stay with me for as long as she can. Please ask her to forgive me."

"You can ask her yourself," he said gently. "If forgiveness is necessary. Perhaps it is the other way around as to who should forgive."

She turned to me and her great eyes were liquid with pleading, though she said nothing more. I felt increasingly exasperated, but no longer as emotional as I had earlier. Whatever her pretense, it was not as a daughter that she wanted me in her house. She wanted me there because she was afraid of something, and I was for the moment some sort of buffer between her and whatever trouble she feared.

"What are you afraid of?" I asked pointedly.

A nerve twitched near the corner of her mouth. Her fingers

played with two silver pins on the lapel of her jacket. Pins, I noted, that depicted the two masks of tragedy and comedy.

"We cannot help unless you tell us what is wrong," Gunnar added.

"I—I've made a terrible mistake. Perhaps I've ruined my own life and that of others. Now I can only live from day to day. I ran away when I came up here, but that was only make-believe. There's no place to run where the whisperer won't follow. I know that now."

Here on this bright veranda, with diners around us, and sunshine outside, with family groups at the white tables on the terrace, young couples with knapsacks walking hand in hand, all seemed wholesome and normal. Laura's words had a melodramatic ring. Yet—I could still remember last night with a terror that could be fully recalled.

"Laura," I said, "I heard the voice last night. It sounded in my room after I'd been asleep for a while. Who is playing this trick?"

She had paled visibly and her hand fumbled at the silver pins in a blind, lost way. "I'm afraid," she said. "I'm bitterly afraid."

"Then you must move out of that house," Gunnar told her practically. "My mother would welcome you at our home. You must come there to stay for a time—until whatever troubles you is cleared away."

"Thank you, my dear. But I would never be permitted to leave. I've trapped myself. It's as I've told you—I can only live from day to day. If Leigh will come and stay for a while, this will help me, perhaps save me for a time."

"Save you from what?" I pressed her.

She shook her head. "I only know that if I'm left alone the sword will fall in some way and I will be destroyed."

I waited for Gunnar to calm her, to try to reassure her and deny so nebulous a danger. He did not. He was concerned for her, and he did not disparage her words. Nevertheless, though he did not offend her with reassurances, I had the feeling that he did not take the ominous tenor of her words too literally. He knew there was trouble, but I suspected that he thought it mainly of her own making, and he knew she liked to dramatize. If he believed this, then she really had no one to turn to —except me. *I* could believe that some evil lived in that house in Kalfaret.

"If you want me to, I'll go back with you," I said.

I was surprised at my own words. I hadn't meant to speak

them. Gunnar was looking at me with guarded approval. I knew he had not forgiven me, but he could at least endorse my going back to the house with her. Laura's smile was tremulous and touching. I glowered at them both and wondered what was wrong with my head that I should make so reckless an offer.

"This is what I came for," Laura said. "I hoped you would come back. Thank you, Leigh."

I did not trust her in the least. She would always find the means to get her way and to use others. That was her nature. That I might let her use me did not make me pleased with myself.

The waiter brought our sandwiches, and they were small works of art—rounds of bread thickly buttered, then topped with an array of tiny mayonnaised shrimps, anchovies, cucumber, tomato and lettuce, all arranged like miniature flower gardens. Like good Norwegians, we drank beer with our meal. For the time being, all that was ominous left, and we seemed like anyone else dining on top of Flöyen that day. Outwardly, we seemed that way.

"While Leigh is here, I must make plans for you both," Gunnar said, though I knew it was Laura he planned for, not me. "There is still snow on Ulriken and you must come up there to visit my hut. Tomorrow is Saturday—let us arrange for it then."

"Miles has never been up the mountain," Laura said. "I would like to show it to him."

"But of course. You must bring your husband and his sister as well. We will make it a cheerful day, and you will feel well and strong, with no fears."

Laura nodded agreement. "Yes, this is the way it has to be —living from day to day. And Leigh must have some outings. We'll come, Gunnar. I'll persuade Miles."

No one had consulted me. He leaned toward me, showing that hint of exuberance I'd seen coming up the mountain, when he had forgotten his anger with me in his own private response to nature. The look became him, and I had an unexpected wish that it could have been for me.

"You will see something of winter in Norway, and this you will enjoy. You have the proper clothes to wear?"

"I'll loan her whatever she needs," Laura offered. "We're not far apart in our sizes. When we go home we'll look over my clothes together, Leigh."

"Then for next week we will plan a theater party," Gunnar

went on, and again I knew he was planning for her, trying to get her away from that house. My presence was only the excuse he used. "I will get a box and—"

"No!" Laura was shaking her head. "Not the theater. I haven't been to the theater in years, and I've no wish to go."

"As I say, I will get a box," Gunnar went on calmly. "And you and Leigh shall sit together in front. Everyone will look at you and whisper, and you will hear your name spoken. You will know you are not forgotten."

She was still trying to shake her head, but a slight smile had parted her lips and there was something in her eyes that remembered what it had once been like for her.

"At the hotel," I said, on impulse, "when I asked the porter where Laura Worth lived, he knew at once. I called you an American actress, and he reminded me that you were half Norwegian and belong to Bergen now."

Once more Gunnar gave me his approving smile, even though he did not trust me, and I shook myself in inward disgust. Why was I now playing this game—trying to coax her and help Gunnar in his efforts to get her away from the house in Kalfaret? I had not really changed. I didn't like her any better than I had in the beginning, and I must not let this pretended softening toward her go too far. Nor must I sacrifice my own strong purpose in some foolish effort to please Gunnar. If I did that I couldn't bear myself.

"We'll see," Laura said.

Gunnar nodded at her firmly. "You will wear your most beautiful gown. And in the *Tidende* the following day they will print that Laura Worth appeared in a box at the National Theater looking more beautiful than ever."

"You almost make me believe it can happen," she said, and they smiled at each other across the table.

It was hard to believe that this was the woman who had fainted yesterday at the sight of a gown—or a candlestick. That she had clawed across her own portrait with a pair of scissors, and that this morning I had seen her fling a paperweight through a picture window with a spectacular gesture of rage. My sense of confusion and disbelief returned. Only here and now was real. Nothing else.

But our luncheon could not last forever, and all too soon we had finished our coffee and were rising from the table. We would not have to walk down the mountain, Gunnar said. We would take the funicular one station and then walk along the hillside to where his car was parked.

We threaded our way across the terrace, and Laura went first, walking with that arresting grace which made heads turn to look at her. Gunnar bought tickets and we found a red car waiting at the platform.

He helped us into a seat which ran crosswise of the car. The vehicle was built on a slant to match the steep hillside, with the seats in tiers like steps. The doors closed, there was a humming of machinery and cables and we started down the mountainside track. Trees and rocks rose to meet us as we slipped past, and the highest row of houses drew near. In a few moments we had reached our stop and were out on the platform. From the street, where we stood for a moment, we watched the car descend, while its opposite number—a blue car—came up from below.

We had only a short walk to Gunnar's car, and then I was climbing in the back seat, because I had no wish to sit with them, while he and Laura sat up in front. It could have been such a lovely morning, but at least I was not the same driven girl who had rushed desperately to meet Gunnar earlier. I was still disturbed and resentful, and I had forgiven neither of them, but I was no longer wildly distraught, and I felt better able to deal with the house and its occupants than I had a few hours before.

Chapter 8

My new confidence lasted a very short time. Gunnar did not come in. He urged Laura to let him know about the possible trip up Ulriken the next day—Saturday—thanked us for our company, and drove off. Laura stood at road level near the foot of the steps, and watched him go.

"If I were twenty years younger . . ." she said, and looked at me.

"As it is, he can't see anyone else when you're around," I told her lightly, and ran up the steps toward the house. I did not in the least welcome any matchmaking efforts on Laura's part.

"I must tell you sometime about his wife, Astrid," she said, mounting the steps behind me. "A lovely, charming girl. Her death was a tragedy from which he hasn't recovered."

I didn't want to hear any more about Gunnar. I certainly didn't want to hear about his wife.

"What has happened now?" Laura asked.

Irene Varos waited for us at the door as we followed the walk along the side of the house. The moment she ushered us in, the climate of the house engulfed me again. Irene's expression was enough to tell us something was wrong.

Irene crossed the inner hall and stopped at the door to the room which contained Laura's memorabilia.

"You must look," she said to us both.

Laura cast a yearning glance at the stairs—her line of escape—and sighed deeply. "I used to be fond of this house. I'm not any more. Coming back here is like returning to prison."

"Perhaps you make your own prison," Irene said dryly.

We stepped past her into the room. It was not shrouded in gloom as it had been when I'd first seen it yesterday. Windows and garden doors stood open to the warming air and light. Not even the Tiffany lamp burned overhead. In the center of the room stood Laura's trunk that she had locked yesterday.

The lid was propped open, the contents spilled out upon the floor. Someone had unpacked the entire trunk in a thoroughly untidy manner, so that clothes and objects had been burrowed into and tossed out in any order. Dresses of rich materials hung over the lid and the sides. Boxes and pictures and a file of letters were spread carelessly about on the floor mixed with a scattering of costume jewelry.

Laura's look was strained, but at least it did not appear that she would faint. "Who did this?" she said to Irene.

"Mrs. Jaffe." Irene was curt. "I heard sounds from this room a little while ago, and I came in to find her tossing out the contents of the trunk as you can see."

Laura picked up a dress and shook out its blue folds. I had stood back, watching her, and she tossed me the dress across the room.

"I wore that one night in Stockholm—about a hundred years ago," she said. "Hold it up—you can still see the streaks made by the rain that night. The water marks never came out. I could never wear it again. Not that I'd have wanted to."

I dropped the soft stuff from my hands as though it burned me and let it fall across a chair.

"What did Donia say when you found here here?" Laura asked Irene. "What was she looking for?"

Irene answered uneasily. "She said she was looking for—evidence."

"Evidence? Evidence of what?"

"She wouldn't say."

"I shall take this up with Miles, of course. Her behavior is outrageous. At least she might have put everything back."

"I told her to leave it," Irene said. "I wanted you to see what she'd done."

"All right—I've seen it. Will you put these things away, please."

A note of strain had come into her voice, but she was still a stronger, more confident woman than the one I had seen yesterday.

"I'll help you pack it away," I said to Irene.

"So that you too can rummage through my past?" Laura asked me.

"If you want to call it that."

She gave me a slight, regal nod of her head. "At least you're honest. When you've satisfied yourself, come upstairs and we'll begin our talking."

"I'll do that," I said. We were back on our basis of antagonism, and that was good.

She started toward the door, and then turned about slowly. Since she'd entered the room, she had not once glanced toward her portrait in its place on the wall. Now she walked directly to it.

"Turn the picture around, please," she said to me. "Since you told me what happened I haven't come here to look. Now I must see for myself."

Irene came quickly to her side, watchful of what might happen, but Laura seemed composed as I turned the picture about so that the beautiful face looked out at us, with that dreadful scarring underneath.

I heard the sound of her indrawn breath as she stared at the cruel defacement. Then she reached out and touched the empty square that waited on the diagonal for the third X.

"Whose turn is it?" she murmured, as I had asked myself. "Who is X?"

"If you made those marks, you're the only one who can know that," I said.

Her composure was fading. She looked a little ill as she stared at the portrait. "No! I would never do a thing like this. Not even in my sleep. Tell Leigh I'd never do it, Irene!"

"I've always thought you couldn't have done it," Irene said. "Would you like me to help you upstairs?"

Laura shook her head and walked toward the trunk, where she stood staring at the spilled contents. "If I am O, then I've only to make my mark in that space and block X forever. Only I'm afraid it isn't going to be as easy as that. When you're through here, Leigh, will you come to me upstairs?"

"I'll come with you now, if you like."

"No—let me have some time alone. I must think about this a little."

"What good is thinking?" Irene said angrily. "Mrs. Jaffe must be sent away!"

Laura turned from us and went out of the room without replying. We heard her steps on the stairs before we roused ourselves and began our work of repacking the trunk.

I knelt on the floor, folding and stacking, while Irene worked with a furious energy that made her drop things once or twice.

"Do you think it could have been Mrs. Jaffe?" I asked quietly.

"This? Of course it was. I found her at it."

"No, I mean the picture."

Her hands were still for a moment as she folded a dress. "You said you came in last night and found Miss Worth here, and that Dr. Fletcher appeared soon after?"

"Yes. She had the scissors in her hands, but someone might have put them there. Or she could have picked them up from the floor."

"Was there time for this damage to the picture to be done while you were outside?"

"Perhaps—it must have been done quickly and roughly. Still—I don't think so. I don't think Laura would have had time, even if she only pretended to be asleep."

"When else were you out of the room?"

I remembered. "When I took a bath earlier. I must have been gone for half an hour. When I came back, someone had been here. The windows and doors were closed, and the picture had been turned back to face the wall."

"I did those things," Irene said. "I made the room ready for the night. But that took only a few moments. Afterwards, I didn't return."

"Then it could have been Mrs. Jaffe. I didn't look at the picture again. What will happen if we ask her, challenge her?"

Irene made a snorting sound. "She'd lie, of course. Her one purpose is to make trouble. She hates to see her brother married to Laura Worth. She is a neurotic woman."

"But wasn't it she who nursed Laura and cared for her at the time of her collapse twenty years ago?"

"Her brother is a doctor. Mrs. Jaffe would do what he asked, under his supervision. Now it's different. She's older and more unhappy. And God knows why they married each other."

"What could Mrs. Jaffe have meant when she spoke of evidence?"

Irene had picked up the gown of Venetian red which Laura had worn in *The Whisperer*. She shook it out and held it up to the light.

"She was only trying to frighten Miss Worth, to upset her. Mrs. Jaffe is a fine one to be talking about evidence. She treads on dangerous ground."

I stared at the warm red of the gown in her hands. "What do you mean by that?"

For a long moment she returned my look. Then she flung the dress over one arm and crossed the room to a long table on which large scrapbooks were stacked. They were not orderly scrapbooks, all of one shape and size, like those Ruth had used to collect Victor's reviews and write-ups, but volumes of haphazard style. When she found the one she wanted, Irene carried it to the sofa and sat down with the book on her knees. Riffling through the pages, she stopped at one and shoved the open book toward me.

These were clippings from a different paper than the ones I had seen in my father's study. The paragraphs Irene indicated had to do with Miles Fletcher and his sister when they had been questioned about his whereabouts on the night of Cass Alroy's murder. The written account was different, but the facts were the same. Miles had been at a theater with his sister at the time Cass must have died. His alibi was indisputable.

I looked at Irene. "I've read the reports before. This tells the same story. So what do you mean?"

She pressed her lips together as if in disapproval at my obtuseness. "I've always believed that something is wrong with those reports. I don't believe Mrs. Jaffe's evidence."

"But they were seen together at the theater that night. There were others who testified to that. Friends who saw them at the theater."

"Coming out of the theater," Irene said. "Under the marquee outside the theater."

"No—there was a woman who said she saw them together during the play."

"A patient of Dr. Fletcher's," Irene said scornfully.

"That doesn't necessarily mean that she'd lie—perjure herself. Why should you have such a suspicion?"

"Miss Worth has talked to me," Irene said. "When I first knew her she talked a great deal. Over and over and over—the same track. How did it happen? What occurred on the set that night?"

"Does she think Miles was not at the theater during the play?"

With a quick gesture Irene took the scrapbook out of my hands and closed it, carried it back to the table and set it down.

"You're a journalist," she said over her shoulder. "Why am I talking to you? None of this can be published. It's not to be spoken about."

"I am also Laura's daughter," I reminded her.

She came toward me across the room, her eyes searching,

questioning. "But not, I think, a daughter who loves and cherishes?"

"How could I be that?" I raised my hands and let them fall in my lap in a helpless gesture. "She has hardly won that sort of devotion."

"You asked me about Mrs. Jaffe. I said only that she's a fine one to speak of searching for evidence. And I showed you the reason. That's all. The matter is ended."

"And it's of no real importance any more, is it?" I said.

"It will always be of importance to Miss Worth. She's haunted by the past. The truth will either free her or destroy her, but she must still search for it."

"What a strange thing to say—that it could free her or destroy her. How can that be possible after all these years?"

She shrugged her shoulders and returned to the trunk, the red dress still over one arm. "I suppose it's a matter of blame. I suppose there's some sense of guilt for her in what happened. Two men who quarreled over her, perhaps. I've heard her say that she blames herself." Irene gestured toward the portrait which hung with its face toward the wall. "When she does wild things, perhaps they are because she blames herself for her own past actions. She must punish herself for the past."

"Why do you turn the portrait to the wall?" I asked. "How long has that been going on?"

"Since her marriage," Irene said. "She thinks her husband cannot love her as he once did because she no longer looks like that. One night we found her here weeping before the picture. He turned it to the wall himself, and I've kept it that way."

As she rose from placing a stack of garments in the trunk, she crossed the room deliberately to turn its face once more to the wall. Now, more than ever, the picture needed to be hidden from view.

"Sometimes," Irene said, "I've been afraid that she may turn some punishment upon herself. That's one reason why I agreed with Mr. Thoresen that you should come here. In some ways you seem to have done her good. In others, I'm not sure. You have your own reasons for being here."

I said nothing, and she shook out the red dress again, examining it with care for any tears in the material, any decorative button that might be missing, any sign of moth damage in the bands of caracul. Then she began to fold it up.

"Don't," I said on sudden impulse. "Don't put it away. That

dress fascinates me. I've seen the film of *The Whisperer* more than once—and—do you suppose she would mind very much if I tried on that dress?"

Irene regarded me in some surprise before her expression softened. "It isn't necessary for her to know. I'll air the gown and press it for you. You'll look well in it, I think."

I thanked her and went to work again, kneeling on the floor beside the trunk. I was not sure what reason lay behind the impulse that had moved me. I only knew that I had a strange wish to see myself in that red gown which Laura had worn so marvelously in the picture made from my father's book. The dress had originated in his book. He had even called it Venetian red. And when the picture was made, Laura Worth had insisted that she wear a similar gown in the scene where she came down the staircase and into the parlor to find her husband dead. Because she knew the story so well, the dress must have lent verisimilitude to the scene, even though it was being filmed in black and white.

Without my being aware of what they did, my hands had picked up a sheaf of letters which lay scattered on the floor. An open sheet caught my eye—the words, "My Darling Laura —" written in my father's hand. I looked quickly away from the page and began to fold it up. When I glanced at Irene, I found her watching me with that unexpected softening toward me still in her face.

"You can read them, if you like," she said.

I gathered the letters together hurriedly and slipped the packet deep into the trunk. "I don't want to! They're not mine to read."

She contradicted me. "They're yours. You came from the two people concerned, didn't you?"

"I can't read them without her permission," I said. "Even then, I'm not sure I'd want to read what he said to her. It might make me all the more angry with her."

Her suspicion was quick to rise. "You're angry with her?"

"Why wouldn't I be?"

"You are both too much afraid of the past. Perhaps it's good for her to acknowledge having a daughter."

"Have you read the letters?" I challenged her.

She did not seem to mind. Her attitude toward me had become more gentle, and for the first time she seemed to accept me with more liking and trust.

"I haven't read them," she said. "I'm concerned only with

the present. As long as I've known her, she's never looked at those letters. But she doesn't throw them away."

I gathered the few remaining things from the floor near me and dropped them into the trunk. "I'd better go upstairs. She'll be waiting for me."

"Yes," Irene said. "I'll finish here. And I'll have the dress for you later today."

But I didn't rise from my knees at once. Something was troubling me. Something I should remember about the trunk. I had the odd feeling that something was missing. It came to me suddenly.

"Where is the candlestick?"

"Candlestick?"

"Yes—the candlestick with the fanged dragon coiled around the stem. It was wrapped in that red dress when I took it out of the trunk yesterday. I saw Laura herself put it back in the trunk. The sight of it seemed to disturb her. But it's not here now."

"Perhaps Mrs. Jaffe has taken it away," Irene said. Her tone was low, restrained, as though she held something back. She put away the rest of the things and closed the lid of the trunk.

"Why would Mrs. Jaffe want that candlestick?" I asked.

Again there was that slight shrug of thin shoulders. "Miss Hollins, you'd better go upstairs to Miss Worth. She sometimes becomes impatient if she's made to wait too long."

Irene knew something about the candlestick and why Donia Jaffe had taken it, I felt sure. But she didn't mean to tell me her thoughts, and I asked no more questions. I left her and went quickly upstairs to Laura's bright bedroom.

She was waiting for me, stretched in the chaise longue, her shoes kicked off, and she seemed to have put aside both her shock at seeing the scarred portrait and her annoyance with Donia over the trunk.

"What a lovely morning we've had," she said when I came in.

I stared in the direction of the picture window. "It's already been mended!"

"Of course. I asked Irene to have it taken care of before I went out. I'm glad we didn't need to wait. I don't like to be reminded of such a performance."

I didn't want to be reminded of my own performance.

She did not question me about the trunk, or about Donia Jaffe, and I told her nothing of my exchange with Irene. We were meeting on a totally different plane, and I let it go at that. The unpleasant things must be returned to, but I would let her be free of them now.

"What sort of plan will you follow for your chapter about me?" she asked.

"A plan will come later. I like to collect my material first, and then see what sort of form presents itself. And of course I try to think of what the public will want to know about you."

"Do you really think anyone cares?"

I saw that she was not being coy. She really did not know what her name still meant in America.

"At home you're a legend," I said. "Like Garbo. There will be a lot of interest if you break your silence, and excitement if you ever agree to make another picture."

The thought made her laugh softly. "I would like to believe you. So tell me what this supposed public would want to know about me."

"They'll want to know how you look, of course. And what your life is like now. Whether you miss the days when you were famous and popular. Perhaps we can start with that. Do you miss them?"

She closed her eyes. "I stopped missing that life a long time ago. It was very hard work, you know. A good deal of it was tedious and frustrating. One spent so much of the time being prepared for a scene—the dressing, the makeup, the hair. And then there was the endless waiting for a scene to be shot. Most of the time there were several takes while the director tried to bring out exactly what he wanted in the actors. And there were always the jealousies, the petty rivalries."

She sounded as if she talked to convince herself.

"I should think it would be hard to get into the right mood under such circumstances—with all that battery of a work force around you to furnish distraction."

"I learned to shut it out. But I've seen good actors from the stage go to pieces under the strain of trying to concentrate and react properly under a camera's eye. Of course I used to insist on absolute silence on the set when we were rehearsing any scene I was in. I didn't mind having people around, if they would just be still and let me get ready for a scene. I suppose I had the faculty of slipping into a character quickly and summoning the emotion I wanted. Or at least the outward evidence of it. I never belonged to the method actor's school. Of course one must study the character, understand it, but a good actor knows how to portray what he wants to portray. He has to feel what he's doing, but part of him has to stay watchful, and in control, or the performance can become maudlin. There are those who say that if you really cry, no one else will. By the time they shouted, 'Quiet everybody—this is a take,' I was always ready for the real performance. Unless something had really upset me."

She was silent, undoubtedly remembering occasions when she had been upset.

"That happened when you were making *The Whisperer*, didn't it? The news accounts said Miles was in the studio that afternoon, and that he quarreled with Cass Alroy."

"He had no reason to like or trust Cass," Laura said unguardedly. "And Cass was treating me dreadfully that afternoon. Nothing I did pleased him. When we saw the rushes, we knew the scene would have to be shot over the next day."

"Do you know why Cass came to the studio that night?"

"Because he knew I was there, of course. But that, my sly young reporter, is as far as I mean to take you."

I switched promptly to another topic. At least she had taken me a step closer to my objective.

"Do you remember any particularly difficult scene you played—are there any stories about them? About other directors and actors?"

She began to talk quite freely and for the first time we were at ease with each other. I could do my job, and she could do hers without the conflicts and strains that had existed between us previously. Perhaps we had Gunnar's outing up the mountain to thank for that. He had freed us for a little while, enabled us to be at ease with each other on this professional plane. The other plane was submerged for the time being. All that area which held a night in Stockholm, Victor Hollins's letters, the birth of a baby had sunk below the surface.

She talked to me easily while I made busy notes and she seemed to enjoy the talking. She summoned old stories out of her memory—stories I had never seen in print—and she bestowed them upon me. There was an occasion when her company had gone on location in the desert while making *Sands of Fortune*, and she'd had a terrible quarrel with her leading man. Her eyes grew rapt with memory as she lost herself in a mixture of amusement and indignation. There was her evident satisfaction too in working well, and her resentment when she felt a director misdirected her. What a marvelous face she had for portraying every shading of emotion. Yet it was all done with the restraint of the film actress. On a stage one had to be larger than life. In the movies there must be an underplaying that would keep the large screen from making the slightest expression an exaggeration. One played to the camera, never beyond it.

She was using all her skill now as she talked to me, playing bits and pieces of roles for me, showing me the human side of being an actress, as well as the professional. Sometimes my pencil forgot to move because she held me so completely. I was the perfect audience.

When she stopped for breath, I leaned forward in my chair. "You ought to go back! They're waiting for you out there. You'd be marvelous on a screen again. The country would flock to see you. The world would pour in through theater doors."

She stared at me out of her dark, slightly sunken eyes, her lips parted, her breath coming quickly. For a moment she was visualizing such a return. Then she shook her head.

"It's all over. I'm too old to go back."

"You're as old as it pleases you to be. You're Laura Worth. You'll never be old!" I could hear the fervent belief in my own voice.

Her smile was wistful and I saw that the old longing was still alive. Perhaps no dedicated actress ever lost it completely. In Laura the fires had only been banked.

"Last night when I stayed in your room downstairs," I told her, "I found the blue shoes you wore in the desert scene in *Sands of Fortune*. There were still grains of sand clinging inside them. The past isn't so far away."

Her eyes were swimming with tears. "You make me feel that I may still be alive, after all. But I mustn't listen to you. I know how impossible such a dream would be."

By this time I was carried away by my own passion. I walked about the room, gesturing and talking, arguing. According to me, it would all be so easy. A word dropped here and there, the electrifying of the public, the offers coming in. Why—she could undoubtedly pick and choose her picture company. There were new directors who would still revere her work and respect her talent. They would be eager to work with her.

I paused before the picture Gunnar Thoresen had painted, my attention momentarily caught by the tossing ship, rock-bound coast, the stormy skies and spume-wreathed waves—

but it was suddenly Gunnar's face I was seeing, his voice I was hearing.

"What are you doing? What mad thing are you doing to a woman who has already been beaten by life to an extent she can hardly bear? What do you think would happen if she went back into films and failed—as she almost surely would in today's picturemaking?"

The words died on my lips and I dropped my enthusiastically moving hands. When I turned about slowly and stared at her across the room, her eyes were closed again—as though she watched a dream, and there was a touch of high color in her cheeks. I remembered who she was. Not Laura Worth, the actress, whom I could honestly admire, but the woman whom Victor Hollins had loved, and who had pushed him away because of her ambition. The woman who had refused to keep her own child—a woman greedy for fame and success and a career. Heartless when it came to others. Even, perhaps, with a death upon her conscience.

She opened her eyes and looked at me and her words came tremulously. "You almost make me believe it's possible, Leigh. What a strange thing if you should be the one to send me back into films."

I turned away from the painting and returned to my chair, picked up my notebook, made a great business of writing something in its pages. Quite dreadful possibilities had opened before my eyes. If I were the one to persuade her to go back, to pick up her career again—and she failed, as something told me she very well might—I would have managed a punishment for her greater than any I could have imagined when I left New York, so grimly determined.

But I couldn't be as base as that. I couldn't be!

Or could I?

"Tell me about the time when you were making *Maggie Thornton*," I said. "Everyone remembers that picture. It's one of the greats. Did Victor Hollins like what you and the director were doing? Did you have any arguments?"

She left her new dream and went back to the old one. Her face glowed as she talked about that time. Arguments? There had been battles, apparently. Victor, who was not very temperamental, had nevertheless fought for his story—fought Laura and fought the director. There had been compromise in the end, and perhaps the picture was the better for it. Either extreme might have been wrong.

"When it was over, we needed that trip to Scandinavia," she said. "There were wounds to be healed."

And a new wound to be dealt. There was confusion in me again, that old tearing between love and hate. I was glad there was an interruption when Miles Fletcher tapped on the door and came into the room. His black hair was sleekly combed across the top of his head, and I could imagine him giving it his concentrated care. As usual the thick mustache on his upper lip hid the expression of his mouth, and his shoulders were slightly hunched as he came toward us.

He gave me a barely courteous greeting and crossed the room to kiss his wife's cheek.

"You're looking better," he said to her. "There's color in your face."

She touched his hand with affection. "Because of my daughter! She admires my work. She thinks there is still a place for me in films. She believes the public wants me back, and that there are directors who would ask for me if I were available."

From where I sat I could sense the anger rising in him. He turned his head to look at me directly, and I was slightly shaken by the fury in his eyes.

"What idiocy is this?"

So challenged, I defended my position. "There's nothing idiotic about it. For some reason I don't understand, Laura has cut herself off from the thing she does best. She is still a great actress. That hasn't changed. Why shouldn't she go back?"

When he would have answered me, Laura rose quickly from her chair and leaned against his shoulder, gently pleading.

"No—don't be angry with her. This is only dreaming. She knows that too. It's far too late for me to pick up a career again. The women of my age who are still acting have done so all along. For me there's been a hiatus. But Leigh has been good for me. You can see that. She's better for me than any medication. We're beginning to fill her notebook with material. I didn't know how much I had to tell her."

Somehow I felt enormously relieved. Laura could look realistically at the matter of returning to Hollywood. She had already put my siren words out of her mind. A danger—for me, as well as for her—had been removed.

Miles slipped an arm about her and he withheld whatever outburst he might have intended for me.

"You're overexcited," he told his wife. "That's not good either. There's false energy in that—and collapse later. How long are these interviews to take?"

"Oh, very long!" she answered him lightly. "Isn't that true, Leigh?"

I nodded agreement. "It's true enough. Perhaps I won't stop at one chapter in a book. Perhaps I could do a complete biography of Laura Worth. There's never been one, and it's certainly time."

"What a lovely idea!" She was plainly delighted.

Miles Fletcher was not in the least delighted. "That's impossible! Do you think I want my wife's entire life put into print for the public to read?"

She wilted at once, and I knew that she, who carried herself so proudly and courageously, had been held up to shame by her husband.

"This would be the biography of an actress," I said. "I'm not interested in writing about Laura Worth's private life."

"An actress is also a woman," he told me coldly. "You could hardly do her justice if you thought otherwise."

"Perhaps it would be possible, Miles." She was suddenly pleading, as I'd never seen her plead. She actually seemed to care what this man thought. She wanted to placate him. "My life hasn't been all that dreadful."

He looked at her coolly, questioningly, and I could see her concern for whatever he might be thinking.

"Anyway, I'm not sure a book is possible," I said. "Let's take it a little at a time, and see how it goes."

Quickly, Laura changed the subject. "Miles, Gunnar Thoresen has invited us all to come up to his hut on top of Ulriken tomorrow. You and Donia, and Leigh and me. You'll come, won't you?"

At least he seemed to have no objection to Gunnar. He agreed, though a little grudgingly, and Laura seemed relieved.

"Thank you, darling. Will you tell Donia?"

"Why not tell her yourself? If it comes from you, she'll feel more welcome."

Laura's expression changed and some of her spirit returned. "I don't want to ask her. I don't care whether she comes or not. Do you know what your sister has done now?"

Miles stepped away from her with the air of a man beset by woman-problems in which he had no wish to involve himself. "I don't know, but undoubtedly you'll tell me."

"No—not I," Laura said quickly. "You tell him, Leigh. You're not prejudiced, as I might be."

Miles went to Laura's small desk and pulled out the painted chair with its seat of striped silk. He sat astride it facing us both.

"All right—suppose you tell me," he said.

Everything about this man made my hackles rise, and I found that I enjoyed telling him about Donia. I explained how Irene had found her strewing the contents of Laura's trunk about the room downstairs. And when Irene had asked what she was doing, she had said she was searching for evidence. Later we found that she'd taken away the brass candlestick with the dragon decoration.

Miles rose from the small chair with a suddenness that set it rocking. He was no longer uninvolved.

"I'll talk to her myself," he said and went out of the room.

I had to know what was about to happen, and I followed him.

By the time I reached the hall Miles was in Donia's room, and I stepped opposite the open door. He stood facing his sister, with the brass candlestick on a table between them. Donia had taken the trouble to set a candle in the holder and the wick was lighted. The flame swayed in the draft from the window, smoking a little.

"What are you up to now?" Miles demanded of her. "Why did you forage into the contents of Laura's trunk?"

He towered above his sister across the table, and Donia seemed tiny by contrast. Her brown, rather wizened face was screwed into a grimace and her big dark eyes snapped brightly, venomously.

"I found what I was looking for," she said, and touched the candlestick. "Isn't this what you've wanted for so long?"

"If you're here to cause trouble, I'm going to send you home," Miles told her. "Take that candlestick downstairs and put it where you found it. She's been disturbed enough by the sight of it."

Donia bent her boyishly shorn head and blew out the flame with a puff that exaggerated her grimace.

"You know why, don't you? Anyway, you can't send me home. You don't dare."

Miles turned his head with a quick, watchful movement, and saw me standing there. He crossed the room in two long strides and closed the door sharply in my face. I went back to Laura's room and found her lying on the chaise longue. But she was not apathetic now. She waited for me anxiously, and some dark excitement seemed to drive her.

"Tell me what happened!" she cried the moment I stepped into the room.

I told her what I had seen and heard, including the words about the candlestick.

She put her hands over her face. "If they know about the candlestick, then it means that Miles must have been in the studio that night. I think I've known all along that this must be so, though I've not wanted to admit it, even to myself. I don't see how they managed the alibi, but Donia must have lied for him. He could have been at the studio and still have reached the theater in time to appear to be coming out with her after the performance. This is why my portrait has been scarred. To frighten me, to threaten. If the X is marked into that place—it will mean the end of everything for me!"

"Hush!" I said. I went to kneel beside her. The wild rose fragrance she wore was in her hair, on her skin, as I put my arms around her and held her till she quieted. I half expected her to push me away, but she did not. She made no response, but she suffered me to hold her until the shivering stopped. Then she removed herself gently and rather proudly from my arms. But she was still afraid.

We had reached the verge of mystery, the precipice that led to murder. Fear was tangible in the air around us. Laura was afraid, and I was afraid for her. But she had no wish to cling to me now, and I stood up and moved away from her.

"What can a candlestick have to do with what happened that night?" I asked.

She answered without caution—because she had accepted me. "The candlestick was the weapon that killed Cass Alroy."

I stared at her in disbelief. "How could it have been? The police, all the newspaper accounts, always gave the same weapon. That iron doorstop in the shape of a cat. The same doorstop that was used on the set of *The Whisperer*, was the weapon which killed him. Wasn't it?"

She turned her head helplessly from side to side. "I don't know! I don't know!"

"But then what about this candlestick?" I pressed her. "Where does it come in?"

"I carried it away." The words were hardly more than a whisper. "Oh, I was so strong in those days! I always knew what to do. I could always take charge when I had to—and I was afraid of nothing. I put the candlestick in my dressing room with a candle in it, and no one ever noticed it there. Not the police. Not anyone. There was no need to look for another weapon—they had the doorstop. But I always kept the candlestick—I suppose as a sort of—well, evidence."

And Donia Fletcher had been looking for "evidence."

"But I don't understand any of this," I said. "I don't understand why any of it is important now."

My words seemed to rouse her to an awareness of me. She sat up on the chaise longue and there was a deep entreaty in her eyes.

"I've forgotten how young you are. You were hardly more than a baby when all this happened. When Miles comes back, it's better if you know nothing, understand nothing. You mustn't speak a word of what I've said to anyone. Not to Donia or Miles or Irene. Not to Gunnar."

She was growing frantic and I had to reassure her. "I promise," I said.

She relaxed a little, but once more her hands covered her face in distress. "When will it stop?" she murmured. "When will there be an end to it? When will I know?"

"Don't," I said. "Please don't be so upset."

Somehow she seemed as fragile as a doll, and as breakable. There was an urge in me to save her from whatever threatened, to protect her from unknown dangers. I moved toward her again.

We heard Miles's step in the hallway, and Laura waved me back. "Don't, Leigh. He mustn't find us in a touching mother-daughter scene."

I managed to be well away from her when he walked into the room. Laura lay back on the chaise longue, with not a hair ruffled, and no sign remaining of the shivering woman I'd held in my arms a few moments before. It was I who was shaken now—and shocked. Shocked by the words she had spoken to me, and by my own protective reaction toward her.

"I've talked to Donia about the trunk," Miles said to his wife. "And I've told her to put the candlestick back where she found it. Sometime you must tell me why that candlestick's existence worries you. But Donia had no business looking through your things. I'm afraid she has an insatiable curiosity." He glanced at me with distaste. "Perhaps my wife and I can be alone for a little while?"

She threw me what might have been a look of entreaty, but

I could not tell whether she wanted me to go, or to stay. Anyway, I had no choice. I went quietly out of the room and left them together.

Donia Jaffe was crossing the hall, carrying the brass candlestick in both hands. The candle had been removed. She smiled at me with a certain bright triumph, and I followed on her heels down the stairs, went with her into Laura's room. Quite calmly she opened the trunk and dropped the candlestick into it.

"At least I was able to go through nearly everything," she said cheerfully.

I stared at her. There seemed to be nothing I could say.

When she had lowered the lid of the trunk and turned the key in the lock, she carried the ring of keys back to the sandalwood box, and dropped them inside. Then she whirled to face me.

"So we're all to go up on Ulriken tomorrow? What a charming little party that will be! I suspect that Gunnar Thoresen has no idea of what he's letting himself in for."

"I think he can handle whatever comes," I said.

"It's possible. I like these strong Norwegian men. But we may put him to something of a test. See you later."

She went out of the room and left me standing there, staring at Laura's trunk with the candlestick hidden from my view. I felt beset by danger on every side. Laura's fears were real. Her haunting was real. The past was not done with or finished. It was hanging over her now, though I couldn't be sure where the danger lay, or what form it might take.

But there was even more to frighten me. I couldn't tell which alarmed me more—the knowledge that I might inflict the ultimate revenge upon Laura Worth if I chose to pursue the road I'd started down and encouraged her in an effort to recapture her career, or my awareness of the strange opposing emotion which had seized me when I knelt beside her and held her in my arms. The latter was a betrayal of myself and my father to a bitter degree, and it dismayed me to think that I might be so weak a person, after all. The girl who had knelt beside Laura wasn't me. I was the other one—Victor Hollins's daughter. The one whose anger would never die.

Now, at least, I knew there was something to be learned in this house. Something which grew out of the past and had some desperate bearing on the present. Something which might put a stronger weapon than I'd ever expected in my hands.

Donia had gone through the trunk, but I had not. I had helped to pack away certain items, but I hadn't handled everything. There had been more packets of letters than those from my father, and I shrank less at the thought of reading them than I did over those Victor Hollins had written. There were no rules of conduct to restrain me now—if my purpose was clear.

Drawn irresistibly, I went to Laura's dressing table and opened the sandalwood box. Donia had dropped in the keys, but when I took them out I saw that a folded piece of paper had been thrust beneath them. Curiously, I drew it out and opened it.

The sheet was of plain, light-colored wrapping paper, and block letters had been scribbled across it in red crayon, like a child's scrawl. The words leaped out at me.

DON'T YOU KNOW WHO O IS?
ONLY MEDDLERS NEED TO WORRY.

The crimson letters seemed to burn on the paper, and as I read them over a new pattern began to form itself in my mind.

Laura had been trapped into seeming to have defaced her own portrait, but neither she nor Irene believed she had done it. Laura believed, however, that the threat was against her—that she was the O whom X threatened. Holding this sheet of paper in my hands, I knew better.

The portrait was hung here in this room with me. I was the one who would look at it, not Laura. I was the O who faced some hidden threat. There was someone who didn't want me in this house—someone who whispered in my room at night, and who had treated Laura's lovely portrait to vandalism in order to frighten me.

I started to tear up the note, and then thought better of it. Here, indeed, was "evidence." I put it away in my handbag, postponing any decision as to what I would do with it. I was dealing with a cunning and psychopathic mind given to childish means of threatening me. There were ways of dealing with such a mind and coaxing it to betray itself.

On a table near the window lay the scissors which had been used to scar the picture. I picked them up and looked at the blades. The same bits of canvas and pigments still clung to the tips. Smiling a bit grimly to myself, I went to the picture and turned it outward on the wall. The X space was still empty. Carefully, I scratched an O into the waiting square.

Now X was neatly blocked from winning the game. Let whoever it was make what they liked of that.

I thought no longer of going through the trunk.

Chapter 9

The household was in a bustle the next morning in order to be ready by the time Gunnar called to take us up the mountain. Laura, as usual, did not come down to breakfast, but ate lightly in her room. Donia, Miles, and I breakfasted in the dining room, and we were all slightly wary of one another.

Only Irene was in no rush, since she was not coming with us. Her position in the household was never quite clear-cut. Miles and Donia both had a tendency to treat her as an employed housekeeper. By Laura she was accepted on a more intimate basis. How she herself felt about her position, I didn't know. She preferred to serve us at the table and eat her own meals leisurely by herself later. Yet she displayed no attitude of inequality with those she served.

The moment I finished my coffee I excused myself and went to my room to put on my borrowed winter clothes. I got into Laura's beautifully cut brown ski pants, and a tan sweater with a bright zigzag design in green. We'd found that a pair of her brown boots fitted me comfortably, and I was lacing them up when Irene tapped at my door.

When I called to her she came in, bringing the Venetian red gown from *The Whisperer*.

"I've pressed it for you," she said, and went to the wardrobe closet that occupied a space against the wall. It was a closet which held some of Laura's clothes, and she pushed them along the rod to make way for the red dress. "Miss Worth saw me pressing it, and she also wishes to try it on."

I stared at her back in surprise, and realized that something had agitated Irene. The very stiffness of her shoulders and neck hinted at some control she was exerting over her own feelings.

"But I thought she hated the sight of that dress," I said. "I thought she didn't want to be reminded of anything connected with *The Whisperer*."

146

Irene hung the dress on the rod, and turned slowly about. "I don't know what's happened to her this morning. It's not that she's merely excited about the trip up the mountain. It's as if she has grown suddenly younger. She's a different woman today."

"But that's fine, isn't it?" I said.

"I don't like it."

"Why not? Why should a change for the better worry you?"

Irene's thin, solemn face trembled into lines of concern. "She's talking too recklessly. She's speaking of returning to Hollywood."

"Oh, no!" My cry was involuntary. I tied the laces on my boot and leaned against the sofa back, waiting for Irene to go on.

"She says you've told her it's possible for her to become a star again. She believes you. She says nothing is going to stop her." There was restrained accusation in Irene's tone.

"But yesterday she said she was too old, and that it was too late," I protested. "What's happened to change her mind?"

"She's done some rearranging of her own thoughts. She's discarding facts and replacing them with a dream. She's convinced herself that all America is waiting for her. It's completely mad."

I agreed that it was, and I felt both hot and cold at the same time because of my own self-questioning.

"She'll get over it," I said. I didn't know whether what Irene was telling me was good news or bad. There was that tearing in me which pulled me in opposite directions, and I couldn't seem to face one steady course.

"If you've encouraged her in this direction, then you must undo it," Irene said sternly.

The contrary pull tugged at me. "What if it's perfectly true that there's an audience waiting for her?"

"Miss Hollins, if there's an audience for her in America, they want her as the legend they know. They want her young and beautiful as she used to be, and enormously talented."

"Talent doesn't die," I said.

"But it may grow rusty. She's not strong enough to face the changes she'd have to make. She'll only be humiliated, defeated."

This was what I thought myself, and I said nothing.

Irene moved toward the door. "Miss Hollins, as her daughter, you must persuade her against this terrible foolishness."

The doorbell sounded, and she went to answer it, leaving me staring at the disturbing visions that had risen in my own mind. From across the room the scarred portrait watched me with lustrous dark eyes, the lips softly parted and faintly smiling. The face of a woman who waited eagerly for love. I hardened myself against its spell. Perhaps she had waited for love, but she had also thrown it away. The O, freshly marked, seemed to glow against the canvas.

Out in the hall I heard Gunnar's voice and I hurried into the warm woolen jacket Laura had loaned me, tied a bright scarf about my head against the wind that would be blowing on top of Ulriken, and went into the hallway.

Laura had just come running down the stairs, dressed in smartly contrasting black and white. Black ski pants and a white sweater, over which she had flung a black leather jacket of expensive make. A black and white wool scarf was knotted about her neck. Her everyday clothes might have a vintage touch, but her sports garb was obviously smart and in fashion. Even her visored cap of white leather looked as though it might have come from a fashionable boutique.

She went to greet Gunnar, who was resplendent in a red sweater and gray skiing pants. Then she gave me an embrace of equal warmth which left me standing stiffly with her arm about me. She sensed my lack of response and stepped back, though her expression showed only a faint amusement. She didn't really mind.

Watching, I saw what Irene meant. There was no apathy left in this woman, but neither was there the keyed-up nervous energy I had seen earlier. Somehow, during the night Laura Worth had come together and was all of one piece, solid. She was a woman of confidence and assurance and gaiety—all of which were based on something she believed to be real in herself. Her ravaged face gave the illusion of youth, her movements were strong and sure, her voice filled with that smoky quality that had electrified her audiences. Gunnar saw the change at once, and he threw me a quick look that was questioning, perhaps a little suspicious.

"You look marvelous, Laura," he told her. "You look like Maggie Thornton."

He could not have paid her a greater compliment and I had a wish to pinch him, to make faces at him—to do anything so that he would not encourage her further.

"It's all thanks to my daughter," Laura said brightly. "Leigh has made me see that I mustn't waste my life any longer. There's an audience waiting for me in America. They know me. They will welcome me home."

For once Gunnar was taken completely aback. She accepted his silent staring as approval and nodded her white-capped head in the assured manner I had seen so often on the screen.

"Yes! I'm going back to Hollywood—or to whatever its equivalent is today. There are those with influence I still know. I'll begin writing letters at once. I'm going to let the world know that I'm available."

Gunnar gave me a long, cool look and regained his quiet self-possession. "I do not like this, Laura. I do not think I will be happy to see Laura Worth playing character roles—grandmothers, dowdy old women, perhaps. You have given something special to the world which still exists. I think you must not take this magic away."

His words convinced her not at all. "What nonsense! Gunnar, my dear, you don't know picturemaking as I do. There are many fine starring roles for the mature woman. Of course I shall not take the first offer. I shall be very sure of the story and my role in it, and of what actors I shall play opposite."

Miles, coming down the stairs with Donia behind him, heard her last words.

"Don't fool yourself!" he said sharply. "Do you think you'd have any choice in the matter? Of course they'd give you a try. If you want to go back, there'll be a huge buildup. They'd exploit you in one picture to satisfy the public's curiosity. And after that—pfft! The sooner you get this idea out of your head, the better."

For just an instant her confidence faltered, but she answered him with dignity. "Even if I have to go alone, I must do this. But I had hoped you might come with me."

Miles said nothing more, but his dark look gave no consent, no approval.

For once, I found myself in full agreement with him. But it was clear that Laura was off on her own wild course, and no mere words were going to alter her direction. I had a sudden swift vision of myself as I might become—a woman who rode headlong, whose wearing of a bit was sure to be between her teeth. The picture did not flatter me.

Donia, her small person enveloped in an oversized plaid jacket and yellow trousers that were slightly baggy at the knees, had come bouncing down the stairs behind her brother.

She looked from face to face with the alert air of the born troublemaker, and when she spoke she took us all by surprise.

"Don't listen to them, Laura. Of course you'll be stupendous in pictures—as you always were. You mustn't let anyone discourage you."

Laura accepted this strange bedfellow calmly, without being impressed. Her manner told us that she needed neither encouragement nor discouragement now. She knew her own course and she meant to follow it. Watching her, I felt a little sick inside. I remembered the ugly note I had found last night in the sandalwood box. It was in the pocket of my jacket now. I wondered even more sickly which one of them had left me that scrawl.

Irene had packed a lunch basket for us to take up the mountain, and we all trooped out the door, with Gunnar carrying the basket. Laura ran ahead toward the steps, her lithe movements contrasting astonishingly with those of that apathetic woman I had first seen leaning on Miles's arm. Gunnar stayed behind to wait for me as the others went ahead.

"So you have done this?" he said gravely.

I could not meet his eyes. I felt ashamed and abashed, and I hated feeling so.

"I didn't expect her to react in such an extreme way. At first she didn't take it up so seriously."

"Then you must undo the damage, must you not?" he asked me. "She looks wonderful for the moment. But there is terrible disaster and disillusionment ahead."

I turned from him and went toward the steps to the street. This was what Irene had said—that I must undo the damage. I had caused Laura to take this course, and now, impossibly, I must change the flow of a torrent.

Gunnar spoke at my shoulder. "There is such a thing as carrying malice too far. I did not expect this extreme from you."

I couldn't answer him. Anger was rising in me and I could feel my cheeks burning hot, feel the tension of my own body. Yet at the same time there was a stinging behind my eyelids. I blinked fiercely. Once I had wanted this man's approval and liking. Yet all I could do was move farther away from winning either. They were all blaming me—except Donia—and yet I had not really been as guilty as they thought. I *had* started the torrent on its course, but I'd done it impulsively, sincerely—and now there was no way to turn it about. I had only to watch Laura to know that.

Gunnar's car waited at the foot of the steps. Laura and Miles sat with him in front, while the lunch basket, Donia, and I were packed into the rear. As the car started off, Donia nudged me slyly.

"You're doing very well," she whispered. "You want her to destroy herself, don't you? This is the best way of all!"

I said nothing, detesting her, fixing my attention on the glimpses of Bergen slipping past. I no longer knew what I wanted with the cool reasoning of my brain. Unpredictable emotions seemed to be taking over, leaving me shaken and at their mercy.

We drove along the hillside to the Ulriksbanen—that small building with the strikingly slanted red roof, which housed the cable cars that ascend Ulriken. Laura's and Gunnar's skis and ski poles had been strapped in a holder on the roof of the car, and when he parked he took them down and carried them upright into the station house. There was no need to be burdened with clumsy ski boots, since one wore soft, easy boots for ski touring.

We stood in line with others on the platform, waiting for a car to come down. Behind the station house a waterfall tumbled down black rocks and washed away in a stream. Above, the cables mounted in silver lines straight up the mountain. Once more we had "festival weather," with the sun bright in a clear blue sky and a day that verged upon spring. Already, Laura said, there were crocuses pushing up in the garden.

The small yellow cable car that was to take us to the top slid down into the station with a clashing of machinery, and as many of us as the car would hold got inside. There was a bench at either end, with varnish well worn, but no one sat down. We all stood up to watch the ascent, the skiers with their skis held vertically beside them. Miles, reluctantly, had taken over the lunch basket.

Gunnar saved a place for Laura and me beside a window and we pressed close to the glass. The sharp peak of Ulriken rose black and forbidding out of the snowfields high above us. Its modern communications tower was a landmark that could be seen from all over Bergen, and it seemed to grow larger as we lifted toward it. Beneath the car as we rose precipitously, the lower slopes of the mountain lay brownish-green with gorse and other stubby growth from which humps of black rock protruded. As we rose, we could see the foot trail that wound up the mountain to our right, with climbers already out in their high boots, some of them with staves in their hands.

The group going up in the car was mainly young, with the healthy attractiveness of Norwegian youth. The girls were bareheaded, and long-haired, and the boys often wore beards of various trims and lengths. Laura stood beside me, watching the ascent with the eagerness of a young girl who might never have gone up the mountain before, and I saw the young people look at her and exchange smiles that she returned readily. I doubted that they knew who she was, but there was an arresting quality about her and they responded to the youth she wore like a flag, and which denied the evidence of one's eyes. For the first time, the claim that chronological age had no meaning came home to me.

The height of the mountain was about two thousand feet, Gunnar said. Norwegian mountains were not nearly so high as they looked in pictures, but since they rose straight up from sea level, the impression of height was great. The car moved smoothly as we passed a red gondola coming down, and we waved at the occupants. At least Laura and I waved. The Bergensere in our car took the other car for granted.

Now there were snow patches along the mountain, and the gray-black rocks protruded in sharp contrast. The air was colder, but there was only a little wind at this level. When it was very windy, Gunnar said, the cable cars did not run. Beneath us the great panorama spread out more impressively than ever, with the mountains all around taking on new characteristics as viewed from this height. We could see the distant lakes of the countryside, and follow the winding fjords out to the North Sea. These were not the fjords I'd seen in pictures, with their steep, mountainous sides, but the gentler indentations that belonged to this Bergen coastline. Between Ulriken and Flöyen, the Ice Valley, Isdalen, cut its way, with Svardiket Lake gloomy at its base.

With a slight jerk, the car slid into the station at the top, the doors were opened and we filed out. When we'd climbed a flight of stairs we found ourselves upon an open observation platform, from which snow had been cleared, and now the higher force of the wind struck us. There was a small restaurant and gift shop adjacent, and those who had come up with us scattered in every direction—some into the restaurant, others to observe the view from another platform, some eager to be at their skiing, marching away through the snow with their lightweight touring skis over their shoulders.

Donia had apparently never been up this mountain before, and she bounced about like a child, running from one vantage point to the next. Miles frowned at her childish eagerness and stayed with Laura, Gunnar, and me.

Gunnar had not spoken directly to me since we'd left the house, but now he strove with cool courtesy to point out various spots of interest, and I listened to him politely, hating the barrier that had risen to stop our growing friendship, and helpless to break it down.

"Over there on the left, out beyond Fantoft, you can see the lake on which Grieg built his summer home. The house is a charming museum now. You must see it before you leave Bergen."

Laura smiled at me. "That must be soon. If you're to write that book, you'll have to come to Hollywood with me, you know. Now that I've made up my mind, I want to act as quickly as I can. Perhaps I will take a house in the hills above Los Angeles and stay there while I read scripts. It's much better if I can be close at hand during this time of preparation. So of course you must come with us, Leigh."

Neither man said a word. Gunnar and Miles looked at me with distaste, and I detested them both. But this time I made an effort to join the opposition.

"I'm not going to Hollywood," I said. "And you're not either, Laura. As you said yesterday, this is a dream. It's too late to make it come true."

She threw me a look of surprise—rather sorrowful surprise —as though I had betrayed her. "But you're the one who said—oh, never mind! I don't need your assurances, or anyone else's now. A few days ago I was ready to give up—to die. Now I'm ready to live. I mean to have my chance to live. Nothing is going to change that."

Miles made a growling sound in his throat and walked away from us on the platform. Laura watched him go with a look of sorrowing affection.

"He disapproves," she said sadly. "I'd like him to go with me, but I'm afraid he won't."

Gunnar put his hands on her shoulders and swung her gently around to face him. "Laura, Laura! If you feel you must run away from something, then there is still my house, and my mother waiting to welcome you. You will be safe there. You can rest and become strong again. And nothing you fear can touch you."

She shook her head at him. "No, my dear. That's not the way for me. I know what I want now. I know what I must do. But first I must placate Miles a little. He's displeased with me and he mustn't stay that way. Wait for me here."

She followed her husband across the platform, walking with that grace which was characteristic—an arresting figure in black and white. Heads turned as always. There was a lump in my throat and again that hotness behind the eyes.

"What if you're all wrong?" I cried to Gunnar. "What if she's right and ought to have her chance?"

He shook his head at me. "You know better than that. But I am disappointed in you, Leigh Hollins. I had hoped that knowing Laura would change you, make you more forgiving."

I choked on my own tears. "There's too much to forgive!" I cried. Let him believe what he pleased. What did I care what this stubborn Norwegian thought!

He began to talk to me quietly, impersonally, as though I were a tourist whose acquaintance he had just made, and his very manner helped me to blink away my tears.

"Do you know that every year Bergen has an event in which all who wish set out to climb the Seven Mountains? We meet at a certain place and each man and woman tries to complete the route—up one mountain and down, and then up the next. I have done it more than once and I have my blue and white certificate with the outline of the Seven Mountains to prove it."

"I'm sure that's very inspiring," I said tartly.

He smiled at me without mirth. "You are angry. I think I am a little angry too. Come—let us start across the snow. We can walk to my hut. The crust is hard enough, and there are many ski and foot tracks. This high air is clearing to the mind—we will all feel better for moving about. Look—Miles and Laura are waiting for us."

Laura and her husband stood at the edge of the platform where the snow began, and she was waving to us. Donia came bouncing across from another point, and we started over the snow together. I could not tell whether Miles had been placated or not. He looked rather sullen and still disapproving.

The bank plunged steeply down from the high point that gave Ulriken its frontal peak, to level out in a shallow, snow-filled valley. A second peak rose opposite, black and rocky and patched with snow. There were tracks to follow and Gunnar took the lead, now allowing Laura to carry her own skis in good Norwegian fashion. Miles followed Laura, who needed no help, as we marched in single file, with Donia and me bringing up the rear. Up here the skiing was all cross-country, or touring, as was most common in Norway, and several skiers went striding past us as we traveled the high valley at the top of the mountain. There was a club house up here, and many skiers were members.

Around a turn, and across a snowfield hidden from the cablecar platform, we came upon Gunnar's small red hut. A thick blanket of snow quilted the roof, and long icicles hung from the eaves. He unlocked the door and when we were inside he went at once to light the waiting logs in the fireplace.

The hut was composed of one large main room, rustic in its furnishings, with a rug patterned in green and brown set diagonally across the rough floor. There was a rustic table and several chairs, and bunks along one wall. My eyes were drawn at once to a painting over the mantel, and I knew this was Gunnar's work. This time it was a snow scene, with his own red hut glowing against a stormy sky.

"Do you always paint storms?" I asked as he worked at lighting the fire.

The kindling caught, and tongues of flame licked upward to the wood, flaring brightly. He put the fire guard in place and stood up, dusting his hands.

"Perhaps I live too quiet a life," he said. "Norwegians are naturally adventurous, so I like to get a sense of conflict and struggle into my paintings. In Norway we must always fight the elements."

"That's one of my favorite pictures, Gunnar," Laura said. "Next to the one you've given me. Leigh, you should see some of his others. This young man has wasted his talent, just as I have done. But it's never too late to change."

Donia was moving with characteristic energy about the big room, examining everything, touching and poking. Miles dropped rather glumly into a chair, watching Laura. She turned to him suddenly.

"You won't mind if Gunnar and I go off for a run, darling? This will probably be our last chance for this season. Perhaps the three of you can walk around a bit."

"We'll manage," Miles said without enthusiasm, and I noted that the look Laura gave him was anxious.

Somehow, I had not pictured the fact that Gunnar and Laura would go off together and I would be left in this unwelcome company. I decided that I would go out on my own and plod about in the snow. In the open, away from the others, perhaps I could sort out my confused emotions.

Laura was impatient to be off, and when Gunnar had instructed us about keeping the fire burning, the two of them went outside, put on their skis and glided off across the snow, using their ski poles. I noticed that cross-country skis left the heels free, so they lifted at each stride. For a few minutes I stood at a small window and watched them go, feeling forlorn and uncomfortable. I was popular with no one at the moment.

Behind me, Donia had curled herself close to the hearth, warming her hands at the hissing blaze, her wizened little monkey face glowing in the firelight. She sat cross-legged, talking to Miles without turning around. As usual, she tried to make trouble.

"You can see, of course, what Leigh is up to?"

Miles merely grunted. Donia was apparently used to this reception of her words, and she went on with light malice.

"You're very good at ingratiating yourself, aren't you, Leigh? Flattering her like that! Laura accepts you more and more as her daughter. She's turning to you, relying on you. And now that you've convinced her that she can go back into pictures, she adores you. That's very clever of you, Leigh. Your mother is a wealthy woman. And as I recall, Victor Hollins left very little of the money he made in his lifetime for his family. Laura hasn't been like that. She has investments abroad, and money in Swiss banks. And wills can always be changed, isn't that true, Miles?"

"Shut up, Donia," Miles said.

I'd turned to stare at her in astonishment, and I saw the look of venom she flung at her brother. She scrambled to her feet without another word and went out of the hut, turning her coat collar up about her neck, her legs in yellow trousers bright against the snow.

Miles rose and closed the door that she'd left rudely open behind her. Then he came back to his chair beside the table, making no comment on his sister's outrageous behavior.

"Sit down, Miss Hollins," he said.

It was still cold in the cabin and I'd kept on my woolen jacket. I thrust my hands into its slit pockets as I did as Miles asked. My fingers touched the crayon-scribbled paper I'd thrust into one pocket. Whatever was coming, would be unpleasant, I knew, and I felt annoyed with Gunnar and Laura for leaving me in this predicament.

"Perhaps it's time we talked," Miles said.

"I don't think talking will serve much purpose," I told him. "You've made it plain from the start that you didn't want me here."

"And I was right, don't you think?"

"How can you say that? After you talked to me at the hotel the other day, I took a taxi to Kalfaret. I saw you and Irene bring Laura out of the house. She looked scarcely alive. She was a sick woman, with no hope, no energy—nothing. Now she's Laura Worth again. Isn't that an accomplishment? And isn't it because I've come here?"

"Perhaps a slow recovery would be safer. A recovery based on a real improvement in her health, rather than on nervous stimulation."

He was a doctor and I couldn't very well tell him that there was nothing wrong with her health. I held to a disbelieving silence, and after a moment he went on. Once more I was aware of his eyes that seemed to hold a pale gray light in their depths.

"It's difficult to be sure of your motivation, Miss Hollins. I think Donia exaggerates—but how can we be sure? You've encouraged her to return to Hollywood and she's taken the bit between her teeth."

"What I said was said impulsively," I told him. "Afterwards she wouldn't allow a retreat."

"I would like to believe that you mean her no harm," he said, and I knew this was not what he believed at all. "The worst possible thing that can happen is for her to return to Hollywood."

"Why?" I asked bluntly.

The gray eyes flickered. "Quite aside from the obvious fact that it's too late for her to take up an acting career again, there is the danger of opening up an old murder case. Reporters would be on her like wolves."

"Danger to whom?" I asked, remembering that it had been hinted that Miles's excellent alibi was not as good as authorities had thought.

He stared at me for a long moment, and the only sound in the world was the crackling of the fire across the room, the only movement the flickering of shadows cast by the flames. An uneasiness stirred in me, and I was aware of his big hands folded grimly into fists on the table between us. I wished that Donia had stayed in the hut.

He spoke abruptly, roughly. "How can I persuade you to go away? You work in the commercial world—would a sum which would pay you well for this lost effort serve to make you leave? You have no love for Laura, obviously, but I realize that you hoped to gain something from this interview, and I would be willing, within reason—"

He was just as bad as his sister. I struggled with my further sense of outrage as I interrupted him. "Why are you so anxious for me to go away?"

"I have Laura's interest at heart. You haven't. From the first that's been evident. Now you've done her more injury than you can realize. You must leave as soon as you can, and I'm willing to make it up to you if there is a money loss in your leaving."

"You must really be desperate to make an offer like that!" I said heatedly. "I'm not to be bought off!"

His hands clenched and unclenched. It was a moment before he answered me.

"It's necessary to protect my wife, at whatever cost," he said.

I made my attack swift. "Then why did you let her believe that she'd done that terrible thing to her portrait—that scarring with the scissors?"

"It wasn't I who told her what she'd done. Though of course she would have to know it eventually."

"But she's sure she didn't do it. She has told me so, and Irene supports her."

Again he gave me that long, cold stare. "You were there. You saw. She had the scissors in her hands. She was holding them when I came into the room and found you both there."

"They could have been placed in her hands earlier. Or she could have picked them up."

He seemed about to deny this, and I went on quickly.

"If that cruel game has any meaning, who do you think X is?"

"The game can be dismissed. She was unconscious—she didn't know what she was doing."

I reached into a pocket and took out the folded sheet of paper I'd found in the sandalwood box.

"Do you think Laura wrote this and left it for me to find?"

The ugly, childish scrawl lay on the table between us. He

could read what it said, but he did not touch it. His face had taken on a closed look that neither accepted nor admitted. I could sense that fury against me was rising in him.

"Why do you want to keep her captive?" I demanded.

He shoved back his chair with a roughness that startled me, and suddenly I was afraid. I left my own chair and went to the door. In an instant I was outside, running along a track where I wouldn't sink into snow. A little way off Donia was trying to build a snowman with an air of gleeful enjoyment. The snow was wrong for her effort, but she didn't seem to realize the fact. She stood up to stare at me, patting snow between her mittens.

Miles didn't come after me. When I looked back, I saw him standing outside the hut, with icicles dripping from the eaves over his head. After a moment, he disappeared inside and closed the door.

"It's a good thing to run when he loses his temper," Donia said cheerfully. "Laura's rages are nothing when you compare them to the fits of anger my brother can go into. He's been boiling up against you for some time." She looked pleased over what had happened.

"Do you know which way Laura and Gunnar went?" I asked her curtly.

She pointed, grinning, but for all her cheery manner, there was spite in her eyes as she watched me. I turned my back on her and followed ski tracks that led across the snow. The walking was not easy, and in a little while the sturdy effort gave me some release. I tried to put the encounter with Miles out of my mind. Perhaps I'd been frightened over nothing.

Up here it was as though I were at the very top of the world. Nothing of Bergen or the seacoast was visible. Only more mountain peaks with their frosting of snow rose around Ulriken, extending endlessly into Norway. Flöyen, alone, tree-covered, except for its rocky face, and not as high as the other peaks, was almost free of snow, the black of its rocky cliff, the dark green of its firs and pines showing dull beneath the sunny sky. Immediately around me stretched the snowfields, and skiers were busy crisscrossing them, moving with knee bends that sent them striding across the snow. At a little distance I could see Gunnar's red sweater, and Laura's black and white. They were moving with surprising ease up an incline, as cross-country skiers do, and I knew they would be out of my sight in a moment. There would be no use trying to follow them. But as I watched, they reached the top and made a turn to start the run in my direction. I waited where I was and they had gone no more than a few yards when I saw Laura's body twist as she plunged into a sliding fall. She cried out and her voice came to me faintly. Already Gunnar had slid to a stop and was turning about. In a moment he was out of his skis and kneeling beside her.

I knew she was hurt. I began to run across the snow, sometimes plunging to my knees where the crust broke to let me through, so I tumbled harmlessly several times before I reached them. She couldn't have been badly hurt, I told myself. The snow would ease her fall, and she had not been going fast. But I did not like that twisting of her body, and I floundered toward her frantically.

When I reached them, Gunnar had helped Laura to her feet and she was examining her ankle gingerly.

"Are you hurt?" I cried, churning through the snow to get to her.

Gunnar and she both turned to watch my approach, and Laura smiled reassuringly. "I've twisted my ankle, but I don't think it's serious. Don't hurry like that, Leigh! You look as though you've taken a few falls yourself."

I began to brush the snow from my pants and jacket, aware for the first time of my own emotional state, which was completely mindless and out of hand. I'd rushed toward her like —like a child hurrying toward an injured mother. The realization shocked and quieted me before I betrayed myself further.

Gunnar bent above Laura's ski to see what had caused her fall, and when he looked up at us, his eyes were grave.

"The cable which holds the boot to the skis has been damaged," he said. "Just on one ski. At best, you couldn't have skied for long, Laura. At worst, you could take a fall—which is what happened."

Laura stared at him, her eyes frightened. "Now will you believe what is happening?" she asked him. "Will you believe this was deliberate?"

I thought of the scarred picture and the whispering voice, the lettered paper. There had been no real danger in any of these things—only a tormenting. A tormenting that might eventually drive a despairing woman to some wild act? But Laura was not despairing any more. Or was she? As Gunnar removed her other ski I saw that all the earlier gaiety and elation had gone out of her. Fear had returned—a fear that was even greater than before.

"Don't you understand?" I said to Gunnar. "Someone wants her to be frightened and helpless. I don't know why, but it's true. It's as if she were being prepared for something."

Gunnar did not disparage my words, or deny Laura's obviously fearful state, but I sensed that this sort of maliciousness was outside his knowledge and experience. He was a man who lived in a well-balanced world, a clear, sane world where such things did not happen.

Laura clung to his arm, trying her foot carefully. "I want to get back to your hut and take off my boot, please. Miles will know what to do. But, Gunnar, my dear, make plans for me during the next few days, as you said you would. Help me to get through this time until I can leave for the States."

Gunnar put his arm about her and looked at me questioningly over her head. He had no weapons with which to fight so nebulous an evil. He seemed to ask for a help I didn't know how to give.

"I'm already making plans," he said. "I was able to get a box at the theater for Wednesday night. And Monday I will take you both to visit my mother. I am taking the day off. But, Laura, it would be better to tell us what is happening to you, would it not? Surely the matter can be righted if we know who is tormenting you."

Laura shook her head almost violently. "No, no! I will leave for Hollywood soon. The past is over. It's done with. It mustn't involve us all again. The results would be too terrible to bear. Miles doesn't want to return, and I won't ask him to, but I'll go alone if I have to."

"Was Miles in the studio that night when Cass Alroy died?" I asked her directly.

Until that moment she had been treating me warmly, almost with affection, but now she looked at me as if I were the stranger I'd told myself I wanted to be.

"Of course he was not in the studio. That's ridiculous. He was at the theater with his sister that night. Everyone knows that. What are you trying to do? What trouble are you trying to stir up now?"

I felt far more comfortable in the face of her irritation with me than I'd felt over rushing toward her so heedlessly. This was the way I wanted it to be.

"Your husband just tried to bribe me into going away," I said. "Why is he so afraid of me?"

"If I thought I could succeed, I would bribe you to go away myself!" Gunnar said. "You have done enough damage for now."

He and Laura started ahead through the snow, Gunnar carrying skis and poles on one shoulder, and supporting Laura with his free arm, leaving me to consider the shock of his words. I plodded along in their tracks. Laura limped as she walked, and their progress was slow.

The clear air in this high place, the beauty of clean snow and surrounding mountain ranges no longer lifted my spirit. I told myself repeatedly that now I was going to feel a great deal better. I was no longer trying to please anyone but myself. That was the cause I should have held to from the first.

Laura tired before we reached the hut, and when we came to an outcropping of rock, Gunnar helped her onto it and she lowered herself cautiously to sit on a stony ledge and rest her foot. Gunnar sat beside her, watching her in concern, while I stood aside in the snow, as if I were not one of the party.

"Shall I loosen your boot?" Gunnar asked.

"No. The swelling had better be contained until we reach Miles. It's not very painful when I can rest it."

Another car had brought skiers to the top, and several boys and girls went swishing past us across the snow. If I ever visited Norway again, I would learn to ski, I thought irrelevantly. But of course I would never come this way again, and certainly I would never ask Gunnar to teach me. The thought depressed me further—without reason.

Laura turned her head and looked up at me. "Do sit down, Leigh. You give me a crick in the neck. And there's something I've wanted to talk to you about."

"I'd rather stand," I told her.

For a moment her clear, lustrous eyes studied me. Then she turned her head so that she did not look at me and spoke in a voice so low that I could hardly hear her.

"Will you tell me about your father's death, Leigh? I would like to know."

The rush of angry blood to my temples made me a little dizzy. The last thing I wanted to talk about to Laura Worth was my father's death. She had no right to know. She especially had no right to know that he had spoken her name at the very end, and thus hurt Ruth cruelly.

"You had better tell her," Gunnar said, quietly stern.

I told them both then. But I held back what was essential. I said curtly that he'd had a heart attack while working on a novel which he had hoped would reinstate him in the public eye. I had read the chapters he'd written. It was a very good novel, and it was tragic that he could not finish it. My mother and I got him to bed and we called the doctor. But it was too late. He died in my mother's arms.

When I was small I had called Ruth "Mama." But when I was older I called her "Ruth." After I knew about Laura Worth I was never able to call Ruth my mother. But I called her that now, and I repeated it.

"I see." Laura had drawn up her knees and she rested her forehead against them. She had taken off her visored cap, and her brown head with the thick coil of hair at the back looked somehow vulnerable and touching—to anyone but me. I distrusted her very attitude. She was asking for sympathy, for pity. But I was on guard now, and I gave her none.

After a moment, she spoke. "Thank you for telling me, Leigh. I would always have wondered. I'm glad it was a quick death and that he didn't suffer. I'm glad his family was there."

Gunnar put a light hand on her shoulder and I knew she had won the sympathy she wanted—from him, at least.

In my bitter and perverse state of mind I sought for some means of wounding, of stabbing into her very vulnerability. I had to stab her out of my own pain.

"While we're speaking of husbands and wives," I said, "will you tell me what happened to Miles's first wife?"

Gunnar made an impatient sound. Laura did not raise her head, but she answered me.

"She's dead."

I don't know why I asked the next question. Perhaps I simply wanted to make her talk about what might be distasteful to her.

"How did she die?" I asked.

Only then did she look up at me, her eyes clear and somewhat questioning. "She died a suicide. She fell from a high balcony in their Hollywood home. It was Donia Jaffe who found her." Laura held out her hand to Gunnar. "If you'll help me up, please. I'm ready to go on now."

Again they went ahead of me, and again I plodded behind, thinking in some surprise about what I had just learned. I couldn't help wondering what had driven the first Mrs.

Fletcher to fling herself to her death from a balcony. And what had Donia Jaffe been doing on the scene in her brother's house?

Chapter 10

Although she limped badly, Laura made it back to the hut. Just before we went inside she asked me to say nothing to Miles of the damaged cable.

"I'll tell him later," she said. "For now, let it seem that we think it was an accident."

Miles and Donia sat together before the fire, apparently engaged in some sort of family wrangle, which broke off as we came in. They were clearly not getting along well these days.

Miles noted Laura's limp at once, and seated her in a chair, where he could strip off her boot. We all watched while he examined the slightly swelling ankle, pressing for any tenderness about the bone, comparing the injured ankle with the sound one. Then he sent Gunnar to break a few icicles from the low-hanging roof outside the hut. With these he made an ice pack by wrapping them in a towel, propped her foot on another chair and said he did not think the injury was severe. There was probably no fracture.

Several times while he worked over Laura, I found myself studying Donia. As usual, she was never still. She would watch her brother for a few moments, and then move restlessly about the room. Finally Gunnar, perhaps impatient with both of us, suggested that Donia and I unpack the lunch basket—and that gave us something to do.

Laura was behaving cheerfully, bravely—as of course she would. The first shock of weakness had passed, and if the fact of that intentionally damaged clamp was troubling her, she hid it well. She told Miles almost gaily that we were all going to the play at the *teatret*, the National Theater, on Wednesday night. Once the festival started, the theater meantime would be preempted for musical performances, but in the meantime *Arsenikk og Gamle Kniplinger* was playing—the Norwegian version of *Arsenic and Old Lace*, and that would be fun. Miles was not notably enthusiastic.

"We'll see if you can walk by then," he said.

When Laura's ankle had had ten or fifteen minutes of the ice pack, Miles bandaged it snugly with one of his own handkerchiefs, and insisted that she sit with the foot raised until we left for home.

Strangely enough, in spite of accidents and uneasy emotions, we were all hungry, and we ate the lunch Irene had packed, and enjoyed it. Nevertheless, a damper had been placed upon our further activities. If Miles had expected to walk about the mountaintop with Laura, that was now out of the question. And if I had hoped that Gunnar and I might do the same, that opportunity too was gone. The barrier between us was higher than ever, and I suspected that he would want no time alone with me. Now our one intent was to get Laura safely down the mountain with a minimum of discomfort to her.

Donia and I packed the remains of the lunch in the basket, while Miles put Laura's boot on, fastening it loosely.

Just before we left the hut, I remembered something and began to look about for the note I had left upon the table. Miles saw me searching.

"I put it in the fire," he told me sardonically.

No one seemed to notice the interchange. I should have taken better care of that sheet of paper. Certainly I shouldn't have left it with Miles.

When we were ready we all set off across the snow toward the cable-car station. Donia led the way, leaving us behind in her nervous hurry, with Laura leaning heavily upon Miles as they followed in her wake. I waited with Gunnar while he checked the fire and locked up the hut. Then we started after the others, with Gunnar once more carrying the skis.

As we left the hut he stopped beside me for a moment and, unexpectedly, his look was not as cold and critical as it had been.

"You are having a bad time," he said gently. "Sometimes there is a pain contained in growing."

"I don't know what you mean," I said, and turned to follow the others.

"Yes, you know." He came up beside me. "You are torn between two directions. You do not know which way you must go."

This time I answered him hotly. "I know very well which way I must go."

"I think you are not sure. But I think you will win out in the end."

"Yes," I said. "I'll win out in the end." But I did not mean what Gunnar Thoresen meant, and we did not speak to each other for the rest of the distance to the cable car. After that moment of gentleness, he had turned from me again, and I couldn't help that. I had, indeed, grown. I wasn't the same person who had come up in the cable car. Something in me had hardened against Laura. The very fact that I had come so close to giving myself over to her had stiffened all my resolve. Yet I felt somehow depressed, and very cold here on this mountaintop.

Our party was going down in the cable car alone, and several cement blocks were put into the car to add weight and keep it from swaying on the descent. This time Laura sat down on a bench in relief, and Miles sat beside her. She seemed grateful for his attention and help, and I wondered at the misplacing of this late affection on her part. Donia occupied her own window, and I mine. Gunnar stood apart, and I felt thoroughly alone, and not a little unhappy and rebellious.

The steep slope of the mountain slipped by beneath us. The up car went past on the opposite cable. The slanting red roof of the Ulriksbanen rose toward us from below. An afternoon sun touched the roofs of Bergen and made the Seven Mountains glow with light. This was one of the most beautiful towns in Europe, I'd heard Laura say, and I could believe it. But it was no place for me. I was no longer sure that I would be able to write a chapter about Laura Worth, let alone do a book. I was beginning to know her too well, and I could no longer separate actress from woman.

I think the same sense of depression lay upon us all as Gunnar drove us back to Kalfaret, for we did not talk, and our thanks to Gunnar for the outing were on the restrained side, even though Laura tried to rally a little enthusiasm.

Irene met us at the door and noted Laura's injury at once. She almost shouldered Laura's husband aside to help her up the stairs. Miles followed and Donia ran after them. Gunnar and I stood alone in the dark inner hallway, and he held out his hand to me.

"We will go another time up Ulriken," he said. "It will be better then. In the meantime, watch over her."

Everything had changed and I could give him my hand in no such bargain. I shook my head. "She's not my responsibility. I'll be going home as soon as I'm able."

"So you are running away?"

I started to answer, but a sound came from upstairs that

chilled my very blood. Laura was screaming as I had never heard her scream before. Gunnar raced up the stairs and I went after him.

In her bedroom Miles stood holding Laura tightly in his arms, trying to still her shuddering sobs. Irene hovered nearby, adding her pleas for calm as she too tried to quiet Laura. Donia stood apart and one quick look in her direction told me that her expression was one of elaborate innocence.

"What happened?" Gunnar asked of Irene.

She shook her head. "Miss Worth came through the door into this room and began to scream." Irene glanced about helplessly. "I don't see anything which might so upset her."

I looked for myself—not at eye level, as the rest of them were doing, but around the floor. At once I saw the china cat. It sat as a doorstop before Laura's open bedroom door—a large, heavy cat of frivolous pink china, with a nose of deep rose, and blue, heavily lashed eyes. It was not made of iron, as that other had been—the cat supposedly used to murder Cass Alroy—but it was a doorstop in the shape of a cat.

"There you are," I said to the others, and touched it with my foot. "I think this is what must have frightened her. I haven't seen it here before."

The others stared and I tried swiftly to read their faces. All except Donia looked shocked and upset. She looked sly.

"Get it out of here," Miles ordered. And then to Laura, "It's all right. There's nothing to be disturbed about. This is undoubtedly some prank of Donia's." He looked angrily over Laura's head at his sister.

She had begun to sidle toward the door, but Gunnar stepped into the opening, quietly blocking her way.

"It will be best if you tell us," he said.

Her slyness fell away, and she looked a little frightened, and as though she might burst into tears. "It was only a surprise for Laura that I bought in a store on Torgalmenning," she wailed in a protest of innocence. "It was such a funny pink cat, and I thought it might please her. She's been annoyed with me lately, and I—I wanted to make it up to her for the trunk and—"

Laura raised her head from Miles's shoulder, released herself from the restraint of his arms. "I'm sorry," she said weakly. "I'm still far too nervous. Donia probably never thought—"

"She thought," Miles broke in, but he was studying his wife

rather coolly and objectively—as any doctor might look appraisingly at a patient.

Gunnar had stepped aside in the doorway, and Donia gave a curious little squeal—like a small animal fleeing the hunter —and hurled herself out of the room.

Laura limped across to the chaise longue and sat down, raising her booted foot to its cushions. "Please go away," she said. "Please go away—all of you except Leigh. She can help me now, if she will. I don't want anyone else."

Miles started to object, but she turned her face away from him. I think Irene, too, wanted to stay, but Laura would have none of anyone but me. And I didn't want to stay at all.

Gunnar spoke to me quietly before he went out. "I would like to know how she does. Will you call me tomorrow at home, please? And on Monday, so if Laura is able I will come to bring you both to visit my mother."

I merely nodded at him, and they all went away. When Irene had carried off the pink china cat and closed the door, I went to stand beside the chaise longue, looking down at Laura.

"Why did you want me to stay? There's been enough playacting between us."

She took off her visored white cap and dropped it on the floor. Her brown hair waved softly back from her forehead and her eyes were wide and a little staring. I suspected that she was still suffering from the unnerving shock of coming upon that china doorstop.

"You detest me thoroughly, don't you?" she said.

"Let's say I find very little to like about you," I agreed. "Except as an actress."

She nodded as if in satisfaction. "You despise and detest me, but you would never injure me. Not deliberately. I can trust you."

This was astonishing and it was not what I wanted. "If you mean that I'd never physically assault you, that's right. But you'd better not trust me on any other score."

"That's a bargain, Leigh Hollins." She held out her hand to me in an open, boyish gesture.

I wanted to repudiate that open hand. I wanted to repudiate any trust she might place in me. Instead, I gave her my hand reluctantly, and felt the warm clasp of her fingers about my own in the sealing of some bargain I did not want to make, and did not understand.

"Now, if you'll help me off with my boots and bring my slippers," she said.

How accustomed she was to being waited on! I helped her out of her jacket and brought the slippers from the adjacent dressing room, between Miles's room and her own, and loosened the boot from about her swollen ankle.

"Irene should be doing these things for you," I said curtly.

"Irene is against my going to Hollywood. She'll lecture me, and I don't want to listen to her. You want me to go. You believe I'll follow my new dream to complete disaster—as Miles and Gunnar do. But you'll encourage me to go for that very reason."

I was rougher with the other boot. I pulled it off and dropped it on the floor with a clatter. She was always ten steps ahead of me in whatever direction I moved.

Miles tapped on the door and came in. She looked up at him guardedly. I think she had begun to distrust everyone.

"We're going to bandage that ankle properly," he told her, and went to work coolly and expertly.

I slipped out of the warm jacket she had loaned me to go up the mountain, and went into the dressing room to get her caftan robe. I pretended to be busy at the dress rack, but through the door I watched Miles while he was working. If he had any affection for his wife, he was not showing it now. When the elastic bandage was snugly in place, he stood up beside her.

"Stay off that foot," he ordered. "Keep it elevated all the time."

"Of course," she said meekly. "Thank you for your concern, darling."

He gave me his usual look of distaste and went out of the room without answering her. When he'd gone, she sat up, swung her feet to the floor, and stood up lithely.

"Ah, that's better! The bandaging helps. There's nothing terribly wrong with my ankle. But we'll let them worry a bit."

She moved to the center of the room with scarcely a limp and stripped her white sweater off over her head. Then she got out of the black ski pants, entirely casual about her undressing, and slipped into the caftan I held for her. Its sand-colored folds engulfed her body gracefully.

"Now then," she said, "we will begin."

"Begin?"

She paid no attention to my echoing of the word, but crossed the room to a bookcase, picked out two volumes and brought them back to the chaise longue, where she sat down.

When she had rifled through the pages of one, she handed me the open book.

"There you are—*Hedda Gabler*. I've always wanted to play her in a film. Not that they'd ever let me. Ibsen's not considered popular these days, except in the theater. But he stands for Norway, and it's always good for me to start with Hedda when I want to get the feeling of playing a part again. I adore her. A marvelous role. A thoroughly unscrupulous woman."

I stared, holding the pages blankly in my hands, while she opened the second volume to the same play.

"We'll read the scene in Act IV, where Hedda tells Tessman that she has burned Lövborg's manuscript. Then on through the end where she realizes that history is going to repeat itself and there's nothing left for her."

"But I can't—" I began, "—I can't possibly—"

"Of course you can. We'll read together. It doesn't matter that you're no professional. All I want is to be cued. I can still remember most of the lines. Ibsen wrote for actors. He's never as effective when read to oneself. He knew what an actor can do with a pause, with the silence between speeches. There's more to acting than the reading of words. Let me show you. Begin. Take Tessman's line—"

I slammed the book shut. "I'll do nothing of the sort. I won't play audience for you. What sort of woman are you? A few moments ago you were screaming with the utmost realism because you'd found that china cat against your door. And now—"

"I was good, wasn't I? I brought you all running."

"I think you're lying," I said. "Your screaming was real. What I don't understand is how you could forget it so quickly."

Her veined hands smoothed the pages of the book she held on her knees. "It was real, yes. But don't you see that I must try to forget. I must try somehow to get through the next few days, perhaps weeks, without being destroyed. Help me with *Hedda Gabler*."

"Tell me first why the doorstop made you scream."

"You're making me remember." Her tone was almost petulant. "It was the shock, of course. You know that an iron doorstop in the shape of a cat was the weapon which killed Cass Alroy?"

"Yes," I said. "I've seen that iron doorstop."

Her eyes widened. "You've seen it—what do you mean?"

"It's there forever in the film of *The Whisperer*. There in the early scenes. But not at the end."

"No, not at the end." Her hands were clasped tightly upon the pages of the book and she did not look at me. I could sense the tension mounting in her, rising once more toward explosion. By this time I knew the signs.

"Why did you scream?" I said.

She sprang up and the book of plays went flying. "Because I killed him! Because I killed Cass with that iron doorstop, and it will be on my conscience forever!"

Hysteria was mounting, the moment coming when she would hurl something wildly, or begin to scream again. I put my hands on her shoulders and shook her hard.

"Stop it! Stop it at once. You're talking nonsense. You couldn't possibly have killed him. That doorstop was too heavy for a woman to have used as a weapon. I've read the reports."

Beneath my hands she quieted, shuddering, fighting for control. "I killed him," she repeated. "For twenty years I've wondered if I could ever say those words aloud. And now I have. To you—to the one person who will never betray me."

"But you couldn't have!" I repeated. "It wasn't possible—" and then I thought of the candlestick, the sudden sight of which had made her faint only yesterday. "Was it the candlestick, then? You could have lifted that? Did you strike him with the candlestick?"

She shook her head violently. "No! No, I didn't use the candlestick. I only carried it away so it wouldn't be found there. That and the gun. I hid that too and no one ever looked for it. I still have it here in this room."

"Gun?" I was echoing her again.

"Yes. He meant to kill me, I think. I hated him before that picture was over. We were never lovers, as the papers said. I—I made fun of him, taunted him. He was close to being psychopathic, though I didn't realize that at the time. He'd already been through one scandal a few years before when he'd been sued in a divorce case. He didn't care about much of anything, and he had the idea that I—that I was interested in Miles Fletcher. When I saw the gun, I knew what he'd meant to do."

"So if you did—kill him," I said, still disbelievng, "it was in self-defense."

"No!" She was shaking her head again. "If I killed him it was in calculated cold blood. For twenty years I've tried to make myself believe that wasn't true. I've run away endlessly.

I couldn't face films any more, or acting. I knew I'd go to pieces. It was better to let my successes stand. But now I've admitted the truth. Now I can rest."

"I don't understand any of this," I protested. "Why do you say *if* you killed him—as if you weren't sure?"

"That's of no importance. You're my confessor. There's relief for me in speaking out. But we'll do nothing more about it. Neither of us. You have to understand that. We can't."

"Because you're afraid of what the law might still do to you?"

"There'd be a penalty to pay. I'd really be finished then. But it's not only that."

"Does Miles know?" I asked her.

Her expression told me that I'd touched a sensitive nerve.

"He can't *know*, but perhaps he suspects. He loved me once, and he saved me when I was desperately in need. But what he suspects comes between us, and there's a growing malice in him that frightens me. Sometimes I think he believes I have spoiled his life. There's an even worse malice in his sister. Undoubtedly he's talked all this over with her in the past. That's why she brought that doorstop and left it in my bedroom. She knew how much it would shock me."

She was silent, lost in some dark thoughts of her own that she wouldn't reveal, even to me. There was more here—something she would not touch upon—perhaps because she felt it was dangerous. It was not entirely the past which haunted her. It was the present.

"Irene has hinted that Miles might have been at the studio the night of the murder," I said, "and I think Donia knows that. Perhaps she's even suspicious of her brother. It's likely that she doesn't suspect you at all, but just knows that anything connected with what happened that night frightens and upsets you. It's in her character to make use of that."

"Yes," Laura said. "That's true. I've grown too easily frightened and I must begin to overcome all this. I must begin tonight. If I'm to go back to Hollywood, I must learn to control my own emotions. There will be questions asked of me by the press. Everything will be dredged up again—I know that. So I must learn how to be strong enough never to be shaken."

"First you'd better get out of this house," I said. "Gunnar is right. Let me call him. I know he'll come and take you to his mother."

"No, Leigh. From now on I'll be safe here because you are

going to stay with me. You're going to bring your things upstairs and sleep in my bed tonight. The chaise longue will be fine for me. You're my guardian angel now."

"You're out of your mind," I said. "If you knew how I really feel about you—"

"Poor Leigh. To hate so much. I know quite well how you feel. But you're Victor's child—and you won't hurt me. Whether you like it or not, you're my wall of safety. So help me to begin what I must do. Go downstairs and fetch me that costume I wore when I played Helen Bradley in *The Whisperer*. Irene tells me you've shown an interest in it. I found her pressing the dress, and I got that out of her. She says you wanted to try it on. But now it is I who am going to put it on. And if foolish little Donia still has the china doorstop, you can bring it back and set it against my door. I want you to find the candlestick as well and bring it here. The time has come for me to face everything—to face down all my fears. All these things should have lost their power over me years ago. Now you'll help me to see them as they are—no more than inanimate objects, with nothing in them to frighten me. I'll be free then—and safe. No one can touch me unless they can reach my mind. Hurry, Leigh. Go get all these things and bring them to me."

I was not ready to hurry, not ready to accept. "First I'm going to get out of these hot ski clothes," I told her. "And then I want to think for a while. I haven't decided what I must do."

Her face was partly in shadow, and it wore that solemn, deeply concerned expression that I knew so well. When she looked like that she was striking, but not really beautiful. And then she did the same thing I had seen so often. Without warning, the brooding look lifted and she flashed her quick, unexpectedly radiant smile—and beauty looked out of her face.

"You haven't any choice, Leigh," she said. "You will do what Victor would want you to do. Come back to me quickly."

I turned from her and went out of the room and down the stairs. A trash basket sat in the lower hall and someone had dropped the china cat into it. I had a momentary qualm about picking it up. I couldn't yet believe Laura's claim that Cass Alroy had died at her hands, but the cat doorstop made me feel squeamish. Nevertheless, I lifted it out and carried it into my room. Irene was standing in the dining room door, watching me, and she came after me at once.

"May I come in?" she said. Her look was upon the cat, and she bristled with questions I gave her no time to ask.

"Laura wants it in her room," I informed her lightly. "And I'm to bring her *The Whisperer* gown. She's going to try it on. She'd like the candlestick too, please. I believe it's in that trunk?"

Irene uttered astonished words in her own tongue, and then gave up and came to help me find what I wanted. When dress and candlestick and china cat had been heaped upon my sofa bed, Irene went to the portrait which I'd left hanging to face the room. When she started to turn it about, I stopped her.

"Let it alone. Let the game stay visible."

Her eyes studied the picture and I heard her soft exclamation. "Someone has marked in an O!"

"Yes—to block the game."

"You did this?" Irene asked.

"Of course. Now X can never win."

"I'd like to believe that. But real actions are not a game."

"Laura knows who X is, and I think you must have guessed as well."

She looked at me across the room, and for a moment I thought she might speak out. Then she moved toward the door.

"I'm not sure," she said. "It would never do to make a mistake."

After she'd gone, I stood for a little while staring at the door. I had told Laura that I wanted time to think, but I didn't seem to be thinking. Not even about that game of naughts and crosses. I was behaving as though Laura had placed some hypnotic spell upon me, and I was helpless to do anything except her bidding.

Where was the Leigh Hollins I knew? How and when had my own identity managed to get lost before the whirlwind impact of Laura Worth? I had not caught up with the changes that were sweeping me ahead of a gale I'd not been able to stand against.

When I was dressed in my own sweater and skirt, I went to the bookcase where Laura's scrapbooks were kept, and took out the one which covered the time of Cass's death and the period afterward. I drew a chair near a window and sat down to leaf through the book. What I was looking for, I didn't know, but Laura's words had perplexed and mystified me. Perhaps the direct statements of old newsprint would right matters in my own mind. She had told me to come back quickly, but I would let her wait. I would let her wonder what I might really do.

The account was familiar as I read the words, but more of it had been recorded in these pages than my father had pasted into his scrapbook at home. I read further details about the investigation, and as I turned the pages something startling came to light. Other hands had been at work here. Someone had gone carefully through these pages and cut out small sections here and there. Scissors had been at work again and again. Mostly the excisions were slight. Yet they were sufficient so that I could not tell what the cut-out paragraphs had referred to. After a moment of leafing I went to the door and called Irene.

When she came in, I showed her the mutilated pages and she took the book from my hands with no apparent surprise, to examine the remaining print carefully.

"If you've looked at these clippings before, perhaps you'll remember what is missing," I said.

After a few moments she gave the book back to me. "I don't remember. But if it's important to you for your writing, perhaps you can ask Miss Worth. She'll surely know. Though she may not tell you."

"But who could have done this?" I persisted. "Have you any idea?"

For a moment I thought she might not answer me. Then she reconsidered. "Perhaps it's better if you know. Miss Worth has done this cutting."

"Are you sure?" I asked.

"I came on her clipping these pages one time when you were out of the room."

"Then it's been done since I came here?"

Irene inclined her head gravely.

"But why? She's begun to tell me a great deal. Why would she want to conceal something about that time in Hollywood if it's something that appeared in print?"

"She doesn't tell you everything, no matter what you think," Irene said quietly. "She doesn't tell me everything either. There is something she wants to hide."

I knew this was true. Whatever Laura said, whatever wild confidences she offered, there was always something missing that kept the pieces from fitting together. It was this fact, I realized, that had made Irene confide in me. She wanted to know too. Her next words confirmed my thinking.

"All these years there has been no way to help her, because

she will never speak of the thing that really troubles her. Perhaps now she's closer to reaching for help than ever before. Perhaps it will be to you, her daughter, that she'll turn."

Once more Irene was evidencing a softening of her manner toward me. I was no longer the enemy who might injure Laura. She was beginning to regard me as an ally.

"Early on Monday morning," she went on, "I'll go shopping at the market on the wharf. Perhaps you'd like to come with me? You can't see much of Bergen when you stay so close to this house."

"I'd love to come," I said readily.

"Then we'll persuade Miss Worth to let you go."

I closed the scrapbook, which was telling me nothing, and carried it back to the table. I did not want to answer her too sharply or hurriedly, but I wanted to make my position clear.

"I don't have to ask permission. I believe Mr. Thoresen is coming to take us to visit his mother later that day. But early in the morning I'll be free."

My hands moved idly over other scrapbooks in the row. Irene watched me for a moment and then went away. I pulled another volume out and laid it open on a table, began to leaf through it idly. From page after page Laura's face looked out at me. There was a benefit at which she had appeared, a burglarizing of her house when jewels were stolen, an account of a party she had given in her spacious home in the hills above Hollywood.

Famous names leaped out at me from the pages. She had known everyone in those days. Not merely those in her own profession, but the great of the world had paid her homage, been her friends. I knew all this, of course, but seeing these printed accounts made it seem real for the first time. Laura Worth had moved in circles that never opened to the average citizen. She undoubtedly had fabulous memories of the distinguished of the world. My father had known some of them too, but he was more the introvert who did not care for large gatherings of people in his home. There was so much which Laura, the actress, still had to give me, if only I could find my former concern with her from the viewpoint of a writer. Too often lately my emotions crossed all lines, spilling over in a mixture of anger and resentment and pity and . . . but I had no name for all the things I was feeling toward her.

I ran through several more pages, and was about to close the book when a printed name caught my attention—that of Cass Alroy. I began to read with renewed interest. None of this account appeared to concern Laura, and it was dated several years before Cass became director for *The Whisperer*. Apparently he had been sued as corespondent in a divorce suit that had taken a rather nasty turn. The man who had sued him was an actor named Arnold Jaffe. The woman accused of infidelity was his wife, Donia. I bent over the book, reading with rapt attention.

Jaffe had won his suit and his divorce, and the report carried the matter no further. What had happened to the rather torrid love affair Donia had conducted with Cass Alroy was not revealed. One thing did emerge during the law procedures, however. Donia's brother, the distinguished Dr. Miles Fletcher, had stood by his sister throughout the affair, and there had been an occasion when he had threatened to give Alroy a thorough beating. There was no telling whether anything had come of that.

I closed the scrapbook thoughtfully and returned it to its place. I was not sure whether Laura had known Miles and Donia at the time of the divorce. The ramifications were interesting, however. Miles's quarrel with Cass Alroy had been of long duration and Miles must have been thoroughly disturbed to find the man directing Laura's picture, and upsetting her so that she had been ill on the set during the filming that had taken place on the day Cass Alroy had died.

By this time I had several matters to question Laura about, and she had been left waiting long enough.

I flung the Venetian red costume over my arm, and picked up the candlestick and the pink china cat. Then I carried everything upstairs to Laura's bedroom, glad to meet no one along the way.

Laura had been busy while I was gone. If her ankle hurt her, she ignored it. She had pushed back all the furniture so there was a large free space in the center of the room. Her cheeks were flushed from her endeavor, her eyes bright. I set down my armload and looked about in surprise. On the low coffee table which had been relegated to a corner stood a gleaming object—the golden statuette of a man holding a sword, and I knew what it was at once.

"Your Oscar!" I cried, and went to kneel on the floor beside the table, where I could examine the precious symbol without marking its shining surface with fingerprints.

Laura laughed at the sight of me. "You're bowing before a graven image! I'm not sure it means all that much."

"It means something in your case. It acknowledges your performance in *Maggie Thornton*."

She came to stand beside me, looking rather sadly at the figure of the manikin.

"Of course it's satisfying to win an award. I can still remember how excited I was that night. And how I forgot the few words I'd tried to prepare ahead of time—in case I won. When the moment came and hurled me up on that stage, all I could do was burble."

"You thanked Victor Hollins," I said. "I've read about that."

"Yes—he'd gone out of my life by that time, but much of the credit would always belong to him."

"And I had been born." How well I knew those dates!

She said nothing to that, but picked up the shining figure. "Do you know that I nearly sent this to your father after I brought it home? But I knew very well that he would only have sent it back to me."

"There should have been a twin," I said. "You deserved the second Oscar too, for *The Whisperer*."

She didn't deny it. "Perhaps I can rectify that."

I looked up at her sharply. The slight air of sadness still lay upon her as she studied the golden figure.

"The trouble with an award is that the time and cause for receiving it are so quickly past. It's like having a photograph taken. We are so quickly older than our pictures. By the time an award is won, or a picture is taken, we're already changing, going on to other things. It's natural to want what is newest to be our best. There's never any standing still—we go on to higher ground, or we slip back. And there's always disappointment when the new achievement doesn't match the vision we held. There's been frustration for me in looking back at *Maggie Thornton* as my best role. I wanted new roles that would be as great. I wanted a finer achievement."

"And you had it in *The Whisperer*. The mere fact that circumstances kept you from winning hasn't taken away from what everyone knows was a stunning performance."

"Twenty years ago! What can it mean now? That's why I want to return. That's why I value your gift in bringing me back to life and ambition."

There was an outward glow upon her that made her beautiful, and an inward longing looked out of her eyes. I got to my feet and walked away from her across the room. When I looked back she was still holding the Oscar in her hands.

"You may not always be lonely," she told him whimsically, and set the figure on the table. Then she turned to me. "I see you've brought everything I asked for. We can begin."

Here we went again! There was no use opposing her. "With *Hedda Gabler*?"

"No! I've thought of a better idea. And I've found the books."

She flew to a bookcase and picked up two identical volumes that lay upon its top. I recognized the jacket of my father's book with a sinking heart.

"Here!" she said and held one of them out to me. "I've marked the passages. Sometimes Victor wrote dialogue as though it was to be played on a stage. The script for *The Whisperer* used whole pages of the book verbatim. I'll be Helen, of course, and you can read the other roles. I'm sure you'll be more at home with these words than with Ibsen."

I didn't want any of this, didn't like it. But there was nothing to do but humor her. While she paced the room as Helen Bradley, I sat in a chair and read the lines between her speeches. Her first cue came from a clumsy young maid who was new in the Bradley house, and terribly nervous of the master. Helen, already frightened herself, went into the business of reassuring a young girl who was terrified. In the scene, the maid was kneeling on the floor, polishing an iron doorstop in the shape of a cat.

Laura finished the speech, moving about the room in her elegantly flowing caftan, yet giving something of Helen's aura even now. Her walk had changed, her manner of holding her head and shoulders made her a different person.

"Tonight we'll use the china cat," she said, breaking out of character. "Tonight you can be dusting it while I read the lines."

"Tonight?" I turned the book face down on my lap and stared at her. "Laura, what are you up to? What do you mean to do tonight?"

There was only a faint edge of nervousness in her laughter to give her away. "Tonight I'm going to prove to you all that I'm still Laura Worth. All you unbelievers are going to come up here to this room—Donia and Miles and Irene—and I'm going to show you what I can do. Perhaps I'll phone Gunnar and bring him here too. In the meantime, I want to read the scene with Robert Bradley, where Helen realizes her danger. I can almost remember the words. Give me the end of his speech, Leigh."

I knew the passage she meant and found the page. I read Robert's deceitful words and heard the stilted sound of my own voice. She picked up the response easily, but I found some comfort in the fact that she stumbled, that the depth of passion wasn't there as it had been in the picture.

"That was not very good," I told her flatly when she paused.

Her brilliant smile erased the somber look of Helen Bradley. "Of course it wasn't. I'm only feeling my way, remembering the words. I always hold something back in rehearsal. Otherwise I'd waste the very essence of a role where it doesn't really count."

I listened to her warily, with all my suspicions alert. It was true that she was being carried away by this sudden desire to prove herself an actress, but I sensed that there was something more. There was some hidden motive in what she planned, and the high excitement which drove her had its roots in more than the desire to perform. Nevertheless, I went along with what she wished. I read the lines which cued Helen Bradley's speeches as woodenly as possible, and now and then I faltered deliberately over the words. This was a safeguard for me. I didn't want her to catch me up in the emotions she was able to generate in those around her. I wanted to contribute nothing to her performance. It would be better for her if she fell far short of her intent. I wouldn't interfere with her, but I wouldn't help her either. I would remain neutral.

We must have worked for an hour and a half, by which time she was letter perfect and did not need the book. We had rehearsed the short scene with the maid, and two other scenes in which Helen and Robert Bradley faced each other before his death. When she would have continued into another scene, I slapped the book shut. It was better to shake her belief in herself now, before she carried this through.

"That's enough. This is completely futile. You haven't anything to support you—no actors, no Victorian house, no stairway—nothing! You will make them think you ridiculous and you'll wind up crying yourself to sleep."

"In that case, I shall keep you awake all night, since you're to stay here in my room. But I'll let you rest now. At the very least, I've given you a marvelous scene for your book. Now you've watched Laura Worth at rehearsal."

I snorted in a thoroughly unpleasant way, and she smiled at me as she went to her bedroom telephone and called Gunnar. He was out, but she conducted an animated conversation with his mother and was apparently assured that Gunnar would wish to be at Laura's house tonight. I sulked while she talked and gave her my darkest look when she set down the telephone.

"I understand you very well," she said, still keyed up and swishing about the room in her sand-colored robe. "You'd like to see me return to Hollywood and meet with disaster. Of course that's obvious. Oh, I realize that wasn't your first intent when you told me I ought to go back. You were sincere then. The other thought came later. Now it's predominant. What a lovely way to get even with me for everything I've done to you—done to Victor! That's the general idea, isn't it?"

I glowered at her. Let her think what she pleased.

"And I will prove you wrong," she told me. "I will prove all my doubting Thomases wrong."

I'd had enough. To attack along a side road that had served me once before was my only resource.

"Why did Miles's wife commit suicide?" I demanded.

She seemed to stop in full flight, ceasing her performance as Laura Worth, the star, shedding it like a garment she put aside. She crossed the room and flung herself at full length upon the chaise longue.

"So you want to talk? Is that it? You want to ask more questions."

"I'd like a few answers," I countered.

"Very well! Kate Fletcher was hopelessly neurotic. Miles had taken her to the best psychiatrists for years, and it had done no good. She imagined that she had a fatal illness, though nothing was seriously wrong. She killed herself because she could not face dying of a sickness she didn't have."

"Is that what Miles told you?" I said.

"Of course it's what he told me. And it was common knowledge as well. He'd endured a miserable marriage for years."

"Apparently Donia was imposed upon his first wife too? Since she was in the house and was the one to find Mrs. Fletcher's body on the stone patio."

"I doubt if Donia added to Kate's mental well-being," Laura agreed. "But Miles has promised me that Donia will be sent away from Bergen before long. Not that she's likely to drive *me* to suicide."

I considered that. "You've said that a few days ago you had given up—you no longer wanted to live."

"I was frightened of a good many things. I'd lost my courage. Now I have it back. I know I must rely only on myself to save me."

We were back to the old question. "Save you from what?"

"From someone who wants to pay me back, who wants to punish me for what has happened in the past. But it won't be possible now. You'll stay with me. And I'll go to Hollywood alone."

"What about your husband?"

"Since he doesn't want me to do this, it's better if I go alone and prove myself. Once I've done that——" She lifted her hands in an expressive gesture and let them fall.

My road of attack had led nowhere, and I chose another path. "I've been reading through some of your old scrapbooks downstairs. I was surprised to find the connection between Cass Alroy and Donia Jaffe."

Laura did not seem particularly taken aback. "That is rather surprising, isn't it? But of course you didn't know her when she was young. That lively, little-girl air of hers was more fitting then—and quite appealing. Her face hadn't become so thin and wrinkled. In fact, she was a plump little thing—very pretty, really. But too dependent on her brother, too devoted to him, even then. And with no judgment at all. Any woman of judgment would have stayed far away from Cass Alroy. *I* should never have touched him as a director. My whole life would have been changed if I hadn't been prevailed upon to use him for *The Whisperer*." She was silent, remembering, regretting.

I prodded her more gently. "Under the circumstances, it was a good thing that Miles's sister was at the theater that night. Otherwise, she—or he—might have made a prime suspect."

"That's true, isn't it?" Laura roused herself. "But she *was* at the theater. Any more inquisition?"

"Just one other thing," I said. "In one of your scrapbooks there are whole pages where small deletions have been made. Irene says you cut them out recently. Which means there is something about the aftermath of Cass Alroy's death that you don't want me to know."

She lay quite still in the chaise longue and nothing about her expression or her manner changed. Nevertheless, I knew instinctively that she was on guard again and that I had come close to that key to whatever it was she continued to conceal.

"What persistent curiosity you have!" she said lightly. "All public figures have areas in their lives which they don't choose to reveal to the journalist. There are, of course, certain matters

I don't want you to write about. I told you in the beginning that you were not to open Pandora's box."

"You've opened it yourself," I reminded her. "You've told me you killed Cass Alroy."

A faint shudder seemed to run through her. "I haven't let myself forget, and now you won't let me forget. But you'll tell no one. You'll certainly not write this in your chapter."

"You trust me too much," I said.

With a swiftness that took me by surprise, she left the chaise longue and came toward me across the room. When she was very close she put her hands lightly on my shoulders and looked directly into my face. There was unexpected entreaty in her dark eyes, and her lips trembled.

"Who else can I trust?" She was pleading now—as I'd never seen her plead. "You are my daughter."

It was the first time she had called me that directly and I was shocked by the flood of emotion that poured through me. Shocked—and saved. Because I remembered something. I remembered a film of hers that I had completely put out of my mind for years; that I'd forgotten because it was necessary to forget. Now the memory came rushing back.

I had been in my early teens when I saw the picture. It had been called *Long Year's Turning*, and in it Laura Worth had played a young mother. The child who was her daughter had been about eight years old. There had been a divorce situation, and the little girl was about to be parted from her mother. I could remember vividly how the child had perched upon the edge of a sofa, resisting her mother, while Laura knelt before her, with her hands resting upon the child's shoulders, peering into that rejecting young face. She had spoken heartbreakingly of her love for her daughter and her wish for her to grow up in the love and safety of her father's home—even though it might mean never seeing her again.

I had wept bitterly through most of the picture, though I was old enough by that time to know that it was all play-acting, and had nothing to do with me. Now Laura stood with her fingers on my shoulders in that very same gesture, with the very same look upon her face. A sick, bitter anger tightened my throat so that I could hardly speak.

With a roughness that must have hurt her, I struck her hands away and pulled back.

"Don't try that!" I choked. "Do you think I didn't see that picture you made when you played a mother for the only time in your life? Don't you think I can recognize an old scene when you play it again?"

Her face began to crumple—like that of a child who has been rudely hurt. She put one hand to her throat and her eyes were wide and staring, as if she held back her tears.

I ran toward the door. But before I went out, I turned back for an instant.

"I've done one thing for you, at least. I've marked an O in that game downstairs. I've blocked the game for X," I told her—and flung myself out of the room, down the stairs and out of the house.

The front garden was empty and I went to sit in a wooden chair in the sunshine and the open air. I put my arms about myself and rocked my body back and forth, back and forth, though this was something I had not done since long ago when I was a child and had longed so desperately for my real mother.

Chapter 11

I couldn't eat my dinner that night, though Irene brought a tray to my room to tempt me. I know she was curious as to what had happened, but she did not prod me to talk. She reported that Laura had plans for this evening, and that Dr. Fletcher and Mrs. Jaffe both seemed upset about what Miss Worth intended to do. Irene said nothing about the role I was expected to play, and I wondered if I should throw the whole thing off by simply refusing to take part.

Around eight o'clock Laura sent Irene to fetch me upstairs, and I went, however reluctantly. I had steeled myself thoroughly against her, but I had also recovered my own equilibrium to some extent—as Laura must have recovered hers. She would realize by now that the one role she could never use to sway me was that of mother. She had been right in the beginning when she had said there need be no sentimental mother-daughter relationship between us. In her devious way she had tried eventually to use that very relationship to get what she wanted. My own reaction had informed her sharply of the foolishness of such a pose. I didn't think she would try again.

Her room was empty when I stepped into it, and I found there had been more rearranging of furniture. At one end, chairs had been drawn up for the audience of four people whom Laura expected. The other end had been given over to the effect of a bare stage—so that Laura could use it to represent whatever scene she wished. The only props were the dragon candlestick set on a small table, and the china cat placed where it might presumably hold open a door. No effort to achieve spot or footlights had been made; indeed, the lights had been turned low, undoubtedly for the sake of flattery.

As I stood looking about, Laura came in from the adjacent dressing room, and even though I was prepared, I caught my breath. The gown of Venetian red suited her perfectly. Her hair had been dressed in the Victorian style Helen Bradley had worn, puffed high above the ears, and drawn into a soft coil on top of her head. She had even cut a fringe of short bangs across her forehead for the occasion. Her cheeks were pale, as Helen's had been, but she had powdered carefully, and used lipstick and eye makeup to gain the effect she wanted. Her own beauty had been subdued to the role of the character she meant to play.

When she saw me waiting near the door, she did not, as I half expected, pretend that nothing had happened between us. She simply stood where she was and studied me coolly, critically.

"I like that beige wool. It becomes you. You could do with a little more weight, but your bones are good. Like mine. The dress needs a touch more. Let me see."

She went to her dressing table in the small room and opened her jewel box. In a moment she was back with the two silver pins she'd worn that day on Ulriken—the tiny masks of tragedy and comedy. She pinned them impersonally to my dress, and stepped back to appraise the effect.

"Victor bought me those in Strøget in Copenhagen. I still wear them for luck. They were his own award to me for *Maggie Thornton.*"

I would not look down at the small pins. It would have pleased me better not to wear them, but I offered no objections. It didn't really matter.

"Can you go through with this tonight?" she challenged me.

If she could, I could, and I told her so.

She nodded with a certain serenity. "Yes—you have strength when it's needed. We'll both be able to pretend that we didn't try to stab each other this afternoon."

I held to a stony silence, following her about, listening as she instructed me. She indicated a straight chair where I was to sit at one side of the "stage," so that the center would be free for her to move about. Only at the very beginning was I to take any part in the action—when I knelt by the imaginary door and polished the doorstop that should have been made of iron. Otherwise, I would sit in my chair and give her the lines of the other two characters—the maid and Robert Bradley.

"Irene will bring them upstairs when Gunnar comes," Laura told me. "I'll be out of sight—so I can make a proper entrance. You'll introduce the scene as I've suggested, and then we'll begin."

"Why are you doing this?" I asked.

Her gaze rested upon the china cat. "I've already told you. I'm going to prove something."

"About yourself as an actress?"

"Perhaps even more." She went to the pink china doorstop and bent to touch it with a hand that was quite steady. "Perhaps I'll also prove that I can't be frightened or intimidated any longer."

The doorbell rang—which meant that Gunnar had arrived. Laura looked at me with sudden panic that belied her words. Then she laughed at herself ruefully.

"Stage fright! Even a movie actress can have that, you know. And it's a good thing. It means I'm keyed up, ready."

She stepped into her dressing room, and I waited uneasily while Irene brought the others upstairs.

Donia came into the room first, giggling in her nervous way—though she fell silent enough when she saw the pink china cat. Miles was obviously in a black and glowering mood. I think he would have stopped Laura if he could, but she had gone beyond his domination, and he knew better than to try. Gunnar greeted me gravely across the room, and he did not seem pleased. Once his eyes met mine with a reproach that I could not face. I wished I could make him understand that what was happening was no longer my fault or doing.

When the other three were seated, Irene took a chair a little apart, and they all stared at me with mixed expectancy and no approval.

I told them what I'd been instructed to tell—that Laura meant to try an experiment tonight, that she wanted to find out here in her own home whether she had any ability for acting left. Since we had all seen the film of *The Whisperer* at one time or another, she had chosen some scenes from that picture to enact. She hoped they would bear with her and be tolerant.

Donia applauded my words with malicious enthusiasm, and then stopped abruptly as I went to kneel beside the china cat. I bent over it with my polishing cloth, feeling more than a little absurd, and sensing the uncomfortable awareness of my audience. These were grown-ups being asked to take part in a fanciful charade, and I wondered if anyone could command their belief under such circumstances.

Laura came into the room and I looked up at her as I'd been told to do. In one hand she carried the tall dragon candlestick, with a white candle burning in the socket. The wavering light struck warmth from the red of her gown, and lighted her face mysteriously. If she had any tendency to limp, she controlled it, and her long gown hid the bandaged ankle. One of the four who watched gasped softly. I couldn't tell which one. I began to read my lines—only a few awkward words to tell her how fearful I was of the master of the house. The sound of my voice fell upon the silence self-consciously, and someone creaked his chair in embarrassment.

Then Helen Bradley began to speak—and no one moved or gasped or creaked a chair. She had the power still. Perhaps she would have been even more magnificent on a stage than she'd been in pictures. Victor Hollins's words on Laura Worth's lips formed once more their old magical combination. She played the scene through with very little help from me. When it was over and she had placed the candlestick upon a table, I left the china cat and went to my chair.

There was no problem about setting the scene or introducing the characters. With her own skill and magic Laura set the stage and peopled it as well. Even though it was I who read Robert Bradley's words, I could have sworn that she addressed another actor—that the scene was complete. She talked to thin air, and our imaginations summoned the necessary figure as though he had been there in reality.

Helen Bradley was perhaps thirty years younger than Laura Worth, but the voice that spoke the lines was the voice of a young woman—a particular young woman—and one forgot the lined face, the sagging flesh.

I recalled that I had seen just this sort of magic evoked on unlikely television talk shows, when some truly great actor took up a book at the m.c.'s urging, and created a mood and a person through his reading of a playwright's words. It was not so strange, after all, when the gift was there.

During one long speech, I stole a look at our audience of four. Gunnar watched in mingled wonderment and uneasiness. I'm sure he did not want her to be as good as she was, for fear she would be hurt later. Miles's pale gray gaze was rapt upon her, and I thought perhaps he saw another, younger, Laura whom he had known long ago. Donia seemed pale and tense. Unexpectedly, there were tears in Irene's eyes. She had not known Laura in her days of stardom, yet she too was responding to a great performance—remember as she might where this experiment was leading.

Laura's timing of the scenes was perfect. There was no attempt to give too much. Only one or two quieter sequences, only a single long dramatic scene was attempted. Then it was over. Laura slipped away to her dressing room, and I crossed to the table and quietly blew out the candle. There was no applause. I saw Donia raise her hands to clap, and then think better of it, and let them fall. Not one of them had seen what he'd hoped to see—Laura's failure and humiliation. They had witnessed the performance of a star and they knew it and did not like it.

It was I who broke the silence. "She's even better than she used to be," I said, and heard my own words in mild surprise.

Miles began to grumble aloud. "There's no pressure here. None of the exacting circumstances of filming a picture. None of the tension of a Hollywood studio. Even Miss Hollins can read lines creditably in this atmosphere."

Donia took it upon herself to contradict. "I think Laura was splendid under any circumstances. Why not let her go back to Hollywood and see what happens?"

Gunnar shook his head sadly. "She has lost nothing of her talent in the years. But over there she still has everything to lose and very little to gain. Her reputation stands at the top. There is no point in pulling it down as circumstances might do."

Irene said nothing at all. She had recovered from her moment of emotion. Perhaps she, of us all, knew best the extraordinary will Laura Worth could exert if she chose. Perhaps she, of us all, realized that nothing any of us said or did really mattered. Laura would do what it pleased her to do. By tonight's effort, she had sought to convince, to perhaps cajole us over to her side. But if no one stood by her, she would nevertheless do as she intended.

After a few moments Irene rose and went to the door. "If you'd like to come downstairs in a little while, I'll have coffee and cake for you in the dining room."

While the others began to talk a bit stiffly among themselves, I left them and went to the dressing room. Laura had painstakingly unzipped herself from the red gown and slipped into the caftan again. She was still alive with excitement—an excitement totally suppressed during her performance—and she pounced on me at once.

"How was it, Leigh? How did it go? What are they saying out there?"

"They're not saying anything," I told her. "I think they're stunned."

"Then I succeeded? I really proved what I wanted to prove?"

"For a pocket-sized performance, I think you were terrific.

Perhaps better than you've ever been." Whether I wanted to or not, I had to give her that.

Her eyes were alight with triumph and she was completely confident. "I know! An actress does know when she's giving her best. You can feel what comes across from those who are watching. Sometimes in the studio the entire crew would applaud me after a scene. It isn't necessary to have a theater audience to know when you're good. But I always want to hear. We can never get enough of praise. We are the most insecure people alive. And I know that you, of all of them, would tell me the truth. Perhaps you even wanted me to fail—the way Miles and Gunnar did. But you'd have to admit the truth."

I spoke without emotion. "Yes, I have to admit the truth."

"Now I've let them know," she went on. "They've seen that I'm not frightened any more. They can realize that no threats are going to shake me. They can do their worst, and it won't matter. That's even more important than the performance."

"They?" I repeated.

She would not answer me. She leaned toward the mirror, fluffing out her bangs, tucking in a tendril of hair. Idly I picked up the red gown from the chair where she'd tossed it, and was aware of her watching me in the mirror.

"Put it on," she said. *"The Whisperer* costume—put it on. You wanted to."

I shook my head. "Not any more. Not after seeing you wear it again."

She came to me and unpinned the small silver masks she had loaned me, dropped them into her jewel case. "Please—because I'd like to see you in it."

Because she'd like to make fun of me, I wondered. I had no wish to put that gown on now—the contrast between us would be too great. But she was already plucking at the back zipper of my beige wool, and I gave in to her reluctantly. She dropped the Venetian red gown over my head and I slipped my arms into the tight sleeves. With no difficulty she pulled up the zipper—since I did not fit the gown as snugly as she did. It had been a little tight for her—it was slightly loose on me, yet the difference between us in size was very little.

She turned me about before her big mirror, looking over my shoulder while I regarded myself doubtfully.

"The gown calls for a brunette—like you," I said. "A blond bob is all wrong. Helen Bradley would never look like this."

Quickly she caught up hairpins from the container on her

dressing table and began to wind and pin my hair on top of my head. So rapt was she in her play, that she might have snipped bangs across my forehead if I'd let her.

"You're playing with dolls," I said. "And I'm not a doll. Remember that."

She laughed and thrust in the last pin. "There! You do look a little like me after all. Run down stairs and show them! Quickly—run!"

I pulled myself out of her hands. "Don't be absurd. This is your idea, not mine. I don't want to resemble you. I want to be myself!"

"You're getting excited, Leigh. Look—I'll put your dress on, and you'll wear mine, and we'll go downstairs for Irene's coffee. You look beautiful, really. You should wear rich, strong colors. Go down and let Gunnar see you. He'll never have another chance to see how dashing you look in red."

She was the most impossible woman I had ever known. Until I'd come here, I'd thought of myself as strong-minded, but Laura Worth could tear down on one like a torrent in flood, with all the overpowering force of a natural element behind her. It was easier to consent to her absurd wishes than to oppose her.

"If you'll stop pushing, I'll go quietly," I said. "But you're to come down at once and tell them what this is all about. Or at least what you think it's all about."

"I'll be there in seconds," she promised, and I went reluctantly out the door.

The hall was dim and there was no one there. Feeling unutterably foolish, I caught up the skirt of the red gown with both hands and started down the narrow, turning stairs. Someone came out of a room above and crossed the hall behind me, but I did not turn. I was busy picking my way down the steps, making an effort not to be tripped by the long skirt of the gown.

There was only an instant in which I felt a presence behind me. There was no time to turn, to save myself—only that instant of awareness, and a whispering voice.

The thrust from behind came full and strong in the center of my back. I pitched straight over and down the steep stairs. I must have struck the wall of the narrow turning with my shoulder, and then slid the rest of the way to the lower hall.

I could not have lain stunned for more than seconds before I came to myself and struggled to sit up. The tableau which had formed in those seconds was frozen around me. Gunnar stood in the living room door. Miles had come out of the dining room. Irene was at the rear in the kitchen door, while Donia and Laura stood above me on the stairs. At once the tableau broke up, and Gunnar reached me first.

Laura called to him from above. "She must have tripped on that long skirt. She's had a dreadful fall. Bring her up to my bed."

I felt dizzy with shock, and I couldn't speak, let alone think. Gunnar gathered me up in his arms and I was aware only of his strength and the lovely safety of being held by him. While he climbed the stairs, carrying me, Laura ran ahead and flung back the spread on her bed. Gently he lowered me to the softness of eiderdown, and drew a pillow beneath my head. I looked up into his face and wanted him to stay like that—considerate, not angry with me, gentle.

"Why is she wearing this dress she would trip over?" Gunnar asked Laura.

"That was a whim of mine. A foolish one. I should have known she wasn't accustomed to a skirt that reaches the floor."

My trembling had lessened a little, and I could lie quietly. Except for Irene, the others had followed us into the room, and my eyes sought Donia's face—and found her hovering at her brother's elbow, watching me with a lively, unpitying interest. Now I was able to speak.

"I didn't trip over the gown," I said. "Someone pushed me from behind."

There was an intense silence in the room. Then Irene came in to bring me a cup of hot tea, and while I sat up to sip it, Miles grumbled under his breath about women with neurotic imaginings. Donia regarded me in uneasy alarm, and sidled out of sight behind Laura.

"Besides Laura—who wouldn't have pushed me—there was only one person on the stairs," I said.

The other four stared at Donia with varying expressions.

"This is nonsense—" Miles began, but Laura interrupted him.

"It's not nonsense. It's more of the pattern that's been plaguing us. If Leigh says she was pushed, I'm sure she was."

Donia looked more than a little frightened. "But I was in my room! I only rushed out when I heard a crash."

"You were there on the stairs when I came out of my room," Laura pointed out. "I was putting on Leigh's dress, so

I was delayed. But you were there, Donia, when I came out to see what had happened."

"But why would I push her? Why would I—"

"Because you saw the dress and in the dim light you thought it was me?" Laura said, questioning.

Donia made a small squealing sound, and Gunnar spoke to her gently.

"Did you perhaps hear anything when you came to the stairs? If someone pushed Leigh and then rushed past her to the floor below, you might have heard the running."

Donia snatched at this lifeline. "Yes—yes, I think I did hear something. But I was looking down at Leigh, and—and I didn't notice whether anyone crossed the lower hall."

Was she making it up or not, I wondered. Or had she seen and did not mean to tell?

Miles was watching his sister doubtfully. "We can't afford to make mistakes about this, or to guess wildly. We're dealing with a very grave situation."

"That's what I've said all along," Laura agreed bitterly.

Irene was more concerned with me. "You're rubbing your shoulder. Have you hurt it?"

"Not badly," I said. I'd struck it during the fall, but it was no more than slightly bruised.

She looked about at the others quietly, calmly. "What we are dealing with is a murderer," she said.

Donia gasped, and Miles caught Laura as she swayed against the bed.

"That's enough," he said curtly to Irene.

She paid no attention to him. "It's time someone spoke out and told the truth. During the last two months these miserable little tricks have been played upon Miss Worth again and again. Someone is trying to injure her. Someone who carries the memory of a terrible crime."

"No, Irene—no!" Laura cried. "Don't say anything more. Let it alone. Please—for my sake!"

Irene went on implacably. "Now it's getting worse. Miss Hollins is lucky. She might have been more seriously hurt. People have been killed by falls like that. But since Miss Worth doesn't wish me to say anything more, I won't."

She turned stiffly away and walked out of the room. Her words of accusation seemed to hang heavily in the air. Laura began to weep softly with her hands covering her face. I saw the strange look exchanged between Donia and Miles. Perhaps it was distrust and suspicion that grew between them.

Perhaps it was something else. One of them knew about the other, yet for some reason neither would speak out. I was sure there was no longer any liking between them—only a deep and growing distrust.

Gunnar stood a little apart, and he, at least, was concerned for me. As Miles bent to comfort Laura, he came to the side of the bed where he could speak to me softly.

"Perhaps it would be better for you to go home to New York as soon as you can, Leigh. In the meantime, our invitation is to you, as well as to Laura. If you care to come to our home tonight, leave this house—"

"No," I said. "But thank you, Gunnar. Tonight I'll stay with Laura. We'll be together in this room."

"That will be a good thing," he said gravely. "Good for you both. You are becoming friends, I think."

I contradicted that at once. "Not friends. Only reluctant allies. Because I mean to help her to get to Hollywood, if that's where she wants to go."

I could sense his stiffening against me. I'd finished the tea, and I lay back on the pillow so I didn't have to look at him and watch the accusation growing in his eyes. There was nothing at all I could do about Gunnar and that gave me an empty, lost feeling. In a moment I was afraid I might be weeping like Laura.

He leaned toward me again, his voice dropping to a whisper. "Be careful, Leigh. There is madness in this house. You and Laura must be out of it soon. You will feel well enough to come to us with Laura tomorrow?"

"I'll try to come," I said, and kept my face turned from him.

Astonishingly, he bent and kissed me on the cheek. I turned to him in surprise, and he laughed softly at my expression.

"You see—we Bergensere are not as reserved as you think! But of course you are my ward—put into my hands by Victor Hollins. And it is permitted to kiss one's ward."

He was laughing at me gently, even though he had not forgotten the gravity of the situation in this house, nor my encouragement of Laura, which he disapproved. I had to smile in return, and felt the trembling of my lips.

"There," he said, "—that is better. I will see you tomorrow, Leigh. Take care of yourself tonight. And of Laura. Tomorrow we will plan. This cannot go on."

He said good night to Laura and Miles, and I saw that Donia had escaped from the room. When Gunnar was gone, Miles returned to regard me impersonally as a doctor. He seemed to think I was little the worse for what had happened. I did not trust him at all, and I was glad when he went away.

When they were all gone, Laura sat in a chair and stared at me. My beige wool, which she had struggled into, did not particularly become her, any more than I felt the Venetian red became me.

"We'd better get back to being ourselves," she told me. "I'll slip out of this dress and then help you out of the costume. I wish now I hadn't asked you to put it on."

"Which one of them pushed me?"

She was struggling with the back zipper of her borrowed dress, her face flushed with the effort. "Don't you know?"

"Of course I don't know! If I knew, I'd speak out. I wouldn't sit silently by and allow this to go on."

"That's what I'm afraid of," she said, and disappeared in the direction of her dressing room.

I lay looking around the room which had so recently played the role of theater. The partly burned candle stood in the dragon holder. The pink china doorstop still held open an imaginary door. And the dress Laura Worth had worn in *The Whisperer* clothed me as I lay upon the bed. But everything had changed. I could still feel that vindictive thrust of two hands in the center of my back. I could feel myself falling forward into nothingness.

She came back into the room wearing her caftan. "Are you able to turn over so I can manage the zipper?"

I lay still, staring at her. "Do you really know which one it was?"

"Of course I know. I've know all along where the threat to me lies."

"Then why can't you tell me, so we can deal with it?"

She touched the ruffle of bangs across her forehead, and I saw the hesitant, half-frightened gesture that was purely Helen Bradley.

"Because I'm not as brave as all that. Not yet. Though I'm trying to be. I'm trying to face whatever has to be faced. There's the slim chance that everything will be all right if I don't speak out. If I can run away to Hollywood alone. Not that being alone means any real safeguard or escape. It can all crash around my head at any moment. But I have to take that chance. Irene was right. We're dealing with a murderer. Someone whose heart is full of hatred. You're in danger now, as well as I. Because you've decided to stand by me."

"How do you know I'll stand by you? Don't forget what you said earlier today about our stabbing each other."

She shook her head at me. "That is a private war. As mother and daughter we're sure to strike out—to stab. Neither of us accepts this unfortunate tie. But you can't help the other thing—your admiration for Laura Worth, the actress. I don't know how it happened, but somehow you grew up with that. And tonight it was confirmed—for me. I saw it in your face. You don't want to send me back to films because you think I'll fail. Now you believe I can succeed, and you want that for me. As I want it for myself."

How much better she understood me than Gunnar did. Perhaps better than I did myself. But I said nothing and she went on.

"Because you'll now back me and help me, you're in danger too."

I had the memory of those hands at my back, and I knew what she said could very well be true. But for tonight we would be together. I sat up and slid my feet to the floor. When I stood up I felt dizzy for an instant. When I'd steadied, I turned my back and Laura ran the zipper down.

"I'm sure Helen Bradley never had it so easy," I said. "In her day there would have been dozens of hooks to undo."

I put on the negligee Laura gave me, and she rang for Irene. When she came, Laura asked her to bring my night things from downstairs, and then help to make up the sofa for Laura to sleep on tonight.

I tried to protest that I could sleep on the sofa, but Laura would have none of that.

"Dr. Fletcher will not be pleased," Irene said dryly, but Laura only smiled enigmatically.

Miles himself came in again when Irene had gone out for the last time. He looked soberly about at our preparations for the night.

"The girls' domitory, I see."

Laura explained lightly. "Leigh isn't feeling well since that dreadful fall. I want her near me tonight." She said nothing of the fact that this had been planned long before the fall.

Miles kissed his wife good night somewhat remotely, and for just a moment she clung to him. Then he went through the dressing room into his own bedroom, closing the far door behind him.

I had watched alertly, and when he'd gone I asked the question that had long puzzled me. "Are you in love with him, Laura?"

She smiled at me rather sadly. "The enemy within the gates! That's what you are, in a sense, aren't you? But an enemy on only one plane. That's why I can trust you. In a lifetime, Leigh, there are different kinds of love. I've known several of them. I need Miles in my life. No matter what happens in the future, I think I will always come back to him. You see, I don't really care what he is like any more. I only know that I need him. Perhaps someday we can be friends. As we once were."

"Before Cass Alroy died?" I asked.

"Perhaps," she said. "Perhaps that's one reason I want to go back to that time. Miles thought I was marvelous in those days. He liked the idea of an attachment to someone who was successful and world famous. Now I'm nothing—nobody. But I mean to change that."

"Even though he doesn't want you to?"

"He believes I'll be humiliated and hurt. He sees trouble ahead for me. Tonight I hoped to change his mind, but I haven't succeeded. So now I must go ahead on my own and do what I have to do."

"Will he try to stop you?"

"He's already trying to stop me. But I shan't permit him to succeed."

"I wonder if he's afraid of more than your possible failure?"

"Yes—he's afraid of the truth. As I have been. Now, no matter what happens, it must be faced. You're helping me to face it."

I was not sure about that, not sure about anything. Not even sure of what truth she meant—except that it had to do with the death of Cass Alroy.

I picked up the nightgown and robe that Irene had brought upstairs for me, and went to the door. "You'll be all right for a little while?"

"No one will touch me," she said. "Not tonight."

I went across the hall to the bathroom. All the other doors were closed and I moved quickly, keeping away from the stairs. When I was ready for bed, I returned to Laura's room.

She stood at the balcony door, looking out over the lights of Bergen and I went to stand beside her.

"It was very successful tonight, wasn't it?" she asked.

I felt my shoulder. "Successful is rather a strange word."

"No—no! I mean my performance. It was only a pocket-sized performance, as you say, but—"

I gave her the praise she wanted because I could understand her endless hunger for applause. That was the way she was made. She could not help herself, and because this hunger was once more alive in her, she would probably be successful in feeding it.

"I meant what I said earlier," I told her. "Tonight you were better than ever."

She nodded her agreement without false modesty. "That's because I've had these years in which to grow and mature. I have something to bring to my work that I lacked before."

She turned back to the room and switched off the lamps, one by one. Then she settled down upon the sofa, and I think she went quickly to sleep. I stretched out in her big bed, where the mattress had just the right resistance to my body, and tried to think about all that had happened, tried vainly to find the answers. But the aspirin I'd taken was making me feel drowsy and relaxed, and I went to sleep remembering Gunnar's arms when he carried me up the stairs, his kiss upon my cheek. It had all been casual—meaning nothing. So I dreamed about him intensely.

Sometimes a dream can waken us to reality. What is vividly felt during sleep can seem comforting, fulfilling, exciting, and though it can't always be remembered and grasped when we awake, it can nevertheless make us newly conscious of some truth not previously understood or accepted. I awakened warmed by the happiness of my dream, and even as it slipped away from me, I knew and accepted for the first time what I was beginning to feel about Gunnar, what I had always thrust away so that I needn't look at it. In these few days something had happened to me that had never happened before. Now I didn't try to fight the knowledge, as I might tomorrow when I was fully awake, but gave myself warmly to a new awareness of myself as a woman who could, after all, fall in love, and I fell asleep hoping the dream would come back to me.

It did not. I dreamed instead of something anxiety-ridden and disturbing, though it too fled when a sound from outside penetrated my heavy sleep. It was long after midnight. I opened my eyes to pale light beyond the windows and lay very still. Someone was in the room. A shadowy figure loomed against the light from the picture window—a figure that moved toward my bed. As silently as possible I rolled to the far side and clung to the edge, stiff and waiting. Hands crept toward me across the pillow, shadowy arms extended in my direction, searching, searching.

Quite suddenly the voice whispered through the room, "*Listen . . .*" and once more, "*Listen . . .*"

I flung myself off the bed and fumbled for the nearest lamp. Light flooded the room and I whirled to face the bed.

She stood there in her long-sleeved lacy nightgown, her hands patting futilely at the pillows as though she searched for something. It was Laura who stood there, and she was sound asleep. Yet it must have been someone else who whispered—someone across the room. Whoever it was had gone. The door to the hall stood closed as we had left it, and while the dressing room door was open on this side, the far door to Miles's room remained closed. Laura had not heard the voice. Her sleeping face was empty of alarm, expressionless. She made no sound.

I went around the bed and took her gently by the arm. She did not waken as I led her back to her sofa bed. She was tranquil beneath my hands and allowed herself to be tucked under the covers without awakening. When the eiderdown was over her, I went to the hall door and opened it softly.

There was no one there, as I had known there would not be. The other doors were closed and blank to my inquiry. Yet I knew that behind one of them the Whisperer waited, listening as he had warned others to listen.

I went back to my bed and lay awake for a long while. The pattern made so little sense. Mischief, mischief. But growing stronger and more dangerous. I was glad that today we would be visiting Gunnar and his mother. We would get away from the house. And—I would test my earlier dream.

Birds were singing in the garden by the time I fell asleep.

Chapter 12

When I next awakened, I found Laura already up and dressed. She came to stand beside the bed.

"How do you feel?"

I sat up and stretched widely. My body was stiff and sore from the fall and I suspected bruises would be appearing. But I knew I'd limber up when I moved around. I was all right.

"I'm fine," I said. "How are you?"

"My ankle feels only a little sore. I'll come downstairs for breakfast this morning. I'm tired of being pampered. Gunnar won't be here until eleven—have you any plans for earlier in the morning?"

"I told Irene I might go marketing with her. But perhaps I'd better not leave you alone."

She considered that for only a moment. "I'll come with you," she decided. "It's true that you should visit Bergen's fish market, and I would enjoy it too. It's a flower market as well, you know, and for fruits and vegetables—and town gossip."

I slipped out of bed and put on my robe. "How did you sleep?" I asked casually.

Her smile was bright, unclouded. "Wonderfully well. I felt safe with you in the room. No sleepwalking, no voices, no bad dreams."

"That's fine," I said, and went across the hall to the bathroom.

Irene stepped out of her room, stopping me at the door. She put a finger to her lips and looked toward the other closed doors. Her thin face wore its usual solemn look.

"Come into my room a moment, Miss Hollins."

I wanted to wash and dress before I contemplated either old problems or new ones, but her manner was urgent and secretive, so I followed her reluctantly.

Her bedroom was of modest size, comfortably furnished with fine old things that must have been in the house since the

201

time of Laura's mother. The draperies and bedspread were on the austere side—a dull slate blue, and three photographs of Laura Worth smiled from neat frames hung against one wall, all of them autographed. Irene did not ask me to sit down. When she'd closed the hall door she turned to me earnestly.

"Was there any trouble last night?"

"She walked in her sleep," I said. "But she doesn't remember it. I was able to get her quietly back to bed." I hesitated, wondering whether to tell her any more.

"At what time was this?"

"I haven't any idea. After midnight, I'm sure."

"Could she have gone out of the room, do you think? Before you found her, I mean?"

"I don't know. I was sleeping soundly."

"Someone opened my door last night."

I waited, knowing what would come next.

Irene nodded. "Someone who whispered one word—'listen.' "

"Whoever it was came to our room too," I told her. "I heard the voice when I found Laura near my bed."

"I've never believed in this voice before," Irene said. "But now I've heard it myself."

"Do you suppose Laura could do this whispering?" I asked.

"It's possible. But she claims to hear it herself."

"And you've never heard it before?"

"Never. I thought it was Miss Worth's nerves and imagination."

"Yesterday you spoke out rather strongly," I said. "You pointed out that we were dealing with a murderer. Perhaps now someone's warning you."

"I can take care of myself. I'm not afraid—except for her. What I said was true. The person who killed that man in Hollywood is here in this house. I'm sure of it."

"Then it's the same person who pushed me on the stairs."

"I suppose so," Irene agreed. But she was not really thinking about my fall. Her entire concern was for Laura.

"Which one of them is it?" I pressed her. "I can imagine Donia doing these things, but not Dr. Fletcher. Yet neither of them was in the studio in Hollywood that night. Neither would have anything to fear from the past."

She regarded me darkly for a moment and then changed the subject.

"Are you coming to the market with me this morning?"

"Yes—I'd like to. Laura will come with us. So she won't have to stay alone while we're away."

Irene accepted the change in plans with approval. "That's good. It was not you someone pushed on the stairs last night, Miss Hollins. The costume made it seem that you were Miss Worth. But perhaps it's fortunate it happened that way. She's not as young as you are. The fall might have injured her more severely."

"Anyway, we mustn't leave her alone," I said, and went off to the bath.

While I got ready to face the day, I tried to think of nothing. Especially not of dreams, especially not of Gunnar Thoresen. I did not want that warmth which relaxed my will to engulf me again. Gunnar could never mean anything to me. He did not really like me, and very soon I would go home and never see him again.

When I was dressed, Laura and I came downstairs to breakfast. She brought with her the dragon candlestick she had used last night, and placed it on a table near the garden doors in the dining room. I knew why. She didn't want to keep it in her bedroom, but she wanted to set it out in plain sight to prove she was no longer afraid of it.

Donia and Miles were already at the table. Miles rose to seat us and inquired how I felt this morning, and how Laura had slept, how her ankle was doing. I let Laura's statement that she had slept well stand, and said nothing about what I had seen and heard. Our plans for going to the fish market with Irene were discussed, but I couldn't tell whether he and Donia were pleased or displeased. Our talk was rather purposefully light and unconcerned, yet I sensed tension beneath the words. No one had forgotten yesterday.

I was glad when the meal was over and Laura and I went to change into slacks and sweaters. When we got into the car Irene took the wheel and we left Kalfaret and drove past the old tollgate and into the center of town. We drove down wide Torgalmenning, past its arcaded shops, central mall, and great Seamen's Monument commemorating those who had served Bergen from the sea. Irene said the moment it was warm enough Bergen would become a city of flowers, and great buckets of them would be set out in the mall, with bright umbrellas and tables.

There was parking space near the market and we left the car and strolled among the flower stalls where fragrant wares were shown in small, glass-sided carts that were banked with flowers. All over the busy market were brightly colored canopies, roofed counters and stalls where produce and fish were being sold. Everything was sparkling clean and neat, with no sign of litter anywhere. Norwegian flags flew from tall poles, and the Jubilee flag with its castle towers on a shield, fluttered in the wind, celebrating Bergen's nine hundred years. Through the open market area were granite blocks surmounted with bronze lions snarling and lashing their tails.

Laura bought an armful of lavender rhododendrons from a dealer who made change from the huge purse that hung from his shoulder like a woman's handbag. The market was built at the end of Vågen, that arm of the sea that reached deep into Bergen. Fishing boats bobbed on the water, sometimes three deep from shore, while along the quay the few gabled warehouses of old Bryggen which had survived destructive fires gave a flavor of the medieval to the scenes. Once the Hanseatic League had flourished here and this had been known as the German Wharf. All around the busy central scene rose the Seven Mountains, and I could see the funicular climbing to the low buildings on top of Flöyen, and the tall communications tower rising from the snows of Ulriken.

Laura insisted upon carrying her flowers back to the car herself, and Irene and I moved on toward the fish sellers. When Laura was out of hearing Irene turned to me abruptly.

"I have decided to tell you," she said. "It is better for you to know. Safer. So you can be on guard. Both of them were at the studio that night twenty years ago."

I stared at her blankly and she went on.

"Mrs. Jaffe had tickets for the play that night, but the woman she meant to go with disappointed her, and at the last minute she asked her brother to accompany her. Instead, he persuaded her to drive him out to the studio. Whether she went through the gates or not, I don't know. He went to the sound stage where Miss Worth was spending the night in her dressing room. He must have followed Mr. Alroy onto the set. What happened after that, I don't know."

"But aren't there guards at the studio gates? How could he get in and out, and not be noticed? The newspaper account said Cass Alroy checked in openly at the gate, but there was no record of Dr. Fletcher coming in. His alibi was never shaken."

Irene shrugged. "I have never heard about this part."

"How do you know any of it?"

"I heard them talking one day shortly after they moved into

Miss Worth's house. They didn't know I was home. They were quarreling, as they seem to do frequently. There is something Mrs. Jaffe holds over Dr. Fletcher's head. Perhaps it is her knowledge of what happened that night."

I could see Laura coming toward us through the crowd that thronged the market.

"None of it matters now," I whispered to Irene. "But thank you for telling me."

"You don't think murder still matters?" Irene said. "Do you believe there can ever be rest over the years when such a crime has been committed?"

There was no time to answer her. I suppose all I really wanted was to put my head in the sand and shut away everything that belonged to the past and which Laura herself wanted to forget.

She came toward us with that gallant, arresting walk, and my heart turned over strangely. I had a quick premonition of something terrible in store for her, and I could not bear it. She came at once to take me by the arm and I was more gentle with her than I'd ever been before.

"Come along," she said. "We must visit the fish!"

We left the flower carts and walked past counters where aproned men were chopping and cleaning fish on reddened boards. Along the water's edge were tanks where live fish were swimming. Where we walked, the ground was wet with rivulets from the buckets of water that were being thrown over fish counters. Long shining knives rose and fell, so that the chopping sound was all around us, and that babble of voices in a strange tongue, surmounted only by the screaming of the gulls. Oddly enough, the smell of fish was slight and not offensive. Laura said this was because the fish were really just out of the sea, and because everything was kept so clean.

This time it was Irene who made purchases. Pink-fleshed salmon was wrapped in newspaper and then placed in a plastic bag for her to carry. Nearby several small boys sat at the water's edge, eating cooked shrimp and tossing the tails into the water, where gulls swooped down upon them. There was an amusement booth with a lighted wheel to spin and gifts to win. There was a magazine stand flaunting Wild West comic books in Norwegian.

As we moved on toward the fruit and vegetable section, Laura met a women whom she knew, accompanied by a small girl. The child bobbed the curtsy with which she'd been taught to greet her elders, and while Laura and her mother conversed, she talked to me shyly in the halting English she was learning in school. The fish market had always been a place for social exchange and the meeting of friends.

When Laura's acquaintance moved on, we watched Irene as she bought small round tomatoes and knobby cucumbers, crisp green lettuce, bananas, oranges and lemons. Laura and I were pressed into service to help carry her purchases, and Laura seemed thoroughly alive and filled with enjoyment over all she was doing. I saw Irene cast a glance at her now and then, as though she distrusted these high spirits and wondered what was coming next. I wished I'd had time to ask whether Laura knew of Irene's claim that both Donia and Miles had gone to the studio that night before they had taken care to let themselves be seen coming out of the theater.

Laura's voice broke into my thoughts. "To be truly happy," she said, fingering a plump tomato, "one must be able to savor small everyday events. When we live with tragedy, that ability is wiped out. I love being able to relish this market again."

I tried to match her mood. Once more I attempted to put all that was ominous out of my mind, to tell myself that it didn't matter. The sunny day and blue sky, the shining water and cheerful throngs, all served to deny that life held an under layer which threatened storm and calamity.

All the while as we moved about, the thought of Gunnar went with me. Not faced and accepted as it had been last night after my dream, but disturbingly present. I could not let it surface completely. I was afraid to look at it too closely because this was a problem without solution to which I was betraying myself and all my long-held convictions. Yet it was there, with me constantly.

When we were laden with all we could carry, we returned to the car and piled ourselves and our burdens into it. Again Irene drove as we turned toward Kalfaret. Beside me in the seat Laura seemed eternally young and filled with the very enthusiasm of youth. I could only pray that everything would be right for her, and that she was not flying headlong toward disaster—as I myself might be, in a different way.

We drove past the park and she laughed at the sight of Grieg, leaning on his familiar cane as he stood on his pedestal, with a pigeon perched on his head. She pointed out the flower beds, and once she made Irene pull over to a curb so we could watch a marching band of youngsters go past. There was nothing to give evidence that this was a haunted woman, and

I marveled at her ability to be caught up in the joy of little things.

Back at the house, in the hour or two before Gunnar would call for us, we spent some time—at Laura's insistence—on my book, my interviewing. Not that I any longer needed to "interview." She seemed to know what I might find useful, and she plainly enjoyed telling me stories of the past. It was not all triumphant. She was realistic about what her life in Hollywood had been like, and she didn't try to gloss it over.

In many ways that life had been hard and rough. Stars had been considered the property of the studio, and were often treated as such. There were the early risings and long hours that often left her exhausted, and with time for nothing but her work. There were sometimes primitive trips on location. And the fact that she had been thrown into enforced company with men and women who were sometimes ruthless in their determination to hold their own positions and climb at all costs. The competitiveness could be ugly at times. Then there had been the gossip from columnists, and magazines whose maws must be forever filled with stories, whether true or not. But there had been warm and genuine affection too. There had been unexpected loyalties. And appreciation. A camera crew, a makeup man, script girl, hairdresser, who recognized Laura as a pro who appeared on time and kept no one waiting, who was willing to work as hard as anyone else in the studio, star or no star, and who held temperament to a minimum when she was on the job. The glamour which the public saw wore thin very quickly when you went to work on a set. There others knew the truth about an actor which could never be concealed.

I let her talk and listened absorbed. I said nothing about the thing Irene had told me. Perhaps Laura already knew. I walked on thin ice and took care not to crack it through.

When Gunnar came, I found it hard to meet his eyes directly. In the night my dream had seemed reality. Now dreaming must be battened down. The longing to touch him and be near him—these new longings which had suddenly surfaced—must be denied.

He asked at once how I felt and seemed pleased to find Laura and me so amiably inclined toward each other, and physically in good health. But I didn't want to be approved merely because I was being unexpectedly nice to Laura Worth.

In the car, Laura and I sat beside him in the front seat, with me in the middle, and I tried to give myself over to the pleasant aspects of the outing. For a little while all else could be left behind.

Gunnar's house, where he had once lived with his wife, was situated on the water in a northern section of Bergen. It was a low modern house with picture windows that fronted on the town fjord. A gracious living room with soft-toned woods and beige carpets looked out upon black rocks piled in a wall against the water. Outside, a path led down to a small beach, where salt water lapped the sand.

Mrs. Thoresen greeted us warmly and made me feel welcome at once. She was a tall woman, not beautiful, but with an air of assurance that was in its way equal to Laura's. Norwegian women were well emancipated, and were often partners with their husbands in working out their mutual lives. Gunnar had said that she interested herself in serving the city, and I could imagine her running committees, meeting difficult problems with good judgment and capability. Her English was excellent and she spoke with the same British accent that Gunnar had acquired. I could see how proud she was of him, and how her eyes followed him as he moved about the room —yet there was nothing fatuous or smothering about her affection. She granted him the right to be himself, as she was independently herself.

As we sat in the pleasant living room that had once belonged to Gunnar and his wife, my eyes were drawn to a silver-framed portrait on the piano. Without question, I knew that the smiling blond girl who looked out of the frame was Gunnar's wife, Astrid. I didn't want to see her face, to know what she had been like, and after that first glance I did not look toward the piano again.

"It has been too long since you have visited us," Mrs. Thoresen was telling Laura. "I am glad to see you looking well and happy. And I am pleased that you have brought Miss Hollins to visit us. Gunnar has told me so much about your father, Miss Hollins."

I wondered what he might have told her about me, but if his words had been less than approving, she did not show it. When we had talked for a little while she led us to the dining section of the long living room and served us an attractive light luncheon of open-faced sandwiches, decoratively arranged.

Laura plied Mrs. Thoresen with questions and kept her talking about her work in helping with the youth center in town, where city-bound boys and girls in their early teens could have a place of their own to come to any night of the week. They came to play games, to dance, to learn something of the social graces—perhaps to escape from home as young people anywhere were so often eager to do.

"We permit no visiting adults, as a rule," Mrs. Thoresen said. "Only the couple who run the center are present. Parents are kept away because this is a place for the young people themselves. It has worked out well. There is less breaking of street lamps, less vandalism and damage to cars among these children. Most of these particular young people will not go to the university, but may attend schools of their own choosing— a beauty operator's school, a waiter's school, a school for mechanics."

Apparently Laura had gone to the center once, not as a visitor, but to talk to the young people about what it had been like to be a movie actress in America. English was taught in all the schools, and afterwards the boys and girls had been eager to practice their English by talking with Laura.

The luncheon hour passed serenely enough. At least I hoped I was outwardly serene. My new awareness of Gunnar was always with me. I watched him when he did not know I was looking at him. I studied his long, good-looking face, and the way his brown hair grew back from his forehead. I listened to the deep tones of his voice, and was aware of his hands, long like his face, with slender, prehensile fingers that I knew could be both gentle and strong. I was lost—and knew I was lost. For the moment I did not care.

After lunch, Laura told Gunnar to take me outside and show me the beach—she wanted to talk to his mother. Thus imperiously dismissed, he smiled at me and led me outside through glass doors. Purple and yellow crocuses were up in the tiny garden, and the forsythia was heavy with yellow buds. Already the snow on the mountains looked thinner, more patchy. These days of sunny bright weather were bringing spring to Norway.

The effect of my dream was upon me again—the feeling that I did not want to think and weigh, but for this little while I wanted only to be with this man whom my father had loved, and toward whom I had been drawn from the first.

We climbed down a stony path and he took my hand to help me over a boulder that blocked the way to the beach. I jumped down from the rock and for a moment stood close to him, almost within the circle of his arms. He stepped back from me deliberately and I stood on the sand beside him, not wanting to look at him after that moment of involuntary rejection, staring instead at the small boat drawn up on the beach, at the water which lapped cleanly at our feet. Gunnar began to talk to me quietly, and I knew in silent rebellion that once more he would speak only of Laura.

"After her performance last night, what did you think?" he asked.

I raised my head defiantly and looked across the water toward the nearest islands. "I think she proved what she wanted to prove."

"And what she hardly needed to prove—that she is still an actress," he said.

"She proved more than that. Now Miles will have to accept the fact that she must have her chance. She'll let nothing stop her."

"How do you feel about that?"

I looked at him directly then, challenging him. It would be better for me if he made me angry again. "I think she should do what she wants to do."

"Even if she fails?"

"She has the right to failure," I told him.

"I believe you would still like to see that happen. I believe you would encourage her along this course."

"It doesn't make much difference what you believe," I said stiffly.

"I know that, Leigh. You make it very clear."

He walked away from me across the sand and put one foot up on the overturned boat. I felt curiously alone and abandoned. Even though I'd wanted to challenge and anger him, there was an aching in me that was an adding up of all the times in my life when I had felt unutterably lonely. Not Ruth, not my father, no friend I'd ever had, could make up for that empty loneliness. All because of Laura! That was what I'd always told myself. These feelings of loss and emptiness had been stamped upon me and out of them had grown my futile angers, my suspicion of anyone who tried to reach me, to crack through the shield I wore to guard myself against further hurt and rejection.

But now something had happened to the shield. Without warning it lay in shards about my feet and I found myself exposed to emotions I'd never felt before. With these feelings came a sharp realization—self-realization. I was not alone because Laura had let me go and forgotten me, and therefore no one could love me. I was alone because I had never been able to love. Not even my father. Not even Ruth. I was alone, not because I had been rejected, but because I had always been the one to reject. I had not even loved myself.

There was a searing clarity in this new knowledge. It was frightening, unnerving. I had a wild impulse to run to Gunnar's arms. I wanted to plead, "Hold me, protect me—don't let anything touch me!" But so foolish a gesture would only alarm him and would not help me. It was not protection I needed. What I needed was the strength to become vulnerable. The strength to love where it was dangerous to love—both Laura and Gunnar.

I spoke to him quietly, and heard the unfamiliar quiver in my voice. "It isn't true that I don't care what you believe. I care very much. You were my father's friend, and I wish you would be mine. Something is—happening to me. Something inside myself—since I've come to Bergen. It's new—and frightening. I need time to understand it."

His guarded look did not lift, but he spoke to me more gently. "Perhaps what your father hoped for is happening to you, Leigh."

I tried to ponder my own feelings aloud. "It doesn't matter any more that I don't mean anything to her as a daughter. I understand that well enough. What matters is that I'm coming to know her and I can feel an affection toward her. Not only because she is Laura Worth, but because she is both my mother and a woman in her own right."

Suddenly tears were running down my face and I knew they were tears of release, bursting from a spring that had been frozen for most of my life. Gunnar came to me across the sand and put his arms about me as I'd longed to have him do.

"It would be good if your father could be here now, if he could hold you like this."

I didn't want him to hold me as my father might have done. But that didn't matter either. Where there had been no one and nothing, there were now two people whom I could care about. Either could hurt me, humiliate me, turn away from me. And that didn't matter either. The thawing of the ice had gone too far to be stopped, and I wept against Gunnar's shoulder, while he stroked my hair and held me till I quieted. Then I stepped back from him of my own accord and wiped my eyes with the big handkerchief he offered me.

"It hurts a great deal to love," I said wonderingly. "I never knew that it could be such a hurting thing."

His smile was grave. "Yes. It is a hurting thing to love," he said, and I knew he was remembering Astrid.

"Just the same it's better to be alive and able to be hurt." I felt my own astonishment that I could say such words and believe in them.

"And now, because you have this new feeling about Laura," Gunnar went on, "you must help the rest of us to discourage her from this mad thing she plans to do."

For a moment I stared at him helplessly. I was discovering something else about my own feelings. There was loyalty as well as love.

I shook my head vehemently. "No! I'm on her side. If that's what she wants, she must go back and face her world, and become what she's now prepared to become, as she never was before. I think she may be the greatest actress in America today—if she has her way."

He was truly angry at that. I saw the storminess of his own harsh country in his eyes. I saw what he believed and knew that he would not change. All that I'd said about love had been canceled out because he still thought I meant to punish Laura, that I wanted to see her bring about her own self-destruction.

I had meant to tell him what had happened last night, and what Irene had told me this morning. Now I would tell him nothing. I turned away, as angry as he—and desperately hurt. I walked back toward the house and he came after me on the path with his long strides, in time to open the doors for me, icily polite.

We found Laura and Gunnar's mother talking placidly in the living room where we had left them. From the frame on the piano Astrid's face smiled at me as if in recognition. Now I would have liked to know about her. I wanted to know what she had done when Gunnar froze into an imitation of his own Norwegian winter. Or had he never frozen against her? She had a gentle, smiling face. What had she been to him? How much had she loved him? All these things I wanted to know—and never would.

I looked across the room at Laura, and saw her, not as the actress I'd admired, but as a woman. Tempestuous, unreasonable, often self-engrossed and self-indulgent—yet with so much more to her complex nature than I had been willing to concede. She *had* been strong enough to recognize that, for her, her work must come first, and that she would destroy any who came too close to her. For the first time I realized that such decisions were not ruthlessly made, not made without pain and sacrifice—but out of her own self-knowledge. Other women who had the same drive to become stars had tried the opposite course, and often their lives were strewn with broken marriages, and children even more bitterly damaged than I had been. Laura, at least, had not attempted marriage until she was free of Hollywood.

She must have sensed my attention upon her, for she glanced at me across the room—and gave me her famous smile. It was the smile of Maggie Thornton, but I knew something else about it now. It was, first of all, Laura's smile. My own lips moved into a strangeness, an expression with which I was not familiar, and I knew I was smiling back at her in a new way. She recognized the difference, and read it better than I did.

"You see!" she said to Gunnar, with a small triumph in her voice. "We're friends now, Leigh and I."

I knew very well that she took pride in subjugating me. But for once I didn't bristle. I would learn to accept what she could give, without asking for too much more. And, however clumsily, I would give her in return something she had never before known—and perhaps would not value—the affection of a daughter.

"I am not sure that you are friends," Gunnar said darkly. "You perhaps give your trust too easily, Laura."

She smiled at him, paying no attention to his words, though I knew now that he did not trust me, and that he would undercut me with her at every turn.

"Gunnar, play your fiddle for us—for Leigh," she commanded. "I'm sure she's never head a Hardanger fiddle."

He went to a cabinet and took out the instrument. Then he brought it to show me with cool courtesy, explaining that the peasant fiddle had been known in Norway as early as the 1600's. It had eight strings, four being understrings. The flat bridge was beautifully inlaid with mother-of-pearl and topped by a crowned lion's head. It was in the town of Hardanger that these fiddles had first been made, and so they bore its name.

"A country friend taught me to play it when I was very young," Gunnar said. "The volume is strong. It is best heard outside."

He opened doors that gave upon the rocky wall which held off the sea, and stepped through them. We sat indoors and listened to him play. The music was strange and lively, the country melodies rather like the sound of Scottish tunes played on the bagpipe. This was the sound I had heard that night in Kalfaret. It was music to be danced to, but it also had a wild, almost mournful, undercurrent that belonged to the mountains and valleys and fjords of Norway. Even though the bagpipe was a wind instrument, and the Hardanger fiddle stringed, the music was polyphonic and very like.

I watched Gunnar as he played, and felt the pain of new knowledge and awareness. It was a pain from which I did not rebel, as once I would have done. The novelty of feeling fully alive—or letting myself be vulnerable—was something I would not reject.

Laura tapped her foot to the tunes and smiled her delight. "You should see the dances in full dress," she told me. "The peasant costumes are different for every region, and they are unbelievably beautiful. The men dress up as well as the women, and it's all quite exciting. If you were to be here longer we would go out to Fanaseter when the season begins and watch them dance the old dances there on the farm. We would eat goat cheese, and those tiny delicious waffles made in the shape of a heart and served cold. But there's no time, no time."

Gunnar heard her and stopped his playing, came inside. "Why is there no time?"

"I've already sent off several letters," she told him. "I have begun to make arrangements. I won't wait. I'll follow up my letters in person. And Leigh will go back to New York."

"Having done as much damage here as she can possibly do," Gunnar said, no longer troubling to be polite.

Laura came up from the sofa and went directly to him. "Oh, no! You don't understand. Leigh has brought me to life. She has challenged me, disapproved of me, shaken me into being alive. She has made me see that I was being sorry for myself and playing the coward. Now I am willing to take the risks I must take. She has brought me out to meet life again."

"All these things your marriage did not do for you?" Gunnar said.

His mother stirred on the sofa and spoke to him firmly. "Come now! You must not say such things to our guests."

"The time for politeness is past," Gunnar countered, equally firm. "You don't know everything that has been happening, Mother."

Laura came to me and touched my arm. "It's time for us to go, Leigh. Gunnar is in one of his dark Norwegian moods."

She went to Mrs. Thoresen and kissed her lightly on the cheek. "I will see you again before I leave, and we will try to have a good visit. Gunnar, where are our coats, if you please?"

She made her exit with dignity and if his words about her marriage had pierced her guard, wounded her, she showed it not at all. He drove us in silence back to Kalfaret. When he got out of the car at the foot of the steps, Laura pulled down his head and kissed him on the cheek as she'd done his mother.

"You'll be over being cross with us soon. I'm looking forward to a lovely evening at the theater Wednesday night. Shall we take our own car and meet you there?"

Her pretty ways were always winning, and he smiled at her wryly, agreeing. For me he had hardly a glance as I said good-bye and followed Laura up the steps.

Above us the house waited and the familiar sense of foreboding descended upon me as we followed the walk along the side and waited for Irene to let us in the front door.

Chapter 13

That night the rain began, and I found out what rain was like in Bergen. It rained all the next day and the waters of the harbor and the lakes turned an angry gray. Clouds boiled down over the mountains and Ulriken was lost in a black canopy. Rain beat upon the crocuses in the garden, upon the sleepy slanting roofs, and water rushed along the gutters. The traffic did not cease its flow, nor did the Bergensere stay indoors because of the weather. Rain was a normal condition and it deterred no one from his purpose.

Laura remained undepressed by the lowering weather, but I began to feel trapped and restless. Now I had too much time to think, too many things to weigh and question, unfamiliar emotions to cope with. I left Laura alone hardly at all, and whether her new husband liked it or not, I slept in her room at night. She wanted me there and I made no effort to oppose her wish.

Nothing had really changed between us except inside myself. Perhaps I was a little gentler with her, but she was still tart and imperious with me. She knew that something had given way inside me, but she took no advantage of the fact. If anything, she held me even more at arm's length, making it clear that for her I was a journalist, and nothing more.

Apparently the rain bore down heavily upon the other members of the household as well. Miles and Donia snapped at each other, Irene watched them with suspicion and restrained herself with difficulty from being rude to Donia. I suppose we all watched one another. All, that is, except Laura. Since she knew where danger lay, she relaxed in my company and managed to laugh in the face of whatever might threaten her.

The matter of a passport, plane reservations—all these things she was busily taking care of, asking no help from anyone, knowing the others might impede and delay her purpose. The day of her departure had not been set, but it would be in a week or two, she felt sure.

I made no plans of my own. I had no plans. When Laura left, I supposed I would go back to New York. Whether I would ever see her again, I didn't know—though I would miss her. Now I could accept that. Gunnar I would undoubtedly never see again, and that would leave me with an aching emptiness for a very long time. Once back in New York, I would no longer be the same person I'd been when I left, but I didn't know yet how the change in me would take effect. I could only wonder what good it was going to do me to come alive, to learn how to feel these new emotions, when both the people I could feel most strongly about were soon to be dropped out of my life.

It was late afternoon of Wednesday, the day of the play. We were not to meet at the theater, after all. Miles planned to take us to an early supper that night, which would include Gunnar. I had come downstairs to put on the indigo silk that was the one dressier frock I'd brought along. Laura said Bergen audiences did not wear evening dress for the theater, but she was apparently making her own exception to the rule, for I'd seen the brown and white organza she had laid out on her bed. It was a couturier design of an ageless style. Irene was to help her dress and I was in my downstairs room, clipping carved ivory buttons to my ears and listening to the rain.

Laura tapped on the door, and rushed in breathless, wearing a negligee clasped loosely about her.

"Have you seen Irene? She was to come and zip me up."

"I haven't seen her," I said. "But I'll take care of the zipping, if you like. Do I look all right for the evening?"

She hardly glanced at me, but walked straight across the room to her portrait, where it hung on the wall face out, as I left it these days.

"Look!" she cried, and there was a catch in her voice.

I went to stand beside her and saw that something new had been added to the eerie game. Where I had scratched a cypher to block the game from X's winning, now a large X was cut across the O, negating its purpose.

Laura grasped my arm and her fingers felt like ice, her teeth had begun to chatter.

"Don't," I said. "It means nothing. You mustn't be upset by this sort of nonsense. I'll stay with you. Nothing is going to happen. Someone wants to frighten you, and you mustn't let them succeed."

She stared at her younger self looking out from the portrait—that lovely young woman, so ready for loving.

"It's the beginning of the end," she said. "The final warning. Time is slipping away."

I started to protest, to soothe her, but she turned from me. "I must find Irene. Help me look for her, Leigh."

I didn't see why she should feel such urgency about locating Irene, but I humored her. While she searched one part of the downstairs, I searched another. No one was there.

"She's not upstairs, either," Laura said. "Her room's empty, and Miles and Donia say they haven't seen her. We must find her, Leigh. We must!"

"Perhaps she's gone out on some errand," I suggested. "Why don't you let me help with your dress, and we'll wait for her to come back?"

But she would not wait. "No—I have a feeling that something's wrong. Leigh, put on your rain things and look in the garden—look around the house outside."

Her anxiety was contagious, and I began to feel uneasy as I put on my raincoat and boots, tied a scarf over my hair. She let me out the front door, where I was able to see along the walk that led to the street steps. The side yard was empty. A wild wind had begun to blow, and rain slashed into my face, thrashed the limbs of trees and filled the gray afternoon with a roaring of sound. I squelched my way around the back of the house, where only a small border of space intervened before the steep rise of the hill. No one would have climbed up there and I hurried around to the dining room side, where there was a small garden, with flower beds that were beginning to take on a tinge of green.

I saw her at once. She lay face down on brownish ooze while the rain beat upon her back. She wore no coat, as though she had not intended to come outdoors, and her gray dress was already soaked through. The dark coil of her hair had loosened and lay wet upon her shoulders. I knelt and touched her, called her name. When she moaned softly and stirred under my hand, I ran to the dining room doors, where Laura stood waiting for me.

"I've found her. We'll have to get help to bring her in," I said. "She's lying out there near the flower bed."

Laura clapped a hand to her mouth and stepped back into the room as I passed her.

"Miles," I said, "—I'll get Miles."

For an instant she moved as if to stop me. Then she

dropped into a leather chair and sat there shivering. I didn't stop to get out of my wet things, but ran upstairs, calling for Miles. Both he and Donia came to their doors and stared at me.

"It's Irene!" I cried. "She's lying in the garden near the dining room doors. I think she's been hurt."

Miles ran downstairs, and Donia came after him. Laura remained in her chair, while Donia and I watched Miles go out in the rain and gather Irene's limp body into his arms. We held the doors while he brought her dripping into the room—as Gunnar had carried me only two days ago. Donia ran to spread a wool throw over the living room sofa, and Miles put Irene down carefully. She stirred and reached a hand to her wet hair.

"My head," she moaned. "It hurts me."

Miles bent to examine her and found the bruise at the side of her head. I watched him, feeling as cold as Laura, finding that my own teeth had a tendency to chatter. There had been only soft earth in the garden where Irene had fallen—there had been nothing there, as far as I had seen, that could have caused the bruise on her head when she fell.

I returned to the dining room, where Laura sat huddled in her chair. She looked up with wide, terror-filled eyes.

"It *has* begun," she said. "It's the beginning of the end. That cross on the canvas—and now Irene—"

"Don't fall apart," I told her sharply. "I'm going out to look for something."

She stayed where she was, gripping the carved arms of the chair with tense hands while I went into the rainy garden. I found what I sought almost at once, but there was a squeamish moment before I could lean over to pick up the long brass candlestick where it lay on the brown grass. The last time I'd seen it, it had stood on a table near the garden doors in the dining room, where Laura had left it when she had carried it downstairs.

Rain would have washed all fingerprints away—it did not matter if I picked it up. The curving body of the dragon which writhed about the stick felt cold to my fingers, and the tiny scales formed an unpleasant texture to my touch. I carried it back to Laura.

She covered her face with her hands at sight of it, and I took the candlestick into the room where Irene lay. She looked in my direction as I came in, saw what I carried. There was shock in her eyes as she fixed her gaze upon the dull brass. I gave the candlestick to Miles, though he seemed reluctant to take it, and I watched him, and watched Donia.

"Someone must have struck her down with this," I said. "How did it happen, Irene? You had no coat on—why were you in the garden?"

She started to say something, and then looked past me to the door. I turned and saw Laura coming slowly into the room. Irene closed her eyes and said nothing.

I prodded her, in spite of Miles's disapproval. "Who struck you, Irene?"

Laura came close to the couch and stood looking down at her, so that when Irene's lashes fluttered open she saw Laura there above her.

"I don't know," she murmured. "I don't remember what happened."

Laura had silenced her. It was Laura who would not allow that one name to be spoken.

"You'll be all right," Miles told Irene. "A slight headache, perhaps. I'll give you something to take."

His words seemed forced, too casual for the circumstances. I couldn't endure what was happening.

"Look!" I cried. "We've got to do something! Laura's portrait was defaced. The binding on her ski was damaged. I was pushed downstairs. And now this. Yet no one asks questions or points a finger. What do you all know that makes you keep quiet? Are you waiting for someone to be killed?"

Irene closed her eyes as though the shrillness of my voice hurt her. The other three stared at me, but not at each other.

"No one has been seriously injured," Laura said. "Let it alone, Leigh."

Miles leaned toward Irene, ignoring me. "Would you like to go up to your room?"

If Irene felt pain or dizziness as she pulled herself upright, she suppressed the fact. "Yes, please—I'll go upstairs."

"Take my arm," Miles said.

As he waited for Irene to steady herself, he looked at Donia for the first time, and his sister stared back at him. It seemed to me that a challenge was flung between them—one had challenged, and the other had picked up the figurative glove. But I did not know which was which.

"Are you all right?" I said to Laura.

She seemed to have recovered herself and she nodded almost fiercely. "Yes. If you'll come and help me dress—"

"Do you still plan to go out?" I asked in surprise. "After what's happened—"

"Of course we're going out. Irene will be glad to be left alone. She knows she's perfectly safe in an empty house. Safer than if any of us stayed home."

"How can you possibly—" I began, but she shook her head at me, her expression tense.

"I must. I must," she said. "For a few more days I must."

Miles help Irene to her room, and Laura followed, with me right after her. When she was sure that everything had been done that Miles wished, she drew me into her room and flung off the negligee.

I helped her reluctantly into the brown and white organza. It was a dramatic dress, with a long, flaring hemline, and a scooped-out neck edged with white. She set it off with simple gold jewelry—a necklace and delicate earrings.

I watched her in continuing amazement. I wanted to question her, but I knew it was useless. She had a good suspicion of what had happened in the garden, but she had no intention of telling me what it was. She seemed filled with nervous energy, almost with an elation that I did not understand. It was as if her courage rose with evidence of danger all around her. Irene had spoken about murder, and Irene had been struck down. Yet when I had zipped up Laura's gown, she stood looking at her pale, beautiful self in a long mirror as if this were any evening and nothing eventful had happened.

"The warning of X came to nothing," she said. "I might be dead by now—but I'm not. I'm alive."

I agreed with her dryly. "Two days ago there was another attack. That time I took the brunt. Now Irene has done the same thing. In either case it might have been you. Don't you think you'd better save yourself—and us—by speaking out."

She clasped a filigree bracelet around her wrist, not looking at me. "No. Not yet. I have my plane reservation for Saturday. There are only a few days left to get through. Then I'll be free—safe."

"Does Miles know when you're leaving? Or Donia?"

"Neither of them knows. You'll take me to the plane in the taxi. Then you'll get yourself away from Bergen."

"And leave Irene to their tender mercies?"

"No one will be hurt, once I'm gone. I'm the catalyst. They'll separate. They won't stay in the house."

"I hope you know what you're doing," I said doubtfully. "Would you like me to come with you?"

Her reflection in the mirror gave me a surprised look. "To Hollywood? But of course that would be very good for your piece, wouldn't it? A firsthand account of the return of Laura Worth!"

"Yes, it would be very good," I agreed quietly.

She turned from the mirror, a vision in brown organza, the pallor of her face somehow suiting the gown far better than high color would have done. Only her lips were red. Her long lashes were brushed with black, her lids tinted faintly blue.

"Don't try to look after me," she said. "Except for a little while recently, I've never been the leaning type. I don't want a daughter in my life. I never have. Go back to New York and forget me, Leigh Hollins."

"I'll do that." I answered her carefully, revealing nothing. This was what I'd asked for by giving too much of myself that day at Gunnar's house.

"We'll be leaving soon," she went on. "It's too bad it's raining, but I have a cape I can wear over my dress. And you're ready in your raincoat and boots. It's nearly time to leave. I'll look in on Irene and then we'll call the others."

She was in control of everything—of herself and the situation. She could be hard—without feeling, without empathy. Once she had told me that she must live only from day to day —and that was exactly what she was doing. Perhaps from hour to hour. I wished that for my own salvation I might go back to hating her. But now, though she could hurt me as never before, I was no longer angry with her—but only amazed. She had a strength that made me feel that I was soft clay by comparison. I had ceased to know my own shape and form.

Too often lately there was a sense of tears burning behind my eyes, a sense of yearning, though I wasn't sure what I longed for. Perhaps what I really wanted was the solace of my old protective anger. I wanted my shield back—that shield which had for so long guarded me from outside hurt. Only it was gone now—perhaps forever. I watched Laura, and saw that however misguided she might be, she was beautiful and brave and unbeaten. I wanted to see her escape from whatever tormented her, and I knew I would give myself to helping her in that purpose—whether she thanked me or not. At least she would use me, and for a little while longer I could be near her, I could warm myself at her bright flame. This was a longing which had been in me all my life, and which I'd denied. It had always been a part of my admiration for the actress,

Laura Worth, although I'd convinced myself that it was only the actress I admired.

She was looking at me strangely, questioningly, and I turned away, not wanting her to see too much.

"Are you ready to go?" I said.

The cape she flung about her shoulders was a dramatic scarlet gabardine, with a black velvet hood to protect her hair. She pulled no covering over her fragile slippers and I wondered if they would be ruined on the way to the car.

In the hall she went directly to Irene's room, with a tossed request to me to summon Miles and Donia. I stopped at Miles's door, but before I could rap, I heard voices. I knew he was talking to his sister, and I listened intently, hoping for some betrayal.

"I'll get your plane reservation for home as soon as I can," he was telling her angrily. "I've stood as much as I mean to —we'll have no more of this."

Donia's reply came in a voice so choked that I couldn't make out the words.

"Come along," Miles said curtly, "get your things on—we'll be leaving for the theater soon."

This time I could hear her shrill answer. "I won't go! I'd rather stay home than—"

"You'll come," Miles said and I heard her gasp, as though he might have touched her roughly.

I backed away from the door and as Laura left Irene's room, Miles and Donia came out of his. Donia's head was lowered as she busied herself with pulling on a plastic rain hood. Laura gave her a quick glance and then looked away as we all went downstairs.

We drove through the rain into town and only Laura seemed determinedly gay and lighthearted. This was her defense, I knew—her gallant defiance of whatever threatened her. When Gunnar joined us in the attractive dining room of the Hotel Orion, her insistence upon a festive mood had its effect upon the rest of us. When I started to tell Gunnar what had happened back at the house, Laura stopped me at once, her look a little too bright, her manner imperious.

"We'll talk about nothing unpleasant tonight," she insisted. "This is to be a lovely evening. An evening to remember." And she gave herself to making it so, in spite of any strains that might lie beneath the surface in all of us.

Only when it came to Miles did she sometimes falter into uncertainty, as though she were torn between cajoling and flouting. His response was carefully courteous, but I know that he watched her as though he waited for something he knew might be eventually forthcoming. Some cracking of her guard? I wondered.

I sat next to Gunnar, and he talked to me pleasantly, though he watched Laura's electric manner in dismay. It was as if he too waited for some breaking point.

I have no remembrance of what I ate that night, though the food was good—everyone assured everyone of that. Afterwards we drove in two cars to the theater. Laura insisted that she and I could go with Gunnar, leaving Miles to bring his sister. She seemed uneasy with Miles, and I wondered if he might be putting pressure on her against going to California. I wondered too what quarreling the brother and sister would do on the way to the theater. But there was no telling when we arrived and got out of the cars, hurrying through the rain to the lobby of the impressive gray stone building of the National Theater. Donia looked no more nor less baleful than usual.

In the marble lobby, we waited for the men to park the cars, and Laura made a dramatic figure in her long scarlet cape. She removed her hood and her hair shone glossy and dark beneath the light of chandeliers. All around us people were coming in out of the rain—a quiet, well-mannered audience of mixed ages, though perhaps with few of the very young for this particular nostalgic play. There were glances in Laura's direction, and perhaps there were some who recognized her, but good manners prevailed and we were not disturbed.

When the men rejoined us, we went through glass doors and up red carpeted marble stairs, where busts of the famous looked down upon us from niches in the wall. These stairs were meant for someone dressed gloriously for the evening as Laura was dressed. She went up at Miles's side, the cape flowing, her head held high. I saw Donia's resentful glance as she and I climbed the stairs on either side of Gunnar.

The upper hall ran in a semicircle, and there were paintings on the walls. Our box had its own cloakroom and an attendant sold Miles programs and ushered us to our seats. Laura, Donia and I took the red chairs at the rail, with the men just behind us. Laura chose the seat nearest the audience, and she looked about the filling house with a certain regal arrogance that could only have been worn by a woman who knew her own importance. She was as conspicuous as the blue-curtained stage, and faces turned toward her as the audience settled into red-upholstered seats. Even those in the steep balcony looked down at her, and there was no question of which one of us held the curious interest of the theater. They pretended not to look, and I guessed that she had been recognized.

Behind me, Gunnar chuckled softly, pleased at the recognition. He leaned toward me. "This is what she was born for. She is nearly sixty, and there is not a woman in the house who can match her."

I could agree wholeheartedly. "I think she's wonderful," I whispered back.

Behind Laura, Miles watched in glum disapproval, liking none of this. He heard my words and frowned at me, then bent toward his wife.

Before he could speak, I stopped him. "Let her have her moment in the spotlight. Perhaps she needs it more than we ordinary people can realize."

The house lights began to dim. The old, old moment of theater magic was approaching. In the box across from us two women who had kept well back in the shadows came forward to sit beside the man at the rail. How different from Laura! The outer curtain rose to give way to the inner one and we could see that the head of a bear rug poked roguishly toward the audience from beneath the lower folds of curtain. There was a quieting of chatter, a stilling of rustled programs —the curtain parted and the scene of a house in Brooklyn early in the century was revealed.

It was, perhaps, a Brooklyn house with a Norwegian accent, and when they came onstage it seemed startling to hear the two conniving sisters speaking Norwegian. Nevertheless, while I didn't understand a word, the comedy of the play caught me up. For a little while I could forget Kalfaret, forget that brass candlestick and Irene lying face down in the rain. Teddy Brewster made his famous dash up the stairs shouting, "Char-arge!" in English as he stormed his own San Juan Hill, and the audience roared. The glass decanter played its deadly role, and the romance began to unfold.

During the long speeches I couldn't understand, I sometimes watched Laura, and saw that she seemed as absorbed as a child. The glow of warm, pinkish-yellow light from the stage touched her face, her parted lips, reflected itself luminously in her eyes. She was reveling in this make-believe world that she knew so well, and I was glad that she could be drawn out of herself for a little while, and freed of whatever terror ruled her life.

In the shadows behind her, Miles sat motionless, seeming never to stir. He neither laughed nor applauded. Beside me, Donia was the most restless one in the box. She could not sit quietly in her seat, but wriggled about, staring at Laura, at me, and sometimes back into the box at her brother. I think she was scarcely aware of the affairs which progressed upon the stage.

When the curtain came down on Act I and the house lights went on, Gunnar leaned toward me. "Would you like to walk about? There is a refreshment room, if you care to—"

It was Donia who stopped him with one of her strange little cries. "Look!" she said breathlessly.

She was staring at Laura, and Gunnar and I looked at her too. She had not moved since the curtains had closed. She was unaware of the bustle in the theater, in the opposite boxes. Her eyes were fixed unblinkingly upon the blue curtain, and she was no longer charmed. Miles noticed and he stood up in the box and put his hand on her shoulder, bent toward her. She winced away from his touch.

"They were talking about murder down there," she said softly. "This is a play which jokes about murder."

"Of course," Miles said, but his look upon her was wary. "You know this old chestnut very well."

Laura slipped out of her chair and stood up. "I want to go home. I don't want to see the rest of it."

We stared at her, aghast at this sudden turn. I think Miles was about to take his own firm stand and insist that she stay and see it through, but Gunnar was quicker than the rest of us.

"Of course, Laura," he said. "If the play is wrong for you, I am sorry. Of course you must not stay if it upsets you."

She looked at him gratefully. "Thank you for understanding, Gunnar. This is something I can't help. But I know what I must do now. You must come with us back to the house. You know how to run the projector, and—"

Miles broke in on her words. "Projector! Laura, what are you talking about?"

"I have to watch it! Miles, please don't try to stop me. Now is the time! I have the film of *The Whisperer*. Gunnar will help us. Now—tonight. I want to run it through. I must, I must!"

It was Gunnar who quieted her. "I will come, if your husband permits. If it will help you in some way to watch this picture, then perhaps this is what you must do."

Miles started to protest, but she would not listen. "I want Leigh to see the film," she said.

"I've already seen it several times," I told her, but she paid no attention. She was already making her way up the few steps that led out of the box. There was nothing to do but follow her. Miles was clearly angry, but he could not stop her.

We put on our coats and Laura went first in her scarlet cape. Playgoers parted before her. The very way she moved, swift and sure of herself, opened a way to let her through.

While we waited on the steps for the men to bring the cars, Donia drew a little apart, as if she disliked standing near that dramatically scarlet-clad figure. I was able to speak to Laura alone.

"Why are you doing this?"

Her eyes had a fixed, bright look, and she did not answer me.

"Isn't it dangerous?" I persisted.

"If that's so—" her lips barely formed the words, "then that's how it must be."

Outside, the rain had stopped, and while the lobby behind us was thronged with those who moved about between the acts, the drive before the theater was empty. The two men returned quickly with cars. Bergen streets glistened wet by lamplight as we followed them. On the mountain the funicular crawled upward like a great lighted worm, and among the clusters of bright lights along the hillside Kalfaret waited.

Kalfaret and *The Whisperer*.

Chapter 14

Long ago Laura had purchased expensive equipment for the showing of her films at home to certain select friends. Before she had left the States she had collected the films of several of her pictures, and had them transferred to more durable film. For a long while she had looked at none of these pictures, but now Gunnar set up the screen at one end of the living room, and Miles, glowering and reluctant, helped to move furniture.

Irene had left her bed by the time we reached the house. She was never one to coddle herself, and she came downstairs to see why we were home early. She seemed to have recovered well enough from the bump on her head, though like Miles she was clearly disturbed over Laura's plans.

While she and I were arranging chairs for the "audience," she spoke to me in a low voice.

"You know what this means, Miss Hollins. There will be hysteria tonight. She will make herself thoroughly ill."

"Why does she want to do this?" I asked.

"I think she hopes to smoke someone out of his cover. That can be a possible reason. Perhaps that's what she intended when she put on that little performance with your help the other night. Only she failed."

"I don't understand," I objected. "If she knows perfectly well who is behind what's been happening, why is there any need to smoke someone out? She has only to point her finger."

"Perhaps she's not as sure as she thinks," Irene said. "Or perhaps she intends a wearing away, a breaking down—a turning of the tables. I don't think it will work."

"Irene," I said, "who struck you down in the garden this afternoon?"

She would not meet my eyes, but she had chosen her course. "No one struck me down. I stumbled and hit my head."

"And the candlestick?"

"I was carrying the candlestick."

"In the garden in the rain?"

"Perhaps you have a better theory?"

I hadn't, and when Laura sat down, I took the chair next to her with a greater uneasiness than ever. Miles was on her other side, with Donia next to him, while Irene sat beside me. When Gunnar, whose post was at the equipment behind us, turned off the lights, there was a slight commotion. Donia bounced up from her chair, crying out that she couldn't bear to watch this beastly film, and ran into the hall. Miles went after her and brought her grimly back to the room. After that, she whimpered softly now and then, and when the film began to roll I could see that she had ducked her head and was not looking at the screen.

This was a picture I had seen often enough, but never under such circumstances, and I found myself moved and fascinated by what was going on before my eyes. The young Laura walked across the screen, beautiful, for all her subdued makeup, and there was an aching in me for all young beauty which must be lost so soon. The actor who had played Helen Bradley's husband had been young at the time, but he was dead now, and that added to the sense of another day, another time, a sense of ghostly presence.

The little maid—that bit actress who had never made her way into larger parts—appeared on her knees, polishing the fatal iron doorstop. Her hair was frizzy, her roundly plump face expressed constant fright.

Beside me, Laura's hand slipped through the crook of my arm, and I could feel her fingers pressing into my flesh. I covered her hand with my own, trying to still the emotion I knew was rising in her. Irene was right. It was likely to be Laura Worth whom the watching of this film was most likely to upset. The other night she had been able to speak Helen Bradley's lines when we'd run through those few scenes. But this was very different.

The photography had been remarkable in the picture, and in spite of our small screen, the mood created by the play of light and shadow added to the intensity of emotion portrayed by the actors. I knew the moment when the first whispering voice would come out of nowhere, and I felt Laura's fingers tighten upon my arm.

"*Listen . . .*" said the voice on the screen, and then more faintly, "*Listen . . .*" On the stairs Helen Bradley gripped the rail and looked as though she might faint and roll down the steps. She clung to the rail, supported herself, and managed to descend to the gloomy hall below.

The sound of that voice seemed to echo through the real room in which we sat, but no one in the small audience moved or made a sound. Not even Laura. Only her cold fingers on my arm told me what she was enduring, suffering.

The fourth character in the play was on the screen now— the distant cousin of Robert Bradley, who was visiting in the house, and was in love with Helen. He had been played by a minor actor, who, like the maid, had disappeared from the screen. He was the villain of the piece, of course. I studied his young, rather ominous good looks, but they meant nothing to me. I had never seen him in anything again.

The scene was played where the young, nervous maid dropped her loaded tray in the presence of Robert Bradley. Her round, lugubrious face contorted in fear and she burst into tears, throwing her apron over her frizzy head.

A few chairs away Donia wriggled as she had done at the theater, and her creaking chair played a counterpoint to the eerie sound track that was an accompaniment to scenes that had no dialogue. Even Donia was watching the screen now.

It was strange that a story so familiar should be able to grip us all again as it had done when we first saw it. Just as we can read a book for the second time and be caught up in the drama, even when we know the ending, so it was with this picture. Once I turned my head to look back at Gunnar and saw his face bathed in the ghostly light that was reflected from the screen. He saw me turn toward him and nodded to me as if in reassurance.

But nothing happened. Nothing really happened. Whoever knew the secret of another whispering voice sat utterly still among us and betrayed nothing. All was quiet until the scene where Helen Bradley once more came down the stairs in that long, slow shot where we watched in something close to agony, watched her go into that Victorian parlor where her husband lay dead upon the floor—that scene in which the doorstop was absent as a prop, because it had been used for a more deadly real-life purpose before this scene was put on film.

The camera moved about the parlor, and Laura gasped softly beside me. It panned from a seashell on a whatnot shelf, from the clasped hands of a china paperweight on a table, to the carpet and a pair of feet lying inert with the toes up. Slowly it began to move up the length of that prone body— and suddenly there was a dreadful sound in the room. A sound that was not on the screen.

Laura's hand was gone from my arm. She was on her feet, crying out her terrible words. "I killed him! I killed him! It's because of me that he died! I killed him!"

Gunnar turned off the projection machine and sprang for the lights. Miles took her by the shoulders and shook her sharply, shook her into gasping sobs.

"I knew this would happen," Irene said grimly.

Miles held her as she wept, but there was no sympathy in his eyes, only condemnation.

"I've known it all along," he said grimly, holding her away from him, forcing her to listen. "I guessed it from the first. You could have told me. I would have protected you. I was there that night in the studio, you know. It was my footprints they found. I followed Cass to the studio because I was afraid of what he intended. I got into the grounds while he was arguing with the watchman. I waited inside the gates until he went to the sound stage across the lot. Then I went after him and let myself in. There was a delay because I lost him among the buildings. When I got there it was already too late. I found him lying on the set, and I knew my own danger. I let myself out the fire door at the rear, and when you screamed and the watchman ran to see what was wrong, I got out of the studio. Donia was waiting for me in the car, and we drove back to the theater and were in time to appear with the crowd coming out."

"You might have come to me," Laura moaned. "You might have helped me then."

"I'd have been no good to you. If the police could have proved I was in the studio that night, you know what they'd have done to me. I had to get away. Later you told me you were innocent. You told me you had nothing to do with it. And you came through free. You didn't need help from me. But you could have told me the truth. You could have trusted me."

She wept against his shoulder, bitterly, wordlessly.

Across the room Donia had curled herself into a chair as though she wanted to keep out of the way, make herself tiny and invisible. But she watched everything with her bright eyes —like a frightened monkey. None of us paid much attention to her. As always, Laura held the center of the stage.

"Let me take her upstairs," Irene said.

Miles shook his head. "She needs my attention tonight. You're coming with me to my room, Laura. You're staying with me tonight."

For the first time she tried to pull herself together. "No—no, Miles. I must stay with Leigh. Leigh mustn't be left alone." She flung out a hand toward me.

I think she did not want to face him any further that night, but there was no way to stop him from what he planned. He was darkly adamant and purposeful.

I tried to soothe her. "I'll stay in your room tonight. I'll be right next door, and we'll both be safe enough. You mustn't worry about me."

She seemed to know when she was beaten, or perhaps she no longer had the strength to oppose any of us. She let him lead her from the room. Donia had disappeared, and only Irene and Gunnar and I remained. Irene paced the floor, angry and indignant.

"What insanity!" she cried. "What a ridiculous, mad thing for her to do!"

"She's not mad," I said sharply.

Irene gave me a scornful look. "Of course she's not. Only foolish—to play out the line like that. To put herself into someone's hands. I hope she's alive when morning comes."

She stalked out of the room in the wake of the others and I dropped weakly into a chair.

Gunnar spoke sadly. "What a terrible thing that she has kept this secret upon her conscience all these years."

I contradicted him a little wildly. "It's not true! It's not true that she killed him. I don't believe it for a moment. Not even though she claims it herself."

"What do you mean? How do you know?"

"I don't know. I only feel that there's something terribly wrong in all this. Something we don't understand. I think she's in dreadful danger now. Tonight I'll stay in the dressing room next to Miles's bedroom. I'll stay up and listen—so she won't be alone if she needs help."

I was pacing now, as Irene had paced, and Gunnar came to me. "Leigh, my dear," he said, and put his arms about me, holding me with his strength, his solidity. I put my head against his shoulder and let all the old Leigh whom I'd never really liked ebb away from me.

For a little while he held me, and then he kissed me on the mouth. Not altogether gently. And I kissed him back.

"Victor would be pleased with you," he said when he held me away, and I knew he was laughing at me gently, lovingly. All his anger with me had gone away.

"There is much to be settled," he went on. "You cannot leave Bergen quickly. First, we must find a way to help Laura. And then there is you and me to talk about."

I didn't feel like talking, like settling anything. I didn't feel in the least like being sensible. I only wanted him to hold me, kiss me, melt away the ice. But I think he was a little afraid of me by that time—a little afraid of himself.

"Come," he said. "See me to the door. I will phone you early in the morning. In the meantime, I will plan."

Whatever plans he might have made would have been futile, though I did not know that then. The undertow had already caught us in its grip and was carrying us toward the pounding sea and the rocky shore. We were all aboard that ship in Gunnar's painting.

He kissed me again at the doorway and asked me to watch out for myself as well as Laura.

When he had gone I went back to the living room and stood looking at the blank white screen on the wall. How strange that something which had no reality, that could vanish at the click of a switch had so vital a life of its own that it lived afterwards in the imagination. I could almost hear the whispering voice again, though the house was utterly still. Only the sound of Gunnar's car reached me from outdoors. I felt utterly and frighteningly alone. Except for Laura, I had no friend here.

I went up to her room and found that she must have come in for her night things. The door to the dressing room was closed. I opened it, stepping between scented rows of Laura's garments, to stand listening at the door to Miles's room. I could hear a murmur of voices. Nothing disturbing in tone. The rest of the house was quiet. Donia and Irene would have gone to their rooms. I got ready for bed and then stepped out upon Laura's balcony.

The city still wore the wet, shiny look that is the aftermath of rain, and the lights of the bridges glowed above their own reflections in the water. There were lights in the houses along Flöyen, and on the hillside occupied by Kalfaret. Only the area close about the house was dark and quiet. In Miles's room a lamp near the window flicked on, forming a sudden patch of light in the garden, where there had been only darkness a moment before. Someone sat on the stone wall down there, with a white face upturned and attention fixed upon the window of Miles's room.

I stepped closer to the balcony rail, peering down. Behind me, I had left Laura's room in darkness, so I could not be easily seen. A woman sat upon the wall, and I saw that it was Donia Jaffe. I must have made some sound, for her attention shifted from Miles's room to my shadowy figure on the balcony. There was a moment of stillness, while we stared at each other and only the dripping sound of wet foliage could be heard close by. Then she scuttled across the garden and through the doors beneath the balcony. I went inside and kept very still, listening. I heard her come upstairs and go into her own room.

As I got ready for bed I tried to put them all out of my mind and think only of Gunnar, and of the ice that had melted in me so thoroughly that I could feel warm at the very memory of his touch. But I was not free to think about him with undivided attention. All the events of the evening crowded back upon me and I remembered Laura at the theater—a lovely dramatic figure in her scarlet cape. Laura crying out that this was a play about murder, and she would not stay to watch it. Laura crying out so dreadfully while *The Whisperer* flickered across a screen.

In an effort to distract myself, I looked for Laura's volume of Ibsen plays and sat down with it under a reading lamp. When Ibsen had been a young man he had been appointed director of the very theater we'd visited tonight. He had worked there for a few years, and had written several plays that had been performed in the National Theater before he moved on to Oslo.

The Wild Duck, however, was not an altogether happy choice of reading matter, being about a girl who killed herself upon learning of her illegitimacy. Fortunately, times had changed. Or had they? Had I not suffered self-injury for years because Laura Worth was my mother? Yet now I sat in her room, worrying about her, listening for any untoward sound from Miles's bedroom. But all they did was talk on and on, softly, tensely.

In spite of my will to stay awake, my eyes grew heavy and I drowsed over the book. Ibsen could be as gloomy as his own rockbound country. I needed something light and humorous to amuse me and keep me awake. I pulled the chaise longue over to the dressing room door and stretched out upon it.

But I could not stay awake. Though I left the light on and constantly roused myself to listen to what had turned to silence in the next room, I grew unbearably sleepy. I thought of all the nights when I'd found it hard to sleep—yet now when I wanted to stay awake, this drowsiness enveloped me. I wondered if I should go downstairs for coffee. But I didn't want to leave my post. I couldn't take that chance. All I could do was order my subconscious to be aware, to *listen*. If I did fall asleep, I must be ready to waken at the slightest sound.

So I went to sleep. Soundly. And so did my subconscious.

When I yawned myself awake it was morning. Bright spring radiance poured through the windows and I turned off the reading lamp. Then I ran across the room to look at my watch. Nine o'clock, and there was no sound from beyond the dressing room.

I got into a skirt and sweater hurriedly and brushed my hair with a few quick strokes. Then I ran downstairs and into the dining room. Donia sat glumly at the table and as I entered the room Irene brought her coffee from the kitchen.

"Where is Laura?" I asked.

Donia grunted. "She's gone. He took her off with him. The lovebirds have flown."

I dropped into a chair opposite her, feeling suddenly cold. "Flown where?"

"How should I know? They didn't even stop for breakfast. They just went off together. She looked as happy as a child, and my brother was treating her fondly."

There was venom underlying her words, and Irene thumped her coffee cup down, letting liquid spill over the rim. "Will you have breakfast?" she said to me.

I was anything but hungry, but I let her bring me toast and coffee. From behind Donia's back, Irene signaled me to outstay her at the table. I drank my coffee slowly, buttered wedges of toast, and did not have long to wait. Donia's appetite was as poor as my own, and before long she wriggled out of her chair and hurried away. The moment she was gone, Irene sat down beside me.

For the first time I noticed how pale she was, and saw the

dark circles under her eyes. She was the one who had gone without sleep, and it might have been better if she'd occupied my listening post at the dressing room door.

"Did you hear them leave?" I asked. "Did you see them?"

She nodded gloomily. "They took his car and headed south. Hurry with your breakfast. We've got to go after them."

I felt more hopeful at once. "Do you know where they've gone?"

"To the summer cottage, probably. Out near Fantoft."

That was near the ancient church where I'd first met her.

"What are you thinking, Irene?" I said.

She rose to gather up the breakfast dishes. "The same thing you're thinking. That she mustn't be left alone with him. She's turned completely trusting this morning. Mrs. Jaffe is right. She's suddenly a woman in love, and now he's got her where he wants her. But you saw him last night when he told her about being in the studio. He showed his true feeling toward her then. Anyway, her car is still in the garage and I have the keys. Will you come with me?"

"Of course," I said. I didn't stay to finish my coffee, but rushed off to get ready. When I returned, Irene was waiting for me. We didn't bother to tell Donia where we were going. Only when we reached the street did I look up and see her looking down from the balcony of Laura's room, watching us go. I was no longer worried about her. It was Miles who concerned me now.

We drove into a world miraculously changed after the rain. Spring had exploded in Bergen. Buds tightly folded yesterday were leafing on the trees, the grass was suddenly green and birds were singing in the gardens. On the mountaintops the snow patches were thinning, and the lakes and fjords were a brilliant blue beneath the bluest of skies.

But I had no feeling for spring now. I could not respond to the beauty around me. Halfway to Fantoft, the thought struck me that I had not waited for Gunnar's call, and that I should have called him and told him where Miles and Laura had gone, where I was going. But there was no time now. Perhaps I would phone when we reached the cottage.

In her anxiety, Irene drove more erratically than when I had gone with her to the fish market. We rushed other cars at cross streets, and hurried to take every advantage when it came to speed. She was as worried as I, and it did not help her driving.

The cottage was on a small lake, and to reach it we wound along a narrow side road that ran beside a hedge. The driveway gate was open and we went through and Irene stopped the car. Miles's car was nowhere in sight. Irene had a key and she let us into the small rustic house. The cottage was empty. No one answered our calls.

While Irene searched the other rooms to make sure, I stood in the big main room with its open fireplace and bright scatter rugs on the floor. Pine wall paneling gave warmth and character to the room, and the furniture was sturdy and comfortable. Often in the past this must have been a retreat to which Laura came with pleasure. But she was not here now.

Irene came out of the two bedrooms, rushing past me to the kitchen. "They've been here, but they're gone. Perhaps he's taken her to the church. She always goes there. When she's happy, when she's sad. Always. He knows that. It would be a lonely place to go."

Yes, I thought, lonely—and remembered my first reaction of foreboding toward that spot where the black church stood.

"Is there a telephone?" I said. "I'd better phone Gunnar."

"Yes, you must. But there's no phone here. And there's no time now to go into town. We must find them at once."

I followed her out to the car. "Do you think he would hurt her? Surely he wouldn't harm her in broad daylight—when we know she's with him."

"Everything has been pushed too far," Irene said. "There are no safeguards left."

Again we drove quickly, but the distance this time was short. Irene pulled into the parking space at the foot of the hill, and got out of the car. Miles's car was not here, but she made nothing of that.

"He could have brought her here and then gone," she said. "We may already be too late."

She ran ahead of me toward the steep path that climbed toward the church, out of sight above us, and again I followed her. I had no sense of reality in what was happening. I couldn't believe that Miles had brought Laura here to harm her, and that we might at any moment come upon her hurt and abandoned. I couldn't believe, and yet something in me responded once more to the spell of the place, and terror began to rise in me.

It all looked different from the last time I'd seen it. Where all the trees except the pines had stood stark and bare when we were last here, now every branch wore a green softness of outline. The grass on either side of the path was no longer brown and dead, but starting into fresh spring life. And birds were singing joyously. But when the tall church came into view above us in all its ancient black wood, and I saw again the dragons' heads, the serpents, the mood of ominous fore-warning grew even greater than before. Once Laura Worth had walked here with Victor Hollins, and there had been love between them. But all that was good and hopeful had been dispelled, and evil waited, ready to attack. It had gathered, focused around the outside of the church. If only she had gone inside where it was bright and safe—but the door stood closed above us.

There was no one here. Not even a workman busied him-self outdoors in the area. The groves of trees stood still and empty. No breeze stirred the pine needles. Nothing moved on the hill opposite the church. We climbed toward the enclosure and saw the black stone cross upon its mound, but no one walked about it, no one touched it for sanctuary. No face looked down at us from the low wall around the church.

"Call to her!" Irene said. "Call to her!"

I called Laura's name again and again, but though echoes shouted back, I had no answer from Laura herself.

"She's not here," I said, "or she'd surely answer us. This is a wild-goose chase."

"She may not be able to answer," Irene said darkly. "Search around the church, and I'll climb the hill and see if I can see her from there."

Her fear, her dark emotions were contagious. The sense of dread was growing in me as I entered the enclosure and crossed the paving stones. I circled the church and found no one. My eyes searched the surrounding area below, and saw nothing to catch my attention. As I moved toward the rear of the church, something glinted on the path before me. I bent and picked it up. The object was a tiny silver mask of tragedy —one of those pins Laura liked to wear, and that Victor had given her long ago.

She had been here. That one thing was certain. But had this pin been dropped by chance or purpose. Had she perhaps tossed it down for whoever followed to find?

I began to call her name again. "Laura, Laura!"

The answering whisper came softly, speaking my own name. "Leigh! I'm here. Come quickly."

At first I couldn't tell where the voice had come from. The black-columned walks that ran along each side of the church were empty, and so were the outer walks, the cross-topped mound—everything.

"Here!" the voice whispered again. "Here, behind the church!"

I stepped between two black columns at the rear and saw that beyond the round bole of an inner column a narrow passageway curved inside the rear wall. After bright sunlight, it was utterly dark, but Laura spoke to me and I knew she was there.

"Are you all right?" I said. "Did he hurt you?"

"I'm perfectly all right. No one has hurt me. Come in here quickly."

I stopped only to call out to Irene that I'd found Laura. Then I went into the dark corridor, groping for her.

She caught me by the arm at once. "Oh, no, no! Why did you call her? Now she'll find us all too quickly. Oh, Leigh, now—"

"But it's Irene," I said. "She brought me here to look for you."

Laura's hands were cold on my own. "Of course! She wanted us together. She hates us both. Now I don't know what she'll do. It's Irene I'm afraid of, Leigh. It has always been Irene. There—do you hear her coming?"

We could both hear her, running on the walks, running about the church. There was no time for reason, for readjustment. I only knew at last, and without doubt where danger lay. Laura huddled close to me and we were very still.

Irene had paused at one entrance to the passageway. "I know where you are now. I know you're both in there. Come out at once, or I'm coming in after you."

Laura whispered in my ear. "She has a gun. She took it from my room. Cass Alroy's gun. I missed it two days ago. She'll have brought it with her."

I had to think, to plan—and there was no time. The dark passageway where we crouched had two openings—one on the side of the church near Irene, the other on the opposite side. I began to push Laura toward the free entrance.

"Get out—run!" I told her. "Get away and find help. I'll hold her off here. It's you she's after."

Laura did not argue. She held me in a quick, close embrace, and then ran toward the patch of light around the curving inner wall. I could hear Irene coming in the other way, and I stiffened myself in the darkness for whatever might come. All that was important now was Laura's escape. If I had to fight Irene, I would.

There was something peculiarly horrible about that black figure which blocked the light from this end and came inexorably toward me. She was not the woman I knew, but someone other behind a mask. The thought came to me sharply that I might never see Gunnar again.

Irene's advance had slowed. I knew she must be blinded, as I had been, and I stood in her path, blocking her from Laura. She ran directly into me, and snatched at my arm with one thin hand.

"Which one of you is it?" she whispered hoarsely.

I knew that sound. I had heard that voice in the night commanding me to listen, listen . . . I froze where I was in utter silence. Something cold and metallic pressed against my temple, spelling death, while her other hand sought my identity, touching my hair, my face, the fabric of my coat.

"So it's only Miss Hollins!" the deadly voice whispered. "If you've let her get away, you'll have to pay for it, you know. Come out into the light. Come with me at once!"

She dragged me by the arm with one hand, while the other held that cold muzzle to my temple. We stumbled together into bright sunlight, and above us the dragons and serpents seemed to hiss in triumph because evil was in command. The inner sanctity of the church could not help me now.

For an instant Irene took her attention from me and looked about the empty courtyard. Laura must have made her escape. But now the madness in the woman's eyes grew in intensity. She stepped a little back from me and raised the automatic.

"Why don't you try to run?" she said. "Why don't you try to escape, you stupid child?"

If I moved to run, she would shoot me down. That was what she was telling me. She had gone beyond sanity. I could only stand where I was and try to delay her pursuit of Laura.

"Of course I shall pay you both off in the end," she told me. "Murder must be paid for, punished. And she's a murderer. She told you the truth last night—that she killed Cass Alroy. There's blood on her hands, and blood must be paid for with blood."

I could hear obsession in her voice. Somehow she had learned what she believed was the truth and over the years that long-ago death had begun to possess and twist her mind, crying out for retribution.

"There's no place where she can hide from me," she went on. "And you've been interfering ever since you came. I owe you payment for that. As I owe it to her many times over. I owe it to her for striking me down in the garden the other day. She made me so angry that I might have paid her off then. I had dragged her outside, but behind my back she'd picked up that candlestick near the door, and she struck me down with it. Only she lacked the courage to strike to kill, as she'd done that other time. She held back the force of the blow. And afterwards she was too weak to let me lie there in the rain. There's no iron in her. She had to rouse the house to search for me and make sure she hadn't killed me. But the end's in sight now. And it will begin with you."

Her eyes were wild, staring, utterly mad. She was far more dangerous than a sane woman. Then from beyond her I saw with horror that Laura had come around the front of the church. It took all my control to keep from shifting my gaze in her direction. I tried to keep Irene talking, keep her from turning.

"It was you who scarred the picture, wasn't it? Not Laura! It was you who marked that game of tic-tac-toe across the canvas, and left that crayon message for me."

She no longer had the gun pointed directly at me, since she was quite sure I couldn't get away, and she was willing to talk—with insane pride.

"Of course! And put those shears in her hand. That really frightened her, because she knew what might happen when the game ended. Because I was X. Only it would have been simpler, it would have happened sooner, if you hadn't come. I didn't want her to marry Dr. Fletcher, but after she did, I had to begin closing in. She was desperately afraid I would tell him the truth about her killing Cass Alroy. She was afraid of losing him if he knew. That was the thing that held her silent about me."

"And it was you who damaged her ski, you who pushed me on the stairs?"

Her smile of triumph answered me. Irene had done it all. She had lied to me at every turn to allay my suspicions, fooled me at will. There was a cunning to madness that I'd never met before.

My eyes were wide with staring—staring into Irene's face

so they wouldn't shift to Laura, who was close now—but weaponless, helpless. I blinked and watched that wavering gun.

"If you harm me, you're finished," I told her. "There'll be no escaping such an act."

"Do you think I care? What happens afterwards doesn't matter—once I can stop the two of you. Oh, at first I thought you'd be useful. It was clear enough that you wanted to pay her off, injure her. Sometimes I almost liked you because I felt you were on my side against her. Sometimes I—"

Laura's arm came around Irene's throat from behind. Its grip choked her momentarily, threw her off balance. I dropped out of range as the gun fired with a roar, spattering stone from the enclosure wall. Laura gripped and clung, and they fell together, rolling on the ground. I stamped on Irene's hand, and she let the gun go. After that, she needed both hands for the fighting fury of Laura Worth.

Gunnar and Donia found them there as they came running up the hill, with Miles a little way behind. Gunnar pulled Irene to her feet and she turned her attention to struggling wildly with him. Miles helped Laura up and held her tightly in his arms. She was breathing heavily and her color was high and bright, her eyes shining with the unmistakable light of battle. She had actually enjoyed coming to physical grips with her long-suffered tormentor. She was primitive woman.

Then Irene broke away from Gunnar and ran from us, out of the enclosure, and away from the church.

"Let her go," Miles said. "It doesn't matter. The police will pick her up. There's nowhere she can hide."

Laura came to me anxiously. "Leigh darling, are you all right?"

"You shouldn't have come back," I said. "She might have killed you. She wanted to kill us both."

"Did you think I would run away and leave you to her? Did you think I'd let her harm my daughter? Darling—how little you know about me!"

Suddenly her arms were around me, and we were both weeping. Her tears mingled with my own as her cheek pressed against mine. It was a wonderfully unrestrained and emotional moment. Above our heads the serpents hissed in despair—because evil had been vanquished after all.

Gunnar picked up the gun and gave it to Miles. Laura turned her head and stared at it in Miles's hands.

"All these years I've kept it," she said. "Cass brought it

with him to the studio that night when he meant to kill me. It's all as I told you last night, Miles."

"I know," he said. "I understand now. I'm glad I was able to free you from what you've believed all these years. But now we must go back to the cottage, and you must rest. There'll be the police to call—matters to take care of."

Gunnar came to put an arm quietly about me, and for the first time I realized I was trembling with the aftermath of shock.

"You will be all right now, Leigh," he said. "It is over now. You are both safe."

I held on to him. "But why—why? What has made Irene, of all people, hate Laura like this?"

"I do not know. It is for Laura to tell us. If she wishes."

All this while Donia had hovered nearby, taking no part, her eyes dancing with excitement—but now without malice. Gunnar smiled at her.

"It is a good thing Mrs. Jaffe worried when she saw Leigh driving away with Irene. She phoned me at once. By the time I reached Kalfaret, Miles had returned from Fantoft. He had left Laura in what he supposed was a safe place and come back to the house to let Irene know that she must pack and leave Bergen at once, that she would not be permitted to see Laura again. When Donia informed him that Irene had taken Leigh to Fantoft, we all followed in our cars."

Laura listened to his words and her smile was beautiful. "My daughter tried to save me, Gunnar. Leigh tried to hold Irene so I could get away. But we couldn't leave each other. I could never have run away and left her to Irene. Now I must tell you everything. We will go back to the cottage—and I'll tell you the story of that night in Hollywood so long ago. I'll tell you how Irene came to feel so strongly about something which should have had nothing to do with her in the first place."

We stopped to telephone on the way. Gunnar alerted the police to look for a woman who was unbalanced and dangerous, and told them we would wait for word at Laura Worth's cottage.

In the small house Gunnar lighted the fire and we sat about it, more chilled and shaken than the day warranted. Breaking the stillness that had been laid upon us, Laura's voice took up a very old story.

Time seemed to falter, hesitate, stand still—then slowly begin to roll backward to another day, another place. It was as if we were there, as if it was all happening anew.

Chapter 15

In California, moonlight lay quiet upon the night. The village of small stucco buildings, the replica of a city street, the false-front western town, the great sound stages, all were still and empty. A few lights burned through the studio grounds, and the guard at the gate stayed inside his shelter, expecting nothing to happen—as it never did.

True, the director, Mr. Alroy, had checked in tonight. But he had a right to be there, as had Miss Worth, who was staying overnight in her dressing room in Stage 5. That's where Mr. Alroy was heading—and if something was up between those two, it wasn't the business of a watchman.

A sound stage was not a stage, properly speaking. Sound Stage 5 was a converted Quonset hut—a huge building with an exterior painted pastel pink, and an interior as vast as a basketball court. Laura Worth was lost and small inside it, but she did not mind, and she had no fear of the great, echoing barn of a place at night. This was her world, and sometimes when she wanted to be wholly caught up in the mood of a coming scene, she would stay in her dressing room, sleep there, prepare herself for tomorrow's shooting. After all, there was nothing to pull her back to her home in the Hollywood hills. It was work that was her life, her very breath. She hated all distractions which pressed upon her from outside, or made demands upon her mind and emotions.

That letter which had come from Victor Hollins yesterday, for instance, had been unhappily distracting. She must forget it now. All that was over, smothered, buried in the past. Yet it was hard to keep it utterly buried while she was working on a Victor Hollins novel. And he had enclosed a picture of the little girl, Leigh. She had asked him not to send pictures, not to write about her—to let all that belong to another life, because these things left her shattered for days at a time. But Victor had written that she could not belong wholly to her present life while Leigh was growing up. Someday she must meet her daughter.

So the letter had been a distraction, and the shooting had gone badly. It would all have to be done over tomorrow, Cass had said. And that was another thing, though more closely connected with her work. Cass had been absolutely beastly all through the picture. He had raged at her today, taunted her, belittled her reputation and her ability. Some directors could get what they wanted from an actress by such treatment, but she was not one of them. She had turned wooden, and the scene had been impossible to play. It was a scene of key importance, and it had to be right. She knew that Cass had grown to hate her. She had rejected his personal attentions, and this he could not forgive her for. She suspected him of being unbalanced, revengeful to a dangerous degree.

Today he had wound up by making her physically ill. She had collapsed on the set, and Dr. Fletcher had been sent for. Another distraction. Miles wanted to marry her, and he was far more importunate than Victor had ever been. He would gladly have seen her career come to an end, even though he'd been drawn to her because she was famous and gifted. She was fond of him, but she knew better than to let him come too close.

When he arrived at the studio that afternoon there had been a thoroughly unpleasant quarrel between him and her director. There was already a deep antagonism between the two men because Cass had been involved in Donia Jaffe's divorce suit. There had been threats made between them at that earlier time, and now the blaze had sprung into the open again.

Laura had been disturbed by the underlying fury she had sensed in Cass Alroy. The two men were thoroughly suspicious and jealous of each other, and she had at times sensed something almost pathological in Cass. When she was not angry with him, she was often a little afraid. But the shooting would soon be over, the picture done with. The sooner, the better. She was honed to a fine edge and she needed a rest desperately.

Because of all these things, she had determined to use the method she'd employed several times before when a scene would not come right. She would stay in her dressing room overnight and give herself wholly to thoughts of the script and the part she was playing.

She liked the role of Helen Bradley. For all the character's fears—and they were justifiable—she had an inner strength and courage that made her sympathetic, even admirable. Anyone could suffer terror, but Helen Bradley could face what had to be faced, even at the risk of her life. She was one of Victor's more thoughtful creations.

So tonight she was here, moving about amid the echoing wilderness of camera and sound equipment, shut away from the outside world so thoroughly that nothing from beyond these windowless walls could be heard inside, and nothing here could be heard outside. She could shout her lines, if she wished, and no one would think her mad.

Two or three naked bulbs burned in the cavernous depths, but the island of light that was the set during the day was dim and empty. Laura moved toward it cautiously, stepping over snaking cables, electrical attachments, rounding cameras on their dollies, stepping beneath the booms that moved the mikes about. Overhead, the great lights in the rafters were dark, the catwalks empty, the huge equipment motionless, silent.

It was a strange world, so very different from the mad bustle and noise that pervaded the whole area during the day, until that moment when an assistant director shouted that this was to be a take. Then everything hushed and all attention was focused on the scene to be shot. Laura did not mind the silence, the emptiness now. There was no conflict here, no human demands being made upon her. She could become Helen Bradley and live only in the confines of that small section that was the set. She knew where some of the lights were and she moved to switch them on.

At once the stairs, the hallway, the parlor of the Bradley home sprang into vivid life. By contrast the catwalks grew all the more dim, the cameras and booms were lost in thick shadow. Only the set glowed with light, illumined in every lifelike detail. She could see the chalk marks that would enable the actors to take up exactly the same positions tomorrow that they'd occupied in the last shot.

Bathed by the heat of the lights, Laura stepped onto the set. She stood very still for a moment, willing herself to be absorbed into this make-believe world so that it would take precedence over other reality and become the immediate present.

Far away in the big sound stage something creaked—and was silent. Laura listened for a moment, then shrugged the noise aside. All this metal equipment had a life of its own. Just as the walls of the Quonset hut lived in their own way. Some creaking and groaning was natural as metal cooled, relaxed from the strain put upon it during the day. It was nothing.

Foolish to have this sudden feeling that someone else was here in the building with her.

Quickly she mounted the stairs that were so important a feature in the film. Stairs that ended in a platform that led to nothing. The camera never focused upon them beyond a certain point. From the platform she looked down upon the narrow hallway below and the door leading into the parlor—closed as it would be in the picture. From this high vantage point she could see over the wall of the set and glimpse part of the parlor, but she went down a few steps and put this unreality from her.

Once her hand was on the stair rail she became Helen Bradley. She could feel the role again—it was part of her. Easily, comfortably, she ran through the entire scene. The emotion was right. She knew what Helen Bradley was feeling, yet she was completely in control of her features and movements so that this emotion would be conveyed to an audience as an actor before a camera must convey it. She did not really feel the horror of the moment when Helen discovered her husband's body and knew that danger was abroad in the house, but she understood it, and she would portray it graphically.

Now that the mood was right, she could go back to the cot in her dressing room and go to sleep as she would not have slept at home with the day's failure hanging over her. She stepped out of the set and turned off the lights, leaving only those two bare bulbs burning at this end of the big stage.

There were three small dressing rooms inside the stage, not far away, her own slightly more luxurious than the other two, and she walked toward it through the faint light. At another place on the lot her trailer dressing room waited—almost a bungalow on wheels, complete with shower and tiny kitchen. She always used that on location. But this smaller room was close to the set and more convenient for the makeup men, her dresser and hairdresser. She liked staying here where the work was being done.

Once more, just as she reached the door of her dressing room, she heard a sound behind her. A sound almost like footsteps. She was still for a moment, holding her breath. But nothing else followed and she knew it was only the usual creakings. She went into the room where warm lamplight and a cozy interior awaited her. With the lines of her scenes still running through her head, she got ready for sleep. The sound stage was apt to grow cold at night, and she had brought a long, warm nightgown, and an extra blanket for the cot.

Running through her part had soothed her and put all that was irritating and distracting from her mind. She went to sleep easily, deeply.

When the crash resounded through her dreams, it brought her floating to the surface, not sure whether the sound had been real or not. She sat up in bed—and for a few moments there was, by comparison, silence. But it was not complete silence. Someone seemed to be moving about out there, and Laura wondered whether to go and see what was happening, or to stay here and lock her door.

Then she head the running steps, and a voice calling her name. A girl's voice.

"Miss Worth! Miss Worth!"

She sprang out of bed and flung open the dressing room door. Rita Bond, the bit actress who played the maid, almost fell into the room. Her young, plump face was ashen, her eyes wide with shock and terror beneath the frizzy hair they'd given her for the part. For a moment she couldn't talk, and Laura took her by the shoulders and shook her into making sense.

"It's—it's Mr. Alroy!" the girl stammered. "He's been hurt. There was another man—a big man. I saw him running toward the fire escape door. I—I think it was that Dr. Fletcher who was here this afternoon."

Laura asked no questions about Rita's own presence, but drew on her robe and slippers and went with the girl back to the set. Though it was dimly lighted, she could see the black sprawl of shadow on the floor of the parlor scene. She gave Rita a little push.

"Go turn on that lamp over there," she said, and as the lamp came on she stepped into the set.

Where Helen Bradley would have found the body of her husband, Cass Alroy lay, with a red stain spreading outward on the carpet. Laura knelt beside him, felt for a pulse. There was nothing. No breath, no heartbeat, as far as she could tell. If Miles had done this, it would have been because of her and the scandal would be tremendous. Her quick mind was already seeking among the possibilities, searching for a way out.

Rita stood near a towering camera on its dolly, and its eye seemed to watch the set. The girl was shivering, her teeth chattering, and Laura stared at her speculatively. Could she use the girl, trust her? Involuntarily, her gaze was drawn to the two chairs with the name plates which faced the scene of the Bradley house. This afternoon she had sat there beside Cass while they stormed at each other. A thousand years ago.

She moved about the set, thinking. The gun was there, near Cass's outstretched hand, and nearby lay the brass candlestick, one end of it wet and shining. Laura felt cold, frozen, but she was thinking, thinking. She had no pity to waste on Cass. He had come here to harm her. The gun told her that. She had been increasingly afraid of him during work on the picture.

She spoke to Rita out there among the cameras. "Did you see what happened?"

"No!" The girl managed to still her chattering teeth. "I heard the crash, and when I came toward the set to find out what had happened, I saw that big man running away."

"You're not to mention him to anyone," Laura said flatly. "We must figure out what to do. Why are you here? How did you get in?"

Rita made a choking sound and fought to answer. "I—I wanted to be near you, Miss Worth. I knew you meant to stay here tonight. You said you were going to rehearse your part. And I wanted to watch you. Perhaps to talk to you. You've never noticed me much, except when we're playing a scene. And I thought—"

"So you hid in the building? You watched me rehearsing?"

"Yes! Please don't mind. If you only knew how much I—"

Laura waved her into silence. "There's no time for that now. They'll say I did this, you know. There's been friction all through this picture and Cass has been treating me badly."

"I know," Rita whispered. "I know very well. He would have killed you tonight."

Laura moved about the set, her eyes searching. "Yes. He deserved what has happened to him. But we must save whoever did it. And we must save ourselves."

Her eyes lighted upon the doorstop that held open the door to the dining room at the rear. She leaned over and tugged at the iron cat. It was very heavy. She could never have used it to strike at anyone, but she could manage to lift it in both hands. She felt stronger than she had ever been before, thoroughly clear-headed and in control of her own actions and everything around her. She did not need to think frantically, to try to reason. She simply knew without any doubt what had to be done, and knew she was strong enough to do it.

She carried the doorstop over to where Cass lay and held it several feet above his head. Then she let it drop.

Rita screamed shrilly, thoroughly demoralized. "You've killed him!" she cried. "If he wasn't dead before, you've killed him!"

Laura scarcely heard her. There was too much to be done. The worst part was wiping fingerprints off the doorstop. She used the hem of her robe, but she had to be careful because of the blood. When she was through, she picked up the gun and the candlestick and carried them back to her dressing room. The gun she placed in a purse. It would be safe enough there until she could hide it later. It had not been fired, and no one would be looking for a gun. The candlestick she set openly upon her dressing table. There were candles in a drawer, and she placed one in the holder. She would have to tell the prop man she'd borrowed the candlestick for the night. He'd think nothing of that. She wiped the base carefully with cleansing tissue which she burned in the candle flame. All these things she did quickly and efficiently, while Rita watched, wide-eyed and sick and terrified.

Laura looked at her coldly. "You must say nothing at all about what I've done. When we found Cass you saw only the doorstop lying there. Do you understand? And you saw no one, you heard no running steps."

The girl nodded wildly. "Yes—yes! I won't say anything."

"If you say anything at all, I'll tell them you killed him. I'll say you killed him to save my life."

Rita's eyes were wild with fright. "But that's why I *did* kill him! To save you! I saw him creeping across the set with that gun in his hands. I'd walked about the set after you left, pretending I was doing your scenes, pretending I was you. When I heard him coming, I hid. I knew he was going to your dressing room. I felt as though he was going to kill *me*. So I struck him down. I had to stop him—I had to!"

Laura stared at her across the small room. All emotion had been frozen in her. She could look at the girl and feel nothing —neither gratitude nor angry condemnation. Nothing.

"We will tell the same story," she said in that voice drained of all feeling. "I was asleep and you were bedded down near my dressing room. When we heard the crash, I rushed out to the set, and you came right after me. We saw no one, heard no one running away. But obviously neither of us could have wielded that doorstop as a weapon while Cass was standing. Do you understand all this?"

The girl was trembling, but she nodded her frizzy head.

"We've just found him," Laura said. "There was no candlestick, no gun. Now I'm going to call for help. Come with me."

Together they picked their way over cables and around pieces of spare equipment and old sets. There was an airlock at the door of the sound stage. That meant there were two doors to open. Heavy doors. Laura let the two of them through with the last draining of strength from her body.

The night was cool outside, the moonlight very bright. The sleeping village that was the studio stretched away on all sides. Laura stiffened herself and grasped Rita firmly by the arm as she began to scream.

It was the same screaming she would use later when they finally shot the scene where Helen Bradley came upon her husband's body. And while she screamed the words Rita had spoken earlier came sharply home to her.

"If he wasn't dead before—you've killed him!"

Inside the Norwegian cottage there was silence, except for the crackling of the fire Miles had built in the grate. Laura sat closest to the fire, seeking its warmth as she told her story. Donia had curled herself cross-legged on the floor on the other side of the hearth, while Miles had stayed well back in the shadows. Gunnar sat beside me.

When Laura's quiet voice, carrying so much emotional impact, fell silent, Miles took up the story.

"If you had told me the truth, so much could have been spared you. I'd had trouble finding Stage 5, and I came through the doors just in time to hear Cass crash to the floor. I heard someone running and I found my way to the set. I saw the gun and the candlestick, and I thought Laura had killed him. My presence would not have helped her—it would have made everything worse. I got away as quickly as I could, and held to my silence later. I told my sister nothing, and all these years Donia has believed that I was guilty of Cass's death. Sometimes she has even held this over my head—and I let her. Because of this, she has hated Laura, hated my marriage to her, blaming her for everything."

Donia wriggled her small person. "Even if I'd been sure it was Laura and not you, I'd never have spoken out. I was in love with Cass once. I knew what he was like. I couldn't regret his death."

Laura went on quietly. "The worst part of all was not knowing for sure if I had killed him. Rita could so easily have been right. Perhaps she wanted to blame me and thus save herself. I was still her idol, but she thought of her own self-preservation too. She had strength in her, even then, and she began to nurture it so that she got through the investigation. Her trembling and fright were natural enough, but not once did she let anything of the real secret escape her."

"Do you know what became of her?" I asked.

"She dropped out of my life. I was ill and Miles and Donia were taking care of me. When I recovered I went abroad alone. She came to me in Dubrovnik—my trip was much publicized. Rita Bond was only the name she used for films. When she went home she took back her real name of Irene Varos."

I stared at her in astonishment. "Irene! But—I've just seen her in the film, and there was no resemblance."

"There wouldn't be," Laura said sadly. "She was only seventeen at the time of the picture, and she altered greatly in maturing. All that frizzy hair she wore for the film, the round, plump face, the terrified air—these were not like the Irene Varos she grew into—thin and gaunt, with all emotion repressed. Of course the investigation uncovered her real name, and it was mentioned in some of the later newspaper reports. It was brought out that she came to America as a child with her parents and grew up there. Because of these reports, I had to clip sections out of those scrapbooks when you came to my house, Leigh. I wanted no journalist to discover who she was and try to explore the past. Miles and Donia knew her identity, but they had no knowledge of the real role she played. Miles thought it was his sister playing all these recent pranks.

"When I met Irene again in Dubrovnik, she wanted to come back to the States. She told me she was still devoted to me, and she wanted to go with me wherever I went. She had nothing to keep her in her own country. The man she had wanted to marry had not died, as she claimed. I learned later that she had told him the real story of what had happened in Hollywood, and he could not bear the thought of marrying a woman who had killed. As the years went by she began to blame me for his loss too. And what had happened to her, reinforced my own reluctance—when I met Miles again—to ever let him know the possible truth about me.

"I took Irene along when I went to Norway. We were bound together in a sense. One of us had killed. And recently she never let me forget that it might have been me. She hated and opposed my marriage to Miles, who was connected with that time. I don't know what may have been churning in her mind all these years, but after I married Miles it began to surface. She began to make me believe that I really had killed

Cass Alroy, and she told me she meant to pay me off for spoiling her entire life. In a sense"—Laura paused and flashed a quick look of affection at Miles—"I married Miles for protection against Irene. But that was futile. She made me believe that it was only a matter of time before she told him the truth about me, and caused me to lose him, as she had lost the man she loved. I'm afraid I gave up. I retreated from reality, stopped wanting to live. She began to play torturing tricks on me, trying to push me into some desperate act. Perhaps she would have been satisfied with my suicide. She wanted my death at the end."

Mutely Laura looked across the room at Miles, begging his forgiveness. He smiled at her, and all the harshness was gone from his face.

"All this time I could have told you the one thing that would have freed you," he said. "I'm a doctor, so of course when I found Alroy lying there in the parlor of that set, I examined him. I made sure that he was dead before I went away. What came out in the investigation about the iron doorstop made me know that the second weapon had been planted. But he was dead before that."

"And now I *am* free," Laura said. "I began to believe I could escape from Irene when my daughter came into my life. Leigh gave me courage and belief in the woman I used to be. Even when she showed me her distrust and resentment, she challenged me. She made me want to prove myself to her. Have I done that, Leigh?"

"You've done a great deal more," I said, and heard the catch in my own voice.

She came to me across the room and put a light hand on my shoulder, looked into my eyes. "Ever since you came, I've been afraid of you. Afraid because you had every right to hate—and you had the power to hurt me. I tried to cut you down at every turn so that you'd expect nothing of me—as I expected nothing of you. But after today there can be no more pretending."

"No more pretending," I said. "And now you'll go back to Hollywood and prove what Laura Worth can do. You'll show the world who you are, and—"

She was looking at me in loving surprise. "Oh, no! Not now. Not when I have everything that's real for the first time in my life. I won't want the other any more. It was only an escape from Irene. That's not to say I couldn't succeed if I chose to go back"—she flashed us all a smile of proud assur-

ance—"but I don't want to try any more. There's something
more important. So let Laura Worth stay a legend, while
Laura Fletcher begins to live."

She turned to Miles. Gunnar caught me by the hand and
beckoned to Donia. She came with us through the door, and
then wandered off by herself, turning her back on us. I felt a
little sorry for her because she was alone, and because malice
was part of her nature, as it was no longer mine.

As we stood outside the door for a moment, watching
Donia wander away, a car drew up to the gate and a police
officer got out. He came to us and spoke in English.

"The woman has been found. She is completely demented
and does not know who she is. She thinks she is a child who
has broken her favorite doll."

I shivered as Gunnar directed the officer into the cottage.
Then we turned away together.

There was a path that led steeply down to the water from
the outcropping of rock on which the cottage had been built.
We went down the curving way, with my hand in Gunnar's.

"What will happen to Irene?" I said.

"She will be examined. Obviously she will not be released
to stand trial. The seed of imbalance has been in her since she
was a child. It has already borne terrible fruit."

"Then nothing will need to come out?" I said. "The past
can be left alone—Laura can be left alone?"

Gunnar nodded. "I believe we can see to that. It will not be
necessary now. Everyone has suffered enough. Even Irene."

We were silent for the rest of the way down the path. It led
out upon a narrow, rocky spit, and we sat down on the rocks
with the water lapping gently at our feet—and looked at each
other.

"We must make plans," Gunnar said. "Are you going to
write about Laura Worth?"

I nodded. "Of course. I want to more than ever now. But
only a chapter. A chapter about Laura Worth, the actress. I
couldn't do a book because there's too much that can't be
written about. I could never really do her justice. First, I'll
have to go back to New York. I'll write it there, where I can
find some perspective."

"But you will return," Gunnar said. It was a statement, not
a question. Then he went on, as though he found his own
words inadequate. "It will be necessary for you to return."

He was solemnly in earnest, and I laughed at him with a
slight choke in the laughter. "Yes, I'll return," I said.

He would not move too fast, my Norwegian, but he knew exactly where he was going, even if he was not ready to tell me yet. I would wait until he was ready.

"You are sitting too far away from me," he pointed out, and I moved properly close. "Even in the wintertime you will like Norway, Leigh."

"Even in the wintertime, I'll love it," I said.

And for quite a while we did not think about Laura Worth at all. She did not need to be thought about, worried about, any more. I had a feeling that Victor Hollins, if he knew, would be very happy.